David Hogg

Life and Times of the Reverend John Wightman

David Hogg

Life and Times of the Reverend John Wightman

ISBN/EAN: 9783337400491

Printed in Europe, USA, Canada, Australia, Japan

Cover: Foto ©Raphael Reischuk / pixelio.de

More available books at **www.hansebooks.com**

LIFE AND TIMES

OF THE

REV. JOHN WIGHTMAN, D.D.,

(1762-1847)

LATE MINISTER OF KIRKMAHOE.

BY HIS SUCCESSOR, THE

REV. DAVID HOGG.

LONDON:

HODDER AND STOUGHTON, 27 PATERNOSTER ROW.

EDINBURGH AND GLASGOW: J. MENZIES AND CO.

DUMFRIES: J. ANDERSON AND SON.

1873.

PREFACE.

THE following Memoir has been written as a tribute
of regard to the memory of one with whom I was
associated in the ministry for a period of nearly three
years, and who always treated me with affectionate and
unvarying kindness. It is now upwards of a quarter of
a century since Dr. Wightman's death, and as he had
almost completed the eighty-fifth year of his age, and
the fiftieth of his ministry, when that event occurred, I
have had to consider many customs, clerical as well as
social, which have now undergone considerable change,
and some which have passed away altogether. Dr.
Wightman was widely known for his benevolent and
generous heart, his high classical attainments and
general scholarship, his popular gifts as a preacher,
and his shrewd discernment of character in various
grades of society. As was common with many of his
brethren in the Church, he kept a diary from the date
of his license till almost that of his death, in which he
freely recorded his opinions of what was going on, not
only in the ecclesiastical, but also in the political
world. From certain of these entries it is evident

that he intended them one day to see the light, so that in any reference made to them I have not been intruding upon forbidden ground. At the same time, I have endeavoured to exercise a judicious discretion in what has been selected, so as not to cause offence to the impartial reader, or wound the feelings of any living relative whose ancestor may have come under notice. I have not willingly misrepresented parties, or perverted truth, when there was occasion to notice the leading controversies of the day, my only object having been to recall certain phases of the times of old in connection with the life of a good man, who faithfully served his day and generation, and whose memory is still green wherever he was known.

As several of the anecdotes throughout the volume were originally contributed to Dean Ramsay's *Reminiscences*, I have thought it not improper to reproduce them on my own account. I gratefully acknowledge the ready kindness of Dr. William Chambers in permitting me to extract the substance of two papers on Deaths and Burials, formerly furnished to *Chambers' Journal*. Special thanks are due to D. Mitchell, Esq., of the *Dumfries Courier*, for his valuable assistance in preparing the work for publication.

D. H.

KIRKMAHOE MANSE.

CONTENTS.

CHAPTER I.

CHAPTER II.

CHAPTER III.

CHAPTER VIII.

CHAPTER IX.

CHAPTER X.

CHAPTER XI.

Page

CHAPTER XII.

CHAPTER XIII.

CHAPTER XIV.

CHAPTER XV.

LIFE AND TIMES

OF THE

REV. JOHN WIGHTMAN, D.D.

CHAPTER I.

PARENTAGE AND BOYHOOD—STRUGGLES OF POOR STUDENTS—POPULAR
ERROR ABOUT BASTARDY—GOES TO COLLEGE—BROIL WITH LORD
BROUGHAM—ASSISTANT IN THE GRAMMAR-SCHOOL OF DUMFRIES
—OFFER OF TUTORSHIP IN VIRGINIA—GOES TO LEITH—CANDI-
DATE FOR THE GRAMMAR-SCHOOL OF KELSO—RECEIVES LICENCE
—EXPERIENCE OF PREACHERS—PRIVATE TUITION—RUSTICATES
TO RECRUIT HIS HEALTH—DR. BLAIR AND PRINCIPAL ROBERT-
SON—DISSATISFIED WITH HIS POSITION AS TUTOR—A CHANGE.

THE Rev. John Wightman, D.D., minister of Kirkmahoe, was the son of a Galloway farmer, and from his
early boyhood was trained to agricultural pursuits, so
far as these were compatible with his education at
school and college. He frequently "looked the hill"
in the morning to see that all was well with the sheep,
at seed-time he followed the harrows, and in autumn
he wrought in the harvest-field. He was born at
Glaisters, in the parish of Kirkgunzeon, on the 12th
of August, 1762, the same day, he delighted to remark
in after years, on which George IV. first saw the light.

A

His father, William Wightman, occupant of the farm, was in comfortable circumstances for his position in life, and was esteemed in the district as a shrewd, intelligent, pious man, whose word was as good as his bond, and whose judgment was always respected in matters of important reference. His mother, Agnes Thomson, was a woman in her own sphere a fitting equal for her husband, and who, while devotedly attached to her children, had still the good sense and the firmness not to spoil them for want of correction. John was early destined by his parents for the ministry, and this object was kept constantly in view; not that he indicated any special aptitude for the profession, but rather from a feeling then prevalent, even among the lowest peasantry, of what was considered "honouring God with their substance," by dedicating one of their sons to the service of the Church, though the prospect was oftentimes long and dreary, and the privations undergone severe, before the ardently cherished desire was realized. The eldest son was usually selected for the purpose, unless he had a delicate brother who was not likely to be able for much manual labour, and then all the energies of the household were called into requisition to foster and mature the tender plant. Young Wightman, however, did not come under either of these categories, as he was neither the eldest son, nor was he a sickly child, but still he was the one fixed upon to be an honour to the family, and an ornament to the Church.

In former times a large proportion of the ministers of the Church of Scotland belonged to the lower classes of society, and many of the ablest and most eloquent

of them had their origin from this source. An interesting volume, though perhaps a painful one, might
be written, descriptive of the difficulties and hardships
encountered, the faintings and despondencies experienced, the hopes now high, and again extinguished,
which lay in the way to the attainment of this position.
Nor was the struggle confined to the twofold energies
of wedded life in pushing the aspiring herald onwards
to the pulpit, for even the mother who was never
honoured with the name of wife braced herself for the
contest, and made a noble effort, despite a prejudice
which lay in the way. She laboured at field-work by
day, earning but a scanty wage, and at night she sewed
or spun, to procure the means for educating and supporting her son at college. A popular belief prevailed
that illegitimacy was a barrier to entering the Divinity
Hall, that every student was strictly examined on this
point, and should any one happen to be passed over by
mistake at this stage, he could not by any possibility
obtain license, or be admitted into the ministry. In
short, the Presbytery neither could nor would allow such
a thing. This opinion was founded on a passage in
Deuteronomy, which says, "A bastard shall not enter
into the congregation of the Lord." Notwithstanding
this, however, the attempt was sometimes made, and
not without success, though popular prejudice was still
firm in holding that the real state of the case had not
been known, and no blessing could possibly follow the
ministrations of such a man.

Having finished his elementary education at the
parish school, and being now fully eighteen years of
age, our young friend was sent to the University of

Edinburgh to undergo the usual training for the sacred office to which he was designed. Here he commenced and continued his curriculum till its termination. Students then often made the tour of all the universities, for the purpose, it was said, of taking the cream of these institutions, though to the detriment, we fear, of their studies, by breaking the continuity of the course of training upon which they had entered; but he had no such roving disposition, and Edinburgh was his *Alma mater* throughout. His appearance in all the classes of Arts and Divinity was highly creditable to his diligence and abilities, and attracted the special notice of several of the Professors. Under Professor Hill he acquired a proficiency in the Latin language which was very marked, even in those days when it was common to intersperse conversation with phrases from the Roman poets. He had also a tenacious memory, and remembered almost everything he read or wrote, a striking instance of which we shall give anon. While attending the classes in the University, he engaged also to a considerable extent in private teaching as a means of helping his finances, and he had under his care in this way two lads who afterwards became eminent in their country's annals—Lord Mackenzie, son of the author of "The Man of Feeling," and Henry Lord Brougham, whom all the world knows, but who was one day so mischievous and disobedient, if not worse, that Mr. Wightman took him by the collar and thrust him out of the room, with the anathema, "Begone, you firebrand, you will plague the nation yet!"

In 1785 he was appointed assistant or usher to Mr. Wait in the grammar-school of Dumfries, with whom he continued for three years, becoming by the exercise of teaching still more proficient in his classical attainments. From this circumstance he ever afterwards took the warmest interest in the prosperity of the Academy, the name it afterwards obtained, and till the close of his life he had a delight in privately visiting the class-rooms, when the scholars were allowed by their masters to give him a ringing round of welcome. One of his highest gratifications, and which he could not conceal, was his being appointed by the Presbytery, which was constantly done, to preside at the annual examination of the institution, for which he always prepared a highly complimentary address to the masters, pupils, parents, and others interested in the cause of education. These addresses were always learnedly, ornately, and poetically composed, and from an expression in them which he almost invariably used, some of the more thoughtless of the boys, when they saw him taking the desk in the New Church (now Greyfriars) at the distribution of the prizes, called it "Wightman's officiating at the Sabæan altars." We shall afterwards have an opportunity of giving our readers a specimen of these addresses. In 1787 Mr. Wait having been requested to recommend a properly qualified tutor to take charge of a family going out to Virginia, and to reside with them there for three years, at once suggested the name of Mr. Wightman as eminently qualified for the situation, and he was immediately communicated with; but the terms were not the most tempting for such an undertaking—namely, £30 a-year, with the promise of a present of ten guineas at the expiration of the agreement, should the poor tutor's conduct give satisfaction. Certain expressions in the communication as to what was necessary on his part he considered derogatory in tone to his feelings, and unnecessary. During the interval before his departure he was "to acquire as much knowledge of the French language as possible"—he was "to endeavour to write a steady good hand, which it was thought in six months he might do exceedingly well" —he was "to be a master of grammar in general, and perfectly accurate in the English tongue; and the more he could acquire of the elegance of pronunciation both in English and French, so much the better." All this was required for a short engagement, in a distant land, at an annual salary of £30 with board, and ten guineas more looming in the distance unless a squall arose. Mr. Wightman felt himself insulted, as well as his master who had recommended him, so, suppressing his feelings, he replied that he could not accept the proposals made, as even with the early intimation given, he would be unable to acquire some of the qualifications which seemed indispensable for the situation.

He now left Dumfries, and became assistant in the grammar-school of Leith, presided over by Mr. James Cririe, afterwards Dr. Cririe, minister of Dalton. Still he always cherished the warmest affection for Mr. Wait, and on the death of that gentleman in June, 1804, he inserted the following tribute to his memory in the local newspaper:—"Died at Moat, after a lingering illness, on the 16th instant, James Wait, Esq., late Rector of the grammar-school in this place. He was a man of great integrity, and of a remarkably independent tone of mind. His desire of knowledge

was insatiable, his application in pursuit of it un-
wearied, and his attainments in it truly uncommon.
His acquirements in classic literature, and particularly
in Greek and Roman antiquities have been long and
justly admired; but his knowledge was by no means
confined to ancient learning; his acquaintance with the
history, philosophy, and politics of modern times was
very extensive. He read French and Italian with
ease, and was acquainted with most of the best writers
in these languages, both in prose and verse. He
applied himself sedulously of late to the study of
German, and without any assistance but his grammar
and dictionary, and his own ardent mind, obtained a
very considerable knowledge of that language. In the
course of a year he read Puffendorf's Introduction twice
over, and almost all Luther's Bible. The Idyls of
Gessner, and some other lighter productions of the
German Muse, were quite familiar to him. He was
well acquainted with the history of the families of
the great men in Europe, and especially of the nobility
and gentry of this kingdom. Though his habits of life
were retired to a fault, yet with a few select friends he
was a very hearty and agreeable companion."

While he was assistant in Leith the grammar-school
of Kelso became vacant, when he offered himself as a
candidate for the situation, and being strongly supported by some of the most eminent teachers of the
day, he was very sanguine of success. Mr. Cririe said
—"In recommending him as a teacher, I think I do
the public the most essential service in my power."
Mr. Wait certified that "he was very well qualified
as an instructor of youth, particularly in communicat-

ing the principles of classical literature;" and Professor Dalzel of Edinburgh College wrote, "I think he would make an excellent teacher. He has had considerable experience, from having acted in the capacity of usher to Mr. Wait, at Dumfries, who appears to me to be one of the best masters of a school in this country." He further characterized him as "a very deserving young man." He was doomed, however, to disappointment, a Mr. Taylor being preferred, to whom, with his natural generosity of feeling, though an unsuccessful rival, he offered his congratulations with best wishes for his success. Some few years afterwards the school became once more vacant by the translation of the teacher to Musselburgh, and Mr. Wightman was asked by one in authority, and having a desire to befriend him, to make application again, with a hint that he was almost certain to be appointed. He agreed to consider the proposal, but former defeat had not lost its impression, and he went no further in the matter. His college curriculum was now running to a close, for while he had been engaged in educational pursuits, he had never for a moment taken his eye off the Church. Accordingly, in 1791 he passed his probationary trials before the Presbytery of Edinburgh, and was licensed to preach the Gospel. There were present on the occasion—Principal Robertson, Dr. Henry, the historian of Britain, Dr. Erskine, Sir Harry Moncreiff, Dr. Paul, and other members of lesser note. The subject of his Exegesis, or Latin discourse, was, *An anima humana sit immortalis?* which he delivered from memory, without a single note before him, to the great wonderment of the reverend Court, who declared with reference to the feat, that "they had never so seen it done in Israel!"

After receiving license he had many applications made to him, near and distant, for his "valuable services," even from parties whom he scarcely knew, and whom he certainly never reckoned among his friends. A forenoon, or an afternoon, or a whole day, would be esteemed the greatest favour, with the hint that perhaps something might come out of it, as some influential personage was likely to be present. But, to the reproach of the Church, these "services" were asked, and expected, and received, without fee or reward, as if a poor student, after struggling hard with poverty for eight years, and oftentimes many more, and perhaps paying his last half-guinea as the Presbytery clerk's fee, on becoming a probationer, turned into a sort of clerical chameleon, subsisting solely on air, and the good wishes of those he served for a speedy introduction to some benevolent patron. It was then as now on the licensing of a student, "wherever the carcase is, there will the eagles be gathered together." No doubt, getting license was a great event in the student's career. It was the climax of his efforts in that direction, and henceforth he should be designated by another name. It was to him crossing the Rubicon, and if, with Cæsar, on approaching the bank, he felt that "if he did not cross that river he was undone," so like him also, the joy was great when the passage was safely accomplished. In those days the term *Probationer* had a very significant meaning, much more than now. It implied long years of preaching, travelling, soliciting, and introducing, before the final stage was reached, the presentation to a parish. One of the earliest of these applications for aid was from the Rev. Dr. Hugh Blair, one of the ministers of Edinburgh, and Professor of Belles Lettres in the University. The note was very formal and polite, addressed to "Mr. Wightman, Preacher of the Gospel," stating that "he was suffering from a cold, that his diet was in the afternoon, and that if Mr. Wightman would take it for him it would be a seasonable relief and favour." Of course the request was complied with, and after the service was over the "preacher" was allowed to return to his own lodgings for dinner. "No, no!" was the rebuke we once got from the mistress of a manse, when in our ignorance we confounded terms, "he's nae minister, he's only a preacher."

But though dignified with the title of Probationer, or Preacher, he was still practically nothing else than what he had been before, an instructor of youth, depending entirely for subsistence upon private tuition. His preaching put nothing in his pocket, and as little he thought in the way of promotion in the Church, however complimentary the phrases he received on bidding "Good-bye" to the clerical friend he had been assisting. He was constantly employed in teaching; his abilities as a scholar being so well known that he had more work offered him than he could undertake to perform. He taught in the families of Mr. Henry Mackenzie, of the Exchequer, author of "The Man of Feeling," Mr. Davidson of Ravelrig, Captain Swinton, Professor John Robertson, Professor Tytler, Dr. Craigie, and others, whose sons were attending the High School or the College. His emoluments were at the rate of five guineas a quarter for two hours a day. He was upwards of two years in the family of Mr. Mackenzie, of whom he always spoke in the kindest of terms, such as—"Drank tea with Mr. Mackenzie of the Exchequer, who always makes me happy in his company, and is remarkable for being the great sublime he draws, The Man of Feeling."

His time being thus fully occupied, he had little leisure for private study, but he rose early and sat late, a course of procedure which began to tell upon his constitution. In December, 1791, he makes this note on the subject—"This is a very severe winter of frost, and is compared to the year '40. The thermometer is 14° below the freezing point, my hands are covered with chilblains by rising in the morning at 6 o'clock; but it is difficult to say whether it is better to rise so early or not, for one is not so active during the day on that account. However, it is still doing more like a rational being, than lying till 9 or 10 in the forenoon, as will sometimes happen; and therefore I resolve never to be in bed, if in health, after 6 o'clock, summer and winter, except on some Sundays when I am to preach, as I find my memory is affected by the state of my body, and that it is always most faithful to me when I sleep neither too much nor too little." This resolution he followed out till he was far beyond the allotted boundary of life, threescore and ten.

His lodgings were neither aristocratic, commodious, nor costly. They were first in Candlemaker Row for about a year and a half, but he thought it necessary to change them, and took up his abode in Potter Row, in the house of a tailor, at three shillings per week. The air was freer, and the room larger, than where he was before, and he hoped his health might thereby be maintained, if not improved. It was one of the difficulties that private tutors and probationers had then to struggle with, that of being obliged from circumstances to live in small, confined, and badly ventilated rooms, by which their constitution was enervated and disease engendered, which often terminated in death. He began to be dissatisfied with his position as a mere private teacher, and the more so that there was not the slightest prospect of a church. His divinity study seemed to have been in vain, his time wasted, and his means thrown away. He imagined himself to be a neglected man, not sufficiently appreciated, and doomed to a life of inglorious obscurity.

What he so much dreaded, too assuredly came to pass, notwithstanding the effort he had made to ward it off. He was necessitated to relinquish for a time his avocation of teaching, and to rusticate among his native hills in Galloway, for the benefit of his health. Still, though off duty on what may be called the "sick list," he was by no means idle in so far as preaching was concerned. He frequently officiated in neighbouring parishes, in Newabbey, Lochrutton, Irongray, Terregles, Urr, Colvend, and Dumfries. We find the following entry, under date 1st December, 1792.—"Have returned to town after six months' stay in the country, where I was re-establishing my health, which had been much impaired by sitting late, studying too closely, and living too abstemiously. Had a sort of nervous fever, together with an extraordinary dejection of spirits, to which the above causes contributed, with some of those

disappointments and marks of ingratitude and neglect
to which a life of dependence is subjected. But, by the
goodness of God, and the vigorous exercise of my best
resolutions to suffer no worldly circumstance to disturb
the essentials of my peace, and to expect no more from
man than what is consistent with his own advantage or
humour, I resolved to repose my trust in Providence,
and to render myself independent of the smiles or the
favours of fortune. By these resolutions, the air and
exercise of the country, and the blessing of God, I have
recovered from my fever and my melancholy, and have
returned to the theatre of life, my former business
of teaching, and preaching sometimes as usual." On
returning to town he changed his former mode of
living as a lodger, and boarded with a Miss Hunter, in
Milne's Court, at the rate of £30 a year. This was in
every respect a judicious doing, as he was better fed,
better accommodated, and better cared for, so that his
health, now re-established, was the more likely to be
maintained.

Not long after his return from rustication, he was
asked by Dr. Blair to preach and to dine with him
afterwards, both of which were done to their mutual
satisfaction. After dinner, the conversation assumed a
literary character, in which the religious merits of the
Romans and the Greeks were freely discussed. The
Doctor was greatly pleased with his young friend, and
commended him for his success in studying a portion of
the history of mankind at once so agreeable and instructive. He advised him to prepare a few good
popular sermons on some of the peculiar doctrines of
Christianity, such as the Death of Christ, Faith, and

similar subjects, which might be suitable for sacramental occasions, or for preaching in vacant parishes.
Mr. Wightman left in the evening highly gratified with
the whole day's proceedings. A day or two afterwards
he called upon Principal Robertson, who had requested
him to preach, and he makes the following note of the
interview:—

"Dec. 26th, 1792.—Called on Dr. Robertson, who is now
old and infirm, but who yet displays the glories of the
setting sun. He is a very gentlemanlike man, of easy
manners, obliging and condescending. He has a wonderful
stock of local anecdote, and particular information concerning the whole kingdom, the living history, as well as the
transactions of past ages, which makes him a very interesting character, and his conversation very agreeable. Dr.
Blair and he are two great friends, and cordially interested
in each other's welfare. They will likely live to nearly the
same age, and die almost together. Indeed, Dr. Blair is
already seventy-five, and is more healthy than his aged
compeer, though he is at the same time a few years older.
Dr. Robertson has had an attack of black jaundice, but is
now much better, and out walking every morning before
breakfast, in order to protract his useful and respectable
life. He says he always preaches himself when he is able,
as it is agreeable to perform what one should do. He is
happy to see the preachers so willing to give him assistance.
He has much less of the monk about him than Dr. Blair
sometimes appears to have, as well as less preciseness and
pettiness. Both are good men."

Again the old feeling of dissatisfaction with his position as an outdoor tutor came in the ascendant, and he
was unwilling to suppress it. Since he received license

he had made little addition to his stock of ideas, or improvement in literature, owing to his close attention to teaching, and to the few opportunities afforded him for enlarging his acquaintance with the world, or with books. He had been obliged to trudge from one door to another so many hours a day, and to travel over the beaten tracks of school elementary lessons, except when reading the higher classics with those pupils who attended college, so that the very monotony of his daily life rendered it irksome and even distasteful. Had his aim in life been no higher than a teacher, the matter would have been altogether different; but when he studied and strove for a church, and yet no church appeared, he felt disappointed and chagrined. Not only did he feel his health giving way, by protracting his studies far into the night, on account of the interruptions he met with throughout the day from the desultory nature of his employment, but he found his habits of application considerably relaxed, and a kind of apathy induced, very unfavourable to progress in any branch of learning. When such a day's business as he engaged in was over, one had little disposition to do much by himself, and was often deceived by appearances of having done something when in reality there was almost nothing. It therefore became a question with him whether he would not have been happier with his old father on his farm at home, and enjoying the sweets of social affection with his brother and sisters, where his consequence was felt as a member of society, than he was at present, not only detached from them, but also from the world, though in the midst of the great metropolis, without any prospect of success in the Church, as he was too proud to submit to some of the terms by which advancement in that direction was secured. Still, in the midst of such reveries, he determined to do the best in his power to make his way creditably through the world, never to stoop to a mean or ungenerous action, so as to forego the pleasure arising from a good conscience; to be industrious, prudent, and contented with the condition in which Providence placed his lot. Thus he should be happy independently of the smiles of fortune. The great object of all his studies, kept constantly in view, was that he might be a virtuous man, a good scholar, and a persuasive preacher. In the midst of his ruminations and resolutions, a new phase appeared in his life which put an end to his murmurings against peripatetic tuition.

CHAPTER II.

BECOMES TUTOR IN BALCHRISTIE—CANDIDATE FOR THE GRAMMAR-
SCHOOL OF DUMFRIES—TUTOR IN DUNRAGIT—APPLIES FOR A
CHURCH IN AMERICA—LETTER FROM THE REV. DR. BLAIR—JOINS
THE VOLUNTEERS—GRIEVANCES—REFLECTIONS ON PUBLIC AND
PRIVATE EDUCATION—RESOLVES TO RESIGN SITUATION—LETTER
FROM THE REV. DR. BURNSIDE—RECEIVES PRESENTATION TO
KIRKMAHOE.

MR. WIGHTMAN, to the great relief of his moody
musings, received and accepted an invitation to become
resident tutor in the family of Captain Christie of
Balchristie, in Fifeshire, and at Whitsunday, 1793, he
left Edinburgh for the discharge of his responsible
duties. After a stormy and tedious passage across the
Forth, he landed at Kinghorn, where he found a horse
awaiting him, and in due time he arrived at his new
abode. His reception by Captain and Mrs. Christie
was most cordial and kind, and the accommodation
provided for him was all that he could desire. The
family library, more select than large, was placed at his
disposal, and he was even requested to take it into his
own apartment. This he felt to be a very great boon,
and he resolved to make good use of the privilege
afforded him, so as to redeem the time which he considered had been lost. The portion of the family
consigned to his care consisted of three sons and three
daughters, the two youngest, however, being reserved

B

for a later stage. His interest in the new situation
was the greater, from the circumstance that Balchristie
was the most ancient of all the places bearing the
name of Christie, and that one of the family ancestors,
having been standard-bearer to David I. in one of the
crusades, was highly complimented for his bravery on
the occasion by the king, who bade him for the future
always to act worthy of his name, giving him the sign
of the cross for a crest, accompanied by the motto, *Vita
sit nomini congrua.* He found, as he anticipated, his
young charge very docile and attentive, and, as time
went on, their progress was much to his own satisfaction as well as that of the parents. He frequently
officiated in the neighbouring pulpits, and thereby,
while improving his preaching abilities, he also extended his sphere of acquaintanceship among those
who might have it in their power to place him more
prominently in the eye of the Church. In his anxiety
for the benefit of youth under domestic tutorage, he
projected the publication of something towards that
end, in which he aimed at showing how much depended
upon the parents themselves, in countenancing the
teacher, enforcing his rules, and strengthening his
hands, by a marked desire to uphold him in the
exercise of discipline, and to assist him generally
by approving of what he did. He had found from
experience that there was sometimes two separate
interests in a family—one of the tutor, and another
of the parents—which ought not to exist, and which
could not possibly do so without detriment to both and
disadvantage to the children. A portion of the treatise
was proceeded with, which took the form of dialogue,

but from want of leisure it was discontinued and never resumed.

During the first year of his engagement there, the mastership of the Grammar-School of Dumfries became vacant, by the retirement of Mr. Wait on account of declining health, and he made application for the office. Before doing so, however, he consulted his friend Mr. Cririe in the matter, and it would seem that at this time he entertained some thoughts of entering into married life. The endowments of the office, including the salary of session-clerk, were £60, of which £20 were payable to Dr. Chapman during his life; the remaining £40, with the Candlemas offering, a free house, and wages from country scholars, were all that could be looked to, except what might arise from keeping boarders. But even this was burdened with the expense of an assistant. Notwithstanding this small allowance, Mr. Wait, during his incumbency of some nineteen years and a half, had amassed a sum of £5000. Mr. Cririe had himself been solicited to stand for the situation, but declined, and he left Mr. Wightman very much to his own decision, stating that "he durst not say more than that it would be a certain and honourable situation." By way of joke, he asked him if he would not think of going back to Galloway to assist Mr. Finnan by marrying his daughter and getting himself appointed assistant and successor by means of interest with Heron of Heron. The election was made by competitive trial, under the examination of Professors Dalzel and Hill, who were brought from Edinburgh University for the purpose. Mr. Wightman was not appointed, to his very great chagrin. There were six candidates in all—Mr. Wightman, Mr. Shand (a school-master from the North), Mr. Hamilton (teacher of elocution in Edinburgh, and who had formerly taught an academy in England), Mr. Grierson (master of the free school of Balmaclellan), Mr. Thomson (son of the schoolmaster of Tynron), and Mr. Gray (a student). Mr. Gray was the successful competitor, the Professors recommending him as having answered their questions most completely. Mr. Wightman was exceedingly mortified, and complained that the field of examination was much too narrow, and did not by any means furnish scope for literary abilities; even the very minor points could not be reviewed in the short space of less than an hour, which was given to each, much less the knowledge of antiquities so essentially requisite in the teacher of a grammar-school. The subjects of examination were:—A short chapter of Livy, a few stanzas of an ode of Horace, two or three verses of the Greek Testament, a single sentence out of Mair's Introduction, three questions in Greek, and the same number in Latin. Professor Hill's Synonyms, quirks, and enigmas, composed the rest of the trial. Some of the questions were—What is the *Litera tristis?*—the *Litera salutaris?* What do the letters *N. L.* signify? What means the *theta* in the passage of Persius? What is the meaning of *Poscere vitam libello?* What means *Terra clauditur infans?* Mr. Wightman did not make a good appearance, partly from ignorance, as he said, and partly from natural trepidation, but he acquitted the examinators of all partiality, and doubted not that their decision was honourable and fair. Still he could not but ask himself if these were the *criteria*

by which to judge of classical knowledge and accuracy
in the principles of the two languages. Towards the
close of this year, 1794, Dr. Chapman of Edinburgh
wrote to him, intimating his intention of opening a
small classical academy at Liberton Kirk, and requesting him to take a share in it. He offered him every
inducement, promised to give him the greatest part of
the profits, as he would have the greatest part of the
labour, and to do everything possible for the promotion
of his comfort. This, however, he declined, being
unwilling to accept the conditions proposed, of giving
up all other views, and devoting his attention enthusiastically to the duties of the new academy.

After having been two years in Balchristie, feeling
himself embarrassed on account of the increasing number of his pupils, and having little time for private
reading or study, though in all other respects he had
nothing to complain of, save an occasional want of
paternal concurrence in the coercive measures he
thought necessary to adopt, he resolved to accept an
offer made to him of another tutorship in Galloway, his
native district. Professor Dalzel and Mr. Criric had
been applied to by Captain Dalrymple Hay, of Dunragit, near Glenluce, to supply him with a tutor for his
son—a boy about six years of age—at a salary of £25
per annum. The first offer was made to Mr. Wightman
and accepted, when he immediately left for his new
sphere in the south. Taking a month's holidays for
rustication and visiting friends, he entered upon his
duties at Dunragit on the 14th July, 1795. Here he
found all the comfort and happiness of home; his
pupils were docile and clever, and the parents treated

him with the respect due to one engaged in so important and responsible a work. He commenced with the greatest enthusiasm, resolved to exert himself to the utmost, especially as Mr. Cririe had said in his letter offering the situation, "There is hope that this may end in a kirk." He was very methodical, not only with his pupils, but also with himself. He rose at five in the morning, walked till seven, taught till nine, breakfasted, taught from ten till twelve, studied and read till dinner-time, taught again from five till eight, supped at nine, read till eleven, and then went to bed. "He found it necessary," he said, "to rise with Aurora and inhale the salubrious breath of the spring, to prevent him sinking into the feeble effeminacy which is destructive of all energy of mind and relish of life." From too much confinement previously, he had contracted a delicacy of constitution which made him anxious to regain his former robustness of health, and prevent consequences by which his usefulness might be impaired. Having got wet in one of his morning perambulations, he was seized with a sudden illness, which lasted for two days, and so violent and dangerous were the symptoms that his life was despaired of; but, by the assiduous attentions of Captain and Mrs. Hay, he was brought round, to the great delight of all. This kindness greatly attached him to the family, while a sense of obligation and duty rendered his situation exceedingly agreeable. Though there was only one boy, there were four girls—the youngest ten and the eldest sixteen—to whom also he agreed to give lessons three hours a day; but as they were very pleasant and attentive, he considered the additional charge a delight instead of a burden. Though under the care of a governess, they preferred taking their history, arithmetic, writing, geography, and grammar from the tutor, who felt flattered and encouraged by the distinction thus shown. He had now more leisure for reading, and study, and writing sermons, than he had long enjoyed. Indeed, during his two years' incumbency in Balchristie, he wrote only one discourse, a lecture on the Prodigal Son. He now read very sedulously every new book he could obtain, making critical jottings as he proceeded. He revised his Latin by reading through the whole of Virgil, and he varied the recreation by going over several standard works in French. Of course, the Greek and Hebrew were not neglected, especially when he was preparing for the pulpit. He preached, too, occasionally for the neighbouring ministers, thus keeping himself in exercise for what he trusted would, in the course of Providence, be his permanent profession. His pupils went on most satisfactorily to all parties—his spirits were high, he braced himself for greater efforts, and he thanked heaven that his lines had fallen in such pleasant places.

Still, he was desirous of getting into the Church, as that had been the one object of his whole life, the mainspring of all his studies. He had many clerical friends who had been using their influence for the attainment of this, and he himself left no stone unturned that he might finally succeed. Learning that a vacancy had occurred in an American church, the filling up of which was entrusted to the Rev. Dr. Blair of Edinburgh and his colleagues, he at once made application for the charge, and received the following letter in reply:—

"EDINBURGH, 12th Nov., 1795.—Dear Sir,—I remember you very well, and not having forgot how obliging you used to be to me some time ago, I shall be very well pleased to be of any service to you when in my power. As to that settlement in America, concerning which application was made by the congregation to me, in conjunction with Dr. Baird and Dr. Hunter, I cannot say whether it be precluded or not. The offer of it has been made to a clergyman at some distance, whose final answer we have not yet received. In case he decline the offer, and the place remain vacant, I shall not fail to mention you to my colleagues in that affair, and shall let you know the issue. It is the Presbyterian congregation of Halifax, in Nova Scotia; their salary is £180 per annum; money is lodged with me for the passage of any one whom we send to them; they take him on a sort of trial for the first half year. Their last minister was Dr. Andrew Brown, who was sent to them by Dr. Robertson and me. He lived among them for some years very comfortably, and with very high reputation, and they expressed the greatest regret on his leaving them. He has lately returned to this country, and is just now settled minister of Lochmaben. If you have any acquaintance with him, he can give you full information, and, indeed, we wish to have his approbation of any person whom we recommend to the congregation. I shall be very well pleased if this or any other thing succeed to your wish, and shall, as I promised, let you know if this remain open, and if the choice is likely to fall upon you, in case you shall incline to accept the place.—I am, with best wishes for your welfare, dear Sir, yours sincerely,

"HUGH BLAIR.

"*P.S.*—Dr. Burnside, who recommended you to me some time ago, will probably now be acquainted with Dr. Brown,

and it may be of use that he recommend you to him, in case
this charge remain open, which, however, as I told you
above, is uncertain, as the offer of it, previous to your
application to me, had been made to two gentlemen."

As no other intimation respecting it ever reached
him, he understood that a previous applicant had been
appointed, and he calmly resigned himself to his fate.

It is said that "Hope deferred maketh the heart
sick," but though his had been frequently in this state,
yet it speedily revived under a consciousness that he
deserved better, and that however long the world might
overlook him, it would bring all things right at last;
therefore, he looked forward to better fortune, when it
should please Providence to send it. He had in a
manner become habituated to failure and disappointment in his views, but still, "though cast down, he was
not destroyed." At this time there was the greatest
fear of French invasion, and men were everywhere
called on to enrol as volunteers in defence of their
country. Mr. Wightman sent in his name to the corps,
and soon afterwards wrote a patriotic ballad to the tune
of "One bottle more," which appeared in the *Edinburgh
Magazine* under the signature of " A Wigtownshire
Volunteer." One of the stanzas ran thus:—

> "Ye artists and workmen of every degree,
>   Come rise in defence of your country with me;
>   Let nothing, I pray you, now damp your bold zeal,
>   But arm in defence of the great Common-weal.
>   Great Common-weal, &c."

Bright as was the sky, and beautiful the landscape,
when Mr. Wightman first went to Dunragit, by-and-by
specks of cloud began to appear on the one, and corres-

ponding shadows on the other, which in his eyes considerably altered the witchery of the scene. Little disagreeable incidents occasionally occurred in the way of his profession, which might have been passed over more easily by one of less sensitive feelings, and with a lower estimate of the responsibilities and duties which devolved upon him. Petty grievances, real or imaginary, took possession of his mind, and when this is the case, a molehill becomes a mountain, and the jealous eye looks at everything through a distorted medium. Maternal sympathy was thought to interfere too frequently with preceptorial decree—his independence was not sufficiently recognized—when the parents were absent the children were told to take the head and the foot of the table, while the tutor and governess sat anywhere. James, the pupil, took suspicious headaches when a lesson seemed difficult, and then he was "to be excused." When he was complained of for assisting the maid to milk the cows, the answer was—"It was natural;" he went with the shoeblack to hunt rabbits, but this also "was natural." It was proposed that he should sometimes go to church, but then "this would prevent him from enjoying himself," and so on with other things similar. Now, Mr. Wightman, in his anxiety to become a model tutor, and to train up his pupil in order to be a model gentleman, might have known, with the experience he had acquired, that such things as these were not peculiar to the heir of Dunragit, as every tutor could testify in a greater or less degree. But he was a strict disciplinarian, and had a high sense of authority in the schoolroom, perhaps a little too much with a boy of such tender years. However, after mutual explanations had been made when any little misunderstanding arose, the sun shone out as before, and all was again beautiful as if there had never been a cloud.

It was during one of these temporary overshadowings that he made the following reflections on the subject of domestic and public education:—"A free and open manner is not so much the effect of being under no restraint, as being convinced that the restraint is just and reasonable, imposed without any vindictive spirit, and preserved on all occasions without caprice, no difference of opinion taking place in the matter of execution. Sympathy is the great key of the human spirit, and if all the parties are of one opinion, a boy will acquiesce in suffering the restraint due to his situation, and will possess more confidence than one who is less restrained, but whose feelings have been agitated by sympathizing with a variety of opinions on the subject of discipline. Let your laws be few, just, liberal, and executed with unshaken steadiness, and without the least partiality or caprice, and a free and unconstrained behaviour is the natural and becoming result. There is more danger of caprice and frowardness respectively on the side of the teacher and the scholar in a family, than where both parties are free. The idea that his kindness is not independent, and his corrections liable to a strict and partial review, renders the mind of the teacher uneasy; and from this very uneasiness and ruffled state of mind arise sometimes actions of rigour and severity which he would never think of were he entirely conscious of freedom to do as he pleased. And, on the other hand, a boy is apt to consider all the happiness of his condition as the effect of his father or mother's vigilance in his behalf, and all the pain he suffers to arise from the perverse disposition of his tutor. Hence that coldness and even aversion which we often see between a person who has been instructed in a private family and his tutor, while that same person speaks with affection and respect of him who presided in the public school where he may have studied a while, either after or before the period of his domestic education. This is one of the many arguments for a public education. The reason arises from the wish of parents to avoid all the odium that attaches to punishment, and to be the objects of all the gratitude and affection so natural to youthful minds. Much might be altered for the better in the ordinary modes of domestic instruction. When a tutor enters a family, he generally sees habits which he longs to undo, and replace by others more suitable to young persons acquiring with advantage the principles of knowledge; but he will do well to consider that these habits have been formed by causes which he is not competent to remove, unless he meets with a more hearty concurrence from the heads of the family than is usually to be found. The very accent of their speech, as well as the tone of their manners, have been derived from the company with which they (the children) have been accustomed to associate, and he will find few parents disposed to agree with him in thinking these things faults which they have been used to hear and see every day. The teacher must be satisfied to correct a part, but he must not attempt to grub up and plant anew lest he should raise a dust not easily laid. The children are disposed to think the old way best,

and few parents will think any new way good which
gives a moment's pain to the children, whatever advantages may be supposed to result from such renovations.
A teacher who does not duly attend to this will prove
another Don Quixote, and be bruised by the windmills
he madly rushed on. The manners and ideas of the
country and provinces are to be considered, and any set
of ideas or manners opposite to these, or superior to
them, ought not to be pushed too far against the tide
of custom and general opinion; for on every occasion
you are liable to be overborne by the plurality of
voices; and where the condition of a leader is, in
general, disrespected, no merits will justify any one of
the order to assume airs of more importance than his
fellows. On considering the case of a tutor whom his
pupil had left at home till he should return from a
month's visit to some of his great relations and friends,
it strikes me that young persons should have finished
the most material parts of their education before it be
found necessary to separate the tutor from his pupil in
so delicate a case, and this seems another reason why a
teacher should prefer a public school to a private
family. In the former situation his work goes on,
notwithstanding the absence of some of his numbers,
and he is not reduced to the alternative of moping on
the miseries of his lot, or of having recourse to pursuits
incompatible with, and perhaps destructive of, a taste
in his profession. He is like a sword in the time of
peace, which is eaten with rust and neglected, till the
trumpet sound to arms again. Another argument for a
public education is this:—Before a teacher has gained
that confidence and authority, that importance and

credit in a family, he is too great a man—I mean, he is beyond his rank when he is out of the family—and this is injurious to his happiness; and if he has not this consequence, the pupil is lost or degraded by receiving instruction from one whom he must despise. A public school or academy is best for the teacher in every case."

In the summer of 1797 he had become so utterly tired of his situation that he firmly resolved to leave it, if not to abandon the profession altogether, as a "critical, laborious, degrading, and under-valued employment." On the 9th May he prepared a letter of resignation to Captain D. Hay, in which he stated that the situation of domestic tutor seemed to involve circumstances peculiarly unfriendly to his happiness, that even the liberal and judicious arrangement of his family could not secure him against their real or imaginary influence, and he would therefore resign his office as teacher at the end of July, which corresponded to the time at which he had entered two years before. This letter he deferred delivering in the meantime, perhaps thinking he might change his mind, or that it might be better to find a new situation before he gave up the old. From the light of after years it was evident that he was entirely mistaken in the suspicion he cherished as to being slighted and regarded as a menial. On the contrary, he was held in high estimation, and on his leaving he received from the parents a diamond ring of very great value, and the members of the family, male and female, kept up a correspondence with him for many years after he left, sending him little *souvenirs* of their affectionate remembrance and regard. But he did not know these kindly feelings towards him at the time, or rather, we should say, he blinded himself to the perception of them, not willingly, but from the over-sensitive constitution of his nature. But we are anticipating.

It was on one of these dark days, metaphorically we mean, that the light streamed in upon him with over-powering effulgence. Churches were vacant everywhere, three within the Presbytery of Dumfries— Troqueer, Irongray, and Kirkmahoe. He had applied to several friends to use their influence for him, and some had done so unbidden, but still there was no sign of a presentation. Mr. Cririe had written him that his appointment to Dunragit might end in a kirk, but that seemed to him an impossibility. One day, when sad and ruminating in a lonely place distant from the house, the following letter was put into his hand by a servant who had been searching the fields to find him. It was from the Rev. Dr. Burnside of Dumfries:—

"DUMFRIES, 8th June, 1797.—My Dear Sir,—It is with much pleasure that I have to inform you that I had a call this morning both of Mr. Constable and Mr. Staig, who each of them showed me letters from the Duke of Queensberry, from which it appears that you are to be minister of Kirkmahoe. For this you are indebted to Lady Winifred and Mr. Constable. Mr. M'Morine of Carlaverock and I pledged ourselves that you are a man of good principles both in religion and politics, and that we believe you will make a good and useful pastor for the Christians in Kirkmahoe. So take care and be prepared to act accordingly. When are you coming down to give me your annual sermon? Remember I will expect that favour from you. You will hereafter have less distance to travel for it. The presenta-

tion, which is in Mr. Staig's hands, will be lodged in due
time with Mr. Heron, our moderator. Our next Presbytery
is on the first Tuesday of July, when it will be lodged along
with a letter of acceptance from your Reverence, which I
dare say you will have no difficulty of granting.—I am, dear
Sir, yours faithfully,   W. BURNSIDE."

It is almost unnecessary to say that on reading
this letter his joy was unbounded. There was now
no necessity for giving in his proposed resignation,
and he felt ashamed that such a proposal should
have been entertained. Everything had assumed a
pleasing aspect, and the world never seemed so beautiful before. Eager to announce the grateful tidings,
he hurried homewards with all speed. A small stream
lay in his way, but he rushed straight through it, as
time would have been lost to have sought the bridge.

> "He stayed not for brake, and he stopped not for stone,
> He swam the Esk river where ford there was none."

On entering the hall, in the greatest exuberance of
spirits, he cried out, "Make way for the minister of
Kirkmahoe!—I'm the minister of Kirkmahoe!" Every
one came running to see what was the matter with
the tutor, and hearty were the congratulations he
received from all when he explained to them the cause
of his joy. He felt they were all friends together.
Poor James' feigned illnesses were all forgiven, and
forgotten—even the shoeblack got a kindly smile of
recognition, and the hunting of rabbits was tacitly
acknowledged to be "very natural after all."

CHAPTER III.

ORDINATION—RECEPTION IN THE PARISH—FIRST COMMUNION—DR.
BRYCE JOHNSTON—COMMUNION IN OLDEN TIME—SOLEMN SCENE
AT SANQUHAR—TENT PREACHING—POPULAR PREJUDICE AGAINST
USING A PULPIT GOWN—VINDICATION OF VERACITY IN CHURCH
—EXTRACT FROM DIARY—ATTENDANCE AT CHURCH—LETTER
FROM DR. CRIRIE.

THE PRESENTATION and Mr. Wightman's letter of acceptance were laid before the Presbytery of Dumfries on the 4th of July, and ordered to remain upon the table till the next meeting on the 14th, when they were considered and sustained, and he was appointed to preach in Kirkmahoe on the following Sunday. The moderation took place on the 3rd of August, when the call was signed by seven heritors, one elder, twenty-four heads of families, and other parishioners. One who was both an heritor and an elder expressed his concurrence in presence of the Court. No objections being made, the call and concurrence were sustained, and the subjects of trial prescribed. These having been satisfactorily performed at a subsequent meeting, the ordination was fixed for the 21st September, at Kirkmahoe. The Rev. Joseph Easton, who had been ordained assistant and successor at Troqueer only a few weeks previous, presided on the occasion, preaching from Malachi ii. 7, "For the priest's lips should keep knowledge, and they should seek the law at his

C

mouth : for he is the messenger of the Lord of hosts."
Mr. Wightman, having given satisfactory answers to
the questions put to such as are to be ordained, was
set apart to the office of the holy ministry by the
laying on of the hands of the Presbytery, after which
he received the right hand of fellowship from the
brethren present, and was suitably addressed by the
Moderator, as was also the congregation, on their
respective duties as pastor and people. After the
dismissal, the heritors, elders, and others of the congregation took their new minister by the hand in
token of their friendly welcome and desire for his
success. Mr. Wightman had now obtained the full
accomplishment of his desire, for which he had long
prayed and struggled amid many difficulties, though
still with fewer hardships than some. He was now
thirty-five years of age, and had been six years a
probationer. He had almost given up all hopes of
preferment in the Church, and, as we saw, had nearly
relinquished the profession of domestic tutor in despair.
Only some four months ago he thought his lot a dreary
one and scarcely to be borne; now he is at the height
of his ambition, with his happiness complete.

As the manse was in a bad state from decay, and a
new one was about to be built, Mr. Wightman took
lodgings in the neighbouring farm-house of Kemyshall,
where he remained for upwards of two years. Though
he had been long a preacher, and in that capacity had
widely officiated for his friends, yet his stock of sermons
was limited, as he had been unable to command leisure
for private study to any considerable extent. Accordingly he set himself to prepare a lecture and a sermon

every week, besides attending to the week-day pastoral
duties of the parish. This was no easy task to which
he devoted his energies, for, in addition to the studying
and writing of his discourses, there was also the committing of them to memory, there being the strongest
popular prejudice against the use of manuscript in the
pulpit; and for thirty years he never used a note. His
entrance into the parish was not altogether favourably
regarded by the great bulk of the inhabitants, although
they had not formally objected at the moderation of
the call. He had been recommended to the patron by
one who did not belong to their religious denomination
—he had been presented before he had once preached
in the parish—they had no opportunity of hearing him,
and in no way had they been consulted in the appointment. The first sermon he preached they watched for
his halting, and carefully counted how often, or rather
how seldom, the name of the Saviour was introduced;
they declared it had been mentioned only seven times,
and in other respects they did not consider it up to the
mark of gospel preaching. The subject was the danger
of keeping bad company, preached from the text Prov.
iv. 14, 15, "Enter not into the path of the wicked, and
go not in the way of evil men; avoid it, pass not by it,
turn from it, and pass away." Unedifying as it was
then regarded, when he preached it to them again,
eighteen years afterwards, they considered it so instructive that they earnestly solicited him to publish
it for general benefit. He was not unaware of the
feeling which existed against him, but he strove the
more assiduously to gain their affection by an ardent
and faithful discharge of the duties of his office, and

in the course of time he entirely succeeded. When a vacancy occurred shortly afterwards in the neighbouring parish of Tinwald, the people there expressed a wish that they had him for their minister, which so affected him that for many a day he went to the Tinwald hills to study his sermons for his own folk of Kirkmahoe. The following incident shows how the wind was blowing at the time. One day coming down the parish from a visitation he overtook an old woman who was vainly endeavouring to rehoist a burden of firewood she had laid down for a rest. When she was making a prodigious effort he came behind her unperceived, and aided her by lifting it on her back. Finding it rise so easily, she looked round to discover the cause, when, seeing it was the minister, she said, " Be thou gude, or be thou ill, thou'st dune me a gude turn anyway." The church began to be well attended, and in a short time became so full that seats were not to be had, so that an additional gallery was thought of for increased accommodation. This greatly encouraged him in his work, and he put forth all his strength for their edification, and to merit their good-will. His communion came round, and he made the necessary arrangements. Dr. Bryce Johnston, author of an Exposition of the Book of Revelation, was at this time minister of Holywood, and he preached on the Fastday. The following memorandum is given of his pulpit services :—

"Thursday, 26th June (Fast-day).—Dr. Bryce Johnston preached all day for me from Acts viii. 37: 'If thou believest with all thine heart thou mayest.' The Doctor introduced the subject with a long explanation of the context relative to the treasurer of the Queen of Ethiopia, and then proceeded to show what is implied in believing with the heart. He laid great stress on the word *heart*, and often reminded us that it is nowhere said in Scripture that we are to believe with the *head*. He made a diffuse application of the doctrine of salvation by faith to the occasion of the sacrament, and insisted on the use of means. I thought he was particularly agitated in his sermon, as if he had met with some opposition to his⟨maxims,⟩and I never noticed him so intemperate in his gestures, nor so low and vulgar in his allusions and comparisons. Showing that we can receive knowledge only by the⟨channels God has appointed, he said if we were to shut our eyes we could not see with our ears, and appealed to the audience, that though he just now saw the letters on the munifaction tablet on the wall before him, yet were he to shut his eyes he could not see these letters with his ears, and desired any of his hearers to make the trial! Illustrating the evidence of testimony, he said we believed there was such a city as Paris, and we knew from experience that ⟨Dumfries was near. When showing that we are accountable beings, he said a machine performed the work appointed, but not from any motive—for example, a mill—and he triumphed in this allusion with peculiar exultation. I do not think such methods of illustration, however plain they may be reckoned, are very edifying in the church, and especially on sacramental occasions. He said that God could have made anything to answer the purpose served by another, even common whinstone to have been as good a manure as lime. *Ohe, jam satis!!* Yet the Doctor has talents, and considerable shrewdness in both religious and civil matters."

The Communion Sunday was extremely hot, and in the morning, before public worship began, Mr. Wightman

ordered several panes to be broken out of the church
windows for ventilation, which had a good effect, though
by some it was thought indecent to break church windows, and especially on Sunday. He had them afterwards filled in at his own expense. There was no tent
preaching, which caused some temporary offence to
several individuals, but all was conducted decently and
in order on the part of both ministers and people. There
were eight tables, and three assistant ministers. The
forenoon service terminated at half-past five o'clock, and,
after an hour's interval, Mr. Smail of Kirkmichael
preached the evening sermon to those who remained.
Two ministers had preached on the Saturday, and other
two followed on the Monday, making nine in all employed on the occasion. As the manner of observing
this ordinance in rural parishes has undergone a very
great change, we may glance at the form of procedure
in the olden time.

The Communion, or the "Preachings," as it was commonly called, from the amount of preaching which
attended it, afforded a favourable opportunity for the
exercise of various ministerial gifts in the several
addresses which were delivered. At the close of public
worship on Saturday, before the blessing was pronounced,
the minister himself entered the pulpit and gave some
directions about the next day's worship. This done,
there followed a long and minute recapitulation of the
sermons which had just been delivered, as well as on the
Fast-day preceding. This was called "perlequeing,"
and was considered advantageous to the hearers, as
bringing into a focus before them the lessons of instruction to which they had listened, preparing them for the

profitable observance of the next day's solemnities. No doubt this had a beneficial effect to a certain extent, and the end was so far promoted, but there was, perhaps, another purpose not wholly out of view by the speaker in being so minute. This was the gratification of a little display, showing how much he himself remembered of what had been said (no great achievement after all), and thereby conveying a tacit admonition that those addressed might have done the same, had proper attention been given. Sometimes considerable ingenuity was displayed in dove-tailing one sermon into another, so as to make them appear one continuous whole, when the subjects were far from having a homogeneous character; but this only told the more to the ability of him who attempted it with success. This custom had another phase not so agreeable. It was sometimes discourteous to the preachers, though it generally erred the other way; for where a sermon had been either defective in doctrine, dry in treatment, or confused in style, new matter, illustration, and arrangement were introduced, as if originally given, so that while assuming a complimentary form ostensibly, it yet indirectly rebuked the preacher for his lack of logic and theology. Such defects, however, real or supposed, were sometimes not allowed to pass in silence, and doctrines were controverted as misleading or erroneous. A minister of Lochrutton, in Galloway, was accustomed to speak very freely when engaged in this duty. On one occasion he attacked the discourse which had just been given by an able and experienced parish minister, who was sitting behind him in the pulpit at the time, and tore it to shreds, declaring that it was not at all an exposition of the text, and altogether unsound. The people knew their minister's tendency, and so paid no attention to his strictures, the scarified preacher doing the same.

The Sunday was the greatest of all the days in importance, solemnity, and outward excitement, several ministers arriving to assist in the work. As the neighbouring churches were thrown vacant on that day, the several populations gathered in crowds and were addressed from a tent in the churchyard, while the more solemn part of the service was conducted inside the church. Sometimes, for the greater convenience of the worshippers, when the weather was favourable, the tables were arranged in the churchyard in front of the tent, and the whole duties of the day were performed in the open air. This had a solemnity and sublimity not realized within the church. The simple worshipper looked up without obstruction to the heavens high above his head, while the homage of his heart and the utterance of his lips rose in sweet memorial to the throne of God. The field of death around brought all, as it were, into closer proximity with their God, with the great resurrection, and with those kindred spirits who had gone before to the mansions above. There, seated on the green graves or the gray tombstones, with the dust beneath them, it required but little imagination to consider both dead and living listening to the word of life, or standing for judgment before the great white throne. The old trees around, venerable with age, like the cedars of Lebanon, and the blue vault of heaven above, gave additional impressiveness to the scene, and imparted a charm to the occasion which wrought a beneficial influence upon the hearer's heart. Besides, suitable topics

were often suggested for discourse to those who addressed
the assembled multitude.   Some of the ministers were
very felicitous in adapting their exhortations to the
peculiar circumstances in which they were placed, which
always produced a solemnizing effect.   James Hislop
gives a very beautiful illustration of this.   On one of
these occasions the ordinance was just about to be
dispensed in the churchyard of Sauquhar, which is
picturesquely situated in the bosom of aged trees, and
surrounded by high hills.   The long tables, covered
with snow-white cloths, were filled with devout worshippers, while hundreds were seated around, waiting
till they could be admitted in turn.   The action sermon
and other preliminary devotional exercises were over,
and the minister at the head of the tables had read the
latter portion of the 116th Psalm, usual at such times,
when an awful peal of thunder burst over their heads,
echoing and re-echoing among the hills.   All were
struck with the profoundest awe, and held their breath
till the sound had died away.   It seemed as if the
Almighty was giving an audible approval of the religious
ordinance in which they were engaged.   When all were
hushed in death-like stillness, the minister addressed
them in the following terms:—" My friends, how dreadful
is this place!   This is none other but the house of God,
and this is the gate of heaven.   He before whom we
must appear in judgment, from His pavilion of dark
waters, and thick clouds of the skies, in a voice of thunder
is now addressing us who are assembled around His table;
and I have no doubt that if the thin veil by which we are
separated from the invisible world were drawn aside, we
might discover among these dark clouds where the

thunder is rolling the throne of Him from before whose face the earth and the heavens shall flee away—we might behold on the mountains around us the bright armies of heaven drawn up in their shining ranks, under the banners of the King of Righteousness—we might behold those who have joined with us at this table, whose graves are now rising green beneath our feet, but whose spirits are in glory. I say we might behold them looking upon us with heavenly joy and satisfaction, while we join ourselves unto the Lord in a perpetual covenant never to be forgotten." Every worshipper there might well remember that communion till the latest hour of life. So much was the dispensation of the ordinance in the church-yard appreciated in the parish of Closeburn that when it was proposed by the minister, for the first time, to transfer it to the church, the elders resolutely refused their consent, declaring it "most unseemly that the holy communion should be celebrated in a hole-and-corner way like that." The minister, however, was firm, and while there was the usual amount of tent preaching outside, the ordinance was partaken of within, but other elders had to be borrowed from Kirkmichael to officiate at the tables.

In "Fencing" the tables, what was called the *Debarring* was always lengthened and minute, while the *Invitation* was short and general. The *Debarring* was so called from the several classes of sinners addressed being solemnly debarred or prohibited from partaking of the ordinance. So minute and comprehensive was the enumeration of these classes that one would have thought the tables were prepared in vain, as none could be entitled to come forward with impunity. Profane swear-

ing was very particularly insisted on in all its forms, and
especially in that of minced oaths, which were very
common. One clergyman in the vicinity of Dumfries is
reported to have said, when engaged in this part of the
service—"I debar from these tables all those who use
any kind of minced oaths, such as heth, teth, feth, fegs,
losh, gosh, or loveneuty." No doubt the great object of
such particularity was to preserve the purity of the
ordinance, and prevent the commission of aggravated
sin, though there was a seeming inconsistency in what
followed, the earnestness in inviting and urging communicants to come forward and partake of the memorials
of redeeming love. Indeed, an instance is on record,
when, after the debarring, not a single individual would
come forward, till the minister, seeing his mistake, en-
treated them by saying that he did not altogether mean
what he had said. It is right, however, to mention that
this minister did not belong to the Church of Scotland,
and his own brethren admonished him for his zeal without knowledge.

While the church was filled in every part, pews, pas-
sages, and stairs, the tent was the great attraction, and
the service there began as soon as an audience had
assembled, and was continued by relays of preachers till
the worship in the church was over far towards evening.
Those clergymen who did not require to use notes
always got well on in the tent, for, besides this stroke of
popularity, there was a great oratorical advantage in
being able to lean over the fauldboard, and look at all
around while making some allusion to the sleeping dust
beneath, while those who used the manuscript had sometimes difficulty in keeping it before them from the gusts

of wind that would rush in through the trees. We once saw the papers of a preacher in this position whirled out of the tent altogether, and blown in various directions over the churchyard. The audience ran in pursuit of the lost treasure, while the preacher acted as well as could be expected, and quietly gave out a psalm, which was joined in only by the precentor and himself. The performances of the various preachers were all freely criticized by the hearers on the way home, when the day's duties had come to a close, and their criticisms were often of an original character. Dr. Scot of St. Michael's, Dumfries, was once assisting at the communion in Urr, where the other officiating clergymen were great guns from Edinburgh. Though highly distinguished in his own locality, he exerted himself so as not to be eclipsed by the strangers from a distance. He gave one of his best discourses as a table address, the subject of which was the Resurrection, which he treated under the three divisions, it is Possible,—Probable,—Certain. It commanded the most solemn attention and interest. In the tent he preached from the text, "There is joy in the presence of the angels of God over one sinner that repenteth," and made a great impression. A little band of old women on their way home in the evening, shortened the road by discussing the merits of the several preachers who had addressed them, when a worthy dame, who had not spoken before, on being applied to for her opinion, gave it honestly thus:— "Leeze me abune them a' for yon auld, bold, clear-headed man that spoke sae bonnie on the angels, when he said, Raphael sings, and Gabriel tunes his goolden herp, and a' the angels clap their wings wi' joy. O but

it was gran'! It just put me in min' o' our geese at
Dunjarg, as they turn their nebs to the south an' clap
their wings when they see the rain coming after lang
drooth."

The abolition of tent-preaching on sacramental occasions was one of the greatest reforms in the Church,
and for this we are in great measure indebted to
Burns' satire, "The Holy Fair." The descriptions
there given of men and manners may be thought
more plain than pleasant by some, but thousands can
bear testimony to the truthfulness of his representa-
tions, as having been witnessed in their own parishes
on similar occasions. So far as we are aware, there is
no such thing now in any of the Lowland parishes of
Scotland. It is a thing of the past, and many of the
present generation do not know it even by name.
Would it had always been so! Doubtless the clergy did
not allow, far less approve of, the indecorous scenes which
then took place; and doubtless also they admonished,
and exhorted, and rebuked, in no lenient degree those
accused of their participation, but nevertheless the
custom continued to prevail with unabated vigour, and
amelioration was scarcely to be hoped for, if it could
only be restrained from going further, supposing that
possible. Burns was, however, longer-sighted. He saw
the effect must continue as long as the cause existed,
and therefore, taking one of his sharpest pointed shafts,
he aimed at both, and the world can now testify as to
the result. When the tent at C——, in Ayrshire, was
laid aside from further use, a discussion arose at an
heritors' meeting with regard to its disposal, and it was
unanimously agreed that the sides should be converted

into backs for the communion table seats, which heretofore had been only movable forms. The top, however, from its peculiar shape, presented a difficulty. There was no purpose to which it could be adapted; but, on the suggestion of one more liberal than the rest, it was resolved to present it as a "hopper" to the parish miller. Had it been able to quote Shakspeare it might have cried out in indignation, "To what base uses do we come at last!" The reader will now see the reason why some took offence at there being no tent-preaching at Mr. Wightman's first communion.

There was at this time a strong prejudice among the inhabitants of rural parishes against the use of a pulpit gown, as it was considered a remnant of rank Popery or black Prelacy, and therefore could not be tolerated on any account. One of Mr. Wightman's earliest annoyances arose from this cause. A kind lady of high position in the parish had presented him with a very handsome pulpit gown, and he was extremely proud of the gift, as he considered it a seemly ornament in honour of the service of God; but the people of Kirkmahoe did not think so; on the contrary, it was in their eyes a badge of the Beast, and, with regard to their minister, they held with the poet, "When unadorned, adorned the most." There had been low mutterings of dissatisfaction among them from the first day he appeared in it, but none had ventured to remonstrate with him personally on the subject. The first direct reference they made to it is thus recorded :—

"4th Nov., 1798.—Preached at Kirkmichael, the Rev. James Smail exchanging with me. Kirkmichael church well attended, considering the inclemency of the weather. Infested much with the barking of dogs, and other annoyances, people going out and coming in frequently. Mr. Smail wore my gown in Kirkmahoe, and some spoke of it to him as a dress too like that of the clergy of England, or of the priests of Rome and France. Alas! that in the close of the eighteenth century there should be still persons found in a civilized part of the kingdom of Britain who should measure a clergyman's merits by such matters. But the prejudice is like that against the name of king to those who are intent on establishing or preserving a democratical form of government. Prelate is an odious term to old Presbyterians, and the robe worn is inconsistent with puritanical plainness."

A report had become current in the parish that he was not a man of truth—that he had pledged himself not to wear a gown in the pulpit, and now that he was doing so, no edification could be derived from a man who did not regard his promise, and who set such an improper example before his flock. He was greatly annoyed at the calumny, for it was entirely without foundation, seeing he had never once spoken on the subject, and he could not live under such an imputation. He resolved to give it a denial at once in the most public manner within his power. Seizing the earliest opportunity, at the close of a thanksgiving sermon upon a Thursday, he brought the matter before his hearers, and vindicated himself from the aspersion with which his veracity had been impugned. He said "he had been groundlessly charged with breaking his word by some thoughtless individuals, who alleged that they had heard he had promised not to wear a gown in the pulpit, and this he believed had caused some of them to absent themselves from church. There was no truth whatever in the report, and he was astonished at their listening to such frivolous gossip. If they could charge and convict him of deliberately violating the least of the commandments, he would divest himself of his sacred office at once; but he hoped it had all arisen from want of thought, and he trusted he would never be called on to make such an address to them again. If any should withdraw themselves from the church on account of it, as he feared some had already done, he hoped they would meet again in heaven, in those blissful regions which are beyond the strife of tongues, where the dark surmise would never spring up to separate their friendship any more—where his affection for them would break forth as the light, and where all their weaknesses would be forgiven." When he had concluded, Mr. Patrick Miller of Dalswinton, whose pew was opposite the pulpit, rose up, and after apologizing for speaking in the church, said to the minister that "he knew not the case to which reference had been made, but he would give him this testimony that if any in the parish were dissatisfied with him, they were blind to his merits, and insensible of the blessing which God had given them." This proceeding, however unusual it may be regarded now, was perhaps the most effectual that could be adopted; it put an end to the calumny, and restored tranquillity to the poor pastor's breast. Still it did not reconcile the people to the use of the gown, and some never returned to the church. The following Sunday the precentor was absent, and did not again appear in the desk, without assigning any reason for his conduct, and, about a year afterwards, the following words were discovered written inside the board of the psalm book, "I will be precentor no longer to a minister who wears a black gown."

That this prejudice against the gown was inveterate is evident from the fact that, upwards of a hundred years before, the Synod of Dumfries had recommended the use of it to all the brethren as "decent and suitable." The words were—"The Synod, considering that it's a thing very decent and suitable, so it hath been the practice of ministers in this Kirk formerly, to wear black gowns in the pulpit, and for ordinary to make use of bands, do therefore, by their act, recommend it to all their brethren within their bounds to keep up that laudable custom, and to study gravity in their apparel and deportment every manner of way." So strong is the power of prejudice, that in this case, a whole century, supported by the injunction of an ecclesiastical court, was inadequate to make any impression towards its removal. So great, also, is the importance which is attached to matters of comparatively little value. With regard to the above vindication, it may have been that Mr. Wightman's great sensitiveness of feeling tended to magnify the evil of which he so bitterly complained, as we find him recording a few months afterwards how easily he was elevated or depressed:—"My spirits are affected by matters apparently of small moment. A single circumstance has often rendered me almost unable to proceed, and on other occasions a piece of good news, or some fortunate incident, especially regarding my ministerial character and influence, has made me deliver with a spirit and energy that had rendered me almost a different person from what I was before." From the following extract it

D

seems the people of Kirkmahoe were not easily deterred from attending religious ordinances in the church by the inclemency of the weather:—

"Sunday, 11th August.—At home. Preached two sermons from 1 Timothy iv. 8, and reserved a third for another opportunity. It was a very wet morning. The roads were much flooded, yet the people were well gathered, and I was reminded of the pains which the ancient Hebrews took to attend their temple, passing through Baca's vale, though the difficulty of attending the church was occasioned by a different reason from that which troubled the Israelites. The latter had too little water, but my good people had too much. They had carts to convey them through some of the currents on the road! It pleased me to see their care and attention equal at least to that which they bestow on their secular affairs. It warms my heart in their favour, and makes me wish I could give them instruction in some measure corresponding to the diligence which they use to obtain edification."

This is very creditable testimony to the church-going propensities of the inhabitants of Kirkmahoe in those times, and we believe the same may be said of them still. But, after all, church-going seems to be in great measure a habit, and while one parish is distinguished for attendance upon religious ordinances, another not far distant is noted for its remissness in the observance of that duty. A ploughman who had been a couple of years in the parish of Ochiltree, but who seldom had " darkened a church door," removed into the neighbouring parish of Coylton, and some months afterwards meeting with his old master was thus accosted—"How are ye John? I'm glad to hear ye attend the church now." "Ou ay, Sir, a' folk gangs to the kirk here. Ye're thocht naething o' if ye dinna gang to the kirk."

From various causes, more imaginary than real, however, Mr. Wightman felt a depression of spirits which seemed to be not easily got rid of, and he felt at a loss what to do. He was most anxious and zealous for the welfare of his people, but some of them showed a coldness and rather stood aloof. He thought himself more appreciated in other parishes than his own, which was a source of disquietude to his spirit, and which he would gladly have reversed. He was mistaken in his opinion, but so he thought. In his sadness he made his complaint to his friend Dr. Cririe, afterwards minister of Dalton, who, in a friendly communication to him, said— " I am sorry to find you in so much distress in the midst of so much good fortune; but did you ever expect to be exempted from the common lot of mortality? Popularity is good so far as it tends to make a man useful, but are not you a little too anxious about it? Do you take care that you do not hurt the usefulness of your brethren by appearing a greater orator than they? Let your discourses be solid rather than showy, and you will find them easier to mandate—command ideas, and words will follow. You are not now such a child but that you may be on your guard against damp. You had better place yourself at the mouth of a cannon at once, in defence of your country, than creep into a damp cell in quest of popularity. It is not a man's pulpit labours that I should expect to be the most useful. You mention visiting, but I see nothing of examination. Show yourself really solicitous for your people's welfare rather than for their good opinion. Be rather distant than familiar, but let that distance have no appearance of pride. Remember the great example." He then goes on to give some goodly counsel with regard to the means necessary to protect his health, and concludes with the advice that he should take a wife to look after himself and his house. This letter in a considerable measure restored his spirits, and he went through the parish with greater elasticity of step than before.

CHAPTER IV.

PREACHES ROYAL INFIRMARY SERMON—EXTRACTS—SETS UP HOUSE-
KEEPING—PRIVATE READING—CASES OF SYMPATHY—LOSSES BY
LOANS—DESIROUS OF HIS PEOPLE'S AFFECTION—REFORMS IN
BAPTISM—REBUKED BY AN ELDER—SUPERSTITIONS ABOUT BAP-
TISM—DIFFICULTIES IN ADMINISTERING THE ORDINANCE—
ANECDOTE OF DR. CHALMERS.

THE preaching of the annual Royal Infirmary sermon in
Dumfries seems to have been attended with greater
"pomp and circumstance" in former days than now,
and also with greater pecuniary results.   This is a highly
useful Institution, partly supported by church collections
in the town and country, which are neither so large nor
so numerous as their object deserves.   Mr. Wightman
had the honour of being asked to preach this sermon on
Sunday, 25th August, 1799, which he did in the New
Church (Greyfriars), taking for his text Job xxx. 25:
"Did not I weep for him that was in trouble ?   Was not
my soul grieved for the poor?"   The sermon was fifty-
five minutes long, and was attentively listened to by a
crowded audience, among whom were his Grace the
Duke of Buccleuch, president of the Institution; Mr.
Miller of Dalswinton, vice-president; Lord Hume, and
a large number of the directors, as well as of the surrounding gentry.   The magistrates and minister went in
procession from the King's Arms Hotel to the church,
with a band of music playing before them, and returned
in a similar manner.   At the close of the discourse, Mr.

Wightman made the following energetic and touching appeal on behalf of the Institution:—

"The Institution, for the benefit of which the benevolent contributions of this day are to be applied, affords us an opportunity, which does not always occur, of being at once charitable and useful. The iniquities of the world have sometimes rendered the virtue of charity inefficacious, and turned it from its proper object. Hence the hand of beneficence has been opened at the voice of dissimulation, and the heart of pity has bled at the imagined woes of hypocrisy. Idleness and profligacy by their clamorous importunity have extorted from the benevolent the tribute which was due to complaining industry and to real distress. But here the rich stream of benevolence may flow in a pure and safe channel. We have no reason here to be afraid that the sinews of industry will be relaxed, the spirit of independence repressed, or the public prosperity injured by a fond and misplaced compassion. Here 'mercy and truth meet together.' The original purpose of this charity, to the true and lasting honour of its founders, was to preserve, under divine providence, 'such useful and deserving members of society as might be labouring under the consequences of those violent accidents to which, from the nature of their employments, the industrious part of mankind are particularly exposed; who are often reduced to such circumstances of poverty, attended with such distress of body and depression of mind, as those who have not visited the habitations of the sick in the humble ranks of life can but faintly conceive;' and by affording them, as much as possible, 'every necessary accommodation and assistance,' to restore them to their friends and the community as an invaluable blessing which might otherwise be lost. For this laudable and benevolent end, in the year 1778, an asylum of human infirmity, a place of refuge to the distressed in body and disordered in mind, large, convenient, and pleasantly situated in wholesome air, arose in this place, an ornament to this town, an honour to this part of the country, and a monument of the virtue of those who proposed, and who contributed, to its erection. Thither from every quarter the children of misfortune and distress are brought as to a sanctuary of relief, where they are removed from 'those numerous causes of danger or of death, arising from bad air, confined space, and various circumstances of defective or bad management, which prove so often injurious and fatal, not only to the sick, but also to those who attend them,' where suitable 'measures are adopted,' and due means used, for their recovery.

" The original object of the Institution has always been kept in view, and the consequence has been such as might reasonably have been expected. Its salutary effects have been extensively felt and acknowledged, and it is happily at this day in the full possession of that high reputation to which it is so justly entitled. From the period when the Infirmary was opened till the present time no fewer than 3500 children of affliction have been admitted to its privileges, of whom 1914 have been completely cured, and 530 less or more relieved! And may we not indulge the hope, from the distinguished patronage it receives from the great and good, from the confidence placed in those who conduct its duties, that it will continue to open its hospitable recesses to the afflicted poor, while such are in the land, and, under the providence of God, whose mercy is over all His works, to raise up through successive ages those who may be 'bowed down!' Go, lover of mankind, visit this house of mourning, this house of mercy; take your pictures of distress here from the life, and indulge the sentiments which your heart will suggest on the occasion. Here you will see, among others, the man who but lately was the support of his aged parents, himself, it may be, the father of a numerous family, who depended on his daily industry for their daily bread. See him laid on the couch prepared for such, unable to administer with his own hand even a cup of water to his lips, and still less able to supply himself with his necessary food. Visit him again and again. See him at last, by the patient assiduity of a nursing-mother habituated to practical compassion, and by the labour of the faithful physician, restored, under the divine blessing, to health, and strength, and joy. Follow him to his own home, where he had left his family and all dear to him, who know not whether they should see his face any more in the land of the living. Here yon mingling accents of gladness in the children's announcement of their father's return. See how they receive his welcome blessing, while she, who lately felt almost a widow's sorrow, now in her heart sings for joy, and blesses the God of the fatherless, in whom she trusted! Ye great, ye mighty, ye noble of the land, here is a scene not unworthy of your eye, a family of your humbler brethren, whose daily toil is all their riches, finding bread and raiment to them, with health, a kingdom! who are only less happy than yourselves in one point, as they have less power and fewer opportunities to communicate to others that happiness which they feel! Go on, ye virtuous patrons, and conductors, and guardians of this charity. Be not weary in well-doing, for though the unthinking part of mankind may not appreciate your merits, or the undiscerning judge of your labours, yours is the testimony of a good conscience, yours is the approbation of God, and great will be your reward in heaven—'Inasmuch, as ye have done it unto one of the least of these my brethren, ye have done it unto me.'"

The collection taken at the close of the service amounted to £32. Above forty gentlemen, including

the president and vice-president, dined together afterwards in the hotel, when "several very suitable toasts
were drunk, and the day was closed in a decent and
sober manner." No public recognition is now taken of
this annual sermon beyond a larger audience than usual
in the church where the service is conducted, perhaps
attracted as much by the popularity of the preacher as
by the necessities of the Institution. The parish of
Tinwald was at this time vacant, and the Rev. George
Greig had received a presentation to the living. He
preached in Kirkmahoe, and the following note is given
of his appearance there :—

"Sunday, 20th Nov.—Mr. George Greig, presentee to
Tinwald, preached for me two discourses from Heb. ii. 10,
'For it behoved, &c.' After some remarks on 'many sons,'
with some very pointed strictures on the improper conduct
of zealots, who confine the divine mercy, and judge of it by
their own narrow mind, he described the glory to which
the sons of God are raised in a future state, in its different
properties, light, city, crown, kingdom, &c., which are inadequate to convey a proper idea of the 'fulness of joy.' Mr.
Greig is what we term a flowery preacher, yet his flowers
are not without fruit, but the sure signs of autumnal plenty.
He is a good man, and has a very gainly and respectable
presence. I think he will be a very useful and successful
minister in Tinwald. Everybody liked him as far as I know.
One man, the master of a small school in Tinwald, wishing
to show his learning and judgment, upon his hearing Mr.
Greig modestly declining to describe the blessedness of
heaven, said, 'He went further than he could explain,'
which is one among the many instances of men's attempting
to judge in matters too high for them. I have often remarked
with regret, that a dogmatical assertion from the lips of a

fool gains more credit to the owner among the vulgar than a modest observation, however reasonable, from the mouth of a wise and prudent man. If you wish to gain the applause of fools, you must profess to know everything, and attempt to explain all mysteries; but we should think on the Apostle's remark, 'If I have not charity I am nothing.'"

The new manse being ready for habitation, on Christmas, 1799, the minister, with his two servants, David Henry and Margaret Haining, entered upon possession, and for the first time in his life he slept in his own home. With a humour characteristic of his nature, he afterwards remarked, that he did not experience any unusual emotion from the event, as he had anticipated, beyond the feeling of responsibility attendant upon housekeeping. That feeling, however, was pretty strong, and well might be so. Provisions were dear, servants' wages were high as times then went, and the resources were by no means great from which all expenses were to be defrayed. Oatmeal was 3s. 3d. per stone, and every day was rising higher, till in two months it was being sold at double that price. Butcher meat was in proportion, or rather out of proportion, as many a family could not obtain it. Candles were 9d. per lb., and 20s. were paid for a cart of coals. Over all this inexperience cast its dark shade, for he had never managed in this way for himself, and the future was wrapt in considerable obscurity, if not misgiving; but he resolved to economize as much as possible, and, in a household sense, "preach according to his stipend,"—live within his means. He had been long threatened with a bleeding at the nose, and in order to check this tendency, and avert future evil consequences, he resolved to abstain from animal food, and to live upon the plainest fare. He was perhaps the more easily persuaded to this from the circumstances in which he was placed, the *res angustæ domi,* and the greater credit was therefore due for his determination to act accordingly. He was naturally liberal of hand as well as generous of heart, as his after life amply testified, but he prudently resolved at the outset of his ministerial career to avoid the Charybdis so destructive to the happiness of many on commencing housekeeping—running into debt; while at the same time he wished to maintain the *prestige* of hospitality characteristic of the Scottish manse. He had several kind friends in the parish among the married ladies, who assisted him in plenishing his new abode. One sent the present of a carpet, another table linen, a third a bed, and other articles of utility, so that with his own furnishing he was pretty comfortable. We find this jotting on the subject :—

" 26th and 27th Dec.—I was employed on both of those days setting up furniture and buying provisions for the family. Find the expense of housekeeping is considerable on the most frugal plan one can adopt. I have already laid out on furniture and provisions more than £60, besides what furniture I had in my rooms at Kemyshall, which cost me upwards of £30. Paid £9 for three Carron grates, and in the same proportion other things are dear. Got a bed in a present from Mrs. M'Murdo, of Milnhead, to whom I sent the following lines in acknowledgment of her gift :—

"While journeying through the vale of life your bounty gives me rest,
I'll live secure from care and strife, and nought shall me molest.

Or if, in spite of all your care, grief shall my breast invade,
Such woe will prove but short and rare, and ere next morning fade.
Whene'er life's ills my heart oppress, your kindness will relieve;
It soon will banish my distress, and bid me cease to grieve.
With such regard, let truth be said, I seldom ever met,
And easy lie the giver's head, till I the gift forget."

To this Mrs. M'Murdo sent a very pretty answer, in which she expressed her regret that the gift bore no proportion to her regard, and requested him to consider her one of his friends, adding these lines of her own :—

" It is my trust no thorny care shall e'er your rest invade,
Smooth is the pillow, soft the bed, where innocence is laid."

It is interesting to observe what was the character of his private reading at this time. Many of our young clergymen might take a profitable lesson from his example, in not skimming the surface of theology, but descending into the depths. Turretin and Vitringa, and such like authors, lay continually on his study table, and that he examined them minutely is evident from the remarks he makes upon their writings. Here is an opinion pretty freely, but conscientiously expressed :—

" 22nd Jan., 1800.—Read several sections of Turretin's Latin System of Theology concerning the nature and definition of the term theology, which, he says, though not a scriptural word *formaliter*, is yet one *naturaliter*. Much idle and scholastic quibble is to be found in this work, but here and there a sensible and useful remark may be picked up, as among rubbish one may find a gem or useful utensil. I admire also a certain acumen of penetration uncommon, and a skill of arrangement worthy of praise, as well as the *improbus labor*, without which no excellence can be attained in any department of learning whatever. And considering the time and place where this author wrote, he is one of the greatest divines of his times. I do not agree with him in several of his positions, but these are not essen. tial, I hope, to salvation. I am pleased to see him assert the use of reason in matters of faith, and boldly declare that some rays of natural light have escaped the ruins of the Fall. I am diverted with his argument for using words which have been applied to heathen purposes, drawn from the conduct of the Israelites, who employed the vessels of the Egyptians for sacred uses."

Mr. Wightman was naturally of a most sympathizing disposition towards any one placed in circumstances of affliction or distress, and almost innumerable instances might be given of his great tenderness of heart, though, as he often said, he could never give expression to what he felt. His heart melted at the tale of woe. When he had one day preached in Tinwald, during the vacancy caused by the death of the Rev. Mr. Laurie, he went out of pure sympathy to take dinner at the manse, as the widow and family had not yet removed. The propriety of his doing so may be questioned, in circumstances which must have been painful, from old associations, to the afflicted widow and family, but the motive was laud-able, as he did it with the purest feeling of commisera-tion, and he left them more cheerful than he found them. The manse is not always the paradise which it seems to many, and the generous heart blest with heaven's bounty might oftentimes cheer a gloomy hour, lighten a galling burden, and dispel in great measure corroding care. He preached one day in his native parish of Kirkgunzeon, during the last illness of the minister, Mr. Heron, and he was much moved by what he then saw. "The occasion," he says, "was truly melancholy. Mr. Heron himself in church, scarcely able to sit till the service was over—his breathing difficult—his colour gone—his body emaciated, and many strong appearances of approaching dissolution upon him. His wife and children around him in the seat, and the tears coming now and then into their eyes, as anything they heard touched upon their state by the most remote application. I took a walk with him, after sermon, in the garden. He looked at some pear-trees he had planted, and the improvements he had made, and said in the words of Virgil, 'Whether shall I say? *Nos, patriæ fines et dulcia linquimus arva!* or *Insere, Daphni, pyros: carpent tua poma nepotes!* and as he had hopes of himself even to a degree of sanguineness beyond what his situation seemed to encourage, he thought he might yet say the last of these. All he did and said affected me, and the more as he seemed not to be sensible of his own dangerous condition. His children were a piteous group indeed! and the father's circumstances I fear are embarrassed, at least in some degree." Such are examples of his sympathy and tender commiseration.

The readiness to feel for those in distress was sometimes taken advantage of by those acquainted with this characteristic of his nature, and he was occasionally imposed upon by some with unblushing effrontery. He lost various sums of money by loans to parishioners, who ungratefully treated his goodness by forgetting the obligation and leaving him minus the amount. This and that other one had a trade bill that was about due, and he was applied to for part if not the whole of the money, "just for a week or so, till country accounts were collected," which seemed a difficult matter from the length

of time usually taken in the business. A gentleman-
farmer borrowed £60 of him for three months, compla-
cently saying, " to whom can I apply in my need but to
my own minister?" The three months passed—three
years passed, and he became bankrupt. One day meeting the minister in Dumfries, he had the audacity to
come forward with a jaunty step and a smirking countenance, and say he hoped he would accept the composition offered his creditors. " How much is it?" asked
the minister, and being told half-a-crown in the pound,
he instantly replied that if that was all he might keep
it also, which was accordingly done. But though he
was in this way frequently deceived, he could not refuse
an application if it was in his power to grant it, " willing
rather," he would say, " to lose a little than believe there
were rogues in the parish." A starving poetaster who
knew his generosity called upon him one day with a
fulsome panegyric in the one hand and a begging letter in
the other, at the same time soliciting any cast-off clothing laid aside, on which Mr. Wightman went into the
lobby, and taking down a black coat hanging there, he
presented it to the dilapidated bard amidst a profusion
of thanks. However, on dressing next day for church,
he found to his amazement that he had parted with his
best vestment, and he had considerable difficulty in
making himself respectable for the pulpit.

He now devoted his whole energies to the pastoral
duties of the parish, allowing himself only six hours of
sleep, as if he would literally take the kingdom of heaven
by violence. He studied, and read, and wrote, with the
utmost assiduity, that he might preach to his people not
only suitable and edifying doctrine, but also present it

in a form which might attract their attention and so win
their souls. Nothing delighted him so much as to see
them come out in goodly numbers to divine service on
the Lord's day; and he felt saddened beyond conception
if he heard of them going elsewhere, even for a single
day, as he thought it implied dissatisfaction with his
spiritual teaching. Again and again he gives expression
to such a feeling as this :—" I know not what I would do
if my people were to desert me, for I find my happiness
depends much on their regular attendance at church, and
on every mark of satisfaction with my ministry among
them. Yet what is the *popularis aura?* a breath—a
bubble—nothing; but it requires much fortitude to do
your duty, if that duty is not acceptable to your fellow-
creatures. So that popularity is of much consequence
in this view; it contributes to make you happy, because
you are the means of making them so. Never may I
relax in my strenuous endeavours to do my duty, and
never may I feel the sting of a mind reproaching itself
for indolence or wilful omission of it! I at present possess
the esteem of my people, and the maxim is true in more
respects than one—'*imperium retinetur iisdem artibus
quibus primo partum sit,*' which may be rendered in my
instance, 'The affections of my people are to be kept by
the same means which gained them, by a faithful and
diligent—as far as my frailty permits—discharge of the
duties of my station.'" The general mass of parishioners
are not aware of the stimulus which their presence in
the church gives the minister, however much he may
seem regardless of this. It is cold and heartless for him
to preach to empty pews, and he has little spirit to exert
himself in bringing forth all his resources to a mere

handful of hearers, who perhaps imagine they are patron-
izing him by being there at all, while he, on his part, is
apt to fancy that he is "wasting his sweetness on the
desert air." Mr. Wightman was extremely susceptible
of impressions whether in the pulpit or out of it, and
sometimes felt his mind distracted, during the delivery
of his discourses, by a levity of conduct on the part of
some of the audience, who, from their position, ought to
have known and acted better. How entirely different
is the conduct of the congregation now ! We understand it is the universal remark of stranger ministers
when officiating in the church, that a more attentive
and decorous congregation is impossible. One Sunday
shortly after term-day, a farm-servant, who was new to
the parish, was in church, and on the text being read
out he laid his head down upon the bookboard, evidently
with the intention of having a snooze, but was instantly
roused up by a *poke* from his neighbour, and an audible
whisper, "nobody sleeps here." The poor fellow looked
up in bewilderment, half-ashamed, and half-dissatisfied
that he could not do as he liked.

There had long been a great aversion on the part of
parents to have their children baptized in church before
the congregation, and the minister set himself to the
task of putting a stop to the irregularity; but after many
remonstrances on the subject, which proved of no avail,
he made a resolution, and intimated it from the pulpit,
that he would baptize no child privately within two
miles of the church, except in the case of urgent necessity, certified by the doctor. The radius, however, could
never be exactly drawn, and it seemed on every occasion
to be getting shorter. He threatened to refuse the

E

ordinance, the parents threatened to leave the church and go elsewhere, and the circle became more and more circumscribed. The very grave-digger, who lived almost at the church gate, insisted on having his child baptized at home, on which the facile minister replied—"Ay, ay, what more will ye have me do? ye have now brought me to the very grave's mouth."

Stringent as he was to observe the laws of the Church, at least in purpose, he laid himself open to a breach of discipline, and was not allowed to pass with impunity. He had baptized a dying child to an unmarried woman in great distress, before she had given satisfaction to the church, but on the promise that she would do so on the earliest opportunity. The following Sunday, after sermon, one of the elders called him to account, in a state of very considerable emotion. He said he had been informed, on good authority, that he, Mr. Wightman, had baptized a child to a woman before she had satisfied the congregation, and if this was to be his manner of discipline he could not sit with him in the session. The minister said that he had acted after the Great Exemplar, who said He would have mercy rather than sacrifice—it was a case which he hoped would never again occur in the course of his ministry—that he could scarcely say he would not do the same thing in a similar case, but that he wished it might not occur; and if he was hinting that he should promise not to do the like again, he thought he might venture to say as much. This concession was made for the sake of peace, though it is to be regretted that elders should think it necessary to bring their ministers to acknowledgment. Such conduct weakens the hands of both, and renders the cause of

religion an object of scorn to those who are disposed to
scoff at such matters. The answer pacified the irate
elder, who thought he had gained an important point
in respect to the good of the church, by bringing
the minister to confess that what had been done
was contrary to the ordinary form of procedure in
church discipline. It were well if there were a
greater number of candid and generous-hearted persons who would always suppose the minister *meant*
well in what he did, or, if he went wrong in a
matter of form, that he never erred in point of
intention.

It must not be supposed that Mr. Wightman was
singular in committing such an irregularity in baptism
as that just referred to, and in being speedily called to
account by one of his elders. Something of a similar
kind occurred at the same time in the neighbouring
parish of Tinwald, and with a like result. The elders
were exceedingly displeased with their minister for
having baptized, without their knowledge, the first child
to his man-servant, which they alleged was not legitimate. The moderator, Mr. Greig, reminded them that
a certain period was allowed by medical authorities in
such cases, but he was met with the reply that they had
counted the time, and it was two days more. He said
that the law was, *Semper in dubiis benigniora sunt
preferenda*, but they did not understand Latin, and
regarded his explanation of it with suspicion; so, yield-
ing to their importunity, and gratifying their sense of
office, he consented that the man should receive a
sessional rebuke. In those days the elders *ruled* well
at least, and considered it essentially necessary to adhere

strictly to the letter of the law in administering discipline upon delinquents.

The reason why there was, and still is, to a considerable extent among the lower classes, a strong irrepressible desire to have their dying children baptized, even in the very last moments of life, was not so much out of honour to the Redeemer by having them initiated into the visible Church, as to secure for them a passport, as it were, rendering them admissible into glory, for they believed that unbaptized persons after death could not be received into heaven, and were consequently lost. A similar sentiment was held by the Greeks and Romans, and frequent reference is made to it in their writings. Thus Virgil says :—

> " Hæc omnis, quam cernis, inops, inhumataque turba est:
> Portitor ille, Charon: hi, quos vehit unda, sepulti;
> Nec ripas datur horrendas, et rauca fluenta
> Transportare prius, quàm, sedibus ossa quiêrunt.
> Centum errant annos, volitantque hæc littora circum:
> Tum demum admissi stagna exoptata revisunt."

That this was a superstition of wider extent than Nithsdale is shown by Burns, when, in his description of the famous carousal in Alloway Kirk, he mentions " unchristened bairns" among the accessories of the scene. Instances are given when it was not known by minister or parent whether a living or dead child was receiving the solemn rite at their hands. Mr. Wightman endeavoured by every means in his power to eradicate this belief, by appealing both to reason and revelation. He used all the logic for which he had been famous at college, but here it was of no avail, nothing would convince the mother of a dying child; and when, with tears

streaming, unable as well as unwilling to meet his arguments, she besought him in words almost identical with
those of Scripture, " Come, ere my child die," it was
impossible to refuse.   Perhaps had the other members
of session seen and heard what passed between the
afflicted mother and the minister, they would not have
been so stringent in tithing mint and cummin, and
omitting the weightier matters of the law, judgment,
mercy, and faith, and their earnest minister would have
been saved the humiliation of acknowledging he had
done wrong.   Another superstition which came under
our own cognizance connected with this ordinance was
of the following nature.   When, in administering the
rite, the water fell upon the infant's face, it gave a loud
scream, and after the service was over, the mother
kissed and fondled her child with the greatest affection,
saying, " Ye're gaun to leeve yet, my darling! Ye're
gaun to leeve yet, my darling!"   Judging there was
something under this, we inquired what it meant, and
were told, that if when a sickly child gave a cry on receiving the water of baptism, it was a sure token that
it would live.   We thought that if it was so, the power
of life and death was very much in the hands of the
officiating minister, according to the quantity of water
he used.   Another superstition, which probably is still
universal, was that when children of different sexes
were to be baptized together, the male always received
the preference, as it was believed, and proofs were ready
to be adduced, that if the female was first baptized, she
would in after life wear the beard instead of the other,
a matter greatly to be deplored by both.

Ministers were not at liberty to baptize a child by any

name an eccentric or a fanatical parent might propose.
All names savouring of ancient paganism, and such as
were peculiar to the Deity, were prohibited, though
scriptural names of holy persons might be given. Also
when a clan or tribe fell into disfavour with the king, or
became an eyesore to the country, the name was forbidden
to be used in baptism, in order that as speedily as possible it might become extinct. The clan Macgregor had
become so obnoxious to the country on account of their
cruelties and depredations, that they were proscribed as
"lawless limmers and villains," and no clergyman was
to baptize a child in their name under the penalty of fine
and deprivation. Baptisms were sometimes performed
under circumstances of peculiar difficulty, but still showing "where there is a will there is a way." A former
minister of Kirkgunzeon, when one day out shooting at
a distance from the manse, called at the cottage of one
of his parishioners where there was an unbaptized child,
and, to save the trouble of returning for the purpose, he
offered to do the duty then. There being no water in
the house, and the well a long way off, the minister said
he had some in his flask, and it was used accordingly.
We once heard Dr. Chalmers relate with great zest the
following story of a Highland baptism :—A clergyman
went to administer the rite in the house of one of his
hearers, near which there ran a small burn or river,
which, when he reached it, was so deep and swollen with
recent rains that he could not get across. In these circumstances he told the father to bring his child down to
the burn-side. Furnished with a wooden scoop, the
clergyman stood on the one side, and the father, holding
his child as far out in his arms as he could, stood upon

the other.   The service proceeded, and when the time
came for sprinkling the babe, the minister, dipping the
scoop into the water, flung its contents across, aiming at
the baby's face.   He failed more than once, calling out
to the father after each new trial, " Weel, has't gotten
ony yet?"   Dr. Chalmers wondered what the great sticklers for form and ceremony in the sacraments would
think of a baptism by a burn-side, performed with a
wooden scoop.   We observe this anecdote is recorded
in the fourth volume of Dr. Chalmers' Memoirs, but it
is impossible to realize the humour which irradiated his
countenance when he related it to his students at the
breakfast table.

CHAPTER V.

WHILE Mr. Wightman was intent on the diligent discharge of the duties within his own parochial domain, he was also a keen observer of what was going on in the political world, both foreign and domestic, and freely expressed his opinion of the wisdom or the injudiciousness of those who conducted public affairs. When the news of the death of Washington reached this country he was greatly grieved, saying that the death of that truly great man would be lamented by the admirers of genius, integrity, and patriotism, for he thought that however his exertions had prevailed in depriving Great Britain of one of her most valuable possessions, he had acted from the most thorough conviction and the purest principle, therefore his memory would be held in the highest veneration. It was not to degrade and enslave his native land that he had lifted the sword, as the late usurpers of France had done, but when the object was accomplished, he, like another Cincinnatus, resigned his supremacy, and reposed in the bosom of an honourable retirement, a retirement more illustrious than the monkish seclusion of Charles V., to which that monarch betook himself, and which was applauded by his pane-gyrists far beyond its deserts.

Turning to home affairs, the legislature has been dis-cussing the preliminaries of peace with France, on which the following remarks occur:—"I rejoice at the prospect of a general peace. I fear evils from the licentious prin-ciples that will be propagated through this country in consequence of a free intercourse with France. I know not what to think of the system of government there. It is a heterogeneous mixture in which atheism, Jacobin-ism, old popery, theophilanthropism, true liberty, and mad licentiousness, have all less or more influence upon the public mind, and the genius of Bonaparte himself is not able to rule the chaotic mass, from which some new order of things seems likely to break forth. The Chief Consul's career seems to be near its close. He is one of those luminaries which shine only amid storms and tempests, and shed an awful glare on the elemental war. When peace comes his mind will have no congenial objects, for whatever he may say of social happiness his soul is not tuned for such serene enjoyments. He will likely be murdered by some dark rival or revolutionary cabal, if men are not yet satiated with blood. The speeches of Lord Grenville and Mr. Windham against the peace, and of Mr. Pitt and Mr. Fox for it, are masterpieces of senatorial eloquence. Grenville thus concludes a speech replete with dignified sentiment— ' We are enfeebled, my Lords, but not broken down; we are lowered, but not debased. Some of our outworks have deen demolished, many of them surrendered to the foe, but the citadel yet remains, and while it is defended by the noble courage of united Britons it will bid defiance to attack.   We meet with mortifications and disappointments, but we shall, I trust, preserve our Honour, our Constitution, and our Religion.'   Mr. Pitt in a part of his speech states among other objects of the war this one—'We were desirous of collecting the venerable fragments of that ancient fabric, the overthrow of which entailed so many years of misery on France—we hoped to restore its ancient system—

—— dives opum, Priami dum regna manebant;
Nunc tantum sinus, et statio malefida carinis.'

There is something very happy in this quotation; it reminds one of some of the eloquent flights of Mr. Burke on the same subject.   Mr. Windham in an eloquent speech against the peace insisted that the great aim of France was universal empire and aggrandizement, and that it was not safe to allow them to gratify this desire by peace.   The French adopted various measures, but never lost sight of their aim.   'In all their revolutions, involutions, and evolutions, they pursue the same course, like pigeons which turn in the air, but still pursue their flight.   The figure and the music are not always the same in this dance of death.'   I believe there is no such theatre of eloquence as the British senate.   Every great and noble sentiment is there inspired.   British genius puts forth its strength in the best of causes, the welfare of its country, some one way, some another, but no true eloquence can spring from insincerity.   It is this which renders the harangues of Fox so tedious to those who see his character."

Mr. Wightman cherished an inveterate hatred to the

great First Consul; and notwithstanding his saying that he never let the sun go down upon his wrath, which we believe was as true as can be said of any human being, yet in this case we fear that Bonaparte was an exception, though perhaps the only one. But it should be remembered, that almost every man of Britain, most certainly of Scotland, held the same opinion. Among all classes of society no epithet was too derogatory to be applied to him. His reputation was considered public property, and it was generally kicked about like a football. We shall by-and-by see what consternation he caused to the peaceful inhabitants of Dumfriesshire and Galloway, though at the same time, as it turned out, they were more frightened than hurt. Still, if one is recklessly frightened, he has good cause to take umbrage at the bogle. Let us hear Mr. Wightman again on Bonaparte :—

"7th May, 1801 (Thursday).—The news of Sir Ralph Abercromby's success in the sacred expedition to Egypt is gazetted. This fortunate turn of affairs will, with other late occurrences in the north of Europe, it is hoped, prepare the way for peace, so much to be desired. I think Bonaparte is not to survive long amidst the convulsions to which a republic, not founded on virtue, is subject. Some rival will cut him off by violence, or he will rush on some hazardous enterprize which will prove fatal to him, for he is a meteor which pleases only while it moves, and is destined to spread ruin and terror while it lasts, but is never to enjoy the blessings of serenity and peace, as he does not seem to be calculated to act a part suitable to the prime personage of a nation in peace. When daring and bustle are not needed, Bonaparte will have no existence. 19th May.—Heard that

Sir Ralph Abercromby had died of his wounds in Egypt. A General Hutchinson has taken the command of the troops there in his room. This, I fear, is a bad omen of success on our enterprize there. A great deal of blood has already been shed in Egypt, and more must be shed before we take the country out of the hands of the French. They wish to make it a step to our settlements in India, and a key to the further extension of their boundaries. The 42nd Regiment, I think, a Highland corps, it seems had cut off to a man the invincible band of Bonaparte. The latter had taken all the flints out of their muskets that they might depend on their bayonets alone, yet French enthusiasm was defeated by Highland bravery, and the Caledonian diamond cut to pieces the Gallic steel. Long live the brave Highlanders! they are noble heroes! How many poor mothers in Scotland are now lamenting their sons slain in battle, and methinks, in France even, I see the generous tear fall, and I pity even our enemies."

Peace was proclaimed, but how long, or rather how short, it continued we shall speedily see. In the meantime Dumfries is in a state of ecstacy at the glad tidings, and has no desire to conceal her emotions. Let us hear Mr. Wightman's opinion on the subject:—

" 14th October (Wednesday).—There was an illumination in Dumfries last night, on account of the news that peace had been concluded with France. The populace were very noisy, and some of them a little tumultuous about the streets. The newspapers are full of the most extravagant expressions of joy on account of this news. Some soldiers, in a town in England, actually kissed the wheels of the mail-coach that brought the intelligence. The Opposition prints are full of triumph over the late Ministry and eulogiums on Bonaparte, while they speak of our own country as in a deplorable state of humiliation and distress. I hope we shall recover from the wounds we have received, and that time will allay all our grievances, great indeed. When shall the widows receive their husbands and their sons, and when shall the public debt be removed? But this war has shown the world that Great Britain is an enemy to anarchy and wild democracy, while she embraces peace as soon as she can do it with consistency or safety. I speak not of honour or of glory; I will leave these terms for happier days still. It appears to me that Bonaparte is a man who cannot live in peace, any more than a leviathan on land. The same jealous rivals of his military fame, and enemies of his measures, may plot and effect his ruin. France, I consider, is a great sea without any fixed limits, roaring and swelling after a storm, and which yet may occasion some disasters before it peaceably repose in its channels. Much broil and feud await the inhabitants of France before their interior affairs be arranged and some form of worship be recognized, which, if not established, all will go to wreck, and a deluge of atheism and infidelity will overspread Europe.—*Quod Deus avertat!*"

Notwithstanding the kindness of the married ladies in helping him to furnish the manse, there still remained a great deficiency which he was anxious to supply, and he reasonably imagined they might aid him in this matter also. In fact, the very generosity, sympathy, and affectionate regard they had shown him, increased his desire the more to have the vacuum in his heart and in his dwelling removed. The angel of the house was awanting. Margaret Haining or Jenny Glen might be very good housekeepers, and promote his comfort by all means in their power; but a housekeeper was not a wife, and mere comfort came short of true and full happiness. But, alas! easier thought of than obtained. He lived and died a bachelor, partly from necessity and partly from choice, by which we mean that he remained in a state of celibacy because he did not succeed in certain quarters where he applied for a wife. He could not brook denial, even when it came with no such real intent, and he was too independent of spirit, shall we say proud, to press his suit. A Miss Taylor, the daughter of a neighbouring farmer, a young lady of great beauty and engaging manners, made a deep impression upon his heart, so much so, indeed, that he resolved to ask her parents that they would allow her to become mistress of the manse, even, we believe, before he asked the consent of the damsel herself. Accordingly, one evening he embraced the opportunity and solicited the hand of "bonny Jean;" but though the maternal heart was flattered by the proposal, Mrs. Taylor modestly said, " It is certainly a great honour you do us, Sir, but I'm afraid she is too young for you." "Well, well," said the wooing minister, "ye know best, let it be so," and the subject was never introduced again on either side. No doubt the mother was right, whatever were her feelings in the matter; he was upwards of forty years of age, and her daughter not half the number. He never, however, ceased to cherish a strong affection for the young lady, but which he thought was not reciprocated in the way he wished. He once sent to her, along with a winter rose, a poetical effusion, the close of which was as follows:—

"And when life's November around you shall close,
    And withers the beauty that ravished the muse,
May piety flourish like this winter rose,
    And o'er your last moments its sweetness diffuse!"

Miss Taylor died at Ellisland, whither the family had removed, and her remains were interred in Kirkmahoe churchyard on the 26th February, 1838. On the day immediately preceding her funeral the following was jotted in his diary:—"Miss Taylor of Ellisland, who died of palsy, is to be buried in our churchyard to-morrow. I trust she died in peace, and felt all the comfort in her last hours which I once wished she might feel in those lines which I sent her, when I thought she did not like my attentions so well as I wished. Lord, prepare me for my own latter end, which cannot be far distant!" He was so affected that he could not attend her funeral, but he visited her grave a few days afterwards, and there, sitting alone by her tombstone, an old man at the age of seventy-six, he sought relief in the following strains. What a subject for an artist! Old age mourning at the grave of unwedded early love:—

"Beneath that stone the dust doth rest,
    Of her whom living I loved best;
My voice of grief she cannot hear,
    Nor can she see my falling tear.
O virtuous love, thy powerful ties
    Are made of nought that fades or dies;
With mind's pure essence they're entwined,
    And are immortal too—like mind!
When yon bright sun and circling spheres
    Shall count no more their days and years,
When that strong chain that binds them fails,
    And desolation wide prevails,
Thy mystic ties, so firm and sure,
    Will through eternity endure!"

Another attempt elsewhere was also unsuccessful, but this time the fault lay solely with himself. He went one evening ostensibly to take tea with a family with whom he had been for a considerable time on terms of the greatest intimacy, and, as he supposed, on terms of the greatest friendship; we say ostensibly to take tea, but really to ask the daughter to be his wife. His visit was unexpected, and perhaps household affairs had been undergoing a scrutiny and a renovation, so that the family were scarcely in trim for receiving the minister's visit. The Fates were again adverse! He left without hinting a single word of his errand. And why? When the blooming fair one, who occupied his whole heart, brought in the tea apparatus, she put them on the table with such forcibility that he said he read in the noise she made, "What the plague's brought that body here again?" Young ladies, beware, the rattling of the tea-cups may lose you the offer of a husband. A third effort also failed. He went one day for the same purpose to a house in town, resolved to make an offer of his hand and heart, but, alas! after knocking at the door, he lost courage and fled before his call could be answered. These three instances we had from his own lips, and he said there were a few others which never went further than a dilly-dallying sentimentality.

The result of his failures in attempting matrimony was such as might be expected in one with so generous, warm, and loving a heart as his. The solace he could not find at home he sought elsewhere, and the happiness he saw, or fancied he saw, in wedded life, was all the more aggravating, in that he seemed doomed to celibacy against his will. So we find him dining here and teaing there, both in his own parish and out of it, when he might have been revelling in a paradise of his own. This state of celibacy had two principal results, one of which is to be especially lamented. The first is, that with his extensive classical knowledge, his experience in education, public and private, his great love for the ancient fathers, Greek and Latin, and his fine discernment of their beauties and faults, he might have given the world a work of importance on some of these matters so congenial to his own taste, which would have benefited and elevated his fellow-men, whereas all we have of this character is comprehended in a few occasional sermons, and a slim volume on one of the Epistles, to which we shall afterwards have occasion to refer. The second result was a perfect influx of visitors of a certain caste from one end of the year to another. Teachers and preachers all found their way to Kirkmahoe manse, and to show how much they enjoyed themselves there, they stayed for days and weeks at a time. The fare was homely yet hearty, but the great enjoyment was "the feast of reason and the flow of soul," which was far more appreciated than the other.

With regard to the preachers, they always did something for their bread in acknowledgment of the hospitality they received; they took the pulpit duty for the minister, which was a great relief, and allowed him ample time for his other duties in the parish. In this way he himself, though in the church, was sometimes not in the pulpit for two months, and, on one occasion, for three months in succession. Still it was agreeable to the people; they heard varieties of preaching, and seeing the minister always present they were satisfied that he was there to do his duty if required. Above all things, a con-

F

gregation cannot bear the idea that the minister is in-
dolent, and if it is found that he is exchanging here and
there, they are certain to put it down to that cause.
Now, nothing is more erroneous. There are many things
occurring, of which they are ignorant, which render it
impossible for him to prepare new sermons every Sunday,
and when he chances to repeat a former one, they are
down upon him tooth and nail, as if what was good and
edifying for them one day was not so another, and as
if they remembered what had then been said to them,
and had acted up to the instruction given. We fear
that with many in a congregation their memory is
assisted greatly by a pencil mark in their Bibles at the
text. There was something in the remark once made
by a clergyman in Nithsdale to a young friend who had
officiated for him—" You're a great fool; you are far too
textual—you can never again preach that sermon but
from the same text. I never do such a thing. Nothing
like treating a general subject, for which a dozen texts
can be easily found any time." When a minister is in
church with his people, though another is employed,
they feel he is not neglecting his duty. Mr. Wightman
was therefore never found fault with in this respect.
And then he had such a kind word to say to his parishioners throughout the week on behalf of the preacher,
that they reckoned it a favour they were so highly pri-
vileged in hearing many of the young clergy, "hot off
the irons," as they expressed it.

No guest ever got a hint to leave the manse, however
long his stay. He came at his pleasure and left at the
same. Many a poor probationer was glad of such a City
of Refuge, while his ministerial gifts and graces were

being tested, as it was not then, as now, a rapid transi-
tion from the exercises of the Divinity Hall to the
responsibilities of the pastorate of a parish. Among
this class of visitors was one who paid a long visit every
year, who might have given up all hope of a church had
he not been like a certain portion of the human race
who hold by the maxim, "while there is life there is
hope," but Providence seemed to consider him more useful as he was then engaged than he could be in the
church. This was the Rev. Duncan Forbes, LL.D, a
student-grinder in Edinburgh, possessing an amazing
amount of scholarship, ancient and modern. It was
thought that if much learning had not made him mad,
it made him eccentric, as his speech, actions, and familiarities with the minister far exceeded even the bounds
of friendship. He often interfered with the manner in
which family worship was conducted, and on rising from
his knees would remark, before the servants had retired,
"I say, John, do you call that a prayer you gave us?"
The minister replied in the affirmative, and took no
further notice of the remark, being quite in accordance
with his expectation. The other features of Dr. Forbes'
character may be inferred from this, yet he was of the
highest service to Mr. Wightman in his study of the
Hebrew language, who acknowledged himself indebted
to him for a better acquaintance with the Bible in the
original tongue than ever he had received at College.
Indeed, we have heard him say that he had read the
Hebrew Bible three times through, every word, but that
he knew little or nothing of the language till Dr. Forbes
began his annual visits to the manse. However, always
on leaving, he weeded considerably the manse library of

valuable volumes, which he forgot to return, but he was never reminded of them by the generous lender.

Mr. Wightman had a peculiar pleasure in visiting at the neighbouring manse of Tinwald. There he received from Mr. and Mrs. Greig the warmest welcome, and as the family grew up he became almost one of themselves, and spoke of them in the kindest terms, as "spending the evening with the amiable Mr. Greig and his wife." At Torthorwald manse, also, the Rev. Mr. M'Millan's, though further distant, he was a frequent visitor, where he regarded the minister as a patriarch. "In the manse of Torthorwald," he says, "I always feel myself in the abode of a purer class of beings than the ordinary sort of mankind. The patriarchal simplicity of the minister, his heavenly conversation, his venerable hoary locks, and his good-humoured remarks, always edify and please me." How beautiful! There was in these days greater intercommunion among the clergy than now, except when business necessities, such as Sacraments, and School examinations, or perhaps an afternoon's sermon, demand a personal audience.

As a specimen of his genial goodness of heart and his taste in expressing a compliment, we give an extract from a letter which he sent to Mrs. Lawson, the widow of the former minister, then in Edinburgh, along with a basket of apples, the first season after he took up his residence in the manse:—"I take the liberty of sending you a few apples as a specimen of the fruit of the garden this season. I wish every other thing showed no greater marks of degeneracy among us here than they do. There is one thing which I think is not likely soon to degenerate or decay with us in Kirkmahoe—the warm affection of your old friends in the parish. This is still more fragrant than the best production of your favourite tree. Mrs. Walker and three of her daughters did me the favour of drinking tea with me the other evening, and spoke of you and former times with much interest and affectionate remembrance. We had heard that James was not very well lately, and hoped he was now all right again. I was sorry I was not at home when he and Miss Lawson called last summer. I staid several days at home, hoping for a second call. I trust when you or any of your family are in this part of the country, which many here wish may be often, I shall be fortunate enough to see you and show you some small testimonies of my sincere esteem, for I wish you to consider the new manse of Kirkmahoe is ambitious to resemble the old one as much as it can in hospitality to the friends of religion. I was just going to throw away this sheet on account of the last sentence, which I feared might affect you too much, but as I meant well, though I did not express myself so, I hope you will take my present and letter both in good part, and believe me to be, with much respect, Madam, your obedient and very humble servant, JOHN WIGHTMAN." This was written in September, 1801, and every one acquainted with him will acknowledge that it was characteristic of his nature to the last.

He was very strict and regular in the management of his household, and though he was frequently out in the evening, he never came home late or neglected family worship. He had a strong sense of propriety, and of the dangerous influence of bad example. One night, sitting later than usual, sunk in the profundities of a great folio tome, he imagined he heard a sound in the kitchen inconsistent with the quietude and security of a manse, and so taking his candle he proceeded to investigate the cause. His foot being heard in the lobby, the housekeeper began with all earnestness to cover the fire, as if preparing for bed—"Ye're late up to-night, Mary." "I'm jist rakin' the fire, Sir, and gaun to bed." "That's right, Mary, I like timeous hours." On his way back to the study he passed the coal-closet, and turning the key took it with him. Next morning at an early hour there was a rap at his bedroom door, and a request for the key to put a fire on. "Ye're too soon up, Mary; go back to your bed yet." Half-an-hour later there was another knock, and a similar request in order to prepare the breakfast. "I don't want breakfast so soon, Mary; go back to your bed." Another half hour, and another knock, with an entreaty for the key, as it was washing day. This was enough. He rose and handed out the key, saying, "Go and let the man out." Mary's sweetheart had been imprisoned all night in the coal-closet, as the minister shrewdly suspected, where, Pyramis-and-Thisbe-like, they had breathed their love to each other through the key-hole. It must not be fancied that in this action the minister had malice and took a cruel advantage; the reverse of this was the fact, but he was full of humour, and did it as a joke. The joke, however, turned out earnest against himself, as he very soon found; at the following term Mary gave up her situation, and set up housekeeping on her own account in company with her imprisoned lover, but whether or not the closet affair had any influence in bringing that matter to a crisis we cannot tell.

He relished a joke with the greatest zest, even when

it turned against himself, and none laughed more heartily than he at the following, when in the excitement of the occasion he confounded genders and otherwise failed in his *ruse*. His maid had one afternoon obtained leave to visit her sick mother in the neighbouring village, and had placed upon the study table and the fire all the necessaries for tea, that he might help himself at the proper hour. When she left he bolted the door to guard against intrusion, and was soon absorbed in the mysteries of some ancient folio, when, by-and-by, there was a sound of carriage wheels at the door. He immediately remembered that a Mrs. Wilson and her daughter from Dumfries were engaged to take tea with him that evening in the manse. He rushed upstairs to the servant's bedroom, put on her nightcap, and, throwing up a window, said to those below, simulating the girl's voice as well as he could—" The minister's no at hame; she's awa' seein' her mither." The voice was too well known not to be detected. Looking up, Mrs. Wilson instantly understood the state of affairs, and said, " Come, come, Mr. Wightman, let us in and we shall manage for ourselves !"

The fare was always homely, but the hospitality was hearty, and his genial conversation soon made every one forget what was set before him. It was something like what has been said of the preaching of Dr. Chalmers; at first it seemed coarse and uncouth from the provincial tone with which he expressed himself, but five minutes had not elapsed till everything was forgotten, and the whole soul centred upon the gushing eloquence of an earnest master in Israel. Mr. Wightman made every one feel at home ere he was well introduced.

A great event took place about this time in the annals of the burgh of Dumfries, which has been a source of just pride and self-gratulation on the part of the worthy citizens of the Queen of the South. This was laying the foundation-stone of its present handsome and far-famed Academy, which took place on the 27th of April, 1802, under the auspices of one of its ex-Provosts, David Staig. Among the immense crowd of citizens and others from the country who turned out on the occasion, in holiday attire and enthusiasm, there was none more interested than the minister of Kirkmahoe. He had studied under one of its ablest rectors, the Rev. Robert Trotter, M.A.; he himself had been one of the teachers when the institution bore a less lofty name, and he greatly rejoiced to see the *status* it had now attained. The whole affair passed off with the greatest *eclat*, and at the close of the ceremony a large company dined in the George Hotel, when Mr. Wightman repeated the following verses which he had that day written for the occasion:—

On Laying the Foundation-stone of Dumfries Academy.

" Kind Heaven now marks this moment for its own,
    While on the chosen spot that stone is placed,
And dates a course of ages yet unknown,
    In which its memory shall not be effaced.

" No! 'tis a moment this to thousands dear,
    And thousands yet unborn its bliss shall know,
For here fair Science means a fane to rear,
    Which ruthless Time will blush to overthrow.

" Yes, when oblivion's mantle shall be thrown
    On all the smiling throng now gathered round,
To learned strangers shall its courts be shown,
    Which, while they tread, they'll say, ' 'tis classic ground!'

" And when this fluttering heart shall beat no more,
  Nor yet this tongue such feeble lines rehearse,
The Muses here some favourite's breast shall store
  With all the treasures of immortal verse.

" Through Time's dread vista Fancy darts her view,
  And marks well pleased a long and studious train,
Fresh as the morn and countless as the dew,
  The palm of knowledge eager to obtain.

' A line of sages, too, of sire-like mein,
  Glad she can trace distinguished from the rest,
By Heaven designed in these retreats to reign,
  And stamp instruction ' on the glowing breast.

" Her looks, full-shaded with the olive's wreath,
  On this fair scene Britannia seems to bend,
And soft as o'er Nith's flowerets zephyrs breathe,
  To say—' My sons, now to my words attend !

" ' Love well your country, and its laws obey,
  Religion's sacred voice with reverence hear,
And Learning's ample page intent survey,—
  Fear God, my sons, and have no other fear !' "

This noble Seminary has lately (1872) been enlarged
and improved, to meet the demands of a progressive
age, and is at present equipped with a body of teachers
who, for intelligence, energy, and success, are not surpassed in any educational establishment in Scotland.

CHAPTER VI.

INTRODUCTION OF THE PARAPHRASES—CHANGE IN THE PSALMODY—
DIET OF CATECHISING—ANECDOTES OF SUCH MEETINGS—CUSTOMS
AT DEATH—ENCOFFINING—OLD ACTS OF PARLIAMENT—BURIAL
ENTERTAINMENTS—MODES OF CARRYING TO THE GRAVE—TREAT-
MENT OF SUICIDES—THE DRAIGIE—ANCIENT BURIAL PARAPHER-
NALIA.

IN olden times the good folks of Kirkmahoe seem to
have been greatly averse to what were considered innovations in the ordinance of religious worship, and some
of the females might, in their zeal for Presbyterianism
pure and undefiled, have claimed close kin with Jenny
Geddes and her stool in St. Giles' Church, Edinburgh.
There is a tradition extant in the parish, that while the
beadle was ringing the bell for public worship, some
heroines of the Reformation seized the altar with both
hands, and, having carried it off by their combined
strength, heaved it with one indignant effort into a
neighbouring pool. We have seen the prejudice which
was manifested against the wearing of a pulpit-gown,
and other things came anon which roused considerable
opposition, but eventually passed away. There was
a strong antipathy generally throughout the country to
the use of the Paraphrases on their first introduction in
the service of the Church, as they were considered mere
human compositions, though a little reflection might
have shown the cavillers that there was no greater reason

for rejecting them than the metrical version of the Psalms. David did not sing that which we use, but the prose one; and what are both of these but just portions of Sacred Writ put into measure, to suit the music we consider appropriate for divine praise. But yet simple worshippers could not be brought to see this, and especially those not connected with the Church of Scotland. "Don't sing any of your Paraphrases, and I will come and hear you oftener," said a strong Cameronian to us one day, who occasionally saved the fatigue of travelling some miles to his own church, and also, in some degree, thought to save his conscience at the same time by worshipping near home, while, in addition to all, he imagined a great honour was being conferred in the patronage he gave to the Auld Kirk by his attendance there. However, by a resolute reference to some of these Paraphrases, which he stoutly endeavoured to avoid, comparing the verse with the prose, and showing that the rendering was as close and scriptural as the version of the Psalms was, we obtained a reluctant acknowledgment that the matter was not, after all, so bad as he had imagined.

The first use of the Paraphrases within the bounds of the Presbytery of Dumfries was in Kirkmahoe Church, on the 23rd of January, 1802, when the 11th was given out and sung without any appearance of aversion on the part of the congregation:—

> "O happy is the man who hears
> Instruction's warning voice;
> And who celestial wisdom makes
> His early, only choice.

For she has treasures greater far
  Than east or west unfold;
And her rewards more precious are
  Than all their stores of gold.

" In her right hand she holds to view
  A length of happy days;
Riches, with splendid honours joined,
  Are what her left displays.
She guides the young with innocence,
  In pleasure's paths to tread,
A crown of glory she bestows
  Upon the hoary head.

" According as her labours rise,
  So her rewards increase;
Her ways are ways of pleasantness,
  And all her paths are peace."

In connection with the psalmody of the church, it is deserving of notice that the strongest antipathy also was exhibited to the disuse of reading the line by the precentor previous to its being sung. The schoolmaster had one day, of his own accord, requested the precentor to sing the last psalm without reading the line, which accordingly was done. At the close of the church service one of the elders was very wrathful, declaring the people would be justly angry, and that he and the other elders ought to have been consulted! Some words of an acrimonious character passed among the members of session on the subject, and the result was a resolution that the act should not be repeated. "I believe," says Mr. Wightman, making a note of the circumstance, "we must not persist in this matter, lest the people be provoked to anger by this gentleman because he was not consulted. Oh! oh! how shall a minister act amidst such notions? and what advancement in religious knowledge and practice can be expected while such things are reckoned the weighty matters? This gentleman would resign his office if the practice was to be continued." No doubt something might be said on the part of the elder as well as on the part of the congregation. He had a right to be consulted in all matters affecting the mode of conducting public religious worship, and psalm-books were not so numerous then as now, but still on such occasions it is not becoming to fly into a passion, when a quiet remonstrance or conference on the subject would do equally well.

The first time a repeating tune was sung in the church great offence was taken by some of the people, as it was called a "rant." A stranger minister had preached that day from Psalm cxxxvii. 3, "For there they that carried us away captive required of us a song; and they that wasted us required of us mirth, saying, Sing us one of the songs of Zion." One of the congregation, on his way home from the service of the sanctuary, gave expression to the bitterness of his feelings by saying, "Had the captive Jews given the Babylonians one of their songs to the tune we got to-day, they would have been sent home next morning, with their expenses paid, as a nuisance in the land." Various alterations, we shall not say innovations, have been introduced since then, but the people have the good sense to see that it is entirely for their own comfort, and the more reverential conducting of divine worship in the house of God, and so have given their approval.

In Mr. Wightman's time there were certain customs connected with pastoral oversight which have now fallen into desuetude, but which were thought to be of considerable advantage during the period they prevailed. One of the most important of these was Catechising, or Examination. According to the second book of Discipline "every minister is ordained to have weekly catechisings of some part of the parish," and though this was meant more expressly for the young, yet all ages were included in the common practice. This injunction was faithfully carried out by Mr. Wightman, and though it was a laborious duty, yet it was a very pleasant one after all. The greatest attention was always shown to the minister's comfort, external and internal, and the whole community, literally and figuratively, were at his feet. A Diet of Catechising was a great affair, and every one prepared for it by a careful perusal of the Shorter Catechism. A leaf of that valuable treasury might have been seen in the hands of a youngster in the family, and another quivering under the scrutiny of old grandame, " with spectacles on nose, and pouch on side," in preparation for the grand review, while the milkmaid, in bringing home the cows in the evening, had laid aside her ballad and her lilting, and was carefully conning over Effectual Calling, and what was prayed for in the Petitions. A farmhouse was selected as central as possible for the district, and thither the surrounding families were required to repair on a certain day at a certain hour, as the tribes went up of old to the testimony of Israel. The barn was sometimes used as most commodious, but as the event usually came off in the winter season, the large kitchen was found more agreeable. There all ages and classes assembled, the old and the young, the parents and their children, the master and his servants, the farmer and his cottars, and underwent the ordeal of an examination in the faith, according to the prescribed standard. The scene was in one view a painful one, as the old and gray-headed were placed on the same footing, and in the same position as the youngest. The grandmother and the grandchild were seen side by side, alike trembling in the prospect of clerical inquisition, and while that was being made, the young prompted the old one when at a loss, and even sometimes giggled when they saw granny perplexed. Pray, what was the use of it all?

We are now going to accompany Mr. Wightman on one of his catechising excursions, and will act the part of a surreptitious reporter. It is an early day in December, fine, clear, cold, and the Diet is to be held in Gleddingholm. That part of the parish is very delightful to one with a taste for landscape scenery. The prospect is very interesting, there being a great variety of hills and dales, rugged steeps, rushing streamlets, smoking cottages, and deeply hollowed glens. The view from the heights above Glenmaid, and at Auchengeith, towards Lochmaben and Burnswark, is truly elevating, while the fine elastic air, the clear atmosphere, and tinges of the clouds on the horizon, are charming and exhilarating in a high degree. Queensberry is towering aloft, as if in prideful rivalry, saluting Criffel, and by many deviations the gentle Æ is threading its way onward to the sea. But the moral landscape is still more enchanting, and the reception of the minister by the families he has come to visit in a pastoral capacity is flattering in the extreme. The large kitchen of Gleddingholm is filled with the surrounding families. All are there, old and young. Seventy-seven persons are present, two more than were at the Diet held at Templandhill last week, a hundred and fifty-two in all in less than a fortnight, not a bad testimony of the religious character of the parish. We have said all were there, but yet not all. A farmer has sent out his two men to the plough, and they are absent. He apologizes to the minister, saying that he was later than usual, and he thought he might not come, and as a frost was setting in, and to all appearance this was the last day for some time to come that the plough could be going, he had sent them out, but their families are here. We overhear the minister muttering something, of which we catch the words, "things seen and temporal are apt to prevail." He is sitting in the arm-chair by the fire; a table is beside him covered with a snow-white cloth, on which lies the family Bible. Seated around the walls, on every available kind of seat, the audience have taken their places, like a badly-arranged row of volumes in a bookcase, and the service begins.

After reading a portion of Scripture and offering up prayer, the minister introduces the catechising by stating, that for the soul to lack knowledge is not good, that there is no knowledge like that of religion, that it makes wise unto salvation, and therefore we should endeavour to obtain it. An assembly of learned and pious men, after much prayer and labour, compiled out of the Holy Scriptures a summary of the leading doctrines and duties of the Christian religion, and this the ministers are commanded to teach and explain. He insists upon the necessity of instructing the young. Human society is like a large wood

composed of older and younger trees, when a race of
plants are making their appearance above the surface
among the taller ones—the hand of Time will lay the
axe to the root of the old, and the young must then be
all the wood that remains. How necessary is it, then, to
water and cherish these young plants, that the face of
society may be like a garden watered of heaven, a seed
to serve God while sun and moon endure. Education,
in connection with religion, is the great source of
national, parochial, and family happiness. This is not
a light matter, but one of inexpressible importance, and
parents should therefore co-operate with ministers in
bringing up the young in the nurture and admonition
of the Lord. He then takes up the Shorter Catechism,
and, beginning at one end of the circle, interrogates all
without exception, taking the several questions in order,
and making a short running commentary on each. On
the whole, they are answered pretty well, though sad
havoc is made in syntax and sense. It is evident that
a better knowledge had once obtained on the part of
some, but there is a willingness to do their best. One
round is sufficient, and this being done, a portion of
Scripture is read, prayer is offered, and the assemblage
disperses, thankful that it is over, and that a long time
must intervene till a similar examination comes round.

These meetings were sometimes occasions of considerable theological discussion and ready repartee, when the
catechiser became the catechised, and was put to his
wits' end to maintain his position. As the visitations
were always expected at a certain season of the year,
some of the more dexterous in the district prepared
themselves for the sole purpose of puzzling the minister,

G

and not at all to have some difficulty in divinity or Christian ethics satisfactorily explained. Indeed, in some instances such an explanation would have been a great disappointment, as defeating anticipated victory. Then the questions were so framed and put that a sermon or a treatise would have scarcely sufficed to give a full explanation, and yet a categorical answer was always required. The genealogies of the patriarchs was a grand resort, as was also predestination, free-will, and other intricate subjects, which it required a whole college of divinity professors to explain. A story is told of a minister who on such an occasion resolved to silence an inquisitive shoemaker by asking him a question thought unanswerable. "John, how long did Adam stand in Paradise before he fell?" John saw the object of his inquiry, and immediately replied, " Weel, Sir, if ye'll promise to answer my question I'll answer yours." " Be it so, John." " Weel, Sir, he stood till he got a wife;—How long stood he after?" The minister's answer is not known. Mr. Dickson, minister of Wamphray, was one day catechising at the house of an old man called Peter French, and naturally beginning with the host, he asked Peter, "What is the chief end of man?" To which Peter promptly replied, "'Deed, Sir, I'll no presume. That's your duty; ye're paid for telling us." Peter thereby saved his credit, and at the same time gave all due reverence to his minister. At one of these catechisings, which took place in the church, the name of Walter Hunter was called, as in this case the parties were separately examined. Walter was at the east end of the church among the school-boys— the school being taught there—and he answered in a loud voice, "Here, Sir." "O yes," said the minister, "loud i' the lone was never a gude milk cow." Walter, after some keen interrogatories respecting doctrinal points and moral conduct, was dismissed to give place to another, but before rising he remarked, loud enough for all to hear, "I hae seen a cow that could gie a lilt, and a gude jilt too." A woman answered all the questions put to her by what Dickens calls the staple of American conversation, namely, "Yes, Sir." In order to see how far she would go with this response, she was asked, "Could you see the wind, Margaret?" "Yes, Sir," was the ready reply. Of course her fellow-servants, after going home, twitted her about her examination and seeing the wind, which she still affirmed, and after much banter she appealed to ocular demonstration, saying, "Weel, then, if ye open twa barn doors, will ye no see the wun' blawin' through?"

These diets of catechising were sometimes taken on consecutive days, in which case the minister did not return to the manse at night, but staid in some parishioner's house that he might more conveniently attend the next day's meeting. In this way almost a whole week was spent, before he returned home to prepare for the duties of the forthcoming Sabbath. The minister of Colvend went out one winter on a catechising tour, and took a boy with him to open gates and attend to his horse. At the close of the week, when the little man was about to be discharged, he said to the minister, "Sir, I hae heard you asking mony questions at the houses we hae been at, and I wad like to ask you a question before I gang. What do ye think o' the Fall, Sir?" "It is a mysterious subject, my man, but what do ye think of it yourself?" "I dinna ken, but it was a

terrible thing that the worl' should hae been lost for the
sake o' an apple.   I can gae into Dalbeattie an' get as
mony's I can eat, an' my pouches filled, for tippence.
But do ye no think, Sir, it was awfu' wee buikit o' the
deevil to attack the woman instead o' the man ?   I hae
never thocht onything o' him sin' ever I kent it."   Such
is a specimen of what was once regarded as an important
ministerial duty.   It was perhaps of use in those days,
when the channels of knowledge were not so numerous
as now, but in these times of cheap Bibles, tracts, and
religious magazines, we think the duty is unnecessary;
and it has therefore judiciously been allowed to fall into
desuetude.

But we turn to more solemn customs than those we
have just noticed—solemn because they have reference
to the dead—and however ridiculous some of them may
now appear, we are unwilling to treat them with levity,
or speak of them with disrespect.   They were well
intended as marks of affection towards the departed,
though it may be thought they were the lingering
traces of a barbaric age.   Times, however, are changing
fast, and the incongruous hospitalities of death are
almost entirely gone out of fashion.   People, no matter
how rural now, see that they can mourn without superstition, that mortality comports ill with festivity, and
that the rites of the grave are best accompanied by
social prayer and silent meditation.   We shall now
refer to some of these ancient customs, that rest upon
the mysteries of mortality, and which were in full force
for several years after Mr. Wightman became minister
of Kirkmahoe, but which he ineffectually endeavoured
to remove.   The tenderness felt for the dead still

makes the living fearful to omit any accustomed mark of respect, and hence the tenacity of some of the old rites, which, in calm moments, might be thought " more honoured in the breach than the observance."

It seemed quite a mistake to imagine that when a man's last breath went out there was no more of him with respect to the present scene. As his entrance into the world was attended with certain observances, so his departure from it had even more, there being four stages to be gone through—his last death-bed moments, encoffining, burial, and draigie. These were religiously performed. We can well remember several curious customs regularly observed in connection with death. If this occurred in the family of a farmer, the arm of labour was immediately suspended. The horses were loosed from the plough and put up in the stable; seed-sowing itself, however favourable the weather might be, was entirely interrupted. If the season was autumn, harvest was in like manner stopped. Traffic of all kinds was at a stand-still; and even the poor cottar's children had to seek their milk elsewhere, or take their porridge without it. The dispensation was considered· the signal doing of the Almighty; and not to have entirely suspended labour, would have been thought alike impious towards Heaven and disrespectful to the deceased. The last expiration of the breath was received by the nearest of kin, as it was thought to bear with it the departing spirit; for similar reasons, the last dying accents were faithfully treasured.

We well remember, when a child, standing by the death-bed of a younger brother, seeing our weeping mother lay her face upon that of the child, just as the last sigh was drawn. It was many years afterwards that we learned the secret of this melancholy movement. The eyes of the deceased were closed by the nearest relative—the body, after being washed, was dressed in its finest underclothing—the hands, if a female, were laid over the chest; and if a male, were extended by the side. Upon the breast was placed a plate of salt, which, it was believed, prevented the body from swelling and bursting the bands with which it was bound. This custom was also observed by some of the ancients, but from a different motive, as intimating their belief in a future state—salt being the emblem of perpetuity. The looking-glass was covered with a cloth, lest the relatives should accidentally obtain a glimpse of their wobegone features. The striking pulley of the clock was removed, that there should be no note of the passing hours, and that silence might reign in the chamber of the dead. The cat was incarcerated beneath an inverted washing-tub, as it was understood that if she leaped over the corpse, and afterwards went over a living person, that individual would ever after be subject to epileptic fits. A better reason would have been, to prevent her from attacking the body, as such animals have been sometimes known to do.

Almost every corpse had its *special* visitors, who came for a purpose different from that of sympathizing with the bereaved family. Had a child been born with what was called a cherry or a strawberry mark upon its face, the spot was sure to be speedily obliterated on being submitted to the touch of a dead man's hand. Also, whosoever looked upon the lifeless form, should of necessity touch it, to prevent dreaming of shrouds,

and ghosts, and churchyards. It was sometimes difficult to be assured that the vital spark had fled in reality
and for ever. Every family could relate traditions of
corpses sitting up in their grave-clothes, staring around,
and finally being restored to their friends. The effect
of such traditions was, that the "kistin," or encoffining,
was generally delayed to the latest moment, to afford
every chance of a return to life; and the "waukin" of
the corpse was a matter requiring considerable fortitude,
and attended with no little apprehension. Every one
had heard of somebody's corpse starting up in ghastly
wildness, striking terror and dismay, and requiring the
presence of the minister to "lay" it; and to have *heard*
of such a circumstance, however far remote, was of equal
authority with having *seen* it. The "waukers" kept a
candle burning all night beside the body; and frequent
as well as timorous were the glances furtively cast
towards the bed of death during the silent watches, till
the morning again dawned upon the world.

The encoffining, or, as it was called in the vernacular,
the *kisting* of the dead, was regarded as of greater consequence, and observed with more solemnity in the
olden time than now—religious exercises being considered indispensable. This was the reopening of the
fountain of grief; and if it was not the final opportunity
for taking farewell, it involved the wrenching of another
tie, the complete isolation of the beloved from all that
once was dear. Before this the body might be considered as still holding its place almost in the domestic
circle. The death-chamber could be entered, and the
death-couch visited at will. It occupied a place belonging likewise to others of the family, who should recline

there on its being vacated by its silent incumbent; and in after-days they would tell it was there such and such a one breathed his last. The encoffining of the body was, therefore, the second step in its removal from the family group; it was now consigned to its own particular tenement; it was alone—shut in from all the world, to rest in silence and darkness till another change should come. The lid, however, was not screwed down till the morning of the burial; but few were the visits now paid. The coffin was itself doleful and forbidding; yet the mother would softly steal in with a wistful heart, trem- blingly lift the lid, remove the face-cloth, and kiss and weep over her unconscious child.

It was customary for the minister or an elder to be present on this solemn occasion, who was conducted into the death-chamber to see the body put into the coffin, and offer up a suitable prayer for the consolation of the bereaved family. This was, doubtless, a very appropriate season for such religious exercise, which must have been an important ministrant to the spiritual comfort of the afflicted mourners. The custom, however, had its origin in an Act of Parliament. It is always pleasing to find the Government of a country attentive not only to the temporal but also the spiritual necessi- ties of its people, and especially sympathizing with them in their moments of affliction. It affords, indeed, a great mitigation of our woes when kings are our fathers, and queens our nursing-mothers, making, as it were, our individual cases their own; and, in return for such manifestations of parental feeling, we cannot withhold the gratitude, the loyalty, and the affection which spontaneously arise in our bosoms. But, alas! the Act referred to was not passed with the spiritual consolation and the religious exercise in view ; it was designed for a far different purpose—namely, *for the improvement of the* LINEN *manufacture within the kingdom.* One may smile at the recital of such a cause, and think that so great a zeal for the benefit of the linen-draper and manufacturer but ill accorded with the sanctity of the house of mourning, and was like seeking the living among the dead. But so it was : the deacon, the elder, or the minister, was to intrude his presence, on that most mournful of all occasions, to see that the corpse was shrouded in home-made linen, and not exceeding in value *twenty shillings* per ell.

In the second session of the first Parliament of James VII., held at Edinburgh, 1686, an Act was passed, called the "Act for Burying in Scots Linen," in which it was ordained, for the encouragement of the linen manufactures within the kingdom, that no person whatsoever, of high or low degree, should be buried in any shirt, sheet, or anything else, except in plain linen or cloth of Hards, made and spun within the kingdom, and without lace or point. There was specially prohibited the use of Holland, or other linen cloth made in other kingdoms ; and of silk, hair, woollen, gold, or silver, or any other stuff than what was made of Hards, spun and wrought within the kingdom, under the penalty of 300 pounds Scots for a nobleman, and 200 pounds for every other person, for each offence. One-half of this penalty was to go to the informer, and the other half to the poor of the parish where the body should be interred. And, for the better discovery of contraveners, it was ordained that every minister within the kingdom should keep an exact account and register of all persons buried in his parish. A certificate, upon oath, in writing, duly attested by two "famous" persons, was to be delivered by one of the relatives to the minister within eight days, declaring that the deceased person had been shrouded in the manner prescribed; which certificate was to be recorded without charge. The penalty was to be sued for by the minister before any judge competent; and if he should prove negligent in pursuing the contraveners within six months after the interment, he himself was liable for the said fine. It was also enacted that no wooden coffin should exceed 100 merks Scots as the maximum rate for persons of the highest quality, and so proportionately for others of lower rank, under the penalty of 200 merks Scots for each offence.

As might have been expected, this Act was very unpopular, and was accordingly evaded and infringed in every conceivable way. Those who did make use of plain linen on these occasions, endeavoured to procure it of the finest texture and quality, and consequently paid a considerable price. The encoffining certificates were frequently neglected altogether; others were irregular in their terms, or were not sufficiently attested, and it required but little shrewdness to divine the cause. Within *nine* years it was found necessary to ratify anew, and approve in Parliament, this Linen Act, and to append certain stringent additions and penalties, for the purpose of enforcing its observance. These were: that none should presume to use home-made linen above a certain value—twenty shillings Scots per ell—under the same penalties set down against burying in foreign linen; and that the

nearest elder or deacon should be present at the encoffining, to see that the Act was not contravened. It
was also made statute that no seamstress should make
or sew any sort of dead-linen contrary to the foresaid
Act and its present addition, under the penalty of forty
merks for each offence, for the benefit of the poor.

Twenty years sufficed for this fashion of Scots linen-
shrouds. Whether the linen manufacturers had become
sufficiently well established, and thought they could
maintain their ground without the further patronage
and support of the dead; or whether the woollen manufacturers, instigated by the success of their rivals in the
linen trade, began a querulous bleating around the
throne, in the strain of "fish of one and flesh of another,"
we are not aware; but we find that our sovereign lady,
Queen Anne, in her first Parliament, did, for the encouragement of the woollen manufacture within the
kingdom, rescind the Linen Act of her ancestors, and
substitute a woollen one in its stead, under the same
severe pains and penalties for its contravention as laid
down in the other. Within the last seventy years this
Act was openly and regularly infringed and the penalty
paid, the first item in the undertaker's bill always being,
" To paying the penalty under the Act for burying in
Scots linen;" but he charged only one-half of the fine,
taking credit for the other half, as being the informer
against himself.

This will explain the custom which still lingers among
certain families and in some districts, of wrapping the
remains of their friends in shrouds entirely of woollen;
but we have reason to be grateful for the improved
legislation of our own times in this respect—that such

sacred and solemn duties are not interfered with, that
we are permitted to clothe and bury our dead in whatever manner affection may dictate and means afford.
But the last morning at length came, and the last fond
look was taken by all concerned in the event, and then
the coffin-lid was screwed down, shutting out friend and
foe, and shrouding its unconscious tenant in darkness
and solitude.

The funeral was a great affair, requiring extensive
preparations; and it was a matter of no small anxiety,
during the whole lifetime of some, to have a "decent
burial" at last.   Inviting few attendants, or having less
than a profuse supply of what were termed *refreshments*,
was the greatest disrespect which could be shown to the
memory of the deceased—while the greater the number
and the abundance, the greater was deemed the affection,
and the intenser the grief.   From the desire which all
cherish of being thought well of after death, many submitted to the severest privations, and denied themselves
the necessaries of life for years, that the expense of their
funeral might not fall upon the parish, and that on the
occasion there might be enough and to spare.

When such foresight as that referred to had not been
duly regarded, the relatives, in order to escape the reproach of the community, have involved themselves
in expenses which it required years to liquidate.   The
time usually intimated for meeting was ten o'clock,
and the "gathering hour" not unfrequently exceeded
three hours of the sun.   The consequences of sitting
so long on a winter day in an open barn or outhouse,
after, perhaps, the violent exercise of walking or riding
over several miles of moorland, are not difficult to

imagine.   Far and near, invitations or "warnings" were
given; and as generally two-thirds more were invited
than could be accommodated at once in the largest
apartment, company after company was entertained in
regular succession.   The order of the refreshments was
the following:—Pipes and tobacco—ale, with bread and
cheese—whisky, with the same accompaniments—rum,
with cracker biscuits—brandy and currant-bun—wine
and *shortbread*.   All these were in consecutive order,
and more than one round of each.   If any were intent
on enjoying a double portion of the good things provided,
they re-entered with the company next in attendance,
and had their wants supplied.   The bun and bread
were cut into pieces about three inches square, and
every one was helped to a piece, which he either ate
or pocketed; but as he could not so readily dispose
of the liquid, any man, whose better-half was indisposed
at home, took with him what was popularly called a
"droddy-bottle;" and when those serving came round,
he held out his flask, and said: "Put it in there, and
I'll tak it hame to the wife."   We remember hearing
Mr. Wightman say, that when he came to his parish in
the Vale of Nith, about the beginning of the present
century, at the first funeral he attended there was
assembled in a barn one large company, who had taken
more than *two hours* to "gather."   There were seven
rounds of refreshments, and he was required to "ask a
blessing"—that is, to offer up an appropriate prayer
before every round; certainly, as he said, "a severe
ordeal at the installation of a young minister."   But
Nithsdale was not solitary in this funereal prodigality.
We find the same profuse entertainment was customary

in Carrick, and even a competition among the people as to the sumptuousness of the burial services. In the parish of Kirkmichael, the son of a deceased farmer ordered a whole boll (eight stones) of *shortbread* for his father's funeral; and this would have been prepared, had not the baker disinterestedly persuaded him that a fourth of the quantity would be sufficient. The currant-bun was cut the size of small bricks; and on one of the company remarking, "These are good *gumps*," he replied, with evident gratification, " I mean gumps: my faither, in a' his life, could never thole to be scrimpit in onything, and he couldna hae restit in his grave had he thocht he was to hae a scrimpit burial."

The excessive profusion of meats and drinks on these occasions, under the name of *services*, has been an unseemly blot in the record of Scottish customs, from the twofold character of the consequences which it entailed —the pecuniary embarrassment in which it involved the bereaved family, and the demoralization it produced on those who attended the obsequies. The doctor's bill is by-and-by handed in—the apothecary's account is transmitted—the village carpenter will call in some evening for payment of the coffin—the grave dues must be disbursed ere the churchyard is left—and a long list of articles of mourning for the various members of the family, to make them appear respectable, will fall to be paid to the haberdasher, the mantua-maker, and the tailor. Most problematical is it whether all these charges can be settled without inconvenience; and yet custom has declared, that in addition to these there must be bread and biscuit, and bun and cheese, and ale and whisky, and rum and brandy and wine, and all of

a superfluity. Perhaps the occasion of all this was the
death of a husband and a father, the only or chief support of the family, and whom, for weeks or months, a
sick-bed had prevented from earning a single shilling!
A custom has long prevailed with respect to marriages,
which, we think, might with propriety be transferred to
funerals: every party invited to a marriage is expected
to take a present to the bride. How much better would
it be rather to take a present to the widow! No man
should enter into the matrimonial state until he is well
able to provide for the expenditure which that state
requires. But death comes without our bidding, and
seizes his victim often without the means to defray the
expense of his interment. How would a little present
on such an occasion cheer the widow's heart, and revive
it with gratitude if not with joy!

We have said that when the company was larger
than the apartment could accommodate at once, it was
divided, and one detachment entertained after the other.
Ludicrous incidents sometimes occurred from this circumstance, and from the state of inebriation which so
many liquors induced. The corpse has sometimes been
forgotten altogether, or dropped on the way to the
churchyard. There is a traditional report that at the
boat-house on the Doon above Kiers, in the parish of
Straiton, the company was divided into two portions,
and when all had drunk abundantly, they marched off
to the churchyard, several miles distant. The advanced
party thought the coffin was with the company in the
rear—the rear thought it was carried by those before;
and when they arrived at the Buskin Burn, in sight of
the burial-ground, where it was intended to fall into

order, it was ascertained that the body had never been removed. The same circumstance is said to have occurred at the funeral of Mrs. Hume of Billie, in Berwickshire, an occasion when grave observance was peculiarly called for, as the lady had been barbarously murdered by her man-servant. Several years ago, a funeral company had wended their way for many miles through deep snow, over Eskdale Moor, bound for Moffat Churchyard. On arriving at the burial-ground, they discovered that they had dropped the coffin by the way, the back having fallen from the cart in which it was being conveyed.

The extraordinary abuse of spirituous liquors on such occasions was not confined to the Lowlands of Scotland. Garnet, in his "Tour Through the Highlands," says:— "A person, originally from Oban, had spent some time in the neighbourhood of Inverary, in the exercise of some mechanic art; and dying there, his corpse, at his own request, was carried by his friends towards Oban for interment. On a hill between Inverary and Loch Awe, just above Port Sonachan, they were met by the relations of the deceased from Oban, who came to convey the corpse the remainder of the way. The parting could not take place without a glass of spirits that had been plentifully provided by the Oban party; and before they separated, above forty corpses were to be carried down the hill, in which, however, animation was only suspended, for they all recovered the next day." Within the last few years, in the Western Highlands, at the funeral of one Macdougal, who died at the age of ninety-two, *nine hundred* persons were present, who were accommodated in three houses. Into one were shown

the gentry of the neighbourhood, where were set refreshments in superfluity, consisting of cold tongue,
rounds of beef, bread of all kinds, various sorts of the
best wines, and the costliest spirits. Into another were
shown the respectable yeomen of the place, where a
similar banquet was prepared, but of a less expensive
description. In another assembled about five hundred
of the commonalty, who were each, on entering, presented with whisky and bread and cheese in abundance.
Two glasses did not satisfy many—seven-eighths of the
company became intoxicated: there were here no wines,
but plenty of whisky, with cold and hot water. *Fifty-six
gallons* of whisky were mixed into "toddy." One of
the stewards in the first-mentioned dwelling (our informant) slipped into the last one, to see how matters
were going on. When he entered, the chair was
occupied by a *ruling elder* of some note, who was dis-
coursing in the most eulogistic terms on the merits of
the deceased, and was very enthusiastically applauded
by the vast assemblage. He wound up his peroration
by giving a thump on the table, and calling silence.
Silence being obtained, and while all were eagerly listening, holding up a brimming bumper, he cried at
the pitch of his voice:—" *Gentlemen, here's the health
of Macdougal!*" and the toast went round with three
times three. Though all had been thus entertained,
so much cold toddy was left, that an application was
afterwards made to the proper authorities for leave to
redistil it—which was refused.

Various attempts have been made, in many places, to
do away with this prodigality, and its lamentable con-
comitants; but these have ever been most strenuously

H

resisted.   Some years ago, a clergyman, whose parish
was on one side bounded by the Solway, endeavoured,
with the assistance of his session, to introduce the custom of but *one service* (one round of refreshments). The
parishioners almost unanimously were up in arms.   One
of them sought to have his revenge even after death.   He
bequeathed a considerable sum to be expended in pro-
viding refreshments at his funeral, and he appointed the
kirk-session his executors to see his will accomplished.
The conclave met to consider what line of tactics they
should adopt—whether they should decline interfering,
or discharge the duty with which they had been intrusted.
The result of their deliberations was, not to decline the
trust, but to procure the most expensive wines, so as to
absorb the money in one single service.   On the day of
interment, when the course of the enemy became apparent, the company of mourners rose up indignantly, and,
marching off to the village inn, subscribed among themselves, and lavishly quaffed the mountain-dew, hurling
their anathemas at the kirk-session and their " shilpit
claret."

It was customary to carry the coffin on handspokes, as
it was believed that no horse would ever thrive which
had once drawn a corpse.   The nearest relation walked
at the head, and the next of kin to him went before,
holding the footstrings of the coffin in his hand.   When
the distance to the churchyard was great, the shades of
evening were often descending when the dust was consigned to its kindred earth.   As hearses had not been
introduced, a *long-bodied* cart was used by those coming
from a distance.   But as even such vehicles were then
in their infancy, and not found everywhere, the usual

method of conveying the coffin was to lay it across the necks of two horses, the riders taking care to keep close together, parallel and steady, so that no accident might happen. A funeral party once met with a sad disaster on their way to the churchyard. Coming to a burn in their way considerably swollen from recent rains, and there being nothing but a plank for foot passengers across, when the horses carrying the coffin on their necks were fording the stream, which was tumbling down "fast and furious," one of them stumbled and nearly fell, on which the coffin, a large one, plunged into the current, and was rapidly borne away, to the consternation of all. Of course, there was "racing and chasing" in pursuit of the fugitive down the banks of the burn, some running to this winding and others to that, but on careering went the coffin past them all, till at a very sharp bend nearly half a mile from the ford, it was safely landed, and re-placed in its former position, when the cavalcade again formed in order and moved along. By-and-by, however, hearses began to be introduced, and the progression to the burial-ground was sometimes as rapid as it formerly was slow. It was more like a race than a funeral pro-cession. Such was the case at the funeral of one Macadam, who lived on the Carrick shore, and who was widely known for his obesity—which was so immense, that he could not see his shoe-buckle. He was to be interred in a churchyard about twelve miles distant; and it was doubted whether one horse could draw the hearse; but such was the career at which it sped, that old Mr. Ramsay, the minister of Kirkmichael, burst his horse in attempting to keep up with it, and many *short-cuts* were taken to be in with the hearse at last.

In the olden time, paupers were only conveyed to the churchyard in a coffin, not buried in one. The article in use was what was called a *slip-coffin*, having a movable hinged bottom, which, being let down over the grave, and a bolt withdrawn, the body dropped in, and was quickly covered over, while the box was set aside for future use in the same way. The last slip-coffin remembered in Ayrshire was disposed of in the following manner:—One Maclymont of Auchalton was invited to attend the funeral of a poor person in Maybole, where the body was to be ejected in the usual manner. When they had reached the grave, and the bolt was about to be drawn, he asked what was the cost of the slip-coffin, and being told it was three pounds Scots (or 5s. sterling), he immediately produced the sum, and desired the coffin to be lowered into the grave. Ever since, the poorest individual has been supplied with a coffin.

The use of the *mortcloth* at burials was also a matter of important consideration; it entitled the gravedigger to a certain fee; and many a weary mile did he travel over mountain and moorland, through rain and snow, in fair weather and foul, with the sable covering under his arm. Afterwards, however, when hearses were introduced, the mortcloth was spread over the coffin only at the churchyard gate, and the sexton's labour was thereby considerably curtailed. His weary travels were dispensed with; and he now stood watching by the grave's mouth, or the kirk gate, the arrival of the solemn cortége. As his services were now less, some thought the fee should be less also; and some even refused to use the cloth at all. This was occasionally productive of unpleasant scenes, ill becoming

the place and the occasion.   Now long ago, the remains
of a respectable farmer in the parish of Tarbolton were
to be interred in the family burying-ground, and had
arrived at the churchyard gate for the purpose; but,
either because the coffin was richly mounted, and the
relatives were unwilling that the honour thus conferred
upon the deceased should be concealed, or because the
mortcloth, from long usage, was become "a thing of
shreds and patches," the attendants declined its service,
and prepared to enter the churchyard without it, which
so roused the ire of the gravedigger that, fixing his foot
firmly in the centre of the gateway to oppose them, he
exclaimed, with the feeling of insulted office, "Ye may
tak him hame and bury him like a cow, for without the
claith he shall never enter the yaird!"   The gravedigger
prevailed; the cloth was spread over the coffin, and the
interment proceeded.

Those who died by their own hand were not permitted the benefit of this mortcloth, nor were they,
indeed, allowed any of the rites of Christian burial; but,
coffinless and unmourned, their remains were conveyed
at midnight to the march-boundary of two parishes or
shires, and there deposited in neutral ground, with a
stake driven through the body, as if fixing it to the
earth, and precluding the hope of a resurrection.   There,
in loneliness and silence, they were left, far from the
habitations of men, where no eye should mark the
resting-place and no foot should stumble upon their grave.
Their body was considered vile; the earth which wrapped
them as stained with pollution; and the coarse frame-
work on which they were dragged along was afterwards
burned to ashes.   One who had become weary of life,

and who had terminated his mortal career by suicide in the neighbourhood of Sanquhar, was drawn at midnight upon a sledge for several miles to neutral ground, and there received the melancholy and peculiar rites. Though the interment was made under the deepest darkness of night, yet the circumstance was not concealed. On the following Sunday, bands of profane and reckless men assembled at the mournful spot, dug the body from the grave, and, fixing a rope to the limbs, amused themselves all day by dragging it up and down the hills. When they were exhausted with their inhuman sport, they placed the corpse in a sitting posture against a stone, and as the glazed eyeballs peered out from beneath their half-opened lids, they put a glass to his mouth, calling him to drink, and not sit squinting there! No treatment was thought too inhuman for a suicide.

A tradesman on the Galloway coast, whose wife had committed self-destruction, anxious to have her remains interred as near the churchyard as possible, since he durst not intrude them within it, deposited them close outside the wall; but the next morning, to his horror and astonishment, he found the coffin, with its contents, placed against the door of his dwelling. He applied to a certain Admiral Stewart in the district for advice in the mournful circumstances, who recommended him to say nothing about it, but to take the coffin down to the sea-shore during the night, and deposit it within flood-mark in the sand, when the next tide would obliterate all traces of the grave before morning. This was accordingly done, and the infuriated populace spent the next day in a vain search for the poor suicide's grave.

The farmer's wife of Auchalton committed suicide, by

hanging herself, in the summer of 17—, and the husband, anxious that her remains should be quietly interred in the parish churchyard, had secretly procured the mortcloth to cover the coffin on its way thither. But no; it would not be allowed. The people rose in fury and tore the mortcloth to shreds. They would rather thus destroy than desecrate and contaminate the sheet of the dead. Strange to say, the women were the most ferocious in their speech and conduct towards the remains of the unfortunate deceased. The most conspicuous of all was one Mary Harvey, whose name we record for the reprobation of our readers.

The following notice of a suicide at Oban, which occurred only a few years ago, shows that the old feeling has not yet died out:—" A private of the Argyll and Bute Rifles, named James M'Gregor, whose regiment was stationed at the village of Oban, committed suicide by shooting himself with his musket. He was found shortly after the act had been committed in his room, dressed in fatigue clothes, with a handkerchief over his eyes, and the musket lying between his legs. He had placed the muzzle of the rifle in his mouth, and drawn the trigger with the toe of his right foot, which was divested of the shoe and stocking. The unfortunate man had been observed for some time in desponding spirits, and there was no doubt he was insane when he destroyed himself. The event created excitement in the village, and much contention arose as to the manner in which the body should be disposed of. The Highlanders of the old stock denied its title to Christian burial, and insisted that it should be put into a hole in the corner of some field, with a stake through the breast, according to ancient custom. The managers of the churchyard, however, finally resolved that the remains of the poor insane soldier might be interred in the ordinary resting-place of the dead. This was not to be, however, for, on the following Sunday night, four privates of the regiment, accompanied by an old sergeant, conveyed the body, which was coffined, in a boat out to the Sound of Oban, and pitching it into the sea, returned under the notion that they had thoroughly retrieved the honour of their regiment from the disgrace cast upon it by the act of the suicide." Alas! for the poor soldier: there were more insane than he!

The committal to the grave, the smoothing down of the turf, and the replacing of the monumental slab above the lonely sleeper, did not complete the funeral obsequies. A very important rite yet remained. This was the *draigie*, a term derived from the word *dirige*, conspicuous in one of the chants for the dead in Catholic times. On retiring from the churchyard, the whole company withdrew to the village inn, not to lament over the memory of the deceased, but to have a handsome refreshment. Strange and mournful results have not unfrequently followed the unseemly carousals that now took place. Family feuds which seemed extinguished and forgotten, were revived with more than their original rancour. Genealogies were traced, and pedigrees recounted, with all the fluency and inaccuracy which resentment, kindled by inebriation, could engender. The closing scene of these disgraceful orgies was occasionally the introduction to another funeral solemnity.

In olden times, certain paraphernalia were employed

on the occasion of burials which did not meet with approbation on the part of the Church. On the death of the Earl of Atholl, in 1579, a rumour being general that it was intended at the burial to use a white cloth above the mortcloth, and also for the mourners to have long gowns with stroups (hoods?), and torches, the General Assembly, held at Edinburgh in July of that year, directed two of their number to wait on certain lords connected with the family of the deceased, desiring that all such evidences of superstition should be avoided on the occasion. It was admitted, on inquiry, that the gowns were intended to be used, but not the torches; and the Assembly were desired to appoint two of their number to examine the preparations. They did so, and intimated their opinion that the cross and the stroups were superstitious; to which an answer was returned, that the mortcloth would be covered with black velvet. The gowns alluded to were made of black cloth, and had red hoods; the torches were of wax, and of very considerable length and weight.

By the will of the Earl of Salisbury, executed April 29, 1397, twenty-four poor people, clothed in black gowns with red hoods, were ordered to attend the funeral, each carrying a lighted torch of eight pounds' weight. These torches were expensive, from their size and number, and therefore they were generally provided by the churchwardens, and lent out at so much each. It is not many years since, in some parishes in Ayrshire, funerals were attended by females arrayed in long mantles of black or red cloth, with hoods—doubtless a lingering relic of the gowns and stroups.

These customs were not confined to one locality or

shire, but were the same from the Solway to the Clyde, from "Maidenkirk to John-o'-Groat's;" and no voice was powerful enough, come from whatever quarter it might, to check the tendency in the popular feeling, till, by a very gradual process, the evil has now nearly corrected itself. Though Mr. Wightman regretted the unnecessary expense incurred, and the waste of time before the interment, and exhorted and urged with all his might for a reformation, still he was ready to sympathize with the family in their intended hospitality and kindly respect for the dead: and he would say, as if in apology for what was done, "Old customs are not easily altered, and there is often foundation for them in nature, as well as in expediency, which may not be discovered by a partial view."

CHAPTER VII.

IMPRESSMENT AND THE PRESS-GANG—FORM OF PROCEDURE.—DOINGS AT SEA—RAIDS ON LAND—SERGEANT BLATTERS—FEAR OF FRENCH INVASION — VOLUNTEERING — PROCLAMATION OF BONAPARTE READY—MEN OF KEIR—SERMON BY REV. HENRY DUNCAN—PASTORAL ADDRESS—OFFER OF ASSISTANCE BY PATRICK MILLER OF DALSWINTON.

THE present generation cannot know as their forefathers did the awful import of the term Impressment, and its dreadful ally the Press-gang. Well for them should they never know either of these otherwise than as a word in the household dictionary, referring only to the past, and serving merely to explain the nature of some incident in history or fiction. The one was not merely a legal enactment compelling sailors of all kinds to join the King's ships, but, with certain few exceptions, it extended also to landsmen wherever they could be seized—and the other was not a body of gentlemen fastidiously observant of politeness, or even of civility, in the discharge of disagreeable duty, intimating to some poor fellow, perhaps the head of a family, that his assistance was greatly needed in his country's service, and that they had come to conduct him comfortably on board. No; they were a band of ruffians, a detachment of desperadoes, alike destitute of the feelings of humanity, the fear of danger, and the dread of retribution. On various occasions it was found necessary to have recourse to this method of supplying men for the British navy,

but it was never attended with more than partial
success. Seldom long at rest, with France on the one
hand and America on the other, either engaged in
actual warfare or expecting to be so engaged, Britain
was always scouring her armour from its blood stains,
overhauling her ships, and counting how many men
might be brought upon the battle-scene. These last
were generally defective, and active measures were ever
being employed to supply the want, which was only
effected with the utmost difficulty even when successful,
which but rarely happened. Though the bounty of
regular seamen was doubled and the pay increased, and
men's patriotic feelings were enthusiastically appealed
to, yet it was all in vain. Men were unwilling to engage
in a sea-service of indefinite extent during perilous
times, with the prospect of hard labour, rigorous discipline, severe punishment not always discriminately
inflicted, and where their associates were certain to be,
in great part, the offscourings of the country, the refuse
of the workhouses, and the sweepings of the jails. Men
who had not taken to the sea in their youth could
scarcely be expected to divest themselves of long-
acquired habits on land, relinquish trades and occupa-
tions at which they were expert, and which brought
them a satisfactory remuneration—tear their affections
from family and home, to enter upon a profession for
which they were not adapted, and which they had no
inclination to follow; and all to the old cry of patriotism
and duty, though it required but little penetration to
discover the beggar's wallet and a wooden leg at the
end. Such was not to be expected, therefore there was
no response to the proffered reward, and hence the

necessity of resorting to compulsory measures for re-
cruiting the service.

The first recourse to impressment in Scotland was in
1755, when great apprehensions were excited of an invasion by the French, who had become jealous and
envious of our colonial possessions. During the previous half of the century we had been at war with
that nation fifteen years, nearly a third part of the
time, and a period of eleven years had elapsed since
a cessation of hostilities had taken place. Three
more engagements, embracing other nineteen years of
war with that same people, were yet before us ere
the century should close. Tired of peace, they were
loud and boastful in their menaces, finally throwing
down the gauntlet, which involved another struggle
of seven years. Our land and sea forces were miser-
ably unprepared for any hostile engagement which
might ensue with such an energetic foe, and as the
usual means for raising the forces to a proper strength
failed in their object, the Act of Impressment was passed
to remedy the evil, though at the expense of creating a
greater in its stead. Increased pay and enlarged bounty,
as we have said, had no inducement for men with the
certain prospect of speedy and disastrous war before
them, and hence the necessity of compulsory service
wherever hands could be obtained.

The plan adopted for carrying this Act into effect was
to form gangs of the most desperate characters in the
service, of a greater or lesser number, according to the
scene of their operations, under the command of an
officer, and who, armed from head to heel, should go
forth in quest of men wherever they were most likely

to be found. Of course, regularly bred seamen were their first desire, and when these failed, landsmen were sought for to supply the need. Merchant vessels were plundered of their best hands, sometimes a sufficient number not being left to steer the ships into port. Men who had been long away on distant voyages, and who were rejoicing at the prospect of soon being with their families, were seized just as they were about to disembark and carried off to the fleet, without being permitted to set foot on shore, or see the face of wife and child. The success which attended this method of increasing the forces was not by any means equal to the anticipation. Difficulties were encountered in every quarter, and, as a necessary consequence, little attention was paid by the press-gangs either to the letter or the spirit of the regulations laid down for their direction. Not only was the number of men obtained comparatively small, but their character or quality was miserable in the extreme. Lieut. Tomlinson says that, "After a hot impress of five calendar months, from the 22nd of September, 1770, to the 22nd of February, 1771, besides the advantage of the first surprise, and after sweeping London of great numbers of those idle, dissolute people who commonly enter on board men-of-war at the first breaking out of an impress; and after all the jails had been swept, and the refuse of the kingdom gathered together, they only mustered in their ships about 33,000 men (exclusive of marines) of all denominations, in which were a great many officers, and a very considerable number of servants, besides the complements of all the tenders, &c., so as to make the number of people raised, who really were seamen, very inconsiderable for the

time, and under the very advantageous circumstances
wherewith that impress was favoured, especially when it
was considered that the navy was supposed already to
muster 16,000 men (marines included) when the impress
broke out. But, to his certain knowledge, a very considerable number of those that were raised were the most
miserable objects he ever saw in the navy or ever heard
tell of." At the commencement of this impress so great
a dread seized the sailors in the collier vessels between
Yarmouth and the Nore, that 3000 of them fled ashore
lest they should be impressed into the fleet. Again, at
the commencement of the war in 1793, the whole number
of men obtained by impressment throughout the kingdom, after eighteen months' laborious efforts in this way,
amounted only to some 30,000 men. Every means which
ingenuity could devise was adopted for evading the hate-
ful impress. Desertions, too, were continually taking
place, and to such a degree that it was believed the number of men lost in this way more than counterbalanced
all that had been obtained. Notwithstanding all the
precautions taken to prevent it, the strict vigilance kept,
and the severe punishment inflicted upon delinquents
aiding or abetting in the offence, desertion went on, and
the most daring attempts were made to escape. Many
of the deserters went over to the American navy, and in
endeavouring to regain them often little discrimination
was used between natives and foreigners. The gang
went on board any American vessel they suspected,
caused all hands to be summoned on deck, and carried
off those who suited them, declaring them British subjects, despite their asseverations to the contrary. One
can scarcely form a conception of the numbers who at

various times were seized in this way, but from a list drawn up in 1801, it was found that 1132 American sailors had been wrongfully impressed, and consequently were set at liberty. The impressment of men at sea was always hazardous, as well as difficult, however well armed the attacking party might be. Men would not willingly surrender themselves and their liberty for a service they detested, if they saw the possibility of escape even with a desperate struggle, and, on such occasions, frequently life was not only endangered but lost. The whaler *Sarah and Elizabeth*, of Hull, was returning from Davis' Straits at the close of the fishing season, and when about nine leagues off St. Abb's Head she was hailed by the frigate *Aurora*, and a party of men sent on board of her for the purpose of impressing some of the sailors. The attempt was of course resisted, and the crew, foreseeing what was intended, hid themselves between decks and secured the hatches. The frigate then came alongside the whaler, the hatches were broken up, fighting began, the carpenter's mate of the whaler was killed, and three of the crew were severely wounded.

We now turn from the sea to the land, and in recording the doings there it is scarcely possible to exaggerate the outrages committed in the name of law. Towns were surrounded and kept in a state of siege till a certain number of men had been given up. The sanctity of the Sabbath was violated, churches were surrounded during the time of divine service, nay, even entered, and numbers of the worshippers carried off at the close. Many a man might have said on the Lord's-day evening, as he sat with his wife and family beside him :—

> "No place is sacred, not the church is free.
> Even Sunday shines no Sabbath-day to me."

The press-gang one Sunday entered the church of
Arbroath while the service was going on, and created the
utmost excitement in the seamen's gallery. The minister immediately stopped, and said—"Were it not for
my gown I would do my best to save my friends." An
old dame in the gallery called out, "If I had Crummie's
rung I wad sune lay some of them flat eneuch. Let
them come up here an' they'll get what they're no seekin'
for." Of course the greatest uproar ensued, and when the
gang reached the gallery, the women rose and attacked
them tooth and nail, while some of the sailors flung
themselves into the area and escaped. Marriage parties
were attacked in the midst of their festivities, and the
young bride was left mourning the loss of her husband
ere she had reached her new home. In short, nothing
was allowed to be a barrier in the way to obtain men for
the country's service by land or sea. The only favour
accorded to those who were impressed was their choice
between the two services, for soldier and sailor were
equally in demand; and when the choice was made, they
were bullied and badgered with the profanest language
till they consented to enlist, and their service thereby
rendered sure. Till this was done, their desertion was
almost certain should opportunity occur, and they could
not lawfully be punished for doing so; besides they
required to be watched and guarded to prevent escape.
On shipboard their treatment was harsh in the extreme,
and on their remonstrating they were ordered with the
wildest oaths to go and enrol themselves, and so end it.
Many, therefore, did so to mitigate their misery, while
others held on with obduracy, notwithstanding all they
endured. When once in the clutches of their captors

I

no attention was paid to feeling or comfort, and but little even to the support of life, beyond what was absolutely necessary to preserve existence, till they had reached their destined man-of-war. Their food was scanty and of the worst quality, while their clothing was only what they chanced to wear when they were carried away. On one occasion the captain of a guardship was obliged to put in at Whithorn to have some repairs done for the accommodation of a number of men who had been impressed and taken on board. He went into the town in quest of carpenters for the purpose, but not a single tradesman was willing to undertake the work for fear of capture, and it was only after the captain's solemn assurance that he would return them safe on shore, that two men consented to go with him. They found a number of men stowed away in the hold like so many head of cattle, but without the comforts usually afforded that class of animals. When one of those kidnapped persons asked the captain where their beds were, he pointed with his sword to the deck, and gruffly said, with an oath, "There are your beds." "Very hard to lie upon, certainly, after what you have done to us," was the reply. To which it was retorted, with a volley of profanity, "If you find it hard, you can turn the oftener." The carpenters were safely put on shore, and the vessel sailed away with its freight of unfortunates.

On the outbreak of the impress about the end of last century, it is scarcely possible to conceive the excitement and consternation which everywhere prevailed both in town and country; and for many miles inland the panic was exceedingly great. The hand of labour was almost entirely paralyzed. Servants could only

with the utmost difficulty be procured to attend the
cattle, cultivate the fields, and reap the harvest, while
farmers and their sons were continually on the watch.
Wives trembled, and children quailed as every sun went
down, imagining that the darkness of night was sure to
be accompanied with that more terrible darkness, the
presence of the press-gang.   False alarms, too, not
unfrequently arose from the universal excitement, when
the adult male population of farm-steading and hamlet
fled to the woods, the glens, and the moors for safety,
as did the Covenanters of old in troublous times, and
there remained in concealment, in the retired cave,
beneath the tangled brushwood, or among the brackens,
stealthily visited by some little girl with a supply of
food and a change of stockings under her plaid, till it
was thought safe to venture back to their homes.
Sometimes the one party was as vigilant as the other,
and when the father had crept softly to his arm-chair at
the fireside, after a week's exposure to wind and rain,
skulking from moorland to glen, and from glen to moorland, he was closely followed and pounced upon by the
dreaded gang armed to the teeth.   Entreaties were
laughed at, and supplications vain.   The fact that the
service wanted men, and that they could not be procured except by the use of compulsive means, steeled
the hearts of those appealed to against every remonstrance!though uttered in sobbings and bathed in tears.
To no purpose was the sleeping infant in the cradle
pointed to, and the meal-barrel turned upside down to
show it was empty, and there would be no one to fill it
again, so that starvation was inevitable.   These men
seemed as if they had never lain in a mother's bosom, or

climbed a father's knee. The days of their own youth were forgotten—without pity or a soothing word of sympathy, they tore their victim remorselessly along, while wife and children clung around him, screaming and refusing to let him go. Armed force prevailed—the threshold was cleared—he was dragged away, and the heart-wailings of the sorrow-stricken family followed him far on the winds.

It was the custom of lord-lieutenants of counties, who were instructed by those at head-quarters, to obtain from the different land proprietors a list of those persons who had become eye-sores to the laird, or who had forfeited the goodwill of the neighbourhood, that they might be called on to leave the parish for the parish good, as well as, perhaps, in the end, their own personal reformation. These were first favoured with the attentions of the gang, and afterwards any others that might be found. Many anecdotes might be given of these raids, laughable as well as serious, but we shall give only one as a specimen. The proprietor of Clon-caird, in Carrick, reported that no person could be spared off his estate but one man called James Wilson, subse-quently well known as *Sergeant Blatters*, from his stammering speech, whose ostensible fault was laziness, but the real one, a strong suspicion of his disturbing the game without lawful permission. In short, he was a determined poacher, and practised the arts of netting, trapping, snaring, and shooting, with astonishing dex-terity and success. James lived with his mother, a widow, and was her only child and the delight of her heart. Many a night did he spend sitting astride the "raneltree" in the chimney, while his mother kept

watch at the door; but notwithstanding *his* cunning
and *her* vigilance, he was done for at last.   One bitterly
cold and frosty night James and his mother were keeping themselves comfortable by the fireside, and letting
the game rest in peace, when the dog suddenly challenged the sound of approaching feet.   Too truly
fearing it was the press-gang, in desperation he
scrambled up the chimney to his old roost on the
raneltree, and there in smoky darkness he tremblingly
awaited the issue.   It was indeed the terrible press-
gang, consisting of some six or eight men of very
formidable appearance, who either by accident or design
had stumbled upon the widow's cottage among the
hills.   Their visit was always thought to have been
intentional.   "Cold night on the moor, this, good
woman," said the leader of the gang.   "We are right
glad to see a fire, as we are almost dead with cold, and
we shall take the liberty of warming ourselves ere we
go further."   "I'm a puir lane woman, wi' naebody but
mysel', an' I hae naething to enterteen ye, but at the
farmhouse ayont the hill ye'll be made richt walcome,
an' get a' ye need; I'll let ye see the road."   "Thank ye
for your offer, my woman, but as a fire is all we want at
present, we shall remain where we are," and clustering
around the hearth, they piled on a large number of
peats, which were found convenient in a corner.   James
began to feel uneasy on his lofty perch, as the smoke
with increasing density curled around him.   Lumps of
soot also began to topple down, as he vainly shifted
from one position to another.   "We shall have a change
of weather, for the soot falls," said one of the party, as
a large flake fell upon his hand.   "My old grandmother,

rest her soul, used to tell me so." "We shall soon be suffocated," said another, as the house filled with smoke from the obstruction in the chimney. "'Tis enough to kill one." "That's a fact," cried a voice from the ranel-tree. "I canna stan't ony langer, come what wull,"—and down he dropped into the arms of his pursuers, who did not need the fire any longer, but immediately departed with their charge. In process of time James received his discharge, and returned to his native parish, with the name of *Sergeant Blatters*, and passed the remainder of his life begging from door to door.

For a long time the fear of French invasion, like a mighty incubus, had hung over the land, and kept the inhabitants in a state of incapacity for rightly discharging the duties of life. Those, especially, contiguous to the sea-coast were under very considerable alarm. France had been at enmity with Britain for the long period of nearly 700 years, 250 of which had been actually consumed in war with each other, twenty-three battles having been fought in that time, so deadly had been the hatred, and so vindictive the spirit of our Gallic neighbours. Bonaparte had been making the most terrible devastations wherever he went—misery and bloodshed followed in his wake; and wherever he threatened to appear the utmost consternation prevailed on account of the calamities which were sure to ensue. In a proclamation by the French Directory towards the close of 1797, the people were addressed in these terms:—"You unfortunate Europeans, innocent inhabitants of the plains of Franconia and of the Noric Alps, innumerable victims of the plague of war, in which more than a million of men have been sacrificed, and on which the eye of peace itself beholds this day, on the field of glory, nothing but general misery, universal mourning, and vast despair." He had caused to be proclaimed at the Mauritius his determination to seize our colonial dependencies, and, in repeated boastings, he had declared that he would land upon our shores and subject Britain to his sway. From his well-known ambition and indomitable perseverance in attempting to accomplish whatever he undertook, it was considered certain that an invasion was inevitable, and any day we might see the landing of a foreign foe. What enhanced the fear was the circumstance that rebellion had broken out in Ireland, and large numbers of our soldiers had been sent thither to quell the insurrection, thereby weakening our own defences against aggression, which was daily and hourly expected. In addition to this, French vessels were occasionally capturing ours in the North Seas, and reprisals had also been made, thus fomenting the discord already sufficiently great. False alarms, too, were by no means uncommon, and advantage was sometimes taken of the excited state of patriotic feeling for playing pranks upon the terrified inhabitants. A strange sail seen in the offing by day, or a gun heard at night, which was mischievously fired, was unanimously placed to the French account, and resistance or flight prepared for, as seemed the more judicious or the more likely to succeed. Though there were occasionally false alarms, yet there was just cause for the utmost vigilance everywhere along the coast. It was reported that a French officer of rank had deserted to this country, and had communicated a plan, with full particulars, of the intended invasion, showing that a landing was to be attempted simultaneously at two places in Ireland, in the south and north of England, and also at different places in Scotland, a statement which after events confirmed.

The call for volunteers was promptly and admirably responded to—even before the call was made, the country foreseeing the necessity, great numbers came forward of their own accord and proffered their personal aid. At Newcastle, 60,000 colliers and others acted in this way, and every town, as well as every parish, was more or less zealous in the cause. It is impossible for us to conceive the alarm and consternation which prevailed throughout the kingdom onwards to 1803, when the panic seemed to have reached its culmination. The Bank of England was authorized to suspend payments in specie, an example followed by many others—the theatres were converted into barracks—the Custom-houses were ordered to have their spirituous contents destroyed in the prospect of attack—in the country, horses were to be hamstrung, and the cattle destroyed—the axletrees of waggons and carts were to be sawn through to prevent their use by the enemy—and, in short, every kind of destruction was to be wrought to impede the progress of the invading foe—for all of which ample compensation would be made to the sufferers by the Government. Upwards of 335,000 volunteers were enrolled, and old worn-out veterans retired from the service were sworn in as special constables. Whenever the wind came from the French quarter the coastguards were greatly reinforced, beacons were ready for lighting on every mountain-top, and red flags for hoisting from every tower and spire to rouse the district. These beacons were all safely guarded by night and day, and when an unknown sail appeared in the distance it was scarcely possible to restrain the people from giving the alarm by setting them all ablaze. Once a constant firing was heard at sea during the whole night and the following day along the coast of Cornwall, at the rate of twenty shots a minute. This, of course, caused great excitement, but no invasion followed, and the reason of the cannonading was never known.

So certain was Bonaparte of success in his invasion of England, that he had ready printed in Paris a proclamation, which was to be issued as soon as he had landed on our shores. In some way it became known in this country, and from its nature roused the people to fury against the audacious Corsican. It ran thus:—"Soldiers, the sea is passed! The boundaries of nature have yielded to the genius and fortunes of France, and haughty England groans under the yoke of her conquerors. London is before you!—the Peru of the old world is your prey; within twenty days I plant the tricolor upon the walls of her execrable tower. March! Towns, fields, provisions, cattle, gold, silver, women—I abandon all to you. Occupy these noble mansions, these smiling farms. An impure race, rejected of Heaven, which has dared to be the enemy of Bonaparte, is about to expiate its crimes, and disappear from the earth. Yes, I swear to you that you shall become terrible!—BONAPARTE." If ever "hating with a perfect hatred" existed in the human breast, it was towards Bonaparte, who was thought of as a fiend, and spoken of under every epithet of denunciation in the language. Caricature almost exhausted its ingenuity in holding him up to ridicule, and though he was greatly dreaded, yet there was an eagerness of desire to bestow upon him personal chastisement should he come within reach. A farmer, driving a waggon along a narrow road in Shropshire, was overtaken by a commercial traveller in a gig, who, finding it impossible to pass, shouted loudly for the way to be cleared. No attention being paid to his call, he assumed an air of great importance, and demanded, " Do you know who I am ?" A drawling " Noa " was the reply. " Then I am the great Bonaparte, and no other." Matters immediately changed. " O ho, ho, Mister Boney, is it you ? I have long wished to meet with you ;" and placing his waggon across the road to obstruct the way, he laid hold of the traveller's vehicle and overturned it in the ditch. Leaving the horse kicking for his freedom, he dragged the poor fellow out and gave him an unmerciful drubbing, for which he was called to account at the next town; but nothing came out of it, as the magistrates considered it not illegal to thrash Bonaparte soundly wherever he was found.

It is almost unnecessary to say that the south of Scotland had a very large share of the excitement, and those in the neighbourhood of the Solway shore had seldom their eyes long off Criffel or the sea—the one for signals, the other for ships. Meetings were held in every town, village, and parish for the enrolment of volunteers, and subscriptions of money for the public service. Presbyteries issued pastoral addresses to their people, urging them to be courageous, and in his enthusiasm, a clergyman (the Rev. Dr. Henry Duncan, of Ruthwell), preached in the red coat beneath the pulpit gown, to inspire the young men with a similar ardour in the cause. Volunteers scarcely required to be asked for; it was enough to give time and place of enrolment, and those in charge lost no opportunity of gratifying the youthful aspirants to military fame. Mr. Wightman makes the following note of what was done in Keir on a Communion Monday:—

"15th August, 1803.—Monday—Preached at Keir. The day was good, and the people in general were attentive. A meeting was held in the church after sermon by the Deputy-Lieutenant, Mr. Thomas Kirkpatrick, for the purpose of receiving names of volunteers. All the men belonging to the parish who were present signed. This I consider as a remarkable instance of heroism and loyalty, and it does much credit to the parish."

"30th October.—Read a sermon by the Rev. Henry Duncan, minister of Ruthwell, recommending an ardent and vigorous exertion in defending our country. Many excellent things in it. It glows with disinterested patriotism and benevolence of sentiment. Some phrases taken from Thomas Campbell's poem—'bare our bosoms,' 'deathbed of fame,' and such like. Some fine strokes of eloquence and pathos. On the supposition the enemy were to prevail, he says—'Then may the hand of death find me fighting in the first ranks, surrounded with those brave men of my own flock, who prefer a glorious death to a life of bondage and infamy! Ours is the cause of our country and our God; let our enemies tremble and despair.' It will do much good in this crisis."

The vale of Nithsdale, from its contiguity to the Solway, suffered a sort of intermittent fever of the Gallic type, which was exceedingly catching, and from which there seemed little prospect of a cure. Every blasting of a quarry rock was at once accredited to

French cannon, and the inhabitants never laid themselves down to sleep at night without a strong feeling of the probability that on their awaking next morning they would be all prisoners in the hands of the French. The good folks of Kirkmahoe shared in the excitement of the fever and the fear which disturbed all around. On one of these occasions, when the panic was at its height, every householder, without exception, in the parish, when he rose in the morning found the door of his dwelling marked with a mysterious number which no one could explain. First the suspicion and then the cry arose that the French had landed, and, by means of their scouts and emissaries, had marked out the first objects of their prey. As the day wore on, and inquiries were made, the whole affair was discovered to be a hoax, and one for which no extenuating circumstances could be adduced.

The Presbytery of Dumfries held a *pro re nata* meeting to consider what was right to be done in the critical situation of public affairs. After anxious and careful deliberation, it was resolved that the ministers, seeing their personal presence was not legally required, or expected, should contribute £100 sterling in aid of the public service, and that a solemn and ardent Address should be prepared, to be read from every pulpit at the close of divine worship on the following Sunday. This was accordingly done, and we believe Mr. Wightman had a principal hand in the composition of the document. An extract from it will show what was the clerical spirit in these times, when our rights and privileges as a nation were in danger of being assailed, It reminds us of the times in Jewish history when the priests always went forth at the head of the people to battle:—

"We trust that you will stand forth and quit yourselves like men. You have most sacred duties to perform, and we are persuaded that you will perform them with that energy for which Britons have always been distinguished, and by which they have often made the proudest armies of France to flee before them. On the plains of Cressy, of Poictiers, and of Agincourt, our British heroes, though few in number, made the kingdom of France tremble to its centre. And within our recollection, the cities of Syria and the shores of Egypt have seen the embattled hosts of their *Invincibles* routed and destroyed. And if our countrymen have been so victorious against their enemy on foreign ground, what may they not, under the same protecting Providence, achieve in defence of their country on their native soil! Let not the heart of any man despair, and let not the hands of any be folded in idleness and languor. Let every one consider the sacrifice of his fortune, and even of his life, to his country as nothing more than his duty, and what hath been ventured and sacrificed by thousands of gallant men in a far less honourable and less animating cause.

"We fight, brethren, for our laws, our liberties, and our religion. Our enemies fight for the avowed purpose of massacre and plunder. To which of these causes can the blessing of Heaven attach, and which of them ought most powerfully to inspire the heart with ardour and courage? We fight for our people and the cities of our God. We fight to defend the dearest hopes of our posterity, and to maintain unsullied the honour and glory which, as free men and faithful Christians, we received from our ancestors. We fight to guard from outrage, and shame, and violation, those whom nature hath entrusted to our protection. We fight for that Con-

stitution and system of society which is at once the noblest
monument and the finest bulwark of civilization. We fight,
in short, to preserve the whole earth from military despotism,
and from sinking into an abyss of the vilest barbarism. Such,
brethren, is the cause in which we are engaged, and if it be
successful in its issue, as we trust that by the blessing of God
it will be, we will secure ourselves and our posterity for ages
against the like insolent and injurious attempts, and we may
be the means of awakening to a just sense of their rights
those nations that have been long enslaved, and of enabling
them to avenge the wrongs on the heads of those by whom
they have been so cruelly plundered, oppressed . . . If
this be our conduct, and this the sincere and hearty purpose
of our countrymen throughout the kingdom, we need not
fear what men do unto us. He that is for us will be more
powerful than all they who are against us, and the God of
our fathers will be our God and guardian also, and that of
our children throughout many generations."

The Presbytery agreed that each clergyman should
give his quota of the £100 sterling in aid of the public
services in his own parish in such a manner as he should
think best for the purpose, and produce vouchers of
payment at their next meeting. To the Ministers' Fund
Sheriff-Depute Craigie sent twenty guineas; Miss Kirkpatrick, daughter of the late Sheriff, two guineas; and
Mrs. Sweetman five guineas; to which parties Dr. Burnside was desired to convey the thanks of the Presbytery
for their handsome gifts. The pastoral address was not
issued in vain. After being read from the several pulpits, meetings were enthusiastically held in every parish,
and men and money were liberally offered. One instance
among many is worth recording, from the munificence of
the offer and the character of the man that made it.

Patrick Miller, Esq. of Dalswinton, addressed the following letter to David Staig, Esq., Deputy-Lieutenant for
the district :—

"DALSWINTON, 24th Aug., 1803.

"SIR,—Having expended, in a long course of hazardous
experiments, ten thousand guineas, with a view to benefit
mankind, I am now, perhaps, not so rich as I was; but I am
more careful of what I have—I am a greater economist. As
such, I wish to insure my property, my share in the British
Constitution, my family, myself, and my religion, against the
French invasion. As a premium, I offer to clothe, and arm
with pikes, 100 volunteers, to be raised in this and any of
the neighbouring parishes, and to furnish them with three
light brass field-pieces, ready for service. This way of arm-
ing I consider as superior with infantry for either attack or
defence to that now in use; but as to this Government must
determine. I am too old and infirm to march with these
men, but I shall desire my eldest son to do so. He was ten
years a soldier in the foot and horse service.

"In case of an invasion, I will be ready to furnish, when
required, 26 horses, 16 carts, and 16 drivers; and Government may command all my crops of hay, straw, and grain,
which I estimate at—

> 16,700 stones of hay, 24 lbs. to the stone.
> 1,400 bushels of peas.
> 5,000 bushels of oats.
> 5,080 bushels of barley.

"You will please to transmit my offer to the Lord-Lieu-
tenant of the county. If the French are rash enough to land
on our shores, they will find, to their cost, that riches acquired
by useful and honourable means have not the effect to ener-
vate a people; on the contrary, riches so obtained are sure
proofs of a happy Constitution, and of a mild protecting

Government, to which all wise and good men must necessarily be attached.—I am, dear Sir, yours sincerely,

(Signed)   " PAT. MILLER.

"To David Staig, Esq., D.L."

The French, however, did not come—the panic died away—the horses continued to plough the rich lands of the Nith—the provender stood stored in the stackyard of Dalswinton, and the warriors of Kirkmahoe were not required.   Assuredly these were not times when one could sit under his own vine and fig-tree none daring to make him afraid.   The rustle of a falling leaf, the creaking of a tree in the blast, the hooting of the owl at midnight, filled every household with fear lest the dwelling was about to be assailed.

CHAPTER VIII.

PATRICK MILLER AND STEAM NAVIGATION—MR. JAMES TAYLOR ASSISTS
IN THE INVENTION—MR. WILLIAM SYMINGTON CONSTRUCTS THE
ENGINE—LAUNCH OF THE FIRST STEAM-BOAT ON DALSWINTON
LOCH—PREVIOUS ATTEMPTS BY OTHER PARTIES—DALSWINTON
INVENTION PIRATED—MR. SYMINGTON'S CLAIM TO THE INVENTION
—THE LOCH A STORAGE OF THE OLD ROMANS—INTRODUCTION OF
SWEDISH TURNIPS—TESTIMONIAL FROM THE PARISHIONERS OF
KIRKMAHOE—ADMITTED A BURGESS IN DUMFRIES—HIS DEATH—
ANECDOTE OF SHIPWRECK—ANGEL WORSHIP.

PATRICK MILLER, Esq. of Dalswinton, to whom passing
reference has already been made, was so well known in
his time for his inventive genius, ardent patriotism, extensive benevolence, and agricultural enterprise, that
some fuller notice of him may not be unacceptable to
the reader. Being the largest landed proprietor in the
parish, his position was one of great importance, and he
was naturally looked up to by all with more than a
common interest, as well as expected to make a generous use of the wealth he had acquired. Nor was this
expectation unrealized, for no one was ever more ready
than he to befriend the poor, and to devise means for
their better comfort during the inclemencies of winter
seasons, or when labour was scarce and provisions were
dear. In this and in other respects the minister found
him the strongest support in the discharge of parochial
duties, as he could count with confidence upon his
counsel and pecuniary aid, when cases of difficulty arose,
in relieving the wants of the necessitous. Shortly after

K

Mr. Wightman's entrance upon his ministerial charge, Mr. Miller sent him a donation of £20 to be applied at the discretion of the Session in relieving the wants of the parish poor. This was accompanied by a kind note, in which he referred to "the religious care and fidelity with which their late very worthy pastor, Mr. Lawson, and his elders, had managed for many years the affairs of the poor, and he believed that the same faithful attention and care would continue to be exercised by Mr. Wightman and his Session." This was exceedingly gratifying, and was an earnest of what was to follow.

Mr. Miller was a native of Glasgow, and was born in 1731. A considerable portion of his youth was spent at sea as a sailor, a circumstance which doubtless contributed greatly in stimulating his genius in the direction it took, finally terminating in the invention of propelling sailing vessels by steam. On leaving the sea he entered on business as a banker in Edinburgh, where, by diligent attention to the duties of his office, and the exercise of shrewd sagacity, he acquired considerable wealth, which, to a great extent, was expended on his favourite hobby of an improved system of navigation. After retiring from business in Edinburgh he settled down upon his estate of Dalswinton, and directed his attention to the subject of agricultural improvements in general and mechanical navigation in particular. In close proximity to the house of Dalswinton there was a marshy swamp, which he caused to be formed into a beautiful loch, which will go down to posterity as the birth-place and cradle of steam navigation. The one great idea which filled his soul was the construction and working of a paddle-wheel to propel a vessel in case of danger or in a time of calm. It does not seem that he looked further than this; at all events, it is certain that he had no idea of the extensive use to which the invention would be put in the progress of time.

It has been long and widely believed that Patrick Miller of Dalswinton was the sole originator of steam navigation, and therefore to him the whole merit is due. To a certain extent only we believe that this is the case. He alone devised the paddle-wheel driven by a capstan, but the application of steam as the propelling power was the idea of another, though he (Mr. Miller) gave the orders and furnished the means for carrying the experiment into successful execution. The fullest evidence has been collected from authoritative sources in confirmation of this, but, from several causes unnecessary to be particularized, the facts have not been made sufficiently known. Although, as in many similar cases, he to whom the merit of the invention was really attributable was allowed to pine in poverty and die in neglect, without any recognition of the boon he had been instrumental in conferring upon the world at large, yet it is only just to his memory that the real state of matters be told, which we are enabled to do from the most authentic and reliable source. The following condensed view of the story of the invention, which in importance has been placed side by side with the introduction of cannon, though their respective objects are wide as the poles asunder, embraces all the points of moment necessary to obtain a true estimate of the merits of the respective parties.

After Mr. Miller's retirement from business in Edinburgh, as we have already said, he settled down on his estate of Dalswinton, and being at a distance from the sources of education, he looked about for a properly qualified tutor for his sons, especially as they were about to enter upon a course of study in the University of Edinburgh. His attention was directed to a young man, James Taylor, a medical student, residing in Leadhills, who had been seven sessions at College, and had studied under Professors Andrew Dalzell, John Robertson, Andrew Fyfe, James Gregory, John Bruce, Adam Ferguson, A. Monro, Francis Home, John Black, Dugald Stewart, John Walker, Dr. Cullen, and James Russell. We are thus particular in our notification, as it has been said that Mr. Taylor was only a first year's student on his appointment of tutor in Dalswinton. Mr. Taylor began his curriculum in 1778, and had attended regularly till this appointment in 1785. There is no foundation, therefore, for averring that his knowledge was limited, if he bestowed the usual attention to the prelections of the professors, which his certificates bear he did; and, further, it was widely known that he had a decided taste for mathematics and mechanics. When he came to Dalswinton, Mr. Miller was immersed in the subject of paddle-wheel propulsion, and every day brought him a brighter prospect of complete success. This wheel was driven by a capstan, which required the energies of four men; but so proud was he of his invention that, in 1787, he challenged a Custom-house boat to sail from the island of Inchcolm to the harbour of Leith, as a comparative trial of speed. A Mr. Weddell managed the one boat and Mr. Miller his own. The latter gained by a few minutes, but the men at the capstan were tremendously exhausted. Mr. Taylor was

also on board, and took a turn at the capstan, the fatigue
of which induced him to represent to Mr. Miller the
absolute necessity of devising some other means of propulsion. Mr. Miller replied—" I am of the same opinion,
and that power is just what I am in search of. My
object is to add mechanical aid to the natural power of the
wind, to enable vessels to avoid and to extricate themselves from dangerous situations, which they cannot do
on their present construction; I wish, also, to give them
powers of motion in time of calm. I am satisfied that
a capstan, well manned, can effect this in part; but I
want a power more extensively useful, which I have
not, as yet, been able to attain. Now that you understand the subject, will you lend me the aid of your head,
and see if you can suggest any plan to accomplish my
purpose?"

After long and earnest cogitation on the matter, the
application of the steam-engine suggested itself to Mr.
Taylor, and he immediately reported the idea to the
proper quarter. Mr. Miller at first demurred, doubted
the expected success, dreaded the presence of fire on
board a boat, and referred to a recent wreck off the
coast of Spain, where every fire on board required to be
extinguished, and where such an engine could not have
been of any use. However, after much persistency on
the part of Mr. Taylor, he succeeded in his purpose, and
was requested to make drawings of his method of con-
necting the engine with the paddle-wheels. These
proving satisfactory, he was asked to find out a working-
engineer who would carry the proposed theory into
practice. He accordingly introduced to Mr. Miller's
notice a school-fellow of his own, residing at Wanlock-

head, by name William Symington, who received a commission to have the engine constructed with all convenient speed under the superintendence of Mr. Taylor. After a few months' constant labour the engine was ready for operation, and was removed to Dalswinton. Small it certainly was, having only four-inch cylinders, but still sufficient for the purpose, and on the 14th October, 1788, it was placed on board a boat 25 feet long, 7 feet wide, and furnished with two wheels. Steam was got up, and, amid the enthusiastic cheering of a crowd of spectators assembled at every commanding point of view, the tiny vessel sailed away on the beautiful loch, at a speed of five miles an hour!

For several days the experiment was repeated, and when all parties were thoroughly satisfied with the entire success of the invention, the engine was removed to the house and placed as a drawing-room ornament, where it remained till Mr. Miller's decease, when it was sold by public auction, along with other effects, at the price of old metal, realizing only a few pounds! The boiler, which was of copper, was about 4 feet in height and $2\frac{1}{2}$ feet in diameter, not cylindrical, but oval in form, and was so encrusted with soot that no one could tell of what metal it was composed. Mr. Miller's son, Capt. Miller, had given instructions that unless it brought £3 it was to be bought in, and as only £2 were offered it accordingly came back to him. There was a young man present, of very great intelligence, Mr. William Wallace, now farmer of Kirktonfield, Kirkmahoe, who had the shrewdness to scrape through the blacking, and so discovered the metal was copper. He had been one of the bidders, and was afterwards introduced to Captain

Miller, who allowed him to have it, after a deal of haggling, for the sum of fifty shillings! A few days afterwards Mr. Wallace removed the numerous bolts with which it was constructed, broke the whole up into small pieces, which filled two sacks, and sold them the following week to an English dealer in old metal at 7¼d. per lb., realizing upwards of £7 on the whole concern. A day or two afterwards he was called upon by a gentleman, commissioned by some antiquarian society in Scotland or England, who was authorized to go as far as £40 for the relic, but it was too late. Such was the invention of steam navigation, in which Mr. Taylor was entitled to a very considerable share; and though the whole circumstances of the case were represented to the Government, in the hope that some suitable pension might be assigned him, no notice was taken of the application made in his favour, and he was allowed to pass the remainder of his days, with a wife and children, as we have already said, in poverty and neglect.

It is a mistake to imagine, as many have done, that this was the first attempt in the application of steam power to the propulsion of sailing vessels in all kinds of weather, against head winds, running tides, or through dead calms, although there is no ground for supposing that either of the parties here concerned were aware of the manner in which it had been proposed to be applied. Mr. Miller's own expression, on the proposal being made, that he dreaded the danger of fire on board, showed that he was not yet acquainted with the fact of its employment; and Mr. Taylor racking his brains to discover some substitute for the exhausting labour at the capstan was an equal evidence on his part of his ignorance in the matter. So far, then, as regarded themselves, it was entirely new. Upwards of fifty years previous to the great event on Dalswinton Loch one Jonathan Hulls, an Englishman, took out a patent for constructing a steamboat, and published a full description of it, with diagrams and drawings, in pamphlet form, under the title, "A Description and Draught of a new-invented Machine for Carrying Vessels or Ships out of, or into, any Harbour, Port, or River, against Wind or Tides." The pamphlet is very rare, but an account of it is given in the ninth volume of the "Edinburgh Philosophical Journal." Hulls' proposed steam-tug, for such it seems to have been, from some cause or another was never built, and the contrivance was forgotten in the public mind. In 1782 a Frenchman, the Marquis de Jouffrey, took up the subject, and with more means at command than poor Hulls possessed, he constructed a steamboat 140 feet long and 15 feet wide, which he sailed on the Saone, at Lyons, for a considerable time, but only in an experimenting character, and it soon passed into oblivion. Some three years afterwards, while Mr. Miller was busy paddling his double canoe on his own loch, two Americans, James Ramsey of Virginia and John Fitch of Philadelphia, under the patronage of General Washington, experimented with steam propulsion at sea, but, like the others who preceded them, their novelty lost its attraction, and want of success caused it to be abandoned. The Dalswinton affair, however, three years afterwards, gave a new impetus to the invention, and henceforth it took a firm hold of the public mind, eventuating, through many modifications, in its present form, of equal importance, as has been said, with the introduction of cannon, though many will be of opinion that, in every respect, it is superior beyond comparison in point of humanity and civilization. As Mr. Miller declined to take out a patent for the invention, though strongly and repeatedly urged to do so by Mr. Taylor, all the machinery was open to inspection, and, as was to be expected, the utmost advantage was soon taken of the omission. Parties came, saw, examined, pirated,·and retired, and the result was that other men and other nations claimed the honour of the invention, ay, and reaped its reward.

As the merit of the invention has been claimed on behalf of Mr. Symington, who constructed the engine which first did duty in opening up the world to commercial enterprise by steam, it may not be out of place to state what is the real position of the matter, so far as he was concerned, which, to a certain extent, has been already done, and this we can do, supported by letters of Mr. Symington himself. The ground of this claim is, that he "constructed the engine," but this he did from plans and drawings made by Mr. Taylor, under the superintendence of Mr. Miller. But though he constructed the engine, he made no claim then to the invention, for, in writing to Mr. Taylor regarding it, he calls it "*your invention.*" Here is his own letter, addressed to Mr. Taylor, at Dalswinton, dated Wanlockhead, 20th August, 1787 :—

"But I believe neither this sheet nor my time will allow me to expatiate at any length on this subject, seeing I must make some remarks on *your summer's invention*, which, if made to perform what its author gives it out for, will undoubtedly be one of the greatest wonders hitherto presented to the world, besides being of considerable emolument to the

projector! Great success to you, though overturning my
schemes ; but take care we do not come upon you back, and
run away with them by some improvement. Your brother
John gives a kind of credit to your report, which, for some
reasons, I did not discourage. I must now conclude, &c.,

(Signed)   " WILLIAM SYMINGTON."

It is evident from this that Mr. Symington was not
by any means hopeful of the success of his friend, and
distinctly warned him of the possibility of himself
making improvements upon the invention. But this is
away from the *origin* of the matter; and that he did
make improvements, and did take out a patent in his
own name, surreptitiously, about 1802 or 1803, there is
no room for doubt, though his conscience seems to have
checked him for so doing, as the following letter shows,
written nearly twenty years afterwards:—

" GLASGOW, *9th Feb.*, 1821.

" Sir,—In terms of our former agreement, when making
experiments of sailing by the steam-engine, I hereby bind
and oblige myself to convey to you, by a regular assignation,
the one-half of the interest and proceeds of the patent taken
out by me upon that invention when an opportunity occurs
of executing the deed, and when required.—I am, Sir, your
obedient servant,

(Signed)   " WILLIAM SYMINGTON."
"To Mr. James Taylor, Cumnock."

The following extracts from private letters are also
corroborative of the fact. Mr. Patrick Miller, in a
published narrative of the whole case, some years after
the death of his father, says, in a letter to Mr. Taylor,
addressed " Kinmount House, by Annan, 20th April,

1824—My impression is, that no human being, except yourself and me, can have any claim to either public consideration or remuneration; and I think my memoir will make that clear enough, be the result what it may." In another letter to the same gentleman, written about a month afterwards, he says:—" By circumstances, the origin of which I am not yet acquainted with, I have hitherto been disappointed of an opportunity of having the honour of waiting upon his Royal Highness the Duke of Clarence, to lay before him the history of Steam Navigation, in which I assigned you the place of suggestor of, and sole coadjutor of my father in, this important improvement." Sir Charles Menteath of Closeburn, in a letter of date 5th April, 1834, says:— " I am old enough to have seen the first boat driven by steam in this or any other country. Mr. Miller of Dalswinton, in the county of Dumfries, after his retirement from business as a banker in Edinburgh, continued his favourite pursuit of making experiments with boats of a variety of constructions, and having constructed a twin boat, with a wheel between them, he employed manual power to drive the wheel, which being found inefficient, Mr. James Taylor, at that time tutor to Mr. Miller's sons, I have always understood suggested the notion of employing a steam-engine to put the wheel in motion." The late Principal Forbes, in a letter to Mrs. Taylor, of date 3rd May, 1842, says:—" Your statements and proofs served entirely to confirm and recall my former impressions—namely, that the merit of the invention of steam navigation is due to Mr. James Taylor and to Mr. Miller of Dalswinton jointly. That the actual suggestion was Mr. Taylor's, there seems no reason to doubt." Another eminent gentleman, John Geddes, Esq., writing to Mrs. Taylor on the same subject in 1842, says:—"I think it may be safely said that the first steamboat voyage was made on Dalswinton Loch; and that your husband, in originating the four-inch cylinder-engine there employed, laid the foundation of the immense extent and power of steamboats that now ply on every sea, river, and loch." Extracts from the letters of other distinguished personages might be adduced, but the above may be considered sufficient.

In the face of these letters, we cannot see how the merit of the invention can be claimed on Mr. Symington's behalf, and how the engine of the Dalswinton boat was the one patented by him, except in the sense of piracy, seeing the patent was not taken out for fourteen years after the experiment on Dalswinton Loch. How could he propose to give Mr. Taylor "one-half of the interest and proceeds" of a patent whose merit belonged solely and entirely to himself? We believe that Mr. Symington, who was a most ingenious engineer, improved upon the invention, which is all the merit that can be claimed on his behalf.

We may observe, parenthetically, with regard to that famous loch, which will ever be associated with steam navigation, and which Mr. Miller had originally formed out of a swamp, that, in 1825, when in the possession of Mr. Macalpine Leny, it was thought the pike were destroying the other fish, and the loch was drained, when there were found only two pike, but a great number of perch and very fine large eels. Taking advantage of the drainage, Mr. Leny caused the mossy sludge at the bottom, about eighteen inches deep, to be removed and

spread on the adjoining meadow, for the purpose of improving the soil.   Below the moss was a firm bed of
clay.   The workmen, in the course of their operations,
came upon an oak tree lying across in the soundest state
of preservation, from which the sideboard in Dalswinton
House was afterwards manufactured, as well as other
articles, while underneath and around this prostrate
monarch of the woods was found an immense quantity
of parched grain adhering in large masses, the corns of
which were quite distinguishable, but having been
burned, could not be expected to be so prolific as the
wheat found in Egyptian mummies.   Doubtless these
were the remains of the old Romans in their raid upon
Nithsdale, as, when suddenly forced to decamp, they
usually set fire to their stores, so that the enemy might
not profit from the plunder they obtained.   It is understood that large quantities of that parched grain may
still be found there, as nothing like the whole was taken
when the loch was restored.   The loch, though small,
is very picturesquely situated, being surrounded with
scenery of diversified character, and looked down upon
by the hospitable mansion of the lord of the manor.   It
is the usual resort of curlers in the winter season,
through the kindness of the proprietor, and many a
victory and defeat it has seen, when contending parishes
challenged each other to a " spiel."   The scenery has
been faithfully transferred to canvas by the   artist
Nasymth, of landscape renown.

Two years prior to the invention of the steamboat,
when Mr. Miller was entirely absorbed in working out
his paddle-wheel idea, he constructed a vessel with five
masts, fitted up with paddle-wheels driven by a capstan,

and armed with carronades, which he had also invented
—a kind of gun he so named from its being cast at the
Carron Foundry—and which, in the pride of his heart,
he considered altogether a matchless production. This
he generously, loyally, and patriotically offered to his own
Government, as he thought himself in duty bound to do
so; but the beauty and the benefit of the work not being
appreciated by that stoical body, the proffered boon was
coldly declined, and he accordingly presented it to the
King of Sweden, Gustavus III., who gratefully acknowledged the gift in an autograph letter enclosed in a
magnificent golden box, which on gala days at Dalswinton was always produced for the delectation of the visitors,
and perhaps as much for the delectation of the worthy
possessor himself. But, along with the letter of thanks,
the box contained also a very small packet of turnip
seed, sent out of compliment to the recipient as an
enterprising agriculturist. The seed was carefully sown,
preserved, and sown again, many times in succession,
and hence came the first Swedish turnips produced in
the land, which are now so plentiful and considered so
essentially necessary for the support of stock.

To Mr. Miller's ingenuity the country is much indebted for several inventions besides that of propelling
vessels by steam, such as the drill plough, the iron
plough, the horse thrashing mill, and others, which
doubtless have been greatly improved upon in many
respects since his day. He was an enthusiastic agriculturist, and one of the great objects in this line to which
he devoted particular attention was the introduction and
cultivation of fiorin grass-hay. The inhabitants generally, and the farmers in particular, of Kirkmahoe,

greatly appreciated his labours and the interest he took in the welfare of all around him, and to show their estimation of his worth as a gentleman, and especially as an enlightened agriculturist, they agreed to present him with two handsome silver cups or vases of the Etrurian form, which might remain as heirlooms in his family, and show to posterity the high estimation in which their ancestor had been held. Mr. Wightman, as minister of the parish, and Mr. Thomson, minister of the Cameronian body at Quarrelwood, were appointed a deputation to present the gift and to express the sentiments of the subscribers. Accordingly, on the 12th April, 1801, these gentlemen waited upon Mr. Miller at Dalswinton House, and performed the honourable task entrusted to their care. Mr. Wightman, as principal speaker, addressed Mr. Miller in the following terms:—

"SIR,—When you retired from other useful and honourable stations, and fixed your residence in this parish, you formed an era in its prosperity. You devoted your talents to improvements in agriculture, a science well worthy of your attention, and which you conducted on the most enlightened and liberal plans. Your neighbours and others saw, admired, and imitated the judicious methods you adopted in the cultivation of the soil, and the various branches of rural economy. They not only saw your improvements, but occasionally learned from yourself many particulars which they could not have obtained had you been less accessible in your person, or less condescending in your manners. The inhabitants of this parish, impressed with a sense of these things, have agreed, in one collective body, to present you with a small testimonial of their respect for the patriotism as well as the benevolence of your character, and especially for your eminence in rural science, and your liberal views as a landed proprietor. They have honoured us, the ministers of religion in this parish, who they knew had a place in your regard, with a commission to express to you in the most respectful manner their sentiments towards you, and to solicit you in their name to accept this mark of their respect. We do this most cheerfully, because we ourselves feel those sentiments which we are deputed to express. We are convinced that your character does not depend upon our humble voice. The name of Mr. Miller will be known and dear to posterity. It will continue fresh as the beauty of his fields, and fragrant as their flowers, when we shall have been gathered to our fathers."

Mr. Miller with much generous feeling expressed the high satisfaction he had in receiving such an unexpected and unequivocal mark of esteem from so respectable a body of men, and invited the gentlemen of the deputation to stay and dine with him, which they did, spending the day in the cheerful expression of those sentiments of patriotism, benevolence, and affection which link society in the firmest bonds, and render man the improver and the friend of his fellow-man. On leaving the house Mr. Wightman put his arm in that of Mr. Thomson, and went down the steps together, which Mr. Miller seeing, he bade them good evening in the beautiful words of the 133rd Psalm :—

> " Behold how good a thing it is,
> And how becoming well,
> Together such as brethren are
> In unity to dwell !"

In the year following his steamboat success Mr. Miller had the honour of being admitted a burgess of Dumfries, as the following minute of the election shows :—" 29th

September, 1789.—The said day, Patrick Miller, Esq. of Dalswinton, one of the four new Merchant Council-lors, before being sworn in, was admitted a burgess in the usual manner, and accepted and gave his oath of burgess-ship in the ordinary way, and promised to keep a sufficient gun and sword for the defence of the town when called for; and the Council, for good services done and to be done by the said Patrick Miller, remit the burgess composition payable by him." It is rather amusing to read that an oath was exacted to keep a sufficient gun and sword for defence of the town from a man who shortly afterwards, as we have already seen, offered to give the produce of his estate, and to equip a hundred men for the defence of his country; but we suppose the minute was drawn out in the usual stereo-typed form, and, besides, the authorities of the Queen of the South were not to know the generous outburst of patriotism and benevolence to be evolved afterwards by the highly esteemed laird of Dalswinton. Some idea may be formed of the difficulties he had to encounter on entering upon his estate, from what he says in a letter of date 24th September, 1810, published in the "General View of the Agriculture, &c., of Dumfriesshire:"— " When I purchased this estate (Dalswinton) about five-and-twenty years ago, I had not seen it. It was in the most miserable state of exhaustion, and all the tenants in poverty. Judge of the first when I inform you, that oats ready to be cut were sold at 25s. per acre upon the holm grounds. When I went to view my purchase, I was so much disgusted for eight or ten days, I then meant never to return to this country." Fifteen years afterwards these same poverty-stricken lands, under the

L

improvements of the proprietor, brought £40 per acre, though it is but right to mention that 1800 was known as the famine year.

After having spent upwards of £30,000 upon his inventions, experiments, and agricultural improvements, Mr. Miller died a poor man, almost landless, and without any Government acknowledgment of the great services he had rendered to the cause of civilization and the cultivation of the soil. His death took place at Dalswinton, on the morning of Saturday, 9th December, 1815, in the eighty-fourth year of his age, and his remains were interred in the family burying-ground, in Greyfriars' Churchyard, Edinburgh, on the third of the following month. Mr. Wightman, in an obituary notice of him in the *Dumfries Courier*, says:—"Mr. Miller was well-known for his enterprising and public spirit, and his unabating ardour in endeavouring to promote the welfare of society and the prosperity of his country. The powers of his mind were capacious, vigorous, and active, and were cultivated by an extensive intercourse with men of all ranks, and by a frequent and intense application of thought to almost every branch of political and rural economy. His moral character was sustained by the most respectable and amiable qualities. He was guided by inflexible integrity in his diversified transactions with mankind, and a warm benevolence and generosity of heart rendered him the friend of the afflicted, and a father to the poor. He was a man, and nothing which concerned the happiness of man was uninteresting to him. These estimable and gentle qualities made Mr. Miller the object of general respect and esteem, and have rendered his

death a cause of deep regret to his numerous friends
and acquaintances, in whose affection his memory is
embalmed, and will be cherished with a lasting remembrance."

An anecdote is told of Mr. Miller's experience as a
sailor, on the occasion of a shipwreck. He, along with
a number of the crew, had escaped from the sinking
ship in the long-boat, and had been out at sea for a
considerable time, when their scanty store of provisions
became exhausted, and it was resolved to have recourse
to the terrible expedient of putting one of their number
to death, in order to supply food for the rest, till relief
should providentially arrive. The lots were drawn out
of Mr. Miller's cap, in respect for his being the only
officer in the boat, and the carpenter was found to be the
victim doomed to die. Mr. Miller was exceedingly sorry
that such an exigency had arisen, and such a proposal
had been decided on; but in the circumstances it was
vain to rebel, and he gave his portion of a very small
quantum of wine to the unhappy carpenter in commiseration of his fate. Turning away from the poor
fellow's death-stricken countenance, and looking into
the far horizon, he immediately cried out, " I see a
sail! I see a sail!" All eyes were turned in the same
direction, but they could see nothing. Still he persisted
in saying that he saw a sail, and soon, to their joy, the
sail came within the vision of all, so that the carpenter
was saved, and they were all relieved.

We may here reproduce another anecdote in connection with this family, but communicated elsewhere,
which can bear repetition. Bowing from the pulpit to
the principal heritor in church, after the blessing was

pronounced, was very common in rural parishes down to a comparatively recent period. Mr. Wightman once made a ready and complimentary reply, on being rallied for his neglecting this usual act of courtesy one Sabbath in his own church. The heritor who was entitled to, and always received, this token of respect was Mr. Miller of Dalswinton. On the Sabbath referred to the Dalswinton pew contained a bevy of ladies, but no gentleman, and Mr. Wightman, perhaps because he was a bachelor and felt a delicacy in the circumstances, omitted the usual salaam in their direction. A few days after, meeting Miss Miller, who was widely famed for her great beauty, and who afterwards became Countess of Mar, she rallied him, in presence of her companions, for not bowing to her from the pulpit on the preceding Sunday, and requested an explanation, when Mr. Wightman immediately replied, "I beg your pardon, Miss Miller, but you surely know that angel worship is not allowed in the Church of Scotland," and, lifting his hat, he made a low bow, and passed on.

CHAPTER IX.

WE have now to introduce to the reader one of Mr.
Wightman's warmest friends, Mr. John Crocket, who
afterwards became his co-presbyter, as minister of Kirkgunzeon, and was widely known for his genial humour
and interesting traditions of the times of old. He was
born at Lochhill, in the parish of Newabbey, in February, 1778, and when a boy at school there he was noted
by the minister as being, physically and mentally, peculiarly active. His grandfather, with whom he lived, was
advised to send him to the Grammar-School of Dumfries
as a more fitting sphere for his aptitude in learning, and
thither he was accordingly sent, going and returning on
foot every day, a distance of some dozen miles. At the
age of fifteen he was sent to the University of Edinburgh, where he went through the curriculum for the
Church, taking three sessions in Greek under the distinguished Professor Dalzell. Like others of his class, he
engaged to a considerable extent in private tuition, as a
source of subsistence and financial treasury for the pro-
secution of his university studies. A vacancy in the

domestic tutorship at Dunragit having occurred, Mr.
Wightman was applied to by his old friends Sir John
and Lady Dalrymple Hay to find them a suitable person
for the important situation. He at once recommended
Mr. Crocket, who then filled a similar office in Inveraray,
and who was well known as an accomplished and elegant
scholar, without being vain of his attainments, or osten-
tatious in their display. The following correspondence
on the Dunragit tutorship is interesting for various
reasons:—

MR. JOHN CROCKET TO REV. MR. WIGHTMAN.

"INVERARAY, 24th May, 1801.

"DEAR SIR,—After despatching your last letter I waited
on the Colonel and informed him that I had got an offer of a
very eligible situation, which I intended to accept of. I told
him that several weighty reasons concurred to induce me to
accept of it; and that I had given him the earliest information, so that he might provide himself with another before
my departure, which must take place in the course of a
month. I said that my time with him expired on the 25th
of this month, but that I was willing to stay with him for a
fortnight longer, so that he might receive no inconvenience
from my departure, and that I hoped he would have no
objections to what I had stated. He answered me in the
most friendly manner by saying that I was certainly in the
right to accept a preferable situation, that it was the duty
of every man to look to his own interest in preference to
that of any other person's, that he would be very glad if I
would remain for a fortnight in the family after my time
expired, and that I had done nothing but what was very
proper. He added that I had given him great satisfaction,
that there was no comparison between me and either of my

predecessors, but that I was infinitely superior to both. I could not with a safe conscience pocket that compliment, for I am sensible that Mr. Paul, my ingenious predecessor, and author of the Epistles to the 'Dearly Beloved Disciples,' was infinitely my superior in abilities, and at least my equal in classical knowledge. The truth is, that he would have been, and was, caressed in many families for his facetiousness, good humour, and obliging disposition, but his frank, affable manner gave offence to the sober people of this family, who are always on the reserve, and who do not wish any young man in the family to take even reasonable liberties. My other predecessor was a humdrum, melancholy, stupid, slovenly fellow, so that I am not in the least surprised that he gave great umbrage. I was, however, very glad to find that I had given satisfaction, and that I came off with flying colours.

"Your letter of the 20th I received yesterday, and in the joy of my heart I could not refrain from immediately informing you of the foregoing particulars. I am heartily glad to find that there is a probability of our sojourning for a few weeks with you occasionally. Nothing could give me greater pleasure, and I will be exceedingly happy if Sir John adopts that plan. With regard to the salary I do not care what it is, as that is a matter just now entirely below my consideration. Only let it be sufficient to maintain me decently, and that is all I will require. I am sure I will find no obstacles in the way respecting it. I entirely agree with you that the teacher of youth is worthy of his reward, for it is a laborious and irksome employment. From your account I believe that mine will be more agreeable than what I have hitherto experienced. How old is the boy, and how far is he advanced in learning? How many young ladies are there in the family? From your account they seem to be very agreeable ones. In what parish will we be situated, and what is the name of the minister? I think I shall leave this place about the 8th or 9th of June, and either go to Dumfries or Dunragit as you may think best. I will go by Greenock and Ayr, where I hope to see Mr. Paul, who is now a steady pillar of the Church. I should like very much to see you before entering on my charge, but you will be the best judge whether I should go to Dumfries or not. Mr. Gillespie and his sister present you with their best compliments, and he bids me say that your letter enclosed in the bag would be in Dumfries on Wednesday last. I shall be very happy to hear from you the first leisure hour you can find, as my stay in this place will now be so very short. Begging pardon for the great trouble I give you,—Believe me to be, dear Sir, yours very sincerely,

"JOHN CROCKET.

"Rev. John Wightman,
"Minister of Kirkmahoe, Dumfries."

REV. MR. WIGHTMAN TO LADY DALRYMPLE HAY.

"KIRKMAHOE MANSE, 16th June, 1801.

"MADAM,—I have delayed writing your Ladyship till I could say when Mr. Crocket would be able to enter upon his charge. He is under my roof at this moment, will be all night with me, and is going to visit some of his friends in this district for a few days. He will be in Dunragit this day fortnight, which will be, I believe, the last day of this month, and will begin the auspicious task on Wednesday, the first day of July, which is the time I mentioned to your Ladyship at Dumfries. In my letter I wrote him to be here a week at least before that time, as I thought the vacation long enough. But I find Mr. Crocket wishes to see his friends here, and as I know that all will go on well when he comes, I am less afraid of any inconvenience from a

week's more vacation to my young friend, and assure
your Ladyship you may depend on Mr. Crocket on Tuesday,
the 30th instant. He has sent his trunk by Glasgow,
as I directed him, and it will be at Dunragit before him.
Your Ladyship is too well acquainted with the good effects
of regular and stated hours of attending school not to
be convinced that hours of teaching must be fixed, and
steadily adhered to. I would venture to suggest, from
the confidence you repose in me, that on Wednesday
Mr. Crocket begin teaching my old pupil at ten o'clock forenoon, and continue till twelve, and that no more lessons be
required that day. On Thursday, 2nd July, an additional
hour be given between two and three, or between three and
four—no more that day. On Friday the same, if not another
hour in the forenoon. On Monday next, teaching to begin
at eight o'clock, the hour before breakfast being, I would
think, very profitable. There should be five hours' work
every day. I believe four might do, if none of the ladies
attend, which I hope they will at times. But whether
any of these should be after dinner, or all over before dinner,
I reckon not of great importance. Many teachers, I know,
prefer the latter. Mr. Crocket will consider it rather a
pleasure than a task to assist Miss Elizabeth and Miss Susan
in any arithmetic, or book-keeping, or geography, &c., that
they may choose to study. I had forgot, it seems, to mention
the pecuniary matter, but Mr. Crocket is well satisfied with
£25 per annum. He said he had the same from Colonel
Graham, and £5 as a gratuity, but he does not seem to be a
man who considers money as the leading object. He will be
happy, I am sure, with the emoluments and privileges I
enjoyed at Dunragit, and I am not affecting modesty when
I say that he seems to me at least equally deserving of them.
I do not mean that he may have just all the preceptorial
iotas and dogmas so rigidly arranged as I had, but he has

liberal information, good temper, and adequate experience. Mr. Crocket does not know any of the contents of this. I will speak to him about regular hours, which I reckon necessary.—I am, my Lady, yours respectfully,

"JOHN WIGHTMAN.

"Lady Dalrymple Hay, Dunragit."   •

Mr. Crocket had been scarcely five weeks engaged with his new charge, and was going on swimmingly, when he received the following letter from his patron in Kirkmahoe:—

REV. MR. WIGHTMAN TO MR. CROCKET.

"KIRKMAHOE MANSE, 5th August, 1801.

"DEAR SIR,—I was poring over a part of Dr. Wilson's Hebrew Grammar, with a Parkhurst's Lexicon open beside me, and trying if I could plant a few 'Hebrew roots in the barren ground,' as Hudibras somewhere says, when I received your letter. Though I thought I was agreeably employed, I soon laid aside my books. Wilson, quoting a part of Scripture, closes his preface with 'the letter killeth,' &c., but if I may turn his words to a temporal sense, from so beautiful an application as he makes, I may say, *the letter gave life to me!* Your letter gave more pleasure than I have enjoyed this whole day, and that is not a small portion. I am truly happy that you find everything so pleasing, and even beyond your happy fancy's stretch. Indeed, I know you would be happy. The scene of Castle Kennedy rose to my view, and if I had known the day when so much beauty and virtue were regaling in that inspiring ground, I would have sympathized much with the pleasure they enjoyed. Nature there reposes in one of her most magnificent and favourite retreats. The grand range of mountains on the one

side, and the variety on all sides, not to speak of the interesting spot itself, would not escape your eye. I was there
once, too, but some wet day, or some worse thing, I remember, marred considerably the enjoyment which I saw the
place was well suited to give to one who is born, as Hume
says, to see the bright and not the dark side of things. And
the pile of stones there is still standing! How many ideas
now sweep through my mind! Many a time we brushed
the dews away to meet the sun on Challoch. The view from
the top of this hill is really grand, and if Sir John plant it,
I know not by what name to express the pleasure which one
would feel in looking from a vista open towards the sea.
And the plantation will make a fine object to travellers, and
be seen at a great distance. I will never forget that when
we staid at Park, one of the young ladies, then a very child
(and now no more!), asked me to take her to the top of
Challoch, and I carried her almost all the way up the hill,
while some of the others attended, *nec me labor iste gravabat!*

"Well, Mr. Crocket, you have undertaken really an
important charge, and on your acquitting yourself with
diligence, prudence, and, consequently, I hope, with success,
depends the happiness of two worthy parents, your own
comfort, and if after such motives I might mention another,
I would say *my* happiness. But I need not expatiate to one
who knows the matter experimentally already, and who tastes
the first fruits of a harvest of enjoyment. You are perfectly
right in your idea of the Academy. Literature was not the
leading object there. Commerce was the reigning genius. I
feared that our pupil had not profited in proportion to his
time there, and this was the reason why I did not examine him
when I was there, for I did not like to throw one shade on
the sunshine of his joy at seeing me, as I might have done
had I expressed the smallest disapprobation of anything
about him, or his studies. He is truly an amiable boy, and

I am glad you have already gained his confidence. This is
all in some sense. Without this all is uphill, but with this
all is easy, like the path of wisdom. This very day I met
with some lines I had written on his birth-day, the first
stanza of which was in the following dull, prosaic strain,
but it shows how much I was always thinking about him,
and in no other light does it give me any pleasure on review.
I think it was in descending from Challoch about seven or
eight o'clock I put the words into my pocket-book with a
pencil. Here they are:—

> While yet fresh roses deck yon gates of light,
> And feathered songsters welcome rising day;
> The willing muse attempts her feeble flight,
> And joyful hails the natal morn of Hay!

I leave you to finish the ode, and hope you will rise to a
higher strain of poetry. I think I had not written the lines
on the top of Challoch, otherwise they would have been
better, with the grand view before me. But I forget that
Challoch is not Parnassus!

"You have not been correct about the Sacraments here.
I was at Lochmaben last Saturday, and am to be at Keir on
Monday. I really fear I cannot get away soon, but I cannot
resist the invitation of Sir John and Lady Hay. They never
speak words of course, on such occasions, and, to be sure,
my own inclinations second the invitation very much. I
have been from home several days this summer, and am to be
away first Sunday, though my own church will be supplied,
so I cannot come immediately, but will do my best to come
before September be over. If sooner I can, you may be sure
I will. Present my respectful compliments to Sir John and
Lady Hay, and thank them in your best manner for their
kind invitation. Mr. Heron, the minister of Kirkgunzeon,
died last Friday, and is to be buried to-morrow. If I could

set Mr. Selkirk into my native parish I would do it. I
would have preferred it to this, though the emolument is less,
if it had been vacant at the time I came here. Mrs. Heron
and family are a sight which I can scarcely bear to see in
such distress. I preached for Mr. H. lately. She anticipated the event, and afflicted me much, and the very children
cried when I went away!

"I had a more pleasing task at the examination of the
Grammar-School of Dumfries. I was Moderator of the
Committee, and as Mr. Wait, the late Rector, said, I rode my
hobby-horse *well*. I say *agreeably*, for Rosinanté was in
good spirits, and went almost beyond herself. The boys all
started to their feet when I bade them love their country, and
mentioned Abercrombie.—I am ever, dear Sir, yours very
sincerely,   " JOHN WIGHTMAN.

"Mr. John Crocket, Dunragit."

MR. CROCKET TO REV. MR. WIGHTMAN.

"DUNRAGIT, 14*th October*, 1801.

"MY DEAR SIR,—An opportunity of conveying this to
you free of expense presents itself which I willingly embrace.
My Lord of Galloway is here just now, and Lady Hay has
very kindly promised to procure me a frank.

"Since I wrote you last I have been at Portpatrick, and
spent a part of two days and a night with my good friend
Dr. Mackenzie. He is one of the best companions I ever
met with, for he abounds with humour and anecdote, and
has something amusing or instructive to say on every subject. On the Sunday I went to church and heard the doctor
preach, who pleased me greatly. I have likewise been
visiting the 'little, round, fat, oily man of God' at the Inch,
and heard him preach. He is far inferior to Dr. M., but his
discourses are well adapted to a country congregation. I had

almost lost myself as I was going to the manse of Inch, by taking a near cut, as I thought, through the fields. To use an expression of Sancho's, 'I wandered through roadless roads and pathless paths,' till I fairly lost myself, but luckily arrived at the manse about an hour after it was dark. Mr. Ferguson has got a tall, stout young woman for a wife, and he seems quite a boy beside her. I was wishing that my good friend Mr. Wightman had such another, and I think he will be very much to blame if he does not soon furnish himself with a helpmeet for him. Mr. Ferguson I found a very sprightly, entertaining man, and we spent the evening very merrily. I received many invitations to come back whenever I could find it convenient. His wife, I think, is a very good woman. On Saturday first I am going to spend the afternoon and night of that day with my laughing friend Mr. Learmont, and on the Sunday I have promised to visit Mr. Kennedy of New Luce. I saw him on Wednesday last, and faithfully promised to be there on Sunday, to bear away a part of his preaching and dinner.

" By-the-by, I spent the evening of last Saturday at Mr. Learmont's, and who was there but George Coulter, whom you very probably know. He regaled our ears by playing on the fiddle, but I'll be hanged if I could tell what tunes he aimed at, for we had to ask him at the conclusion of every tune what he had been playing. I found that the man was actually a little cracked, and was astonished to hear him give a sermon on the Sunday replete with good sense, but delivered in a strange manner. He preached upon the ' fear of man bringing a snare,' and though he sometimes wandered from the point, yet his discourse discovered a good deal of original thought. He was very severe on the missionaries, and some of these gentry, terming them a parcel of hypocritical fanatics, who artfully flattered the prejudices of the people in order to gain popularity to themselves. In short, he far surpassed my expectation, and I wish that you had heard him. The missionaries have been preaching for nearly a fortnight past at Glenluce, but one of them is as mad as a March hare.

"Sir John has taken out a deputation (commission) for me to shoot, and for some weeks past we have been very busy at that amusement. We have got a most excellent greyhound, and we have had admirable sport at coursing. The hares are remarkably plenty, and one day, about a week ago, we caught four of them in the course of three hours. The dog and gun will be fine amusement to us during winter. James and I are going on in the same manner as when you were here, slowly but surely. We never lose sight of patience and perseverance, and with these two I think we will be able to do something. . . . . So you are turned farmer; but I think you pay an enormous rent for your land. I will help away with some of the produce when I come to Kirkmahoe. The family are talking of going to Edinburgh in spring, but whether Hay and I go I cannot say. I suppose Lady Hay will not like to want him out of her sight.—I always am, my dear Sir, yours very sincerely,

"JOHN CROCKET.

"The Rev. John Wightman, Kirkmahoe."

With regard to the Rev. George Coulter referred to above, it was universally believed that he was "cracked," but a good man notwithstanding. He was passionately fond of the violin, and appreciated his own performances on that instrument more highly than Mr. Crocket and his friends seem to have done. It was his favourite amusement, and after playing for some time, in an ecstacy of delight he would stride across the room, exclaiming, "Exquisite, exquisite, it makes me almost cry out!" He died in 1817, in the village of Kirkmichael, Ayrshire, without having got a church, but he possessed independent means, and was never in straits. Throughout his last illness he was attended by the village innkeeper, William Christy, who was considered a "skilly person," and who acted as doctor, barber, and apothecary, without charge or any remuneration. Mr. Coulter left a will, in which he directed that his funeral should be conducted on the "old plan," and that there should be a handsome *draigie* to those attending it, given in Christy's, that the profits might in some measure remunerate him for his gratuitous services and the kindness he had shown. The minister and schoolmaster were the executors, and the *draigie* bill handed in to them amounted to the sum of £25. Mr. Coulter, we think, was not the only one "cracked" in the concern.

Mr. Crocket was licensed as a preacher of the Gospel in 1803 by the Presbytery of Dumfries, and the character of his pulpit discourses attracted public attention. His preaching was earnest and impressive, his expositions of Scripture clear and practical, and his sermons especially were characterized by elegance of composition, simplicity of language, aptness of illustration, and pointed enforcement of divine truth. Mr. Wightman said of him, among his first appearances, after preaching in Kirkmahoe—"Mr. Crocket was heard with great attention, and I hope with profit, by the congregation. The style was rich, strong, and animated, and, in many instances, splendid and sublime." Through the influence of the Rev. Dr. M'Morine, of Carlaverock, he was presented to the church and parish of Kirkgunzeon in 1809, on the translation of the Rev. Mr. Rae to another charge, and there he lived till his death, fifty-eight years afterwards, dwelling among his own people, and with no desire to leave them. He ever cherished the warmest affection for them, and went continually amongst them, sympathizing, comforting, and instructing, as their cases required. He was known pre-eminently as a man of peace. His voice was never heard hastily in the stormiest debate on Church politics, but, on the contrary, he always endeavoured to throw oil on the troubled waters. Gentle and forbearing to all, he was still steadfast and immovable when duty called. His memory was remarkable both for facility and retentiveness. A single reading of a sermon or a poem, even not his own, was enough for him to deliver it in public. As an example of this we shall mention an instance of each. When he was a preacher he arrived unexpectedly one Sunday morning at Kirkmahoe manse as Mr. Wightman was about to dress for church. Though in travelling guise, and not intending to take part in pulpit duty, he was strenuously urged to take the day's service, and told that no refusal would be accepted. "The thing is impossible!" said Mr. Crocket; "I have not been thinking of preaching for a month, and I have no sermon with me. I have been engaged with the gun, and I could not preach though I got a kingdom for it. I have preached all my sermons in your church already." "You must preach," was the reply; "there must be no refusal." "Well, well, then, be it so; give me a volume of sermons for half-an-hour, and I'll try what can be done." This was complied with, and at the stated hour he went into the pulpit, and delivered *memoriter* what he had just recently read.

M

The other instance was of this kind. The first time we were introduced to him in his own manse we had driven a distance of fourteen miles through a heavy rain for the purpose of preaching, it being his Fast-day. Every outer garment was dripping, and some of the under ones soaked through, when we arrived; and before sitting down, while some dry habiliments were being sought out, he entertained us by repeating a considerable portion of "Tam o' Shanter," saying that he had never read the poem but once in his life, and that he could repeat it from beginning to end. This little bit of welcome was out of compliment to our having been brought up on the Banks o' Doon, and in the vicinity of Alloway Kirk.

A few Sundays after his settlement in Kirkgunzeon, the Session, in name of the congregation, called upon him, and said that as they had all along been accustomed to hear the sermons read, he need not trouble himself by committing them to memory, thus showing how rational and considerate a people they were. He did not, however, adopt their suggestion, though kindly intended, but thanked them cordially for their proffered kindness. In 1812 he was presented with the freedom of the burgh of Kirkcudbright, "with liberty to him to exercise and enjoy the whole immunities and privileges thereof, as amply and freely as any other does or may enjoy"—an honour which he highly appreciated, but did not take advantage of. As no man is complete without a wife, or a manse without one to look after its internal arrangements, so he resolved to supply the deficiency, and married Miss Goldie, eldest daughter of Mr. Goldie, of Stenhouse, Dumfriesshire, then residing at Isle, in the parish of Kirkmahoe, and connected with some of the best families in the county. It is worthy of notice that Mr. Wright, parish minister of Newabbey, baptized him, licensed him, introduced him at his ordination, and married him. In addition to his glebe he held a farm of considerable extent which lay contiguous, and so highly was he esteemed by the proprietor that the factor received instructions that Mr. Crocket's rent for the farm was not to be raised so long as he chose to keep it. As we have already hinted, he was a practised hand at the gun, and an admirable marksman—a qualification he had cultivated at Dunragit. For many years after his settlement—twenty, we think—he shot over the parish with a success envied by many who had nothing else to engage their attention. An anecdote is told of him having reference to his ability as a sportsman. On one occasion he and the Rev. Walter Dunlop met accidentally in the *Herald* Office, Dumfries, and in the course of some clerical conversation, Mr. Dunlop, who was rather corpulent, said, with characteristic humour, " I hae the better o' you ministers o' the Establishment, for I attended baith your Divinity Hall and our ain, so, ye see, I'm like a calf that has suckit twa kye.' " Ay, that ye are," said Mr. Crocket, "and a braw stirk they hae made ye." Mr. Dunlop felt himself foiled with his own weapon, but jocosely answered, " That's no sae bad, my freen Crocket, but I'll pay ye back for't some day." Not long afterwards, one Sunday morning, the two met again accidentally on the High Street of Dumfries, as the bells were being rung for public worship, when the following colloquy took place :—" How are ye the day, Mr. Crocket? I hope

ye're weel; ye're gaun to preach in St. Mary's, I believe?" "I am; but who told you that?" " Weel, ye
see, Mr. Crocket, I was just coming alang the street,
behint twa mason lads, when I heard one o' them say,
'Whaur'll we gang the day, think ye? will we try St.
Mary's?' 'Wha's to preach there?' said the ither.
'O, it's Crocket o' Kirkgunzeon,' was the reply. 'O,
it's him; he's nae great gun.' Weel, I didna like
to hear you made licht o', and so I stepped up, and
touching them on the shouther, I said, 'Lads, gang to
St. Mary's and hear Mr. Crocket; if he is nae great gun,
I can assure ye he's a capital shot.' Gude day wi' ye."
After walking a few paces, he turned round, and calling
Mr. Crocket, he said, "I hae now paid ye back for the
stirk."

He died in the eighty-ninth year of his age, and
the fifty-eighth of his ministry. Scarcely had any one
such an immunity from the "ills that flesh is heir
to" as he enjoyed. A short time before his death
he remarked to us, when requesting us to preach his
funeral sermon, that he had never had a day's sickness in his life, had never paid a farthing for medicine
or a doctor, having never required either, and had never
been absent from his pulpit during the whole of that
period from illness of any kind. A more acceptable
minister—a more genial, hospitable, and generous-
hearted man did not exist; this was everywhere acknowledged, and the parishioners of Kirkgunzeon found, to
their great grief, that they had lost a loving and sincere
friend when they consigned his remains to the grave.

While Mr. Wightman was a devoted student of the
learned treasures of antiquity, he also kept pace with the

current literature of the day, whenever he could command leisure in the discharge of parochial duty, and he freely made notes of merits and demerits as he passed along.   Poetry was his great resort after the labours of the pulpit, and he declared himself thoroughly reinvigorated after a couple of hours' luxuriating among the beauties of Milton's " Paradise Lost."   Hannah More's " Strictures on Female Education " excited considerable interest on its appearance, and called forth a variety of opinions from the press.   Mr. Wightman immediately procured the work, and the following criticism shows the interest he took in it:—" The authoress lifts a warning voice to the females of the present age, and gives very excellent advice respecting education, both as regards the heart and understanding.   Her manner is bold and energetic, and she appears as an Amazon to fight the battles of virtue and religion.   The air of smartness and irony she assumes rather injures than promotes the great cause of which, in general, she is an able advocate. She frequently speaks of the high and low tone of morals, and the Bishop of London says she writes in a strain of high-toned morality, or some such words, which has afforded Peter Pindar an opportunity of being witty on the subject.   Several writers have thought this book too strict, and in some parts there may be ground for the remark.   Nor does she always avoid the faults she reproves.   She censures the clergy and moralists for too much squeamishness in avoiding certain words, as *sin*, calling it *vice*.   She herself avoids the word *adulterers*, and calls them the persons whom ' God will judge.' She speaks euphemistically of the devil, the world; and the flesh, as ' the enemies of man.'   In a word, she writes with all the elegance of a delicate novelist, while she is treating on religious and moral subjects, and affecting to rescue the age from a weak compliance with the tide of custom in avoiding words which may offend the ears of the falsely refined, as the prophet says, 'speaking smooth things.' As a specimen of her manner, the beginning of the tenth chapter of the first volume seems to be one of the most favourable—'It has been the fashion of our late innovators in philosophy who have written the most brilliant popular treatises on education, to decry the practice of early instilling religious knowledge into the minds of children. They have, &c.'

"As an instance of her smartness already mentioned, when she is cautioning her readers against sending their children to any other source than the Gospel for their Christianity, or letting them set up any act of self-denial as the procuring cause of their salvation, she says, 'this would be to send them to Peter the Hermit and not to Peter the Apostle.' She urges the folly of striving to engage the attention of a dying person to the influence of religion in some such words as these—'Can he be supposed to listen to the voice of this charmer, when he cannot listen to the voice of singing men and singing women?' This kind of opposition or conceit occurs very frequently, as well as a combination of the serious and ludicrous, thus—'Shall they become Christians by accident? Is not this acting on the principle of Dogberry, that reading and writing come by nature?' Such writing as this would tempt one sometimes to think that she is more skilful in the faults and weaknesses of others, and able to expose and blazon them forth to view, than earnest in her wish to reform them or to take the beam

out of her own eye. She pleads strongly for the strict
and appropriate use of terms, and censures using 'proud
day,' 'proud success,' and such like, in the speeches in
Parliament, as being more suitable to the panegyrists of
the battle of Cannae, or some Roman or Carthaginian
victory, than to a Christian orator. But she blunders in
this very thing; she says a 'worldly Christian,' and
apologizes for using the term. This is, then, only to
argue about terms, not things, for Christian means either
a real or professing disciple of Jesus Christ, and a
'proud day,' means a joyful day, so that the word 'proud'
is sometimes used in one sense and sometimes in another,
which is also the case with other terms, as righteous,
perfect, and good.

" But while these remarks are made, it must be owned
that a great many beauties and excellencies are to be
found in the work. The cutting and satirical power
which sometimes appears may be seen from such parts
as the following, when she is censuring the rage for
novel writing, which seems insatiable:—' As Alexander,
on reading the Iliad, found, by congenial sympathy, the
image of Achilles stamped on his own ardent soul, and
felt himself the hero he was studying; and as Correggio,
on first beholding a picture which exhibited the perfection of the graphic art, prophetically felt all his own
future greatness, and cried out in rapture, ' I, too, am a
painter!' so a thorough-paced reading Miss, at the close
of every tissue of hackneyed adventures, feels within
herself the stirring impulse of corresponding genius, and
triumphantly exclaims, 'And I, too, am an author!'
The part of her book where she describes the attempts
to destroy female delicacy and principle, the tendency

of the German writings, is admirably well managed.
The effect produced is not like that of floods, or cataracts,
or volcanoes, where, though the crops are destroyed, yet
the seeds are not so, and there is hope they may spring
again; but the effects of this newly-medicated venom
are subtle though sluggish in their operations, like what
travellers relate of the Dead Sea, a stagnant lake
of putrifying waters. No wholesome blade shoots up
on its shore, and no living thing can exist within its
influence. Near the sulphurous pool the principle of
life is extinguished. We may justly say of this authoress,
in the words of her motto from Lord Halifax, that she
has 'raised her character that she may help to make the
next age better, and leave posterity in her debt for the
advantage it has received by her writings.' Upon the
whole, I have received both pleasure and instruction
from this production, and hope I shall profit by some
of her hints."

With the same author's "Sacred Dramas" he was
greatly pleased, especially with the speeches of David
and Daniel, though he took exception to certain epithets
and phrases employed, and thought some parts of the
work not easily reconcileable with the strict rules of
grammar. On the last leaf of the book he wrote in
pencil the following lines:—

> "Borne on the breeze from wild Carnarvon's steep,
>   Proceeds this minstrelsy? or Deva's stream?
> Does Nature's bard, awoke from death's cold sleep,
>   Warble on Avon's banks? or do I dream?
>
> "No! from where Severn rolls his ample flood,
>   In rival grandeur to the mantling main,
> These notes proceed, and stir my mounting blood.
>   While admiration thrills in every vein.

"'Tis, or a Zion's harp, or Anna's lyre,
  'Tis Harmony's own child that sweeps the strings,
The Song's enflamed with heaven's own living fire—
  'Tis Milton's muse—'tis More herself who sings!"

Of another work by the same authoress, " Cœlebs in Search of a Wife," he thus writes:—

" It is replete with useful remarks and observations, showing a great knowledge of the world. I cannot account for the fine variety of poetical and historical allusion with which the work is embellished in any other way than her having a commonplace-book, where all the quotations are stored under their proper heads. I have admired this before, when reading her 'Strictures on Female Education.' Her style is vigorous and flowing, and indicates a habit of composition. She generally uses *nor* after *neither*, and indeed after negatives in general, but on some occasions she forgets, or seems to forget her usual way. I do not admire the dialogue between Miss Lucilla and Lord Staunton at the summer-house, and her refusal of him on the grounds of religious difference of opinion. She is right, but the colloquy intended to do honour to the doctrines of religion I think has not the effect, at least to that degree the author intended. *Religious Courtships* do not sound well. It might have been the real cause of Lucilla's disliking him, but she was under no necessity to attack his religious principles on the subject. It afforded Staunton an opportunity of acting the hypocrite—of pretending he had not been sincere before. I observe alliterations very frequent in this work, such as Shakespeare and Sophocles, Juvenal and Johnson, soup and sauce, odd and opposite, bent and bias, compassion and compunction, &c. She sometimes introduces different allusions in the same sentence, thus—' The part of the Arcadian nymph, the reading lady, the lover of retirement, was each acted in succession, but so skilfully touched that the shades of each melted in the other without any of those violent transitions which a less experienced actress would have exhibited.' Here the actress and the painter are employed in too close proximity; they are elbowing each other in the same sentence. She uses Providence as equivalent to the term God. The best writers have *it* after this term and *its*, but she uses *him* and *his*.

"It is somewhat pleasant to find the sage Miss More, who in other works speaks so lightly, and with even contempt, of the novel-reading and novel-writing Misses, hitting off all the brilliances of romance in this religious work. She speaks of wiping fine eyes, of starts and confusions, of celestial rosy red blushes, and timid glances, with as much address as if she had used this kind of phraseology all her life. The book is rather useful than otherwise, especially with regard to politics and domestic economy, but in religion, though she says some excellent things against the Antinomian scheme, yet she has such a charity for such weak brethren and sisters that one cannot help thinking she is verging that way herself. She unsays in some measure what she has said, and leaves the reader to infer that she has either been persecuted for supposed Methodism, or that she has a leaning that way, so difficult is it for a female theologian to steer that *manly* course between the Scylla of self-confidence and the Charybdis of Antinomianism. There are several little blemishes in the tone and morality of the work, but, on the whole, I should like my daughter, if I had one, rather to read this than 'Clarissa Harlowe.'"

These specimens are given to show Mr. Wightman's abilities as a critic, and not for any special merit the works under review now possess.

But young preachers are rising up in the district, and

as one by one receives the Presbytery's *imprimatur*, he makes his way to Kirkmahoe manse. The following is noted with respect to the late Dr. Duncan of the New Church (Greyfriars), Dumfries, who had recently received license as a preacher:—

"4th March, 1804.—Dr. Thomas Tudor Duncan, presentee to Applegarth, preached. Lecture, John xiv. 1–5. Sermon, Matt. v. 43. Dr. Duncan is a young man about twenty-four years of age, son of the Rev. George Duncan of Lochrutton. His lecture was masterly, showing great knowledge of human character, and a happy talent of applying the consolations of religion to the wounds of the heart. His style was neat, and his delivery animated. His sermon also showed a great acquaintance with the principles of the human mind. Under the first head, he pointed out some of the offices which evince the duty; under the second, in which he showed that it was Christian, he gave a very animated explanation of resentment as far as it is justifiable, and applied his remarks to the invasion threatened by the French. His prayers exhibited a good heart, and much reverence of the Deity."

Dr. Duncan was a young clergyman of most prepossessing manners, and of refined taste. He had travelled for a considerable time on the Continent, especially in Italy, and was a perfect master of the language of that country. His ordination took place in the ensuing month, at which Mr. Wightman was present as a friend, and who afterwards made the following note of the day's proceedings:—

"Thursday, 12th April, 1804.—Was at Applegarth, at the ordination of the Rev. Thomas Tudor Duncan, M.D. He was ordained by the Rev. Andrew Jameson, minister of

St. Mungo, who preached from Luke xxiv. 26, 'Ought not Christ to have suffered these things, and to enter into his glory?' Mr. Jameson was two years at an Academy in the south of England. He has a great partiality for the English form of worship, and in his prayers and preaching exhibited the mixed character of an Episcopalian Presbyter. He was sufficiently orthodox in the ordinary sense of the term. He said his text was suitable in ordaining a minister of the Gospel, whose only business was to preach and make known among his people Christ crucified. I expected to have heard the sufferings of our Lord described, and the consequent glory, or some such thing, but our young champion for the truth rushed headlong into the depths of controversial disputations respecting the cause of moral evil, and the efficacy of repentance to salvation of itself. On these subjects he descanted at great length, and threw around some detached fragments of the answers which the soundest divines had given to the cavils of sceptics and infidels. After he had waded a considerable time in the midst of a chaotic and heterogeneous jumble of discordant matter, he preferred a prayer to the Father, Son, and Holy Ghost, to assist, illumine, and direct him, and to carry home his subject with effect to the hearts and lives of his hearers, which seemed to be like the prayer of Jonah from the whale's belly (for his subject had swallowed him outright); and letting fall some good things, and some very unguarded things, he flounced on to the end of his discourse. He sang a paraphrase, and then proceeded to ordain Dr. Duncan—his consecration prayer consisting of a very pious and suitable address to God, and was seemingly closed with an address to Dr. Duncan—'We set *thee* apart, &c.,' and then he resumed his prayer and closed anew. He then ascended the pulpit, read from a paper some scriptures from Paul to Timothy, and turning to the people he harangued them in an *extempore* effusion, which he concluded with entreating and conjuring them to accept their minister from the hands of his father, whom he termed a venerable man. The Rev. Geo. Duncan is truly 'venerable,' but unworthy of being treated so unmercifully on this occasion. A large company of us dined at Halleaths. I went to Dalton with my worthy friend Dr. Criric, and returned home next day."

CHAPTER X.

THANKSGIVING FOR NAVAL SUCCESSES—DEATH OF LORD NELSON—
CHURCH VACANCIES IN DUMFRIES—MR. WIGHTMAN A CANDIDATE
FOR THE NEW CHURCH—CALL IN URR—DR. MUIRHEAD AND BURNS
—EXAMINATION OF STUDENTS — ALLAN CUNNINGHAM — THE
FRENCH IN SPAIN—LINES ON SPANISH PATRIOTISM—EXTRACTS.

ON the 1st of December, 1805, Mr. Wightman read
from the pulpit of Kirkmahoe a proclamation for a day
of thanksgiving on account of the late naval successes
which had been achieved, and especially that by Lord
Viscount Nelson on the 21st of October, when that
brave man fell mortally wounded in the hour of victory,
unflinchingly carrying out his immortal and inspiriting
order—"England expects every man to do his duty!"
A court of lieutenancy had been held in Dumfries for
the special consideration of the state of affairs which
had then emerged, and had transmitted copies of their
minute to the several ministers within the bounds of
their jurisdiction, recommending the following Thursday
to be set apart for religious service and solemn thanksgiving, and also suggesting that a collection should be
made on that day for behoof of the widows and orphans
of those who had fallen fighting the battles of their
country. After reading the proclamation, Mr. Wightman,
with his usual enthusiasm in such matters, said to his
people in support of the proposal, that he was certain it
only required to be mentioned to meet with their

approbation, and to insist on its necessity and propriety would be to offer an insult to their understanding and feelings. Their benevolence could not extend to the dead—they were removed beyond the reach of all human sympathy, and required no human aid, but the relatives who survived were the proper objects of their charity, and had a peculiar claim upon their generous consideration. If the measure proposed were carried into effect, it would not only operate as a seasonable relief to many who had lost their whole support and their only stay, but it would stimulate their brave countrymen to fresh incentive in turning the tide of battle from our gates, and in checking the rapacity of audacious ambition. With what ardour would the husband, and the father, and the brother, and the son, engage in fight when they knew that their grateful country would watch over those dearest to their hearts, and provide for their comfort, should they themselves never return. The collection on the day appointed amounted to £14, a sum pretty good for a country parish, where the principal grandees gave their subscriptions elsewhere in the county list. On receiving the first news of the sad but glorious event in which Nelson fell, Mr. Wightman wrote the following lines off-hand, within twenty minutes, in honour of the departed hero:—

THE DEATH OF NELSON.

"As pensive she sat on her sea-beaten shore,
Britannia exclaimed, 'My brave Nelson's no more !
Who now shall be guardian of Freedom's domain,
Since Nile's laurelled hero in combat is slain ?'
Old ocean I heard thus in thunder reply,
As flashed the red lightning all over the sky,

> ' Our Nelson is fallen, but immortal's his name,
> And heroes unborn shall yet rival his fame;
> The bold sons of freedom will guard her green isle,
> They'll conquer or die like the hero of Nile !' "

Some years afterwards, when Mr. Wightman was in Edinburgh, the late Dr. Andrew Crichton, a native of Kirkmahoe, and at that time editor of the *Edinburgh Advertiser*, took him to Nelson's monument on the Calton Hill, and showed him the lines splendidly framed and glazed upon the wall. " Ye have immortalized me ! " said Mr. Wightman. " Yes," replied Dr. Crichton, with a peculiar twinkle of his squinting eye, " as far as rosewood and glass will do it." " It was very cruel of him," said Mr. Wightman, as he told us the incident, " he might have allowed me to enjoy my immortality for one day, without putting a sting in it." The above lines appeared in a local journal, and were very generally approved of, as being succinct, yet comprehensive, and in some degree energetic. Almost every newspaper was crowded with poetry on the subject. The *Star* sternly excluded from every quarter all poetry on the event, declaring afterwards that it could not have admitted a single sentence of prose into its columns had it given even the half of the verses written and sent for publication on the death of Nelson.

Mr. Wightman received many compliments on the first appearance of his verses, and as he was often requested to recite them, these were always warmly renewed. The following graceful tribute to his muse was paid him nearly forty years afterwards, when, with a voice somewhat tremulous with age, but with all the fire of yore, he acceded to the request of a distinguished party to gratify them by a recital with the author's own voice :—

WRITTEN AFTER HAVING HEARD DR. WIGHTMAN REPEAT HIS WELL-KNOWN LINES ON THE DEATH OF NELSON.

"One night as I sat in my chamber alone,
Bethinking of heroes and times that are gone,
Brave Nelson of Nile stood in image before me,
Arrayed in the robes of his undying glory—
His eye, calm and bright, as an unmoving star,
And his brow broadly traced with the furrows of war,
His breast as undaunted, his heart still as true,
As they formerly were when to battle he flew,
When collected he stood, 'mid the cannon's loud roar,
Like a rock in the wave which the surge lashes o'er.
He spoke—and his *voice* was sufficient to show
The *heart* of a *Nelson*, ne'er dreading the foe—
And he said—' I have come from the country above,
Encircled in glory and pillowed in love,
To give thee, my son, the most cherished command
Of him who has bathed in the tears of the land.
To *Wightman*, go, tell, that I wait him on high,
Where the souls of the brave and the good never die—
That an angelic host and a seraphim throng,
Inspired with the love of his soft-falling song,
Heaven's gate now besiege, to re-echo the strain
That he sung while on earth to the Son of the Main.
                              "PAUL K. FORRESTER."

But nearer home an event of considerable importance had occurred, though not by any means so great as that which has just been recorded. The church of St. Michael's, Dumfries, had become vacant by the demise of its reverend pastor, Dr. Burnside, and various influences were at work with regard to the appointment of his successor. The Rev. Mr. Scot, of the New Church, had received intimation from the Duke of Queensberry

N

through the Incorporation of Dumfries, that he was
doing all in his power with the Crown to secure his
appointment to the charge, and was confident of success,
though some time must elapse before the presentation
would be made. Another party had made application
to the same source through the Burgh Member on
behalf of the Rev. W. Thorburn, minister of Troqueer,
and they too reported with equal confidence of success
as to the prospects of their nominee. The town was in
a state of considerable excitement, party feeling ran
high, and the merits of the two reputed candidates were
unsparingly criticised. A short time, however, sufficed
to end the contention, and Mr. Scot was found to have
obtained the goodly heritage. After his induction there
was next a run upon the charge which he had vacated,
and the contention again revived with even redoubled
strength. The emoluments of the two livings were very
far from being equal, but a great deal seemed to be
attached to the name of a town charge both by the
worshippers and the clergy themselves. Mr. Wightman,
after some hesitation, on Friday, 24th January, 1806,
sent a letter to the Provost intimating his willingness
to become a candidate for the vacant church if the
congregation were to be consulted in the matter. He
had delayed taking any measures to obtain the situation
out of deference to his young friend, Rev. Wm. Dunbar,
who had been formerly promised the influence of the
Duke of Queensberry, at the request of the magistrates,
when a fitting opportunity should arise, and it was only
when he saw that this interest was not being used he
came forward on his own behalf. He considered this
delay proved fatal to his chance of success, for on the

week after he had sent his letter of application he found a subscription going on for a Dr. Sibbald, and an application had been made by Dr. Hunter of Edinburgh, and formerly of Dumfries, in favour of a Mr. Thomson at Port-Glasgow. He immediately withdrew his name, and ceased using any means whatever to succeed. He also heard that the congregation of the New Church had sent a very warm remonstrance to Dr. Hunter on the subject, stating that if he persisted in favour of Mr. Thomson his popularity in Dumfries would be lost. Some of Mr. Wightman's friends, seeing the direction in which matters were drifting, soothed his wounded feelings by flatteringly saying that had he applied in time all the trouble, and confusion, and animosity would have been prevented. We very much doubt this from what we know of the congregation. If they were of the same character then as now, they are not willing to accept the first man that offers, or to sell their birthright to the first comer, as a stall-keeper disposes of her apples, but still oftentimes a small matter makes a turning-point in such circumstances, and affairs of religion are no exception. He was, however, glad he had not entered the lists in the contest then going on, as he enjoyed the esteem of his own parishioners, and a degree of comfort seldom met with in a charge so extensive, so intelligent, and so full of responsibility. Dr. Sibbald's subscription served only to exasperate the majority of the people, as Dr. Hunter's application for Mr. Thomson also did. The result was that neither of these gentlemen was appointed, but a clergyman whose name had never been introduced in connection with the affair, and, beyond all controversy, the best of the three, Dr. Thomas

Tudor Duncan, minister of Applegarth.   Mr. Wightman
sought solace in his usual refuge, a Latin quotation from
Virgil :—

> "Non nostrum inter vos tantas componere lites:
> Et vitulâ tu dignus, et hic."

Another church appointment was made during this
year within the bounds of the Presbytery of Dumfries,
that of assistant and successor to Dr. Muirhead, in the
parish of Urr, in favour of Alexander Murray, the celebrated linguist, and afterwards Professor of Hebrew and
Oriental languages in the University of Edinburgh.   At
the moderation of the call on the 7th of November, Dr.
Muirhead himself officiated, preaching from the appropriate text, 2 Timothy iv. 7, "I have fought a good
fight, I have finished my course, I have kept the faith."
At the close of his discourse he gave his audience a history of calls, which was both instructive and entertaining.
After recounting the unhappy effects of popular elections, he observed that they were nothing but preaching
ploughing-matches, and no better than one of their
burgh or county elections, then hotly going on.   He
concluded with a eulogium on Mr. Murray's talents and
moral character, and recommended him warmly to the
congregation.   Dr. Muirhead was a character in the
Presbytery as well as out of it, and was possessed of
eminent abilities of various kinds, but which he did not
always exercise with creditable prudence, as some of his
brethren could testify from experience.   On one occasion
he and Mr. Gillespie of Kells were to preach together
on the Fast-day of a neighbouring Communion.   Mr.
Gillespie delivered his sermons from memory, and, being
the elder minister of the two, according to custom he

preached last. Before leaving the manse for church Dr.
Muirhead inquired of Mr. Gillespie what was his text,
and the heads or divisions under which he treated it.
Having got this information, on going into the pulpit,
to the consternation of Mr. Gillespie, he gave out the
same text and adopted the same divisions for elucidation.
Mr. Gillespie made a very awkward appearance afterwards, but he had the Christian and gentlemanlike
feeling to make no reference to the treacherous way in
which he had been treated.

The same thing once occurred, but unintentionally,
in Mr. Wightman's experience, when preaching on a Fast-
day in Closeburn. He also preached from memory,
and the first minister took the same text which he was
prepared to preach from. When his turn came, on
giving out the same text, he composedly said, "they had
already reaped an abundant harvest from this fruitful
passage of the Word of God, and he would now follow
with a few gleanings." The thing was admirably turned,
and he got the credit of adopting the text on purpose,
and of preaching *extempore*, some of the hearers declaring afterwards that "the gleanings of the grapes of
Ephraim were better than the vintage of Abiezer." The
minister of Colvend having, under some unaccountable
delusion, left his family and his parish for some time,
and no trace of him being found, the Presbytery agreed
to supply the pulpit temporarily, in the expectation that
he would soon appear. The first minister appointed to
preach in Colvend Church was Dr. Muirhead, who, on
doing so, chose for his text, Exodus xxxii. 1, "As for
this Moses, the man that brought us up out of the land
of Egypt, we wot not what is become of him." Mr.

Kennedy, the minister of Terregles, was, like Zaccheus of old, exceedingly little in stature, but in accordance with the law of compensation he married a lady of unusual proportions for her sex, and by name *Grace*. Dr. Muirhead was asked to preach in Terregles on the Sunday after the married pair returned from their marriage tour, a custom known by the name of "kirking the young folk." The whole parishioners turned out on the occasion to see the young mistress of the manse. Dr. Muirhead proceeded with the service, and gave out for text, Ephes. iii. 8, "Unto me, who am less than the least of all saints, is this *great grace* given." It may be mentioned, however, that the better to suit the case, he interpolated the epithet "great" in reading the text. When the late Rev. Dr. Glover of Greenside, Edinburgh, was married, being then minister of Crossmichael, in the Stewartry of Kirkcudbright, Dr. Muirhead was requested to "kirk" him, which he did, taking for his text, 1 Tim. ii. 12, "But I suffer not a woman to teach, nor to usurp authority over the man, but to be in silence"—from which he delivered one of the most extraordinary sermons ever heard from a pulpit, almost to the consternation of the worshippers.

He had the misfortune to come into collision with Burns the poet, when there was hard hitting on both sides, though the poet suffered most. Dr. Muirhead plumed himself on his family descent, and having some landed property he felt more independent than the generality of the clergy, so that presuming on this he often said and did things which would not have been tolerated in any other. He also took a very warm interest in politics, especially when local electioneering

was going on.   During a hotly-contested election in the
Stewartry of Kirkcudbright, about the beginning of
1795, in which Mr. Heron of Heron was the candidate
in the Whig interest, and Mr. Gordon of Balmaghie on
the Tory side, Burns took the side of the former, who
had greatly befriended him previously, and by way of
helping his cause he published three squib ballads in
which the Tory supporters were satirically portrayed.
In one of these he refers to Dr. Muirhead in terms
equivocally complimentary, which no one had the slightest difficulty in construing as the poet intended:—

> "And there'll be lads o' the gospel;
>   Muirhead, wha's as gude as he's true;
> And there'll be Buittle's apostle,
>   Wha's mair o' the black than the blue."

In a second diatribe on the subject he comes down
with equal severity:—

> "And by our banners marched Muirhead,
>   And Buittle was na slack;
> Whase haly priesthood nane can stain,
>   For wha can dye the black?"

Dr. Muirhead was not disposed to let these pass with
impunity, and in retaliation, being somewhat of a rhymster himself, he got printed, in Edinburgh, a sheet in
verse, in which he quotes one of Martial's Epigrams,
giving a very free translation, pointedly referring it to
the character of Burns:—

MARTIALIS LIBER. XI., EP. 66, IN VACERRAM.

> "Et delator es, et calumniator;
>   Et fraudator es, et negotiator:
> Et fellator es, et lanista: miror
>   Quare non habeas, Vacerra, nummos."

TRANSLATION.

" Vacerras, shabby son of wh——,
   Why do thy patrons keep thee poor ?
   Bribe-worthy service thou canst boast,
   At once their bulwark and their post ;
   Thou art a sycophant, a traitor,
   A liar, a calumniator,
   Who, conscience (hadst thou that), would sell,
   Nay, lave the common-sewer of hell
   For whisky : Eke, most precious imp,
   Thou art a rhymster, gauger, pimp ;
   Whence comes it, then, Vacerras, that
   Thou still art poor as a church-rat ?"

It is said that " no publication in answer to the scur-
rilities of Burns ever did him so much harm in public
opinion, or made Burns himself feel so sore, as Dr. Muirhead's translation of Martial's Epigram." Burns, however, had the last word. In the following year Parliament
was dissolved and a new election took place. This time
the candidates were Mr. Heron and the Hon. Montgomery
Stewart, a younger son of the Earl of Galloway. The
hand of death was upon the poet, but the former spirit
revived, and the Epigram translation was not forgotten.
He accordingly wrote another satirical ballad, in which
he represents a pedlar hawking the characters of the
Tory supporters and offering them in the shape of
Troggin :—

   " Wha will buy my troggin,
      Fine election ware ;
   Broken trade o' Broughton,
      A' in high repair.
       Buy braw troggin,
         Frae the banks o' Dee;
       Wha wants troggin
         Let him come to me.

   *   *   *   *   *

" Here's armorial bearings,
Frae the manse o' Urr;
The crest, a sour crab-apple,
Rotten at the core.
Buy braw troggin, &c."

Dr. Muirhead died 16th May, 1808, in the sixty-eighth year of his age and thirty-eighth of his ministry.

Mr. Wightman had an attraction, as we have already seen, for all young men of merit desirous of rising in the world, whatever their profession, and who wished to have the counsel of a friend on whom they could rely as to the best way in which their aim might be attained. The manse was ever open with its homely hospitality, and his heart to welcome them with unfeigned sincerity. His generous nature, his sound judgment, his classical attainments, were widely known, and he was regarded above all in the Presbytery as the student's friend. When trials for license came on he was always appointed to examine in the Hebrew and Greek languages, and his manner of doing so was kindly in the extreme. He would never take a separate book in discharging the duty, but putting his arm round the student's neck, he looked on along with him as the invariable twenty-third Psalm and the Gospel of St. John were waded through. He was not by any means over-punctilious in the correct reading of the words, or the thorough accuracy of the translation, if the general sense was given, and he always finished with a clap on the poor fellow's shoulder, and a " Very well, very well, that'll do." We have heard him say that on such occasions he never put a question to a student which he thought he could not answer, and when there appeared any signs of doubt or hesitancy in the reply, a soft whisper in the ear made all things smooth. He had the same generous feeling in giving certificates of scholarship and ability to candidates for the mastership of vacant schools. "Very thin, very thin," said he, when he had written one of these in our presence, "but conscience will not let me make it thicker." This facile though not perfunctory examination of students was perhaps not altogether to be approved of, but he could not help it, and if the reverend Court were dissatisfied with the form of procedure they could have appointed another, which was never done. His manner contrasted favourably with that of some others, who, however, wanted the ability to dig among the Hebrew roots. Of him it might be truly said, and was said, that "his failings leaned to virtue's side," and his memory is still fragrant to many a minister in the Church who passed under his arm.

One of these applicants for counsel in the way of life was Allan Cunningham, a young man twenty-two years of age, who had been brought up in the parish as a stone mason, and who afterwards became distinguished, as all the world knows, as a poet, a biographer, and a historian. Mr. Wightman received from him the following letter, dated Dalswinton, 11th April, 1806 :—

" Rev. Sir,—According to promise, I have sent you Sharp's edition of 'Collins, Gray, and Cunningham's Poems,' and I am well assured they will give you in reading them the same degree of satisfaction and pleasure which they gave to me. I would have been happy to have seen you at the manse on purpose to converse about some important and laudable matters—particularly to get your advice concerning my future course of life—to direct my reading, &c., for I am in a manner entirely left to my own inclinations in pursuit of what we term happiness, and I may go wrong. I shall be directed entirely by you in everything that tends to my welfare and improvement, for I am not above or below advice. I shall give you some idea of what I make of time when among my hands, that you may form in your mind what kind of being I am. My daily labour, I may say, consumes it all, except what is allotted for sleep and the short intervals for meals, and considerable portions of these are dedicated to reading any entertaining book, provided it says nothing against our religion. Such I carefully avoid. Poetry especially gives me most delight—Young, Milton, Thomson, and Pope, please me best. Social converse with my fellow-creatures I never avoid on any rational subject that improves the mind and sweetens the bitters of life, of which, though young, I have had my share. Sometimes I write a few lines on any pleasing subject that strikes my fancy. I have even attempted poetry, but mostly failed. After public worship is over on Sabbath, you may find me reading in some sequestered spot, far from the usual haunts of bustling mankind, where I retire by myself to be more at liberty in my reflections and contemplations upon the works and goodness of Him who made me. I am, for the most part, cheerful, except when musing upon or reading some affecting book. After returning thanks to God for my preservation, I retire to the embraces of sleep, and rise with a cheerful mind, judging it part of my tribute to my Maker. An honest and cheerful heart is almost all my stock. I fervently adhere to truth, and, to close all, I have an independent mind. These, sir, are the outlines of my way of life as near as I can draw them. Now, to be candid with you, I wish to have your advice concerning books which are most proper to peruse; how to use my time, and, in short, whatever you deem useful to me in life.

If you would be so good as to direct my small share of abilities to flow in their proper channel, I would esteem it the greatest favour your goodness could bestow.   I am certainly much in want of education.   I was taken from school and put to learn my trade at eleven years of age, and I really begin to feel the want of it much.   English grammar I never learned; indeed, it was not in use in the school I was at.   I have spoken of the library to several of my acquaintances here, and they will become members of it as soon as it is instituted. I spoke with all the eloquence I was master of in its favour. —I ever am, reverend and worthy Sir, your devoted servant while   ALLAN CUNNINGHAM."

Mr. Wightman was greatly gratified at this application, as he had known young Allan for several years, and had formed a most favourable opinion of his character. All the family were members of the church, and he was on terms of intimacy with them, not only as a minister, but as a personal friend.   It was therefore with no little pleasure that he sent the following reply, chalking out the necessary literary cultivation of the young aspirant for fame:—

"KIRKMAHOE MANSE, 20th April, 1806.

MY DEAR ALLAN,—I return you your two volumes, with many thanks.   These poems have long been great favourites of mine.   The picture you have drawn of yourself in your letter to me is exceedingly interesting.   I wish you to have a happy journey through life—a smooth road and a serene sky.   We must, however, lay our account with a chequered scene.   The wisest and best of Beings has seen this to be most conducive to our true interests. I approve of your reading poetry.   Goldsmith, in his

'Deserted Village,' says some things very fine on the subject of poetry:—

> 'And thou, sweet Poetry, thou loveliest maid,
> The first to fly when sensual joys invade.'

The reading of poetry should be mingled with other pursuits. It is a liberal recreation, but should not be a business. It is said to be apt to foster, in elegant and ingenuous minds, a romantic delicacy and a morbid sensibility inconsistent with the sober and industrious pursuits of the useful arts and professions. This can be the effect only of an excessive fondness for the creations of fancy; but I think there is not much reason to fear this excess in one who is so much confined, and so properly, to the duties of his employment as you are. You would do well to read books of practical science, and history, and travel, which will guard you effectually against any danger of loving poetry too much. Such books as the following may be worth your perusal, as they may fall in your way, or as you may find it convenient to purchase them:—Dr. Robertson's 'History of Scotland;' Hume's 'History of England,' with one of the continuations; Dr. Henry's 'History of Great Britain;' some of the best tours in Great Britain, or different parts of it; the travels or tours of Moore, Cox, Swinbourne, Brydone in Sicily and Malta, Niebhur in Asia, Vaillant and Sparrman in Africa, Captain Cooke's and Anson's voyages, &c., &c.; and I shall mention a book or two in Divinity—'Evidences of Christianity,' by Dr. Porteous, Bishop of London, by Dr. Beattie of Aberdeen, and by Mr. Addison; Dr. S. Clarke's 'Commentary and Paraphrase on the Four Gospels, with Dr. Pyle's continuation through the New Testament;' or, the 'Family Expositor' of the pious and amiable Dr. Doddridge; Dr. Gisborne's 'Survey of Christianity,' and his other works; the sermons of Blair, Walker, Seed, and Sherlock. These, my dear sir, are a few of the books which you may read at your leisure and still be steady and unremitting in attention to your profession. It is a well-balanced rather than a well-stored mind which bids fairest to be happy. Never lose sight of your religion. This is the grand recipe for happiness :—

' Let fouk bode weel, and strive to do their best;
  Nae mair's required; let Heaven make out the rest.'

While you preserve your independent mind, consider always that stubbornness has no right to the title of independence. I am *convinced your* mind is not of that character. That rude and savage independence which does not attend to the mutual subservience of the branches of human society is apt to meet, in an evil hour, with a rude blast to break it, and ruin follows. Mingle with your virtuous contemporaries and friends, and convince them that one may be cheerful, and yet ' unspotted from the world.' I will be glad to give you my best advice at any time, and am, dear Allan, yours truly,   (Signed)   JOHN WIGHTMAN."

In the meantime Bonaparte is blazing through Europe like a wandering comet, and filling every bosom with dismay :—

" 27th December, 1807.—The French are in Spain. The Royal family of Portugal are sailing towards the Brazils under the protection of the British thunder. The despotism of Bonaparte seems now to be forging a spear for his own destruction. There is a point to which the fetters of tyranny may be drawn, when they burst asunder and recoil on the hand which fastens them. I augur that the day is at hand when Europe will be freed from this scourge of nations. Russia will not long submit to the humiliation to which she is reducing herself. Denmark will forgive what a friend did in a moment of tremendous importance. Austria will recall her cumbrous vigour—and Dr. Henry's 'awful recoil of indignant nations' will be realized; while the tyrant of the civilized world will be hunted from his perilous and giddy height of enormous and ill-acquired power and demonstration. The ensuing year will be memorable for great events. Great Britain, under Providence, will hold out against the world in arms; and although Bonaparte has all the Continent of Europe under his power and at his feet low in the dust, our happy land, like a green oasis amidst the African desert, will flourish and afford the 'oppressed an asylum and a refreshing draught from the streams of liberty."

The following verses on the patriotism of Spain were written a few months afterwards in anticipation of the tyrant's downfall:—

SPANISH PATRIOTISM.

" From Marathon's inspiring plain,
  Where Grecia spurned the Persian's chain;
From where the royal Spartan fell,
  Or where Helvetia mourns her Tell.
Come, Freedom, come on wings of fire,
  And boldly strike the martial lyre;
See where Iberia's sons advance
  To meet the death-doomed files of France!
Heaven's lightning flames in every eye,
  And Gallia's slaves in terror fly.
Lo! far the sky-born vigour spreads,
  Where glory's streaming banner leads!
Hark, loud the patriot trumpet blows,
  One ardent mass the nation glows,
Dread Justice draws her flaming brand.
  See vengeance flashes from her hand!
Indignant nations rise as one—
  The despot trembles on his throne;
His palsied hand the sceptre yields,
  While deep he rues his bloody fields.

Britannia grasps her gleaming spear,
Bids Freedom's sons no danger fear.
Her friendly flag holds high unfurl'd,
And opes a sanctuary to the world!"

This prophetic effusion was inserted in the *Star* news-paper, and from it copied into others, as in some measure descriptive of the universal feeling entertained against Bonaparte at the time. But news have arrived that the Austrians have been defeated by the French and a decisive victory obtained. "Good heaven! After the Emperor Francis and the Archduke Charles had gone forth with their armies, trusting in God, and with a view only to defend their dearest rights, to be driven as dust before the wind by oppressors and tyrants! But I hope the cause of freedom is not yet lost on the Con-tinent. Some living fire lies yet under the ashes which so thickly cover the surface of the nations there, and soon a conflagration will break forth which will destroy the works of the despot of Europe and afford the phœnix of some better order of things to arise out of the com-bustion; for to hope that any good will issue from pacific measures seems to be vain. Spain will surely not yet succumb to the iron yoke, and the Russian Eagle will plume his wings for some bold flight for liberty. Nor will the British Lion cease to raise his voice and shake the dews from his mane!" When news reached this country that a glorious victory had been gained over the French at Corunna, though General Moore fell mortally wounded, cheering on his brave 42nd Highlanders, and calling upon them to "remember Egypt," Mr. Wightman again struck his lyre in praise of the Spanish patriots, and sang, like Moses on the shore of the Red Sea:—

THE PATRIOTS OF SPAIN.

" Iberians sink not in despair,
    Though Gallic legions crowd your plains ;
  Your banners fearless raise in air,
    And boldly spurn the tyrant's chains.

" From Biscay's cliffs, which meet the skies,
    To where sweet Murcia's vales extend,
  Let patriot hosts indignant rise,
    And wisdom with your valour blend.

" Though sullen clouds your sky deform,
    They cannot quench the orb of day;
  Your sun shines awful through the storm,
    And soon will chase the gloom away.

" I see the sky-born flame relumed,
    I hear your martial trumpets sound;
  I see your helms with victory plumed,
    And Freedom's foes bestrew the ground.

" See where the Tagus rolls his wave,
    Of glittering steel a forest moves;
  The British Fabius leads the brave,
    And true to you and freedom proves.

" By famed Corunna's crimsoned shore,
    By all the blood of patriots slain,
  By Britain and the shade of Moore,
    Usurpers shall not conquer Spain!

" 'Tis done! the Gallic bands withdraw,
    Their ensigns in confusion furl'd;
  The tyrant bends to freedom's law,
    And peace returns to bless the world."

With reference to the "British Fabius" it is necessary
to mention that this stanza was written when Lord
Wellington began to move from his quarters towards
Spain, and was afterwards inserted. But we turn again
to the journal:—

" 13th June, 1809.—At this critical period of Continental politics the view of things is not very promising. Perhaps even now the tyrant of Europe is scattering the armies of Austria, and binding his own fetters on the German nations. His troops in Portugal and Spain are resisting but too successfully the efforts of British valour, and a wavering patriotism in defending the rights of these ancient kingdoms against the grasp of insatiable ambition. On the enterprises of the present time depends the fate of Europe, and, it may be, of Britain! I am still of opinion (against hope) that the cause of Liberty and Independence in Europe is not yet lost, and that though Russia has now declared against Austria, yet some event will deliver the oppressed nations, and free the world from bondage. I wait with anxiety for news from Moravia, where some important operations must have already taken place. I wish Sir Arthur Wellesley may keep near the shore, and not go too far into the country after M. Soult. 14th June.—Heard of the famous battle between the Austrians, under the Archduke Charles, and Bonaparte, in which the latter was defeated, and obliged to retire a considerable way from the field near Vienna. I augur well from this turn which is now given to the tide of unexampled success with which the arms of the French Ruler have always been crowned. The spring being now let free, it will rebound with an awful elasticity, and events will likely follow which will place Europe in a different state before long. It is likely Bonaparte will exert his utmost skill and force now. It must be now or never, and he knows that well. But if the Austrians be once more successful, the fate of the tyrant is fixed, and his fetters burst—for ever !"

Bonaparte, however, was not to be so easily vanquished as the above meditations anticipated, and other lands were to smart under his despotism and tyranny ere his career should close. Some two years and a half afterwards we find the following note:—

"23rd Dec., 1811.—The war in the Peninsula is more favourable to the Patriots than it was lately. I still hope and believe the tyrant will never be able to conquer this portion of Europe. The Guerillas, if they were well organized and commanded, would do great things. Bonaparte will not trust his person south of the Pyrenees, unless he has succeeded first in corrupting the leaders of the people, and in paralyzing the strength of the nation. And if he heads his legions, this will be a proof that corruption and intrigue have gone before. But I cannot easily suspect that the heroes of Saragossa, Gerona, and Albuera, will not be succeeded by kindred spirits, and that out of the ashes of these cities, and their brave defenders, will not spring a race of patriots invincible to the bonds of tyranny. General Hill's brave conduct has given new life to the cause in one quarter, and Catalonia is all in arms. We have just taken the island of Java, and the town of Batavia in the East Indies —'Bellum, bellum, horridum bellum!' The sovereignty of the seas would be likely for ever lost by a *peace*, in the present state of things, for the enemy would soon cover the ocean with ships, and man them with his millions; and then one or two battles might reverse the history of naval glory. Dark! dark!"

Little more than four months afterwards we read the following:—

"4th May, 1812.—The affairs of the Peninsula are more prosperous. The brave and skilful General Wellington has, with the heroes under his command, British and Portuguese, taken the city of Badajos, after a siege which lasted a considerable time, after fighting a whole night, losing 1000 men,

and performing deeds of the most heroic valour. This will
inspire new spirit into the minds of the Spaniards. Bonaparte is manœuvring against Russia, but while he is in the
north with his legions, some other Powers will rise against
his tyranny; and I still think that the time is not distant
when his empire will be curtailed, and clipt in some parts,
if it do not fall entirely to pieces. It is an image like that
of Babylon, composed of such heterogeneous materials that
it must soon crumble into fragments, or be moulded into a
more stable form. Austria will not long remain friendly to
her oppressor and friend. The marriage will be a curse and
not a blessing, a division and not a bond of unity."

" 1st November, 1812.—Bonaparte has done in Moscow
what will transmit his name to posterity as the scourge, the
curse of his species—the Nero—the Attila—the Demon of
destruction and hate. He has constituted a *soi-disant* tribunal,
a consistorial, inquisitorial, tyrannical, despotical, bloody,
savage commission within the bosom of an empire to which
he has no claim—tried, condemned, and executed men for
obeying the orders of their own Government! Here the
cloven foot of the fiend, whose deeds of barbarity tarnish the
annals of the war in Egypt, appears. Bonaparte, thy name
is cruelty! Ye Neros, ye Domitians, ye Attilas, ye Bajazets,
ye Goths and Vandals of a barbaric age, hide your diminished
heads! The glare of your infamy is lost in the lurid blaze
which surrounds the head of the Corsican Napoleon! 10th
November.—The Russian General Kutusoff has cut down
a part of the vanguard of the invader's army, gained a decided
victory, and taken many prisoners. Bonaparte has left
Moscow in haste! The tide is now refluent against the
tyrant, and it will swell with redoubled tempests of hatred
and vengeance till it drive him, on its angry surges, beyond
the limits of the Russian territory, while the hovering spirit
of Peter the Great will blow the trumpet of victory and

summon the oppressed nations of the Continent to raise the banners of Freedom and chase the wolf to his Parisian den, howling as he flees, no more to come forth, in prowling capacity, to drink with impunity in overflowing streams the life-blood of men!"

CHAPTER XI.

REJOICINGS AT THE SUCCESS OF THE ALLIES—ODE TO THE MEMORY
OF PITT—BONAPARTE LEFT ELBA—BATTLE OF WATERLOO—COM-
PLIMENTARY DINNER TO THE SCOTS GREYS IN DUMFRIES—
NUPTIAL ODE ON THE MARRIAGE OF THE PRINCESS CHARLOTTE—
PATRIOTISM.

To Mr. Wightman's unbounded gratification, the news
arrived that the military career of Bonaparte was seemingly at a close for ever, that he had been hopelessly
defeated in battle, and been sent an exile to the island
of Elba, a residence of his own choice, there to spend
the remainder of his days in bitter rumination over the
past.   He had followed the tyrant from one battlefield
to another, loading him with the heaviest imprecations
for the atrocities everywhere perpetrated, till every
denunciatory epithet in his vocabulary was exhausted,
and he now greatly rejoiced at the prospect of peace
being restored to the world.   He thus gives expression
to his feelings on the occasion:—

"Friday, 8th April, 1814.—The bells of Dumfries rang on
account of the news that the Allies have defeated Bonaparte,
and, in consequence, have entered Paris on capitulation!
Where shall the tyrant now find a place of safety?   His wife
and son are taken out of town to some asylum, but the
narrow house seems to be the only place which can shelter
him from the vengeance of the Cossacks and the indignation
of the Allies.   The white cockade is now flying, I trust, over
France, and the legitimate sovereign of that unhappy country

will soon put on the crown! Peace will return with the *Lilies* of the Bourbons and reign long over the Continent, undisturbed by the clangour of arms and the din of war!! Amen. 11th April.—The dynasty of Napoleon—the scourge of nations—the Goth of Corsica—is at an end. He has resigned the crown, after the Senate had pronounced him unworthy of reigning, and declared the throne forfeited! His conduct on that occasion was as base and pusillanimous as it was cruel and always tyrannical. He has closed a reign of unparalleled despotism by a resignation of equal meanness and abject abasement. He is to be permitted to retire to the island of Elba, in the Tuscan Sea, celebrated for nothing but its productions of marble and iron; and now it receives into its bosom a composition harder and more untractable than either of these. May he there find repentance for the blood he has shed, if so be there is yet hope. The finger, the hand, the arm, the bare and outstretched arm, of Jehovah was there. Let the isles be glad, and Britain, in the midst of her success, rejoice in her God and King!"

In the jubilation which prevailed he burst into song with the following tribute to the memory of the late Prime Minister:—

ODE TO THE MEMORY OF WILLIAM PITT.

" Father of verse, lord of the golden lyre,
   Give me a patriot's rage, a poet's fire,
   To sing of Freedom's laurels bravely won,
   And plant them on the grave of Chatham's son.
               There shall they grow,
               While Thames shall flow—
               There still be seen,
               Wide-spread and green—
   There Britain's sons shall catch the patriot flame,
   And fan the fire with Pitt's immortal name.

"When Gallia's despot swayed his iron rod,
And vanquished nations trembled at his nod,
With lurid smile he looked across the main,
And vowed to bind Britannia in his chain.
            The Goddess scorned his vow,
            Nor to his will would bow—
            With dauntless look
            Her spear she shook—
Then loud her martial shell indignant blew,
And quick to arms insulted Europe flew."

* * * * * * *

Serenity now reigns supreme in the minister's study,
and his diary, which had become quite obese with war
bulletins and reflections thereon, is now devoted to the
records of a different character. It tells of sermons
preached by himself and others, books read and criticized,
sick-beds visited, funerals attended, infants baptized,
catechisings held, and, in short, the faithful discharge of
pastoral duty in all its ramifications, betokening peace
on earth and goodwill to men. The serenity, however,
is but short-lived. Elba is not the "narrow house"
above referred to, and there must be more turmoil as
well as bloodshed in the world ere peace is finally established. We do not envy the possession of the feelings
with which the following notes must have been written,
after the decided conviction that the power of the despot
had been crushed for ever:—

"10th March, 1815.—Heard that Bonaparte has left
Elba, like Satan from hell, and, with 1000 men or Guards,
has landed in France, and penetrated as far as Lyons! He
no doubt has had promises of concurrence, not only from
many active and restless individuals in France, but also from
some State, or States, who are not satisfied with the arrange

ments made at Vienna. Maddison in America, and Murat in Italy, may also have contributed to raise this Demon of war, this Fury of blood and massacre. The dogs of war may be for a little let slip, but confusion terrible and sure awaits this Corsican prowler. The prisoners who have returned to France, as well as many idle, ambitious, and discontented spirits, may wish to join his gonfalon of death; but the marshals in general will find it their interest to adhere to the present order of things; and all the well-disposed of the people will execrate the tyrant who wishes again to embroil the country in war. The arch Napoleon has chosen indeed an evil hour for Europe to make this last, and to him, I trust, fatal attempt. The discontents of some of the nations at the decision of the Congress have not yet abated and subsided. Britain is agitated by corn-laws; and to these things in Europe, America has been successful over the British troops. Taking all these things together, and the unaccountable delay of crowning Louis at Paris, it was a bold and magnanimous plan, hatched in despair, and hazarded in delirium of mortified ambition, to reverse the order of things once more, to seat himself on the throne which he had usurped, and to rule with a rod of iron a people whom he had insulted. The Supreme Ruler, I trust, will defeat his schemes, put a hook in his nose, and bring back this chief of the children of pride by the way which he came, and bring his counsels to nought."

" 17th April, 1815.—The Allied Powers have issued a declaration that they have no designs to interfere with the internal affairs of France, but they will not treat on any terms with the usurper. How matters may go, it is not very easy to presage. It is not unlikely that the French marshals, with Bonaparte at their head, will muster all the means of a desperate effort to preserve the tyrant on the throne of the Louises. But I have little doubt that the force which the Allied Powers will bring against these desperadoes will be sufficient to discomfit and root up the military banditti who may follow the standard of the usurper. Whether even Louis shall regain his throne seems problematical, but I trust that the dynasty of Napoleon is ended—for ever! There is a race under arms in France which, it would appear, must be cut off before either their own country or Europe in general, or the world at large, can enjoy the blessings of established peace. In the Roman history there is an opinion that the heads of the tallest poppies should be cut off. It may be said that the heads of the most prominent *puppies* now in France should be taken off, and immolated to the *manes* of the innocent victims they have butchered, and offered in the temple of Peace! Bloody and dolorous bulletin!"

"25th June, 1815.—A great battle has taken place on the 18th, not very far from Mount St. John (Waterloo). The arch rebel having laid his plans with his hordes of banditti to cut off the armies of Blucher and Wellington, before the Russians should come up, made a most desperate attack on the former at daybreak, upon which they were obliged to fall back on their reinforcements. The gallant Duke soon made them repent their temerity in attacking him. A decisive battle was obtained—150 pieces of cannon, 2 eagles, &c., &c.!! Napoleon can now no more blame the elements, or circumstances. The place, and time, and manner of attack were all of his own choosing—he often led on his soldiers in person—but a mightier genius was opposed to him, the immortal British commander—*Wellington!* The consequences of this victory are incalculable—the Bourbons may yet be restored—the Jacobins confounded—peace concluded on a solid basis—the false philosophy exploded—religion honoured—and God glorified! It has been demonstrated by experiment on the broadest scale, that among the excellent advantages of true religion, one is, that it ever produces order, fidelity, and bravery on the field of battle, as well as virtue and happiness in the shade of peace. Bas le tyran! Vivent les Bourbons! The Duke of Wellington for ever!! God save the King!!!"

We have no doubt that some of the above epithets and expressions will be regarded as strong, terribly strong, and even such as could scarcely be expected from one professedly a messenger of peace; but it was because Mr. Wightman was a lover of peace he used them, and held in detestation the man who was so recklessly destroying the peace of the world. But the strongest of these designations, and the most opprobrious, Bonaparte applied to himself when addressing the fear-stricken and almost speechless deputies of the Senate on the subject of his future proceedings. " I have 80,000 men," said he; "I have gunboats; I will have no more inquisition, no more Senate; *I will be an Attila to Venice.*" And who was the great model he thus sought to imitate? Attila was a celebrated King of the Huns, who died about the middle of the fifth century. He assumed the title of the " Scourge of God," from the savage heroism, or rather barbarism, with which he attacked, and conquered, and devastated almost every province of Europe, and gloried in dragging at his chariot wheels the kings whose countries he had subdued. In the reign of Valentinian he attacked the Roman Empire with 500,000 men, and laid it in ruins. His desire was to conquer the whole world, but he died suddenly, on the night of his marriage, in a state of intoxication. Such was Attila, as described by historians. None but great

warriors whose ambition was insatiable did Bonaparte
set before him as examples of military renown. Like
another Alexander, the world was too small for his soul.
"Your little Europe," he said, "is but a molehill, and
could not supply glory enough; I will go and demand it
of the East,—of that land of wonders, which alone has
seen great empires and great revolutions, and is in-
habited by six hundred millions of men." What is to
be thought of the man that makes a bloody attack upon
some helpless outposts for the mere amusement of his
mistress, and that she might have her curiosity gratified
by seeing somewhat of the nature of war? Yet here
are his own words in communication with a friend—
"Riding with her one day in the middle of our positions
in the environs of the hill of Tenda, whilst reconnoitring
as commandant of the artillery, the notion suddenly
occurred to me of treating her to the spectacle of a little
war, and I ordered an attack of advanced posts. We
were the conquerors, it is true, but there could evidently
be no result. The attack was a pure fancy, and yet
some men fell in it. Later, I have bitterly reproached
myself with this affair whenever it has recurred to me."
But we cease from making further quotations from his
own words, as we deem what has been given sufficient
for our purpose, to vindicate Mr. Wightman in the
epithets and expressions he employed in speaking of
Napoleon Bonaparte.

The rejoicing consequent upon the glorious victory of
Waterloo was universal and unbounded, as it was believed
that the nations of Europe would now enjoy a solid and
lasting peace. But amid the jubilation which agitated
every breast, there was an undertone of sadness at the

thought that there were many weeping in sorrow at the loss they had sustained, and in the prospect of want, now that the support of the household was gone. Never was a picture more truly drawn than that by Mrs. Opie in her pathetic story of the "Orphan Boy," and especially in the following stanzas :—

> " The people's shouts were long and loud;
>   My mother, shuddering, closed her ears:
> ' Rejoice! Rejoice!' still cried the crowd—
>   My mother answered with her tears!

> "' Oh! why do tears steal down your cheek,'
>   Cried I, ' while others shout for joy ?'
> She kissed me, and in accents weak
>   She called me her ' poor orphan boy!'"

Contributions were everywhere called for and received on behalf of the widows and families of the brave men who had fallen on that memorable field. In the Presbytery of Dumfries it was unanimously resolved and appointed that a collection should be made in the various churches within the bounds for this purpose, which was cordially responded to by the several congregations, the sum of £178 5s. 2d. being obtained and forwarded to the Committee of the Waterloo Fund in London. This was irrespective of public subscriptions received by house-to-house visitation. But though the tempest was over, it was a considerable time before the agitation of the waves subsided—all kinds of provisions kept enormously high, and the labouring classes had the greatest difficulty in procuring food. In many places it could scarcely be had at any price, as the war had consumed almost everything. The prices of oatmeal and grain were not again equalled for thirty-two years, and butcher-meat was never thought of by the working poor. Many a child was put hungry and supperless to bed because there was nothing to eat, and the mother adopted the *ruse* of stilling the cries that pierced her heart by sticking a crumb of liquorice or black sugar upon the thumb of each child, and so, while sucking it, the poor things fell asleep.

Mr. Wightman happened to be in Edinburgh during the following year, when a regiment of Highlanders, who had greatly distinguished themselves at Waterloo, passed up the street to their quarters in the Castle. He was so overcome with patriotic emotion at the sight that he uncovered his head and walked a considerable way alongside of them, hat in hand, every now and again clapping them on the shoulder and exclaiming, "Brave fellows! Brave fellows!" while the tears were running down his cheeks all the time. On the anniversary of that glorious event, a year or two after its occurrence, four troops of the Scots Greys, who had gallantly fought on that memorable field, were quartered for a few days in Dumfries, on their way to Ireland. Embracing the opportunity so happily afforded, some of the leading inhabitants made a liberal subscription for the purpose of giving these veterans a complimentary dinner on that auspicious day. On the preceding evening, for that was all the time they had to prepare, the committee were consulting what they should do for a chaplain, when one of them cried out—"Here comes the minister of Kirkmahoe—a better chaplain for such an occasion is not in all the South." Their request was complied with, and on the following day nearly 200 non-commissioned officers and privates sat down to a sumptuous banquet.

After dinner, Mr. Wightman recited the following verses in honour of the brave men present:—

THE SCOTS GREYS.

"Old Scotia's sons, whose swords and burnished mail
 Flash terror on your foes, we bid you hail!
Warriors of Waterloo, who nobly stood
 Like walls of adamant in seas of blood;
Who checked the Tyrant's pride and crushed his power,
 By one brave charge in one decisive hour!
We hear Napoleon praise the gallant Greys—
 We see his pallid look, which fear betrays—
We hear your shout, which rent the sulphury air,
 And struck his firmest lines with mute despair:—
'Scotland for ever!' with electric roll,
 Rings on our ear and ruffles up our soul.
As when through Soignies forest zephyrs sweep,
 Or curl the expanse of Caledonia's deep,
Our hearts are moved, our spirits wildly play,
 In memory of that grand auspicious day,
When Rose and Thistle, aye, and Shamrock joined,
 To form the wreath which Victory then entwined;
When Fame's loud trumpet, heard o'er sea and land, .
 Proclaimed the honours of your noble band.
From your own mountains we fresh garlands bind
 Of blooming heath, fanned by our Northern wind;
The humble chaplet you will deign to wear,
 And to your graves our warm affections bear.
Safe may you reach old Erin's fertile plains,
 To guard her lovely nymphs and guileless swains;
And happy may you be till life's last flow!
 May virtue in your dying bosoms glow!
When your cold dust is gathered with the dead,
 Soft be the turf that wraps the Soldier's head;
When rest your spirits with the good and brave,
 Sweet be the flower that blooms upon your grave!"

At the conclusion the whole company rose in a body and returned their hearty acknowledgments to the

reverend author.   After they had retired to their
quarters the men requested the officers' permission to
march out on the following Sunday and hear sermon in
Kirkmahoe church, which was granted; but, unfortunately, on that morning, when all had assembled and
were ready to march, a heavy rain came on, which
prevented them from carrying their purpose into effect.
Had it been otherwise, what a memorable day had that
been to pastor and people!   As one after another, to the
number of two hundred, entered with measured pace
the venerable sanctuary, we can imagine the patriotic
man of God involuntarily exclaiming—"Warriors of
Waterloo, we bid you hail!"

Old Anacreon found himself unable to cope with more
than one theme when he struck his lyre, and greatly
bewailed his inaptitude when inclination or circumstances prompted him to change the nature of his song.
He tells us that, wishing to chant the exploits in battle
of the sons of Atreus, he strung his lyre anew, that he
might do full justice to the subject, and he boldly put
forth his hand in a martial spirit, but, to his great
bewilderment, it sounded love alone!   Mr. Wightman
could sing on any theme, his harp being equally adapted
for love and war.   But lately we heard him making the
welkin ring with warlike strains; and though his breast
is still heaving with emotion at the late rapacities of
the ambitious Corsican, yet how gently he sings an
epithalamium on the marriage of the Prince of Saxe-
Coburg and her Royal Highness the Princess Charlotte
of Wales!   The whole kingdom is rejoicing—nay,
the whole of Nature, as well as he, at the happy
event:—

NUPTIAL ODE.

"'Mid war's red ruins now the olive springs,
  Now dove-eyed peace expands her snowy wings,
  Hoar Winter's blasts in sullen march retire,
  And Spring's soft gales the gentle loves inspire!
            Fair Brunswick's flower,
            On Hymen's bower,
            Sheds perfume sweet
            When two hearts meet!
  The lovely violets their petals rear,
  And feathered minstrels hail the opening year!

" Old Ocean's billows in hoarse concert swell,
  And every sea-green Nereid blows her shell,
  While Thames from rustling reeds uplifts his head,
  Pleased to perceive the festive gambols spread.
            Awake the lyre,
            Each muse be fire,
            Let discord cease,
            And love increase!
  On Coburg's Prince bold Wallia's daughter smiles,
  And hope's bright star illumes the British Isles!"

This ode was copied into several newspapers, and was dated "Vale of Nith, May 2, 1816."

Mr. Wightman had a great ambition to write a longish poem, and composed several pieces in this way, some of which, however, never saw the light in print. The following fragment was among his earliest attempts of a lengthened kind in heroic verse, and whets the desire for something more of a similar kind:—

PATRIOTISM.

" From where yon heath-clad mountain props the sky,
  And headlong torrents whiten to the eye;
  Where sails the eagle through the deep of heaven,
  And forest oaks are oft by lightning riven;

P

Where cheerful shepherds chant the rustic song,
Where peers my natal dome the woods among;
Come, Patriotism, come inspire my lays,
And crown thy votary with a poet's bays.
So shall the herd of censors idly rave,
To merge my song in dark oblivion's wave.
He comes! He brightens on the Muse's sight,
The Patriot Power, in majesty of light.
An oaken branch adorns his temples fair,
His snow-white robe streams proudly on the air.
An azure zone, wide-circling, binds his waist,
'God, and my country,' sparkles on his breast.
High, in one hand, an ivy wreath he brings,
The other holds a harp with golden strings.
'This diadem,' he says, 'shall grace thy brow,
This harp the subject soul shall teach to bow.'
Thy mystic harp, sweet power, then let me string,
And what thou deign'st to dictate, dare to sing.
Who can explain great Tully's gentle law,
Which all our heart, in cords of love, can draw,
And, though to earth's far verge we stretch the chain,
Still leads us to our native land again?

        " The exile's eye hence closes not in sleep,
Or opens but to languish and to weep.
The fettered captive hence is taught to smile,
And all his fears and sorrows to beguile.
The mariner, when cast on foreign strand,
Hence moors his wishes in his native land.
When Israel's captive sons their vigils kept,
By Babel's streams they thought of home and wept.
Their sacred harps they pensively unstrung,
And on the boughs of drooping willows hung;
Insulting o'er their bleeding country's wrongs,
Their tyrants cried, 'Sing one of Zion's songs!'
They spurned the mandate with supreme disdain,
For there they could not sing Jehovah's strain.
In Fancy's view the heights of Salem rose,
Where still they hoped for freedom and repose,
When like the rivers of the south was turned

The bondage under which they long had mourned—
When Zion's hills their sacred summits showed,
Their hearts were full, their eyes with tears o'erflowed,
They stood with one consent mute and amazed,
And on their own green confines fondly gazed.
What moved the loud and universal cry,
Which from mount Teches rent the Colchian sky,
When the retreating myriad, Græcia's pride,
Worn by rude warfare, hailed the Euxine tide?
'Twas Patriotism's powerful influence all,
The thoughts of home, deep mustering at his call.

"In yon rude hut on wild Kamtschatka's bay
KING and his friends felt patriotic sway—
When on the half-worn spoon they fairly traced
The dear word 'London,' not by time effaced,
To home and country their affections turned,
And every heart with British feeling burned.
What means yon hoary pilgrim bent with years,
Whose furrowed cheeks are wet with briny tears?
Why does yon ivied oak attract his eye,
Or the meandering brook which murmurs by?
Why does he to yon mossy bank repair
And pluck the flowers which scent the desert air?
Why sits he down among yon ruined walls,
And fondly scenes of other years recalls?
Ah! there his eyes first saw the light of day,
There was his 'careless childhood' wont to 'stray'
Where now the wild bee hums along the green,
And here and there a garden flower is seen,
Where sprigs of eglantine shed sweetness round,
And solitary hawthorn crowns the mound—
With brothers, sisters, and companions dear,
When life was new, he summer bowers would rear,
Or ply with little spade the easy toil,
And emulously dig and dress the soil;
Where'er he walks or turns his glistening eyes,
A thousand forms in wild confusion rise,
In Fancy's sight the soft illusions play,
And mingle in the beam of life's declining day.

" I marked the time-worn stranger, feeble, lame,
Till tottering to the churchyard's gate he came.
There, leaning on his staff, he looked around,
Then faltered forward, lost in thought profound.
He stops at last beside a moss-grown grave,
While on the evening breeze his gray locks wave.
I saw new paleness o'er his visage spread
As he surveyed the mansions of the dead.
So yon pale crescent sheds a sickly light,
Seen through the thickening damps of coming night.
The grassy turf on which his eyes are fixed
Blooms o'er the dust of both his parents mixed.
The sacred spot his falling tears bedew,
As days of youth are seen in dim review.
In Fancy's vision rapt he climbs the knees
Of his fond father, and his mother sees,
With looks parental, kindled at the heart,
And claiming in his happiness a part.
He stands the pleasing frenzy to pursue,
Till he half thinks the dream of fancy true.
His eyes I saw him raise as from a trance,
And half erect with eager steps advance
To where the church with open portals stood,
Which soon he entered in his thoughtful mood.
Within those holy walls, in former days,
He heard Heaven's truth, and joined in prayer and praise.
There oft his soul had owned Religion's sway,
And every wayward passion fled away;
His young ambition there was wont to rise
And scorn to settle lower than the skies.
The preacher's well-known face he seemed to see,
To hear the voice which spoke of Heaven's decree,
The notes of harmony yet flowed around,
Lo! God was there, he trode on holy ground.
'Oh! what,' he cries, 'is all beneath the sun,
To him whose glass of life is nearly run,
If interest he has none in Heaven's great plan
Of love and mercy to apostate man!
But what though time in outward frame should bend,
To meet that dust with which it soon must blend;

What though it should dissolve and melt away,
In yonder low and lonely bed of clay,
If yet his deathless soul aloft shall fly
To realms of endless bliss above the sky!
In Hope's soft bosom shall his flesh repose,
Till Time's revolving centuries shall close.
Then shall at length his slumbering ashes wake,
And his whole frame eternal joys partake!'

" See Israel's warriors on yon mountain's brow,
And Elah's valley stretching green below.
Philistia's sons against them stand arrayed,
Each army on its mountain height displayed!
Look! from the steeps descends a giant form,
Like winter's cloud, and fierce as winter's storm.
Now, in the valley, see he proudly stands,
And sternly frowns on Israel's frightened bands.
Hark! loud as thunder his bold challenge sounds,
While from the hills a hollow voice rebounds.
His burnished mail shines awful on the sight,
And from his helmet beams a brazen light.
High in the air he brandishes his spear,
With patriot shouts his friends their champion cheer.
Shame and chill fear through Israel's columns reign,
For none dare meet Goliath on the plain.
Like some brass column blazing in the sun,
He proudly stands and deems the day is won.
But lo! what stripling moves across the vale,
His golden tresses floating in the gale,
Whose blooming looks no marks of warfare show,
And on whose modest cheek fresh roses blow.
Though come from Israel's camp and harnessed lines,
On him no mail, no burning helmet shines.
His shepherd's staff and scrip, his trusty sling,
Are all the warlike arms he seems to bring.
Yet this young hero from the shepherd's fold,
A Patriot turns—for Israel's glory bold.
The towering Philistine anon draws near,
Nor doubts his sweeping sword, or massive spear;
With threats and curses while the mountains ring,

The son of Jesse triumphs with a sling.
Swift through the air the polished pebble flies,
And smites Goliath—see, he falls, and dies!

" Such, too, the patriots and the heroes bold,
If tales be true which ancient fame has told,
Who, self-devoted, Death's dark shades would brave,
Their country from impending fate to save.
The Spartan band moves in my fancy's eye,
Resolved to defend the Pass, or die.
I hear their lion-hearted leader vow,
That night to banquet with the gods below.
I hear Attilius bid his friends adieu,
His fixed and fatal measure to pursue.
I see the Fabii and the Decii fall,
True to their country, ready at her call.
So falls great Moore on famed Corunna's strand,
So flows his life-blood for his native land,
While Gallia's eagles flap their sullen wing,
And o'er his closing eyes their dusky shadows fling.

" Nor does the Muse rejoice to wheel her flight
Where rival nations and their champions fight,
To dip in human gore her peaceful wing,
Of wounds, and groans, and agonies to sing.
Her emblem in yon dove is better seen,
Which, soaring, bears a leaf of olive green.
But let her country's cause once fire her breast,
She spreads her plumes and ruffles up her crest..
So that domestic bird that leads her brood
Beside the garden wall and sheltering wood,
If hovering kite or hawk she chance to spy,
Or if some surly mastiff trudges by,
Her head she raises and her pinions spreads,
Nor death nor danger for herself she dreads,
But feels new courage through her bosom thrill,
And ready stands her life's last blood to spill."

     *   *   *   *   *   *   *   *

As we have already said, this is but a fragment of a poem on Patriotism, which was originally intended to be drawn out to considerable length, but, like many other intentions, in being temporarily set aside, it was at last forgotten.

CHAPTER XII.

THE CAMERONIANS—MEET AT QUARRELWOOD—THE "FOUR JOHNS"—
WIDE CIRCUIT OF SUPERINTENDENCE—CONGREGATION OFFENDED
AT THEIR MINISTER PLAYING ON THE VIOLIN—DEPUTATION SENT
TO REMONSTRATE—COMMUNION AT QUARRELWOOD—MEETING-
HOUSE ERECTED—DISPERSION—THE BUCHANITES—THEIR PECU-
LIAR TENETS—EXPELLED FROM IRVINE—SETTLE IN CLOSEBURN—
MOBBED BY THE INHABITANTS—RIDICULOUS ATTEMPT AT TRANS-
LATION—RETIRE TO AUCHENGIBBERT—BREAK UP OF THE SECT.

THE Reformed Presbyterians, or Cameronians, as they
were commonly called, occupied at one time too prominent a position in the parish to be passed over with
the mere mention of their name. Though they were
never by any means a numerous body in the Nithsdale
district, yet many came from far distances to Sunday
worship at the village of Quarrelwood, their principal
station. How or why they settled down there for
religious purposes we have no means of determining,
and cannot even suggest a reason for their doing so,
any more than for the hiving of bees upon one tree
rather than another. Instinct is at all times powerful,
and with this body it seems to have been always in
powerful operation, for wherever a fragment of the old
Covenanting banner fluttered there was a gathering of
the clan. Mr. Wightman found them at first rather a
thorn in the flesh, as their aversion to the Established
Church caused some of the more thoughtless of them to
propagate any gossip, however groundless, against his

professional discharge of duty, as well as his private intercourse with his people. He had the prudence not to retaliate, sorely as he felt their calumnies, and we need not wonder that he was extremely sensitive on the occasional absence of some of his hearers on a great field-day at Quarrelwood. Thus he writes:—

"Sunday, 13th July, 1806.—At home. Cameronian Sacrament day at Quarrelwood. Day warm, cloudy—preparing rain. Carnsalloch family returned from London— were in church. The church was well filled, considering the Sacrament at Quarrelwood; yet I was somewhat affected to see the seats of several families empty who live in this end of the parish. I think it is a duty the inhabitants of a parish who profess attachment to the established religion to show this attachment by attending the church, and when sermon is over there, they might with more reason gratify their curiosity and inclination in hearing other teachers. This was the case with my elders and servants, and many respectable persons in the parish, who came first to their own church, and afterwards went to the Dissenters. Such a day as this is a kind of sifting day, which tries the solid grain and the chaff—I mean as to the attachment which persons have for the Establishment, and not with regard to what is really right."

Though for nearly fifty years there was no church for the people to worship in, or manse for the minister to live in, the general body of the members did not seem to consider this a grievance or any privation, for when a building was erected a considerable number refused to enter it, declaring they had been driven to the hills, and on the hills they would remain. Hence the name they sometimes bore of Hill-men, or Mountain-men, which gained them considerable sympathy, as implying hardship and privation. In the course of a short time, however, they thought better of the matter, and agreed to worship with their less refractory brethren within a tenement which shielded them from the weather. What was called the northern and the southern congregations were presided over by four clergymen, all bearing the Christian name of John, and hence commonly spoken of as the "four Johns." These were John M'Millan and John Thorburn, who held the collegiate charge of the northern congregation—John Courtass and John Fairley, who held that of the south-ern. They have been characterized in one of their own magazines as "lovely examples of Christian character, and impressive patterns of ministerial fidelity, who did much to stem the torrent of declining virtue, and pro-mote the cause of truth and righteousness in a bad time." Perhaps the torrent of increasing vice would have been a more appropriate expression; but be that as it may, they appear to have been very able and zealous ministers, and were much respected by those for whose spiritual welfare they laboured, as well as by many outside the pale of their own denomination. It does not fall within our scope to give a history of these clergymen severally, but only to notice them in connection with Cameronianism at the time when it may be said to have flourished in the district in its purest and most original form.

Mr. Courtass, the first minister at Quarrelwood, was ordained at Craighead, 17th September, N.S., 1755, to the charge of the southern congregation, which extended

over an area of nearly forty parishes, so that he might
be said to have had the oversight of a *diocese*, much as
he abhorred the name. The circuit was, indeed, a wide
one, and to allot it to the care of one individual, however
robust his body, willing his disposition, or powerful his
mind, was an utter absurdity. In agricultural phrase, it
was "losing heads gathering straws"—aiming at universal responsibility, as if there were no means of religious
instruction besides. It was cruelty to him and starvation to the people—cruelty, by the toil and travel
imposed, starvation as to religious ordinances, these
being in any one place necessarily "few and far between."
And what was the extent of Mr. Courtass' supervision?
It comprehended "the whole of Annandale and Nithsdale south of Queensberry, and centre of Keir, and a
part of the Stewartry of Kirkcudbright as far as the
Water of Urr, some twenty miles distant from Quarrelwood, to the south-west," an area nearly as extensive as
the county of Dumfries. Nor was this the whole; there
was also a portion of Ireland included, where the minister
had to officiate annually for several months. In the year
following that of his ordination, Mr. Courtass was in
Ireland from July till October, busily preaching, bap-
tizing, and giving in marriage, thereby exercising the
vagum ministerium in its fullest extent. From his
own records, now before us, we find that he officiated in
ministerial capacity at Vow, Drummond, Ballyspalen,
Londonderry, Jarkiveny, Killyleagh, Clochmore, Ardoch,.
Magherafelt, Ballymena, Playmore, Glen of Larne, Done-
gore, Artary, Clendermont, Ballywatick, and Newton-
breda. After a life of wide and active usefulness in
his Master's vineyard, he died in 1795, having baptized.

in the course of his ministry 752 children, celebrated 178 marriages, and preached sermons without number.

A few years after his ordination, the labour being considered excessive for any one man's strength, in addition to the hungry bleating of the flock for larger supply of pasture, and perhaps a desire to increase the fold, the office-bearers of the congregation resolved to appoint a colleague to him, who might occupy some distant district and allow him to be longer at home. Accordingly, we find the following minute in reference to the matter:—"Woodhall, First Monday of August, 1763.—In consequence of a minute, last meeting of Presbytery, appointing the Rev. Mr. John Courtass to moderate in a call to the Southern Congregation at their desire, the Rev. Mr. John Courtass represented to the meeting that, at a meeting of electors at Quarrelwood, 11th July last, appointed for foresaid purpose, he had moderated in said affair, and a blank call being presented, it was unanimously agreed by the electors there present, in name of all their constituents, that the call should be filled up with the name of Mr. John Fairley, preacher of the gospel, which was accordingly done, and said call subscribed by them in presence of the Moderator and two neutral men as witnesses, as is attested on the back of said call; and thereupon the said Mr. Courtass presented the foresaid call to the Presbytery, which was received by them." In December following, at a meeting of Presbytery held at Leadhills, Mr. Fairley was, "in the name and by the authority of the Lord Jesus Christ, the glorious and alone Head of the Church, by solemn prayer and imposition of the hands of the Presbytery, set apart to the office of the ministry," and after receiving the right hand of fellowship from the brethren as co-presbyter, took his seat accordingly, with one Francis Halliday chosen for his elder.

Mr. Fairley's basis of operations was Douglas Water, so that the Quarrelwood district was but occasionally favoured with his ministrations. He was an estimable man, of somewhat peculiar appearance, but highly respected by all classes for his sincere piety and earnest zeal in the work of the Church. The Ettrick Shepherd speaks of him as " the good John Fairley, a man whom I knew and loved. I think I see him now, with his long white hair, and his look mild, eloquent, and sagacious. He was a giver of good counsel, a sayer of wise sayings, with wit at will, learning in abundance, and a gift in sarcasm which the wildest dreaded." While regarded as an excellent preacher, he was specially noted for the roughness of his rebukes in cases of scandal before the congregation, as all such discipline was exercised in those days in accordance with Paul's advice to Timothy —" Them that sin rebuke before all, that others also may fear." His addresses to the delinquents were always more plain than pleasant, except to onlookers who came for the purpose of being amused, and to such the plainer the pleasanter was the language used. A poor creature who had fallen from her integrity was ordered to stand before the congregation on a certain day, and make atonement for her fault in the shape of public repentance. It soon became bruited abroad what was to happen, and on the day appointed a great crowd assembled from long distances to enjoy the scene. Mr. Fairley was apprised of this before entering the tent by one of his elders, and he bethought himself what he would do. At the close of the service he ordered the woman to stand up, in a tone sterner than usual, which was considered ominous of a grand onslaught on immorality in general, and on the trembling culprit in particular. All held their breath in deadly silence, and eagerly awaited the bursting of the storm. Here it is— "Jane Smith, you have committed a great wickedness; go and sin no more, lest a worse thing befall you!" The amusement seekers were greatly disappointed, declared to one another on their way home that he had not done his duty—that he had not rebuked at all, but by his leniency had rather given encouragement to sin. They were well served for their prurient curiosity, and could not conceal their chagrin. Mr. Fairley died on the 18th of April, 1806, in the seventy-seventh year of his age, and the forty-fourth of his ministry, and was buried in Douglas churchyard, a very large number of persons attending the funeral. A few days before his death the ministers of the Presbytery came to see him, when one of them engaged in a very lengthened prayer, during which he called out with a very feeble voice—"Stop! stop! I cannot follow you any longer. Sickbeds and deathbeds cannot do with long prayers; duties should be pointed but not lengthened out"—a most judicious advice, with all the solemn sanction of the distant land in view.

By far the most popular of the Quarrelwood ministers was the Rev. James Thomson, well known as the author of two volumes of sermons of a superior character on doctrinal and practical subjects. His name is still fragrant among those of his flock who survive, now few in number, and like a cardinal point in their creed they are careful to instil into the hearts of their descendants a strict veneration for the memory of the good Mr. Thomson of Quarrelwood. He was the son of a joiner in Kilsyth, and was born in the year 1760. He learned his father's trade, and subsequently found his knowledge of carpentry of immense advantage in the circumstances in which he was placed. He was not, however, destined to be a joiner, except in a high and holy sense, having had an early aspiration for the office of the ministry in connection with the Cameronian body, to which the family belonged. After going through the requisite curriculum at the University of Glasgow, and a course of divinity under the teaching of his own Presbytery, he was licensed to preach the gospel wherever his lot might fall, which soon appeared to be the charge of the Quarrelwood congregation. He was then in his thirty-sixth year. Mr. Courtass had died the previous year, and the office of pastor still remained vacant. In due course he was ordained September, 1796, and entered upon the onerous office with a determination to spend and be spent in the sacred cause. It is not too much to say that the heyday of Cameronianism in Nithsdale was during his incumbency, and in no small degree arose from his great ability as a preacher, and his judicious administration of sessional affairs. While he was equally ardent with his brethren, he was more intelligent in a common-sense light, less wedded to cant forms and phrases, took a larger and more Christian view of other denominations than his own, and consequently made a wider impression of his usefulness as a minister of the gospel of Christ.

Many in the world do not recognize blessings when they are sent them, and would have everything moulded after their bigoted opinion of what is right. Of this number the congregation at Quarrelwood formed a part. The week following Mr. Thomson's ordination they sent à deputation to him complaining that his voice was not solemn enough while preaching; it had too worldly a tone, and they urged him to adopt the *drant* which their late minister, Mr. Courtass, had always used so well. Mr. Thomson was astonished and indignant. He replied that he would employ the tone that was natural and that God had given him, and he requested to be no more annoyed with their interference in such childish matters, and with which they had nothing to do. The deputation retired discomfited. Mr. Thomson was a very fine performer on the violin, and was accustomed to relax his mind after long and severe study by taking an hour with his favourite instrument in the evening, and driving " dull care away." This was, however, too much levity for douce Cameronians, especially for one appointed to minister in holy things, and set an example to the flock. It was not to be tolerated, and at one of their meetings, held without the minister, a deputation was ordered to wait upon him and remonstrate with him upon his conduct, setting forth the great scandal it brought upon religion in general, and upon themselves in particular, who ought to be perfect patterns of true godliness in the midst of a crooked and perverse genera- tion. John the Baptist had lost his head by a dancing girl, and every follower of the Baptist should discoun- tenance the means by which he was cut off from the world. But they omitted to notice two things con- nected with the decapitation—the music supplied to the dancing maiden was not that of a fiddle, and Mr. Thomson played for his own gratification, and not as a dance fiddler, where there was no one but himself to perform in either capacity. Some one was kind enough to inform the minister of the invasion which was about to be made upon his domestic privacy, and he prepared himself for the attack.

On the appointed evening he was on the look-out, and when the enemy were in sight, approaching with authoritative tread, he took from the corner of a lumber-room a large bass-fiddle, and was thrumming over its *thairms* in the most lugubrious and discordant tones, when the deputation was ushered in. "Come away, gentlemen," said Mr. Thomson, "I am glad to see you, for I have been studying hard all day, and I was just trying to get a little relaxation." He immediately ordered in refreshments for the gentlemen, of which they freely partook, and, after an hour's conversation on nothing in particular, save the prospect of a good harvest, they left the minister without uttering a single word of their errand, to report the result of their interview to their constituents. That report was short, but to the point, as all such reports should be. They said "they had waited upon the minister as desired; that when they entered he was indeed playing, but it was on the big, gaucy, solemn, bass-violin, and not on the wee wicked fiddle, as had been represented, and they were sorry they had engaged in the job." Mr. Thomson was never again disturbed either as to his fiddling or his preaching.

Mr. Thomson divided his labours between Dumfriesshire and the Stewartry, officiating in each every alternate month. "In the former, Quarrelwood was the

Q

usual place of worship; in the latter, the places varied according to circumstances for the accommodation of the people. Sometimes he preached at the farmhouses of members in one parish, and sometimes in another—from a tent in the fields in summer, and in a barn in winter. On these occasions he did not need to dwell in his own hired house; he was hospitably entertained by some one or other of the members of his congregation, who considered it a privilege and an honour to have a servant of Christ in their habitation. At Quarrelwood, he lectured from the Epistles to the Hebrews and Jude, and the first six chapters of Revelation, &c.; and in the Stewartry, from Hosea and the Song of Solomon. The attendance on his ministrations was generally numerous when the weather was propitious, particularly on Sacramental occasions. He preached long. In summer the service commenced at eleven A.M. and continued till about five P.M., with three-quarters of an hour of interval. On the Communion Sabbath he commenced the services with an introduction of some three-quarters of an hour in length, preached about two hours and a-half, debarred from the table, invited, and finished the first table service about four in the afternoon. His debarrations were generally minute and lengthened, his invitations comparatively short, alleging in vindication of his brevity in this department that professors are generally more in danger of approaching that solemn ordinance in an unprepared state than of neglecting it altogether. Several of his table addresses were deemed very remarkable, and remembered with intense interest by some of the communicants to the day of their death, and were referred

to with peculiar pleasure as table services from which
they had derived no small satisfaction and benefit." So
says a writer in the *Reformed Presbyterian Magazine*,
November, 1849, and there is no reason to doubt the
correctness of the data from which the above description is given.

There are one or two things, however, in connection
with the Quarrelwood Communions omitted, which we
are enabled to supply. These Communions were famous
in the district, and were attended by large numbers of
people, some of whom came a distance of thirty miles;
and as the services were never over till after sunset, it
was impossible they could return to their own homes the
same day. These far-comers generally started on the
Saturday, travelling all night, carrying provisions with
them, and drinking of the brook by the way. The tent
was placed in an open space, not always in the same
field, but where a level spot could be found for the Communion tables, and a rising ground in front for the
worshippers, somewhat like an amphitheatre. At the
entrance to the field was an array of ginger-bread and
sweetie stalls to captivate the young, while at no great
distance another emporium was open with ready wel-'
come for the benefit of those who thought they required
something more stimulating than ginger-bread and
confectionery. This, however, was not peculiar to
Quarrelwood, but was generally to be seen on similar
occasions almost everywhere. All the houses around
were full of visitors: couches, chairs, lang-settles, and
shake-downs being in requisition, and as the Monday
preachings were stayed for, it was Tuesday morning ere
many reached home. There was, therefore, the greater

part of four days consumed in the observance of this solemnity, but then, in the eyes of the worshippers, all the sacrifice they made, the travel they performed, and the fatigue they endured, added to the worth of their worship, and was therefore submitted to with the most religious zeal. Though this ordinance was dispensed only in summer when the days were long, yet the sun had always sunk in the west ere the solemnity was brought to a close; for as it was a day set apart for a special purpose, it would have been undervaluing the blessing, and almost sacrilege, to have dismissed the great congregation before the shades of evening necessitated a truce.

We said that Mr. Thomson found his knowledge of carpentry an advantage, and this was especially the case in the erection of a meeting-house and manse, which were only put up after he became minister. The greater portion of the joiner-work of these edifices was executed by himself. He made his own household furniture, the pulpit for Hightae, in the neighbourhood of Lochmaben, constructed more than one barometer, and even attempted a thrashing-machine to be driven by hand. But these things were not at all appreciated by his people, and though he preached to them sermons of two hours' duration, yet they thought that he often spent his time otherwise than for the edification of his flock. He died suddenly at Quarrelwood on the 18th of April, 1810, in the fiftieth year of his age, and the sixteenth of his ministry. He was buried in Kirkmahoe churchyard, where a gravestone records that "he was a man of distinguished talents, of profound theological knowledge, and of eminent piety. In private he maintained an

unblemished character.   He was a powerful and faithful
preacher, and his discourses always showed deep thought
and extensive research.   He was a diligent, affectionate,
and most exemplary pastor, although his flock was widely
scattered, and his congregational duties were, therefore,
peculiarly laborious."

Mr. Thomson was succeeded by the Rev. Mr. Jeffray,
a clergyman of great ability and varied talent; but
preachers began to be more plentiful, and new stations
being appointed for the greater convenience of worshippers, the congregation began to decline, the minister
resigned his charge, and henceforth the famous Quarrelwood meeting-house was entirely deserted, the worship
there having run the prescribed term of human existence—threescore and ten years.   If these were not sincere and earnest men in their religious principles, we
know not who are; they went ten, fifteen, and twenty
miles, every Sabbath-day, to worship the Lord their
Maker, and did not consider it any hardship to do so.
No doubt some may say that such things partook largely
of fanaticism or bigotry, but such harsh judgment ought
not to be so readily expressed.   True, they might have
worshipped God as acceptably in their several parish
churches as at Quarrelwood or anywhere else, but they
had a principle to carry out on which it may be said
their denominational existence depended, and they
deserve credit for the sternness of attitude, the singleness
of purpose, and the devotedness of heart with which that
principle was maintained.   They seemed to keep constantly before them that saying of Scripture, "No man
having put his hand to the plough, and looking back, is
fit for the kingdom of God."

Along with this respected body of Christians we would notice a sect of a far different description, a sort of Latter-day Saints, who invaded Nithsdale towards the close of the last century, but who did not succeed in attaching followers, except, to our astonishment, a few from our friends the Cameronians. They are known in history, for they are otherwise extinct, as the Buchanites, whose head was an illiterate and immoral woman, who, by her volubility of speech, hypocrisy, and assumption of divine origin, imposed upon a small knot of persons whose gullibility only equalled in greatness the impious daring of their female founder. Their whole story is ridiculous in the extreme, in some points painful, and in others important in an ethical view; but as the last of the sect in this country lived till far on in the present century, and was the custodier of all their documents, the information regarding them may be relied on as authentic. From these documents, and a pretty full narrative drawn up by the only survivor, the late Mr. Joseph Train produced a very interesting volume, entitled "The Buchanites," to which we are indebted for much of our knowledge with respect to that peculiar and self-deluded body of religious fanatics.

Elspath Simpson, or "Luckie Buchan," as she was familiarly called, was the daughter of a wayside alehouse-keeper in Banffshire, and was born in 1738. Before she was three years old her mother died, and her father having again married, she was put out to the *fremit*, where, as soon as she could herd a cow, she was assigned the duty. A distant relation, after whom she had been named, gave her a little instruction in reading and sewing, but at an early age she gave evidence of vicious propensities, which she maintained on principle till the time of her death. At Ayr she inveigled into marriage a working potter, called Robert Buchan, who soon had cause to repent of his indiscretion, as her vows of fidelity were cast to the winds, and, ashamed of her licentiousness, he removed to Banff, where he afterwards left her, with one son and two daughters, to shift for themselves. She opened a sewing and reading school for girls, and might have succeeded tolerably well had her conduct been in keeping with the office she assumed, which, unfortunately, it was not, and so the children were withdrawn. Strangely inconsistent, she pretended to be very pious, read the Scriptures, attended fellowship meetings, at which she debated on religious subjects, and had frequent discourse about Heaven and the soul with certain female acquaintances, whom she deluded with her hypocrisy and cant. She had been divorced from her husband, and became enamoured of a Relief minister in Irvine, the Rev. Hugh White, whom she heard preach in Glasgow, and whose vanity she flattered in a fulsome letter she sent him, declaring, "I have been more stumbled and grieved by ministers than by all the men in the world or by all the devils in hell; but I have rejoiced many times, by the eye of Faith, to see you before I saw you with the eyes of my body." The result was that, by invitation, she took up her abode in Mr. White's house in Irvine, with Mrs. White's consent, and henceforth had him as her main supporter in the faith she held.

By-and-by she became loftier in her pretensions and bolder in her speech. She declared that she was the Third Person in the Godhead—that she was the woman described in the Revelation as clothed with the sun, and Mr. White was the man-child she had brought forth, who was to rule all nations with a rod of iron—that she had the power of conferring immortality on whom she breathed—and that all her followers in a body would be translated to Heaven without tasting death. She further held that marriage was abolished at the termination of the bestial sacrifices, and that free-love was now the universal command. Maintaining such views and principles, it is astonishing that any one was weak enough to give her a listening ear, but still a number, comparatively small, became her followers. The Presbytery deposed Mr. White from the ministry as being heterodox, and dangerous to the morals of society. The inhabitants of the town became infuriated that such a pest should be allowed to remain amongst them, and insisted upon the immediate expulsion of the whole body, which was carried out under the protection of the magistrates, as otherwise it was almost certain that summary vengeance would be taken upon the delinquents. As it was, when the bounds of the burgh were passed, and the magisterial jurisdiction ceased, the mob with execrations proceeded to maltreat the leaders with the utmost persecution. Mrs. Buchan was thrown to the ground, kicked and tossed, and hair torn from her head. Others were thrown into the ditch, and every indignity and reproach cast upon them. At last, however, they got clear of their tormentors, and directed their steps towards the rising sun, from which quarter they expected the agents of their ascension to come. They made their way by easy stages through Mauchline, Cumnock, Kirkconnell, and Sanquhar, when the journey seemed to become too painful for them. Compared with the exodus of the Israelites they were a small body, only forty-six in number—men, women, and children—but they had higher aims than the land of Canaan, and they cheered one another along. By some unaccountable instinct, such as influences certain animals, they lighted on the farm of Cample, near Closeburn, where the tenant gave the use of his barn till he should need it for his grain; but offering them a site on which to erect a habitation for themselves. This offer they gratefully accepted; and as the barn was soon required, they set about the construction of their own abode, as several artisans were in the body. This is the description of the edifice given by one of their number, Andrew Innes:—"The house was only one story high, and covered with heather—it was thirty-six feet in length, and sixteen feet wide. There was a loft in it, made of poles from a neighbouring plantation, and these were covered with green turf, instead of boards. Something like a bedstead was formed by four boards being nailed together at each end; these were laid flat on the loft, and filled with straw, as soon as we could procure it. We had now two blankets for each bed—one below, and the other as a coverlet. The beds, now more numerous than when in the barn, were required to be placed so close together, that a person could hardly move between them. To the bedroom we ascended by a trap-ladder in the middle of the house. There were only two beds below, in a small closet adjoining the kitchen. Our furniture consisted of two long tables, or deals, surrounded by binks or cutty-stools. In the kitchen was a dresser, a meal-chest, and a few stools. In Mr.

White's closet was a table and a few chairs, intended for strangers." Such was "Buchan Ha'," the name by which it was universally called, even long after the departure of the inmates.

But here no more than in Irvine were they allowed to remain in peace, though extremely obliging to all they met, and working to the farmers gratuitously, refusing even thanks. The community were indignant at their presence, and resolved to expel them, *vi et armis*, some seven months after their arrival, which was done with fell destruction, though no lives were lost. Choosing a moonless night in December, when the ground was deeply covered with snow, about a hundred men ruthlessly attacked the dwelling with bludgeons of various kinds, threatening to set fire to the whole place unless Mrs. Buchan and Mr. White were delivered up to their rage. Seeing these worthies were not forthcoming, they battered in the doors and the windows, ransacked the whole premises, and when the objects of their search were not to be found they drove out all the inmates to the highway, ordering them to return whence they came. After the infliction of much harsh treatment and rude insult, the assailants, as if satisfied with what they had done, retired, whereupon the persecuted victims wandered back to their house, and were no more similarly molested there. Apprehensive of injury, Mrs. Buchan and Mr. White had been previously removed to a place of safety till the riot was over.

Getting somewhat settled down after this disastrous attack, their minds were more and more directed by Friend Mother, as Mrs. Buchan preferred being called, to their glorious ascent at the coming of Christ, which was declared to be fast approaching. Mr. White composed doggrel hymns for the exercise of their vocal aspirations, which were constantly sung with the greatest enthusiasm, as being more divine even than the Psalms of David. These were generally chanted to the air of " The Beds of Sweet Roses," then a popular song. As a necessary preparation for the joyful event, it was decreed that the whole body should undergo a fast of forty days, that they might thereby be purified from all earthly pollution. This was actually carried out to a certain extent, when the legal authorities found it necessary to interfere and put an end to the absurdity. All were reduced to the merest skeletons, except Mrs. Buchan and Mr. White, who, it was known, took their usual food, lest they should become too transparent and shining, so as not to be looked upon as Moses was on coming down from the mount. This was a sad blow to their arrangements, but the arm of the law was stronger than theirs, and they were obliged to submit.

At last the anticipated day of ascension was at hand, and all was activity, and bustle, and joy, in full expectancy of the grand translation to the realms above. Layard tells us, in his story of Nineveh, with regard to a sect of devil-worshippers, called the Yezidis, that on the eve of one of their great religious festivals at which he was present, the devotees washed their robes and their bodies in a stream contiguous to the scene of the solemnity, and next morning they all appeared in white raiment, spotless and pure. So also here, on the eve of the expected ascension, there was rubbing and scrubbing in the Cample Burn, that on the following day the "saints" might appear in comely garments for entering the mansions of the blest. Of course these were white, or what was meant for such. It may well be supposed that there was little or no sleep in the Ha' that night, and by daybreak the surrounding eminences were occupied as situations of ascension. On a particular height three platforms were erected, as if so many spring-boards, for the more distinguished of the body, the centre one being several feet higher than the others, and allotted to the special use of Mrs. Buchan, so that she might gain a somewhat earlier ascent, leading the way, and the flock following in promiscuous order. The whole fraternity, in full expectation of immediate ascent, had had their heads closely shaved, with the exception of a little tuft on the top by which the angels might grasp them and waft them to glory. All were in readiness by an early hour—the platforms were occupied—the floor of the Ha' was strewn with watches and jewellery of all descriptions, as no longer of use—the high grounds were covered, the neighbourhood having turned out its wondering spectators—and the sound of hymn-singing in all its ecstacy rose and floated far away among the hills, the refrain, as usual, lilted to "The Beds of Sweet Roses:"—

"Oh! hasten translation, and come resurrection!
Oh! hasten the coming of Christ in the air!"

By-and-by the sun came forth in magnificent splendour, as if conscious of the glorious event just about to happen. All eyes of the "saints" were turned towards the heavens, and every moment it was expected the sky would be darkened by a cloud of angels on their visit

to the plains of Cample. The sun shone on with increasing lustre, the "saints" gazed with increasing
expectation, and the crowd watched with increasing
wonderment. A slight breeze sprung up, and this
was construed as heralding the angelic approach, the
cause being the action of celestial wings through the
air. "Still they gazed, and still the wonder grew."
The breeze not only continued but increased, though
not a single angel wafted into sight. All at once a
sudden blast swept over the scene; the platforms, with
their occupants, were violently overturned, and an igno-
minious fall put an end to the ascension. Shortly
afterwards Mrs. Buchan was found quietly smoking her
pipe by the fireside, as if no mishap or disappointment
had occurred, and alleging for the failure of the ascension that they were not all sufficiently ready.

This was indeed the downfall of the Buchanites.
The dupes came now somewhat to reason, and a great
many of them went away. Mrs. Buchan and her
remanent family were compelled to leave the locality,
as certain rumours, not without foundation, of the fruits
of their free-love doctrine roused the indignation of the
inhabitants, and we next find them settled on a piece of
ground at Auchengibbert, in the parish of Urr. Their
day, however, was done; the faith they inspired was
exhausted, and it was hopeless to expect any new
recruits, or even to retain the adherence of old ones.
After imprisonment for debt in Dumfries, and other
vicissitudes, Mrs. Buchan died in 1791, and her remains,
after being clandestinely buried in Kirkgunzeon churchyard, were secretly disinterred, placed in a box, and
preserved as a household relic, every now and again

receiving an airing, and a covering of hot flannels, which were afterwards used as a sort of charm when they came to be changed. At last the box—for it could not be called a coffin—with its cherished treasure, was transferred to the earth in the kailyard of Auchengibbert, along with the remains of her only surviving and most devoted follower, Andrew Innes, in January, 1846.

The sect, as we have said, gained no followers in Dumfriesshire, with the exception of a few weak-minded Cameronians, who unaccountably were led astray by their nonsensical doctrines. But in this they were not altogether to blame, as some of their own pastors could not forbear visiting the fanatics, perhaps somewhat out of curiosity, but ostensibly on a mission of proselytism. The Rev. John Fairley, mentioned above, being on a professional tour in the neighbourhood, thought it lay within his sphere to visit Buchan Ha', and endeavour to reclaim the wandering brotherhood and sisterhood there. After waiting for a considerable time, his knock was answered by Mr. White, who was immediately joined by Mrs. Buchan, and in a gruff voice he was asked what he wanted. On answering that he had heard of their being in the place, and had called for the purpose of having a friendly conference, he was sharply told to go about his business, and the door was slammed in his face. A more deluded sect of religionists it is scarcely possible to imagine, and, what is very remarkable, it contained more than one member of cultivated intellect and of good position in society, who yet allowed themselves to be gulled and guided by the artful machinations of an illiterate, a coarse-minded, lascivious, but naturally

-clever woman. On their breaking up, the greater number of them emigrated to America, as if ashamed to remain at home, and unable to bear the jeering of their friends. Mr. White became a schoolmaster in the Far West, occasionally preaching to a body of Universalists; but he never made the slightest allusion to his previous connection with the Buchanites in Scotland.

CHAPTER XIII.

RELIGIOUS EPIDEMIC—RESOLUTION AND SPEECH IN THE PRESBYTERY—
ADDRESS TO THE NITH—EXTRACT—RENCONTRE IN THE PRESBY-
TERY—POORHOUSE SERMON—DR. CHALMERS—BYRON—DUMFRIES
ACADEMY.

DURING the year 1816 a sort of fanatic tidal-wave
passed over the land, threatening destruction to the
interests of religion, but, fortunately, not leaving any
very baneful effects behind. It was a blow insidiously
aimed against Church Establishments, and, from the
thin veil under which it was shrouded, many were ready
to say of it, as of the wooden horse of Troy, "*Quicquid
id est, timeo Danaos et dona ferentes.*" The proposal
was the formation of an association in which persons of
all creeds and of no creed should be harmoniously
blended together for the better promoting of Christian
love, and of more successfully propagating the gospel of
Christ. In short, it was to be the fulfilment of the
prophet's oracle—"The wolf shall dwell with the lamb,
and the leopard shall lie down with the kid; and the
calf and the young lion and the fatling together; and a
little child shall lead them. And the cow and the bear
shall feed; their young ones shall lie down together;
and the lion shall eat straw like the ox. And the sucking child shall play on the hole of the asp, and the
weaned child shall put his hand on the cockatrice' den.
They shall not hurt or destroy in all my holy mountain."

Alas for human fallibility! Under all the display of brotherly affection and Christian love, there was hid a snake in the grass; the principal, if not the sole, object in view was to destroy in the holy mountain. The infection crossed the Border and took a hold in Dumfries. Some belonging to the Presbytery, of whom other things were expected, came under its influence, and if ever that reverend Court did sing, it was evident to every discerning mind that the piece in preparation was, "Let Whig and Tory all agree!" By all means, we say, but let there be an equal agreement, an equal disinterestedness, and on neither side a desired humiliation of the other.

That the movement was not disinterested was shown by the result, as the record of the times too sadly testifies. Mr. Wightman's spirit was greatly moved at the seeming inconsistency of some of his brethren who fell under the contagion, and who were endeavouring to inoculate others with the disease. He accordingly submitted a resolution to the Presbytery on the subject, the gist of which was that they should not connect themselves with any association of persons pursuing such measures, however well meant might be their views, but should discharge their duties diligently and faithfully, following no divisive courses, in terms of the vows they came under at their ordination. At the same time they would carefully, as they had hitherto done, conduct themselves with Christian moderation and charity towards all denominations, according to the sound principles of religious toleration; but they strongly disapproved of ministers of different persuasions mingling their religious exercises of preaching, exhortation, prayer, and praise

R

in the same church, school, or elsewhere, whether with a
view to edify the old or instruct the young, as disorderly,
and not tending to edification; that the great interests
of religion and morality were safer under the steady
auspices of our religious establishment than under the
desultory directions of promiscuous speculation.

Mr. Wightman, in supporting his resolution, spoke
with great feeling and animation; and as he was seldom
loquacious in the Presbytery, he was listened to on this
occasion with unusual interest. We shall give an extract
from his speech, as it is well deserving of quotation. In
comparing those speculators, whose proposal of amalga-
mation he deprecated, to projecting alchemists with
illusive expectations, he said—"From their sublime
fusion, I call it *confusion*, of different metals, they dream
of some kind of Corinthian brass, which shall be more
valuable than all the gold and silver of the temple. But
these fanciful theorists, these benevolent dreamers, if
they would open their eyes, might see that this precious
metal of theirs, such as it is, can be procured only by
desolation, as that of Corinth was, when the city of the
two seas was sacked and burned by the Roman Consul,
Mummius. It can be procured only by the ruin of
everything fair and comely in the buildings of our
Jerusalem. They know not, or consider not, the genius
of the people and of the times. They speak as if we
lived in a golden age. On such romantic and visionary
plans I look with the same suspicion with which I view
the revolutionary flags of our modern constitution-
makers, 'dashing the public eye' with their blood-
blazoned and flaring inscriptions. They promise you
much, but they pay you with less than nothing—they

promise you golden prizes, but they pay you with worse than a blank—they hold out a branch of their accursed tree, laden apparently with rich fruit, shining with apples fairer to the sight and more alluring to the taste than the fabled ones of the Hesperides of old, but they are in reality apples of Gomorrah, hollow and deceitful, or full of sordid dust and bitter ashes. My favourite maxim with regard to such novel and such dangerous projects is, ' *Obsta principiis*,' check them in the bud, and, if you can, extirpate their very stem from the soil on which they appear. A small beginning may lead to a very mischievous result—a minute spark may, if neglected, produce a conflagration which the blood of millions may not quench—the hand of a child may set the stone a-rolling on the top of a mountain which the arm of a giant may not stop when it has gained force with its progress, and ' smokes along the ground.' A small aperture has sometimes let forth a flood which those who first opened a passage for it could not restrain within the bounds they intended. It is somewhere recorded, I think, that so small a creature as a dormouse, by perforating some of the dykes of Holland, let in the sea to overflow and deluge the fairest gardens of the Batavian vintage, and the rich harvest of that fertile country.

" I am not holding up any bloody scourge of persecution, I am not recommending, as it has been indiscreetly insinuated, both in my own hearing and in the public prints, any ' penal laws as props of our religion.' *Non his defensoribus eget.* I am not creating any inquisitorial tribunal to overawe and repress the generous sentiments of freeborn men. I am forging no iron yoke to lay on my brother's shoulders. No! I spurn all such insinuations from whatever quarter they come, and I wish that a certain newspaper, which calls itself 'a great literary engine,' would point its cannon against our common enemy, and not against a brother's breast, and wield its sword with a little more mercy and discretion. I would have repelled the charge by the same means, and with as much publicity, if I had not been prevented by the consideration that those who are at least indifferent about religion, and the avowed enemies of our common faith, and of all revealed religion together, would be gratified to observe anything that looked like a quarrel among the friends of Christianity, and hence be led to strengthen themselves in their courses. *Hoc Ithacus velit, et magno mercentur Atridæ!* I am not that intolerant person which some of those anonymous hints and allusions seem to insinuate. I do not suppose the influence of heaven to be confined to the schools of our own prophets. A prophet may arise in Nazareth. Nursed among the heaven-propping mountains and boldly rushing streams of my native district, I inhaled the breath of freedom with the untainted breezes which fanned my youth, and I have my full share of that love of independence and privilege which glows so warmly in the breast of every true Scotchman, and I wish to withhold from others none of the privileges I myself possess, and especially that high one of serving God according to the dictates of conscience. I am only supporting by my feeble voice the salutary regulations of our Established Church, and to which all her sons are bound by the most solemn vows to adhere. I believe,—and Heaven knows how sincere my belief is,—that without establishments religion would not prosper in any country, and that where the Great Ruler shall please to bless with His favour the Christian religion, He will there ordain that establishments shall arise and be supported by the State. There are others—and those, too, worthy and well-meaning men—who are as sincere as I am in a different and opposite belief, that establishments are so far from being supports of religion, they are actual bars to its purity and prosperity, and operate as so many mounds and partition walls to prevent the universal flow of glory to God and good-will to man. On this controversy I do not mean to enter. I mention the matter only to account for my zeal on the present and on other occasions of this kind.

" If any should think that the enactments and regulations of our National Church are too narrow and confined for their large and philanthropic views, there is a way, and an easy one, to escape from the alleged bondage, and that is, to quit the emoluments, small as they are, belonging to ministers of the Established Church, and expatiate at large in the freedom they may admire; and I would venerate the man who should leave our Establishment from truly conscientious motives and a pure heart. But I am so constituted by nature, by education, and perhaps in some degree by prejudice, that I cannot estimate so highly the man who should retain in his hands the emoluments of an establishment, and follow any course which tends to weaken and undermine that very establishment which he has solemnly avowed to support. Might I hope, then, that the resolution which I have laid before you, or one framed on the same principle and in the same spirit, be adopted and subscribed by us all, as a testimony against the latitudinarian schemes which are projected and acted upon in several parts of the kingdom! But if we shall not be unanimous in adopting this or a similar resolution, those of us who may not approve of it will no doubt enter their dissent and give their reasons for doing so; and these must either be founded on an opinion, right or wrong, that this resolution is unnecessary, there being no such spirit discovering itself anywhere in the kingdom, or, that although the disposition does exist, it is harmless and even beneficial, and not in any degree contrary to the statutes and practice of our National Church. Now, I contend, on the other hand, that the disposition I complain of does indeed exist, and that it is very inconsistent with the notions which I, at least, entertain of the laws and practice of the Established Church of Scotland. I move, therefore, that this resolution, or one framed on the same principle and in the same spirit, be adopted, as a testimony of our fidelity to our ecclesiastical establishment, and of our aversion to any innovations, which, to say the least of them, are of doubtful issue. *Sensibus hæc imis, res est non parva, reponas.*"

This speech was delivered with great energy and emotion, and produced a very solemn effect. The resolution was adopted at the time unanimously, but afterwards two of the members dissented and gave in their names at a subsequent meeting, a proceeding entirely irregular. After this mental strain we may now follow Mr. Wightman's example and seek relief in poetry. We shall take one of his own pieces:—

The Nith.

"O gentle Nith, or by whatever name
    Thou hast in former epochs been known,
An humble muse, scarce recognized by fame,
    Would add a single floweret to thy crown.

"In vain through dusky ages, long gone by,
    Thy rise and shifting channels would she trace;
Thick clouds and darkness meet her aching eye,
    And bid her not by rashness seek disgrace.

"Yet would she ask, in meek and modest tone,
    At what dark era rose thy winding stream?
Where Corsoncon now rears his towering cone,
    To meet at early hour the morning beam.

"In what direction was thy current led,
    When first it issued from its ancient urn?
How did it form its parent pebbled bed,
    And when to other channels did it turn?

"Say, if thy course did always thus extend
    In lengthened beauty to the Solway sands?
Or, with the tide, did once thy waters blend
    Where now Dalswinton's princely mansion stands?

"Didst thou not once pursue thy devious way
    Below where Tinwald's verdant ridges rise,
And through Torthorwald and through Mouswald stray
    To join the firth where Ruthwell's border lies?

"Eastward and westward, say, how wide thy range,
    Where still thy polished stones are frequent found,
In every spreading plain, and, far more strange,
    On every shelving bank and rising ground.

"Can hoary time the wondrous record show
    Where thy eventful history is contained?
Or tell us where thy margin, high or low,
    In lapse of years has either lost or gained.

"How rose the hills which guard thy long-drawn vale,
    And lean their wavy summits 'gainst the sky?
What formed the varied surface of thy dale
    Which now with such delight transports the eye?

"Who built these circles, and who raised these doons
    Which yet are seen on many a neighbouring height?
How many golden suns and silver moons
    Have gilt or silvered them with varied light?

"Did o'er thy strath once spread the swelling deep
    Beneath whose surges sea-born monsters played,
And in its darksome caverns soundly sleep,
    When other fish their hunger had allayed?

"Or was it one dark forest, through whose glades
    In quivered pride the savage archer ran,
While furious tigers crouched within its shades,
    Watching to seize their hated rival man?

"Beneath thy spreading oaks have Druids taught,
    And scholars listened to the British lore?
Have trembling captives to the altar brought
    The standing-stone distained with human gore?

"Have Saxon rites in thy domain prevailed?
    And Woden's race adorned the sun's bright beam,
Or moon's pale ray, when his effulgence failed,
    And seen their gods reflected in thy stream?

"O Nith! in gentle whispers kindly tell,
    What motley tribes along thy frighted flood,
Once met, and mixed, and fought, and stood or fell,
    While thy green margin reddened with their blood?

"What fur-clad chiefs concerted war or truce,
    Smiled in the feast, or in the battle frowned,
Ere yet the rivals, Baliol and Bruce,
    Were in historic page so much renowned?

"Where did the Roman legions o'er thee pass,
    When through thy warlike bands they urged their way,
Where stood their tents, where lodged they on the grass,
    Or did they ever in thy precincts stay?

"The muse, disgusted, turns her crimsonèd wing,
    From savage ire, and deeds of deadly strife—
Her voice she tunes of peaceful scenes to sing,
    Of what adorns and blesses human life.

"When did thy tribes their dens and caves forsake,
    Their wicker shelters, and their huts of clay,
And with a skilful hand commodious make
    The handsome cottage, and the mansion gay?

" When did unsodden flesh and acorns yield
    To viands rich, and food by art prepared,
When first was bread-corn cast upon the field,
    And all thy sons on well-cooked victuals fared?

"O say, sweet stream, when o'er thy smiling lawn
    Did gospel truth diffuse its cheerful light?
When did the day of the Redeemer dawn,
    And chase away the shades of heathen night?

"Did some good friar, by old Augustine sent
    To thy rude natives, the glad tidings preach,
And on the object of his mission bent,
    The gracious plan of free salvation teach?

" From chalky Whithern, or from Lindisfarn,
    Did any holy messenger appear,
Thy painted sons in charity to warn,
    Of coming wrath, and teach them God to fear?

"As when by Jordan's flood the Baptist showed
    That heaven's benignant reign was then at hand,
The mingled multitudes around him flowed,
    And heard his message on the rocky strand:

"So might thy tribes now hear the Saint declare,
  How the redemption was by Christ procured,
How on the cross He our transgressions bare,
  And what dread wrath He there for us endured.

"How shall the muse in worthy numbers sing
  The brighter glories of thy Christian day,
Which made thy borders all with anthems ring,
  To hail the Reformation's holy ray!

"When from behind the murky cloud appeared
  The sun of truth in majesty most bright,
And all thy sons in concert sweet were heard,
  Blessing the fresh and heart-reviving light.

"Her bloody scourge again oppression plied,
  And lashed them sore, while for the truth they bled,
Their faith and patience then were sadly tried,
  But heavenly hope their bosoms never fled.

"The tender muse here sensitively shrinks,
  And dares not in her lay record their woes,
Her heart recoils and sympathizing sinks,
  At the fell rage of their bloodthirsty foes.

"With peace and comfort they have long been blest—
  O may they still enjoy these blessings long!
Beneath their vines and fig-trees may they rest,
  And raise to heaven the glad and grateful song.

"O never may they seek to break the chain,
  Whose threefold links to all such blessings bring,
Which sages wished to form, but wished in vain,
  The golden chain of Commons, Lords, and King.

"O never may they seek to overturn
  The sacred tripod of our envied state,
Lest they should idly weep o'er freedom's urn,
  And sorrow o'er their fallen country's fate.

"But now the sky seems to be overcast,
　　And grimly with the gathering storm to lower,
While yelling demons revel in the blast,
　　Exulting in their desolating power.

"As when some cloud, surcharged with liquid store,
　　Lets fall its weighty burden at thy source,
Thy mazy channel down to Solway's shore,
　　Displays one foaming, raging, wasting force.

"So Demolition, in his dark divan,
　　Plots to embroil thy sons in brutal fray,
Thus hoping to promote his reckless plan,
　　And usher in his dread and dismal day.

"Forbid it, heaven! forbid it truth and peace!
　　The truth and peace that erst from heaven came,
Through all thy dale may Christian love increase,
　　And piety still glow in brightening flame.

"May all thy borders prosper in their store—
　　May pure religion flourish and abound,
Till Corsoncon and Criffel be no more,
　　And thy loved stream shall sink beneath the ground.

"So the rude bard, with calm and tranquil heart,
　　In thy sweet vale his even of life shall spend,
And then at last lay down his mortal part,
　　In hopes of bliss that ne'er shall have an end!"

"Tuesday, 20th Feb., 1816.—I finished reading 'The Evergreen,' a collection of Scottish poems, published by Allan Ramsay, and dedicated to the Duke of Hamilton, the Captain-General, and the rest of the honourable members of the Royal Company of Archers. Mr. Burns has been led by this to dedicate his poems to the members of the Caledonian Hunt. The beauties and faults of these volumes would require much time and labour to point out. In several

parts I could remark one of these old poets borrowing a
thought or two from another, as in the case of the 'Cherry
and the Slae,' the author of which has borrowed from 'The
Vision,' a most noble heroic ballad; and the 'Bard of Coila'
has lighted his lamp at the flame of this old altar—and, indeed,
in *many* places I can trace the print of his feet among the
bushes of this Evergreen *Silva*.   He has evidently studied
the Vision here.   His 'Vision,' in which the Scottish muse
visits him, is inspired by the Vision here recorded.   And
many of Burns' favourite words are to be found in these
two ancient volumes.   He has cast a new light, and put a
more modern dress on some of the thoughts of these kindred
minds."

We have already noted Mr. Wightman's geniality
towards the students, and his efforts to assist them in
passing their professional examinations as comfortably
as the nature of things would admit, and, at the same
time, as creditably as possible for their own reputation,
and their usefulness in the Church.   For this purpose
he invited them to the manse, he read with them, he
lent them books, he gave them advice, and when under
the ordeal of the Presbytery he even whispered in their
ear the answer to a question at which they seemed to
hesitate.   It must not be imagined, however, that in
the exuberance of his friendship for these young men he
was willing that their examinations should be conducted
in a perfunctory manner; so far from that, there was not
one in the Presbytery more ready than he to notice and
lament the want of scholarship visible on the part of
any preacher to whom he listened, at the same time
preserving a judicious silence where he could not conscientiously commend.   On one occasion, however, he

came into collision with his brethren of the Presbytery on the manner in which these examinations should be conducted for the future. A discussion having arisen on the subject, and one member having proposed a certain list of books to be digested and examined on, in order to secure greater proficiency in the ʼrequisite studies, Mr. Wightman's spirit was roused at what he considered too strict and rigorous a vigilance over the minds of the young men, extending even to the books they should read, and he insisted that if the court demanded accurate information and sound views in theology from them, they might be allowed to derive that information and these views from any books they might possess, without being put to an inconvenient expense which they oftentimes could but ill afford, always recommending them to apply to their acquaintances among the ministers for such works as might best promote their progress in useful and solid knowledge, and so successfully arrive at the end proposed—proper preparation for discharging the duties of the sacred office. There were many ways, he said, to our Jerusalem, or the grand capital of our faith, public instruction being only a finger-pointing or sign-post to direct the young traveller the way; yet this did not mean that the road to accomplishment in divinity was by one way, one set of books, or one class of canons of criticism alone. A diligent young man would find his way independently of particular treatises or works of men, however learned and useful in themselves, by studying the Scriptures and reading such books as they might be advised, or as they might find them. The member who had proposed the list rose in a paroxysm of zeal and said he protested against answering a man who had declared that there was a narrow and a broad way to heaven! The word Jerusalem, which had been used in a flight of glowing imagery, had led him to suppose that the heavenly Jerusalem, and the way of justification in the sight of God, had been referred to, a sense which was participated in by another member of court.

Dr. Lamont, of Kirkpatrick-Durham, said that as Mr. Wightman spoke *extempore* he had employed some words susceptible of misapprehension, but that the meaning ascribed to them was not the one intended. We think that a very careless listener might have seen that the words were employed solely in regard to the studies of students and probationers for the ministry. Mr. Wightman was very much hurt at the insinuations thrown out against him, as such attacks tended to destroy their confidence in each other, and the confidence of the public in their order in general. He said it was the prerogative of Him who searches the heart, and it ill became a puny mortal to take into his hand the reed and the line which measure the temple of God, or to hold the awful balance of the sanctuary, and pronounce upon its gold and silver with a tone of arrogance. No individual had any right to consider his own views as a test by which to try the spirit and piety of others. This *rencontre* the more confirmed him in his opinion that too rigorous a scrutiny into young men's belief rather injures than promotes the cause of truth. He resumed his seat muttering sufficiently loud to be heard, "I shall ever endeavour to exert my feeble powers to rescue a young man from the fangs of such inquisitorial examinations and priestly dogmatism. *Amicus Plato, sed magis amicus Veritas!*"

The following extract is in reference to the Rev. Mr. Kirkwood, minister of Holywood, on his preaching the annual Poorhouse sermon in Dumfries:—

"Sunday, 14th October, 1821.—Preached at home, and rode in afterwards to hear the Poorhouse sermon preached by Mr. Kirkwood, who has lately come to Holywood. He took his text from 2 Cor. viii. 9, 'For ye know the grace of our Lord Jesus Christ, that, though he was rich, yet for your sakes he became poor, that ye through his poverty might be rich.' Three things were set forth as contained in the text. (1.) What Christ was. (2.) What He became. (3.) The end of His doing so. Mr. Kirkwood treated his first head with too much minuteness, dwelling tediously on the pre-existent state of our Lord, though some good things were said; but when he came to describe the humiliation of Christ, he grew still more extravagant and loose in his ideas and expressions. 'When our Lord entered on this world,' the preacher said, 'He had none of the trappings of human greatness. What were His retinue and attendants? They were in yonder heavens—companies of angels—beneath the heavens—see them over the plains of Bethlehem—He lay in a place destined for inferior animals—among straw, rubbish, and with the horned cattle—where they fed. At this time there must have been some alteration round the throne, some change in the Godhead—the eternal God was joined to an infant of a span long. Oh! think, think, think on such abasement!' He observed that 'many of the congregation were in darkness—none but spiritual men understood the things he was saying—they were foolishness to them.' (Many thought so, I presume.) 'But,' said he, 'consult the Bible, just take one six weeks' reading of the Scriptures, a chapter or two a day, for example, and then, after studying the Word, say whether I have not been telling you the truth. O think, O think, think, &c., &c.!' A tissue of the same kind of matter closed the harangue, and some notice concerning the Institution for which he had the 'honour' to plead. For my part, I never heard a discourse of which I thought less, and I blushed to see the pulpit made a stage of empiricism, and my religion wrapped in a fool's coat. If this be the way to win souls to Christ, I am sorry that my heart is so alien to the plan. But I grieve that the taste of the times, and even of this hitherto sober part of the country, seems to relish such sort of *eloquence;* and as a proof of this, the collection on the occasion was larger than on any former one of the kind. Thus folly is fostered, and fanaticism rears her distorted head, while sober piety blushes and retires from our assemblies. I am the more vexed, that Mr. Kirkwood is my neighbour, and with whom I could have wished to correspond and hold social intercourse, both in civil and religious matters. He is pleasant in company, and not without learning and various information. May I hope that he will never again outrage decorum and soberness, and that he will become like other modest men. There is a spirit abroad at present which encourages all new and untried methods of attracting public notice, and is greedy of high-seasoned viands both in political and theological entertainments. Some wonderful change is looked for in the religions world, and extravagant preachers and orators at clubs are considered as so many *avant couriers* before the event. Hence every wild and otherwise foolish sentiment and expression is hailed and trumpeted as something presageful of greater things yet to come. What will be the issue of such a fermentation I cannot guess. I look through the loop-hole of my retreat with anxiety on the great Babel, and wish society may not be convulsed and dissolved. Every puny agent contributes to increase the mighty stir and the wild hubbub!"

Notwithstanding the above philippic, Mr. Kirkwood proved a most useful minister and a most popular man among his own parishioners. Having acquired, though irregularly, a considerable knowledge of the diseases which afflict humanity, and the means and medicines which promote relief, if not always effect a cure, and, besides, being at all times ready to give both advice and medicine *gratis*, the manse of Holywood was every morning literally besieged by those from all districts upon whom the hand of disease had fallen with more or less severity, and who were not, from circumstances, enabled to call in a professional physician. In this way Mr. Kirkwood did a vast amount of good, though he had to submit to the reproach of being designated a "quack doctor" by the regular profession. It is not for us to say, in merely relating history, how far this help of the body contributed to the help of the soul. That it did so in many instances is undoubted, though at the same time our own private opinion, if we may be allowed to give it, is, that every man should hold by his own profession, or, as the common proverb has it, "Let the cobbler stick to his last," for in this way the duties of life are always best performed. Mr. Kirkwood had a ready talent of delivery, which is not difficult of acquirement, and he never read his discourses from the pulpit, for, as the initiated knew, he seldom wrote his preparations. Many things, therefore, were said off-hand which never could have stood the test of writing. He died about the end of 1844, or beginning of 1845, but from

S

the time of the delivery of the Poorhouse sermon above referred to, until the time of his death, there was never any great cordiality between the ministers of Holywood and Kirkmahoe. This the inhabitants of the several parishes noticed and remarked on, and were sorry for, and secretly wished it were otherwise. On the west side of the Nith it was said that the other side was jealous of the popularity of their minister, and on the other it was said that the western preaching was "fusionless," and exemplified the truth of the proverb that "a toom barrel made the loudest soun'." We believe that both sides were wrong; but however that may be, we know that "Kirkwood's pills" are sought after to the present day, and that he is still held up by his former people as the greatest preacher that ever adorned the Holywood pulpit.

When Dr. Chalmers left Glasgow for St. Andrews, on his appointment to the chair of Moral Philosophy there, he was entertained at a public dinner, given by his old parishioners and other friends, in token of the esteem in which he was held both as a preacher and an advocate in the interests of the poor. In responding to the toast of the University of St. Andrews, he said she had been described as "an old lady wearing brocade," which elicited great laughter from the company assembled. This having been reported to Mr. Wightman, he sent the following verses to the Doctor, in name of the offended lady, by way of reproof:—

THE OLD GENTLEWOMAN OF ST. ANDREWS TO DR. CHALMERS.

"Dear Doctor, 'tis true an old lady I am,
    My garb is not new, I confess;
But pray, could you not take your dinner and dram,
    Without laughing at me and my dress!

" My Sister of Glasgow is both young and fair,
  She wears neither ruff nor brocade,
But though my old head now can scarce boast a hair,
  My vigour seems never to fade.

" On the height of St. Rule, where I sit in my pride,
  I ponder the days that are gone;
A thousand fair damsels have fallen by my side,
  And left your ' old lady' alone.

" How oft, from my seat, have I marked the sea wave
  Grow white as it chafed on the shore!
How oft, through these towers, have I heard the wind rave,
  Since these puckered garments I wore!

" A border or trinket I'll change as you please,
  But my hood and my mantle I'll keep;
It little becomes you a matron to tease—
  When your ' old lady' naps, let her sleep.

" She rocked your own cradle and dandled her boy,
  As she had nursed thousands before;
Now she trims her brocade and her heart leaps for joy,
  To cherish her Chalmers once more.

" But oh! never let any muslin or gauze
  Around her old person be thrown;
She never will think that she has any cause
  To part with her grave russet gown!

"ACADEMIA ANDREAPOLITANA.

" From the Tower of St. Rule, 20th Nov., 1823."

The following was the passage referred to in Dr. Chalmers' speech:—"I have heard her spoken of as if she were little better than a decayed gentlewoman, who had brought the high origin of her family to bear her up under the decline of her now withered fortunes, that by the prosperity of her more modern neighbours she is now completely overborne, that it is true she has still her gray ruins and her venerable recollections to appeal to, even as the old lady to whom she is compared can still bring forth some venerable relict of her former days, a piece of magnificent brocade, for example, worn at Court by her great-grandmother, or perhaps some obsolete china and other vestiges of antique grandeur, spread out in fair display upon her mantlepiece."

Lord Byron does not seem to have been a favourite with Mr. Wightman, from the loose and licentious character of some of the poet's earlier pieces. On reading one of these, in which the memory of the late venerable sovereign George the Third was traduced, Mr. Wightman sent the following lines on the subject to a local journal. The —— newspaper had said of the king's domestic virtues that they were but a poor thing, and that posterity, looking into his merits, would not find it difficult to reach their bottom:—

BYRON.

"Thy muse, O Byron, like the bird of Jove,
In high ethereal tracts was formed to rove,
To bear the flickering lightning through the sky,
Surveying earth and heaven with piercing eye.
Why are the moral pestilence and death
Shot from her withering glance and poisonous breath?
Oh! why did Genius light in thee his fire,
Or Fancy lend thee her enchanting lyre?
Why did sweet Harmony attune thy lays?
Why were thy temples graced with Delphic bays?
Did Science smile upon thy noble birth,
To scatter vice and misery through the earth?
To shake dire mildew from the Muse's wing,
And blight each moral flower in blooming spring?

Heaven sees the zoneless and degenerate Muse
In vain her guilty artifices use,
Through virtue's paradise her bane to spread,
And turn life's bowers to charnels of the dead.
Religion's citadel no foot unblest
Shall ever enter or disturb its rest;
There heavenly hosts unseen, in phalanx deep,
Wave their dread brands, and faithful vigils keep.
They guard the ashes of great George's urn,
And each unprincipled intruder spurn.
They doom to dark oblivion Byron's verse,
Whene'er it dares his memory to asperse.
So shall it deeper sink in Lethé's stream,
Than even thy moody ————'s drivelling dream!
So vice and Byron are confined to shame,
But George and virtue to immortal fame!"

Here is a glimpse of Dumfries Academy in 1825, showing that it has always maintained the highest position for learning and efficiency among the educational institutions of the country:—

"18th July, 1825.—This day the schools of Dumfries were examined. The Academy was more especially under my eye. The minister of Dunscore, Mr. Brydone, was in the chair as Moderator. Mr. Harkness displayed uncommon ability. He excels in conveying the spirit and knowledge of the Greek and Roman literature to the minds of his scholars. There is much strength in his plan—there is a masculine spirit in it. It is in such a soil the roots of the British oak are successfully fixed. There is here a *'concentus virtutis,'* an aggregate of mind, a confluence of all the streams of literature and philosophy, where all the force of ocean centres, and thunders, and foams, and whirls, and rolls along, carrying all before its mighty tide. There is here nothing barren, bleak, or stunted —all is green, and fresh, and flourishing. There is here no

Dead Sea. All is alive and salubrious, refreshing and beautifying all within reach. All is high table-land, where no points or peaks overtower the other parts. The eye is pleased with the widespreading extent, and the mind is filled with sublime emotion by contemplating its aërial heights. I thought that I had attained almost the summit of perfection in the teaching of the classics, but I find my young friend has found out new and easier paths, where the Muses strew roses, as well as the Graces, and where every step is fragrant, and every advance is easier than the former—where all is beauty to the eye and music to the ear. Dr. Scot, of Dumfries, opened the business of giving opinion, and he gave such a luminous view of the school and its plans as astonished us all. The age of the man, the vigour of his remarks, the liveliness of his fancy, and the correctness of the whole oration, for such it was, were all in the very best style, and have increased the very high opinion I have long had of the Dr.'s industry and talents. We all dined at the expense (I suppose) of the town, and I came home at seven o'clock, pleased with the work of the day."

All the parties here referred to, the scholars excepted, have long since been gathered to their fathers, but the Academy still maintains its high superiority, though at the close of its annual examination there are missed those spirits which of yore loved to glow with such enthusiasm over the honours of the day, giving satisfaction to the teachers, and a perfect Elysium to the taught.

CHAPTER XIV.

ACADEMY ADDRESS—DELIVERY OF SERMONS—UNUSUALLY SULTRY
SUMMER—SUFFERING AND DISTRESS—BETTER TIMES—ANECDOTES
—CONVIVIALITY—POETRY—VISIT TO EDINBURGH—REV. MR.
GILLESPIE OF KELLS.

WHILST we are on the subject of the Academy examinations, we may take the opportunity of inserting a specimen of the kindly counsels Mr. Wightman was in the habit of addressing to the pupils on the eve of the breaking up of the classes for the autumn vacation. These were always rich with classic references and inspiriting encouragement to noble darings, full of religious admonition, and the whole delivered in such an ardent tone of sincerity, as also of affection, that old and young frequently could not refrain from tears, himself being overcome. After eulogizing, in glowing terms, the high state of efficiency in which the several departments of the Academy had been found, and giving the masters his warmest commendation, in the hope that they would be stimulated to perseverance in their important spheres of duty, he turned to the young and addressed them in the following terms:—

"The Academy appears to be in a very promising and efficient condition. It is a bright gem in the diadem of the Queen of the South, a fair and fragrant flower in her garland. We gladly encourage the masters to proceed in their honourable career, to gather fresh laurels in the field of honest fame.

It was long ago observed by Columella, a writer on rural economy, that the ground rejoices to yield its increase when cultivated by a silver plough or ploughshare. The meaning is obviously that the soil is productive when it is duly stimulated and in good heart. So teachers of youth put forth their skill and energies with vigour and success when they enjoy the public approbation, and when their plough has as much silver about it as to make it shine in the furrow. The house or city is always well lighted when the lamps are sufficiently supplied with oil or with gas. We are happy to remark that the principles of religion are not overlooked in this seminary, and that the Church Catechism occupies a due place in the academical system. We hope, and are even confident, that the excellent masters embrace every opportunity of seasoning their lessons with the sweet savour of heavenly truth, and of watering the seeds of instruction from the stream which refreshes the city of Jerusalem. A word in season from their lips in favour of pure religion will fall with peculiar influence on the young hearts of their pupils—it will be as the dew on Hermon, and will cherish the lively green of the soul. I have a few things to say to the ingenuous youth of the Academy, to which, I am sure, they will give careful and kind attention.

"My dear young friends, you are now enjoying very favourable and precious opportunities of storing your minds with useful learning, which, if you neglect to improve, you may have cause to regret when regret may be unavailing. Knowledge is now unbarring the avenues of her rich fields and gardens, and inviting you to gather her choice fruits and her fragrant flowers. She is opening to you the gates which conceal the recesses of her temple, and counselling you to catch the inspiration of the place. She is unrolling to you the ample volume of her book, and bidding you to read and to learn. But, my dear young friends, there is a field in which there is a treasure and a goodly pearl of great price, for which you are to dig as for hidden treasure; there is a garden with pleasant fruits which this dull earth can never yield, and where flowers sweetly blow which never in other garden grew; there is a temple where the sacred fire ever burns, and where a far sweeter incense breathes than ever rose from Sabæan altars; there is a book of knowledge which maketh wise unto salvation, and there is a teacher who teaches savingly and to profit. That field, my young friends, that garden, that temple, that book is the Bible; and that teacher is the great Father of Lights himself, who calls upon you to hear and to obey his voice, to be instructed and to be wise for yourselves. The elegant and romantic Rousseau advises you not to regard any instructions of religion till you are sixteen or eighteen years of age, or at some such period of life. But I trust, my dear young friends, that you will not hearken to that' fascinating voice which comes from the mountains of Switzerland, but that you will rather listen to him who says, 'Remember thy Creator in the days of thy youth,' and to Him who inspired Solomon with wisdom and who Himself is wisdom, who says, 'Hearken unto me, O ye children! for blessed are they that keep my ways.' Consider your responsibility to God, the bounteous Giver of all your faculties and of the means of their improvement. He sees all your actions—public, and private, and secret—He hears all your words, and even the most secret thoughts of your hearts; for, as one of our poets expresses it—

'Our thoughts are heard in heaven.'

Maintain a sacred regard to truth and integrity in all your intercourse with others, and with one another even in your amusements. It is said of Aristides of Athens and of Epaminondas of Thebes, that they never told a lie, even in jest; and Atticus, the friend of Cicero, was celebrated for his never violating truth and justice. And it is recorded of the younger Cyrus, that he was remarkable for his strict observance of truth and justice with his playmates and young companions. Now, if heathens, under their institutions, were so observant of truth and equity, what must be expected of you, my dear young friends, who have such superior advantages, and who are brought up in the bosom of Christian families? Cultivate humility and compassion, amiable in all, but peculiarly graceful in youth. Visit frequently the house of mourning, where the heart is made better; sympathize with the dying parent and weeping orphans, with the afflicted and bereaved heart.

> 'Your minds let truth and justice guide,
>   Your hearts let mercy fill;
> And, walking humbly with your God,
>   To Him resign your will.'

Guard carefully against imprudent anger, against envy, and hatred, and dark revenge. Let all bitterness and wrath be put away from you, with all malice, and be tender-hearted, forbearing, and forgiving. It is thought by some that forgiveness is the same as cowardice; whereas no two things are more different from each other than these. Sir Richard Steele says—'A coward has fought, and even sometimes conquered; but a coward never forgives.' This is a sublime of self-government which the Christian hero alone can realize. Let no consideration of this world's gain ever tempt you to deviate in the least from the onward path of heavenly wisdom. This is a path which the vulture's eye hath not seen—I mean, which the sagacity of worldly wisdom hath not found. Respect your parents, your masters, your magistrates, and your ministers; for they consult your best interests. Love your country and obey its laws. Fear God and keep His commandments. My dear young friends, age and its infirmities now admonish me that it is high time to deny myself the pleasure of addressing you any more on such public occasions. May the good Lord bless you, and help you, and preserve you from all evil. May He enable you to shut your ears against the siren song of temptation, lest your frail bark should be wrecked on some rock, or whelmed in some gulph of destruction. May He be a pillar of fortitude to you by night, and a cloud of comfort by day, and bring you at last to Himself, in whose presence there is fulness of joy, and at whose right hand there are treasures for evermore."

Much has been written and said on the subject of pulpit oratory, as to whether sermons should be read or delivered from memory. There are good arguments on both sides of the question, but the practice is becoming almost universal of using the manuscript, more or less, in all kinds of churches, without any formidable opposition on the part of the hearers. For more than thirty years, as we have already noted, Mr. Wightman preached without a single note before him, and even on one occasion, while attending the General Assembly, he was appointed to preach on the following Sunday before the Lord Commissioner and other dignitaries, which he did eloquently and well, though the manuscript was no nearer him than his sermon drawer in the manse. Still, he thought committing discourses was a great waste of time and wearing of the brain. Here is a reflection on the subject made at midnight on a Sunday after he had delivered, not read, a lecture and a sermon of forty minutes' length each:—"It is now struck twelve at night. All is still, and nothing but the ticking of the clock on the stair is heard. My dear sister long ago, I presume, locked in the drowsy arms of sleep! 'Tired

Nature's sweet restorer, balmy sleep!' I find myself not so able for sitting up late or prosecuting study so long at a time as formerly (*Consule Planco*), and my spirits often sink, especially when I consider how long I have lived, and how little I have done. I have grudged the time spent in committing my lectures and discourses to memory, but my congregation has been gratified, and I may have employed myself in some less clerical avocations. Yet I think my name might have survived longer than it is likely to do, in some literary (Biblical or Theological) productions. My vanity may flatter me, but my reason suggests that posterity will suffer no great loss for want of my lucubrations." This was a calm reflection, and a modest one, after he had been about thirty years a parish minister. Nor was it the only time he had done so. He had made the same often and long before, lamenting how much more good he could have otherwise effected, in visiting the sick, and performing other pastoral duties, instead of mewing himself up in his study for a couple of days every week, conning and committing his task as a schoolboy his Catechism or his grammar. Congregations generally are wiser now, and look more at the matter than the manner of what is addressed to them from the pulpit.

The year 1826 was one to be long remembered in the country from the hardships, and suffering, and distress of various kinds which many of the inhabitants endured. Early prognostications had given them to anticipate an unusually hot and droughty summer, and when the season arrived every anticipation was far exceeded. There had been nothing equal to it for considerably more than half a century, the only one with any resemblance to it being 1762, though even it was not nearly so burning. The summer became scorching to an inconceivable degree, the thermometer ranging from 84 to 90 degrees in the shade, and as high as 125 in the sunshine. The consequence was that all herbage was speedily destroyed, the fields were brown and bare, and cattle had to be driven from one sheltered spot to another where the sun had not acted so severely, and small patches of grass had not withered away. The scenes which took place were very much like the patriarchal customs of old, mentioned in Scripture, as when Jacob's sons drove their flocks from the vale of Hebron to Shechem, and thence to Dothan, in quest of pasture, and when Joseph, going in search of them, was sold as a slave and taken to Egypt. The heat was so intense that in several places of the country peat mosses and forests spontaneously took fire, causing great destruction. This was especially so in the shires of Stirling, Perth, Forfar, and Aberdeen. Half an acre of Mabie moss, near Dumfries, burned for a week. Several mountains in the North also ignited; Lochnagar became all ablaze, the furze covering it bursting into flame, as was supposed, by the reflection of the sun's rays from the cairngorms and other gems with which the place abounded. Others followed suit, such as Benaboard, Benaven, and Glentanner, which burned for several days. In America it was even worse than in Europe; the thermometer was higher, and the heat more insufferable. Ten thousand acres of forest near Boston were consumed by spontaneous ignition, and several woods were also destroyed in the same way in the neighbourhood of the Erie Canal. Showers occasionally fell, but they were too slight to effect any good, and produced no abatement of the intense heat. The heavens continued like brass, and the earth like iron. A lady in Galloway found a duck's nest by the side of a burn, and desirous to have it more closely under her superintendence, took it home, but the duck would not follow. The dame, having a speculative turn, covered the nest with a large slate and set it in the sunshine. In five days the whole brood came out, the mother was brought back, and she took as kindly to the young ones as if nothing unusual had occurred. Water became extremely scarce—many streams were dried up, and wells never known to fail became exceedingly low. Cattle were in a state of starvation, as sufficient food and water could not be obtained. From time to time great thunder-storms came on, followed with showers, which only tantalized human expectations, for when these had passed away, all things seemed just as before.

The atmosphere continued sultry almost beyond endurance, and the harvest prospects were sad and sickening. The wheat crops proved scarcely an average, while barley and oats were far below a half. These last were so short in the straw that they could not bend over the sickle, and had to be mown with the scythe, or, more generally, pulled up by the roots. The result of this was that the meal produced was so full of sand as to be almost useless for human food; nevertheless, when it came to be offered for sale, it was charged three shillings a stone. A man in Maxwelltown was mobbed by the populace for raising the price when he saw the demand was in excess of the supply, and he narrowly escaped with his life. Twenty

acres of uncut ryegrass hay in a field near Dumfries
were sold for the trifle of fifteen shillings. Trade of
various descriptions was at a stand-still, and labour was
with difficulty invented in rural parishes to preserve
families from starvation, although only half wages were
allowed, the unaccustomed hand being unable even for
the performance of half-work. The whole body of
weavers in Kirkmichael, Ayrshire, went a mile out of
the village to meet the weekly carrier from Glasgow to
learn if he had brought them any work, and when they
were told he had twelve webs, and had the promise of
more the following week, they were so overjoyed at the
welcome news, though only a tithe of their number
could be supplied, that they unyoked the horse and
drew the huge cart home. Great rain-falls occurred in
October, and a renewed season seemed to set in, in lieu
of the one that had just gone. White currants produced
a second crop, as also strawberries from plants which
had yielded fruit in June. Gooseberry and other bushes
also budded anew, and so propitious did the weather
become, that a farmer planted a field of potatoes from
seed of the same year's produce expecting a good supply,
and he was not disappointed. The writer remembers
this to have been done in his father's garden, and the
second crop was allowed by all the family to be superior
to the first. Nature appeared to have been wearied out
with the distress she had produced, and now desired to
make some reparation as far as she could.

The Editor of the *Dumfries Courier*, taking a retrospective view of the past season, in the beginning of
November of that year, says:—"Our fields were brown
and bare enough in June, but, fortunately for the country,

they are not so now; the woods, too, though stripped of a portion of their leaves, beseem the shroud better which Autumn weaves, than the bridal robes and livery of Spring; and confining ourselves to vegetable phenomena alone, eighteen hundred and twenty-six may be well denominated *annus mirabilis*. Bunches of roses in the open air—peas, if not beans, blooming and podding at the same time—strawberries covered with fruit and flowers—stubble fields so green that you cannot tell where corn grew—self-sown second crops of barley tempting the sparrows to commit petty larceny—turnips and potatoes so surprisingly large that a hungry man might dine on a root of the one and the hares dig encampments in the side of the other—small birds pairing, crows busy rebuilding their nests and chattering their loves aloud in the rookeries—why, these are things so seldom seen or heard of in November, that we begin to doubt whether certain theorists were right in asserting that our seasons were becoming colder and colder, and assigning as a reason for it, that the whales had formed themselves into a Joint-Stock Company for the purpose of dislodging the masses of ice that hamper them for room in their native seas. In the effects resulting from a *second Spring* the gardens, if possible, outrival the fields, and exhibit phenomena, whether in the shape of fruit or flowers, that will be chronicled and referred to for fifty years to come." This is a most cheering survey, after what has passed during the previous six months, in the dispensation which had befallen the land.

Notwithstanding the strength of mind, the shrewdness of intellect, the energy of speech, the tenacity of purpose, and the sensitiveness of criticism Mr. Wightman exhibited among his brethren in the Presbytery, there was a simplicity in his character which occasionally led him into the commission of acts from which an entire stranger might have inferred that there was somewhere a screw loose in his mental tabernacle, while nothing was further from the truth. It was said that on one occasion, when attending the General Assembly, he had accepted an invitation to dine with Lord Mackenzie, his former pupil, in Moray Place. A very important debate had engaged the attention of the reverend Court all day, in which he had been entirely absorbed, forgetting everything else, when suddenly the appointment flashed upon him, and looking his watch he found it within five minutes of the dinner hour. Rushing into the street, he looked to the one side and the other, but not a vehicle of any description was to be seen save a baker's empty barrow, leisurely hauled along by the united efforts of two young lads. He rapidly waved his arm towards them to come up with all haste, at which they stood still in astonishment, not knowing what was meant— still more rapidly went the arm, and up came the hurley. "I'll give you sixpence to take me quickly to Princes Street!" No sooner said than agreed to. Up he mounted; one before and another behind, they went down Bank Street and the Mound like an express engine at full speed. Arriving at Princes Street, he called out "Sixpence more to Moray Place!" This was too glorious fun to be refused; so at it they all went again, up one street and down another, finally drawing up at his lordship's residence, much to the amusement of the ladies at the drawing-room window, who laughed out-

T

right at the sort of equipage with which their waited-for guest had come. We took the opportunity of asking him, in one of his happiest moods, if the incident was true, to which he replied, in a laughing manner, as relishing the joke, " It's one of the stories that Crocket and Dunbar got up against me—I took it only as far as Princes Street." Mr. Crocket, however, afterwards insisted that he took it the whole way.

When a horticultural show was being held in Dumfries, he was desirous to exhibit a specimen of pears, not on account of their quality but their number, a tree in the manse garden being weighted almost to the ground. He caused the heaviest-laden branch to be carefully sawn off, and, mounting his horse, rode away into town in the greatest spirits, with the precious treasure over his shoulder. At every wayside dwelling, as he passed, the youngsters gave a hurrah and ran after him, while he hurrahed in return, and as he entered the town the hurrahs were repeated by every street arab as he rode along. He was delighted beyond measure at this exuberant exultation, and he thought that if " coming events cast their shadows before," he was certain of a perfect ovation when he reached the exhibition grounds. Alas! for the deceptiveness of all human speculations, on alighting from his horse he found, to his astonishment and chagrin, that every pear had disappeared; that the huzzas with which he had been greeted and followed by the way were for the falling fruit, and, on entering the town, at the ludicrous spectacle of his carrying so prominently an unsightly branch. We can easily imagine him muttering, as he threw it down in disappointment, *Olim truncus eram ficulnus, inutile lignum!*

On no occasion, but especially on that of a wedding
festival, did he ever attempt to mar the mirth of innocent amusement by an austere look or an unkind word.
On the contrary, he gave it all the countenance and
support in his power consistent with his clerical profession and his advanced life. When performing the duty
of uniting two loving hearts "till God should separate
them by death," he was short and pointed in his address,
wisely declaring that it was very probable the parties
specially interested, from the excitement of the moment,
scarcely heard a word he said. When the ceremony
was over, if the married parties had not been guilty of
immorality, he always joined in the festivities and added
to the conviviality of the meeting by now and again
giving some witty saying, or enjoying with zest the
rustic outbursts of humour in others, listening to their
simple singing, and applauding the comely songstress
who did her best, though her voice sadly quavered
under the consciousness that the minister was present.
So we find him occasionally noting in his diary such
matters as these:—"It was a fine warm evening, and
after the marriage ceremony the company went all out
into the garden and had tea—a *fête champêtre*—and a
merry dance. I danced a reel with the bride, though I
had often said that I was going to leave off frisking
under the burden of threescore years and three.

> 'To song and dance I'd bid farewell,
> But for the—Vive la bagatelle!'"

He possessed a remarkable elasticity of spirits as circumstances required, and none more readily or sincerely
carried out the Scripture injunction to rejoice with them

that do rejoice and weep with them that weep. Mournful occurrences affected him deeply, and he generally sought relief to his feelings in poetry. The following pathetic verses were composed on the death of his father, for whom he cherished the most devoted affection:—

My Father's Death.

"Chill o'er the mountain-heath the east wind blew,
  Mute sat each feathered minstrel on the spray,
As near my father's loved abode I drew,
  I met who told me he was lifeless clay!
Farewell! pale form, no more my father dear—
  Thy eyes no more a father's love reveal,
Thy lips no more kiss off my falling tear,
  Thy ear no more approves my fond appeal.

"Deep in the dust that hoary head must rest;
  Green o'er that bosom dewy grass shall grow;
Those knees, my infant seat, with cold earth pressed,
  Must be unclimbed the mouldering turf below.
Suns yet shall rise and set, and nature bloom
  As fresh and beauteous as it bloomed before;
But ah! how dark and dreary is the tomb!
  There shines no sun—there nature blooms no more.

"Thus mourned the Muse a tender parent lost,
  While all the soul to grief was freely given;
But 'midst the ocean where the barque was tossed,
  An anchor lay whose chain was fixed in heaven.
Hope, radiant seraph, calmed the rising storm
  Which shook the heart with sorrow's 'whelming power;
Faith gave a substance to each shadowy form,
  And showed a sky where tempests never lower."

Of similar pathetic beauty is the following Ode respecting family bereavement in the case of a dear friend:—

The Premature Death of a Son.

" As the sweet flower which scents the lawn,
    But withers in the rising day,
Thus lovely was my Henry's dawn—
    Thus swiftly fled his life away.

" And, as the flower that early dies,
    Escapes from many a coming woe,
No lustre lends to guilty eyes,
    Nor blushes on a guilty brow;

" So the sad hour that took my boy,
    Perhaps has spared some heavier doom—
Snatched him from scenes of guilty joy,
    Or from the pangs of ill to come.

" He died before his infant soul
    Had ever burned with wrong desires,
Had ever spurned at Heaven's control,
    Or ever quenched its sacred fires.

" He died to sin, he died to care,
    But for a moment felt the rod;
Then, springing on the viewless air,
    Spread his light wings and soared to God.

" This, the blest theme that cheers my voice,
    The grave is not my darling's prison;
The stone that covered half my joys
    Is rolled away, and he is risen ! "

" Monday, June 5, 1826.—Attended the funeral of Mrs.
Rachel Carlyle, widow of the late Rev. James Laurie, minister of Tinwald. He died twenty-six years ago. I was two
years his neighbour, and preached his funeral sermon. His
skull was entire, as also his under jaw—both of which I took
up in my hand at the grave's mouth (for Mrs. Laurie was
buried in her husband's grave), and many serious thoughts
rushed on my mind, for I had often heard that mouth speak,

and had seen that skull clothed with flesh and hair. I well remember the features of his countenance and the tones of his voice! This scene is rich with matter of serious meditation, and calls on me what my hand finds to do to do with my might, and to consider how soon I may be laid in the lonesome grave. His son James was weeping sore, and his daughter Rachel, Mrs. Wilkin."

Mr. Wightman was indeed very solemnly impressed, and on returning home he wrote the following lines in remembrance of the scene:—

ON HANDLING THE SKULL OF THE LATE REV. MR. LAURIE, OF TINWALD.

"Ah, where are the eyeballs in which brightly glowed
   Humanity's heart-melting beams?
That tongue, ah! where is it, from which gently flowed
   Heavenly truth in exuberant streams?

"Oh! fled are those looks which bespoke the kind heart,
   The features which lighted his face;
And fled, too, that voice unencumbered by art,
   But distinguished by each manly grace.

"Ah me! and is this what remains of my friend,
   And what my own self soon shall be?
Great Father of Lights, O then show me my end,
   And prepare me for meeting with Thee!

"If ever some brother thus pore o'er the bone
   Which at present encases my brain;
I ask of that brother one tear—only one—
   For I wish not to give needless pain.

"But should the warm tear which may drop o'er my dust,
   From virtue and friendship proceed,
Then—though at my grave stand no proud marble bust—
   No other memorial I need.

"'This skull I consign to its low narrow cell,
   To moulder beneath the cold clay—
  Dread relic of him whom I lovéd so well—
   Till the dawn of the great judgment day.''

Here is an account of a visit he paid to Edinburgh, during the sitting of the General Assembly, in 1826:—

"I have been in Edinburgh doing [some little business, and, though not a member, attending the meetings of the General Assembly. One day I sat in the gallery from 10 o'clock A.M. till 11 o'clock P.M., the day on which the *Plurality Case*, as it is often called, was discussed. Overtures from several Synods and some Presbyteries had been given in regarding the union of offices in the Church, especially respecting a minister holding a Professorship in a University. This kind of union has prevailed almost constantly in the Presbyterian Church, and in the Christian Church since the very beginning; but the public mind seems now to be in favour of these overtures, and there is a pretty general leaning among the people, and among many who reckon themselves competent judges, against ministers having any office except the ministry, and the duties immediately connected with it. They who are for abolishing plurality of charges have no objection to a minister having a professor's chair if he resigns his living in the Church when he accepts of the professorship. I believe the public voice will in a few years prevail, if it continues to speak as loud as it does at present, though I lean to the old way. This is at least excusable in a sexagenarian; and especially as I am an alarmist with regard to the proposed disjunction of the Church and the college—the sanctuary and the seminary—the clergy and the schools. I am the more confirmed in my opinion that I see many of those brethren who are most zealous for the abolition of pluralities enjoying what I reckon

much more hurtful to the interests of religion and learning—
factorships, secretaryships, farms, and editorships of magazines and newspapers.   Much reasoning and a great deal of
irrelevant matter was used in the Assembly that day on both
sides of the question, and the vote being called, a large
majority (58) declared in favour of the existing state of things.
Dr. Thomas Chalmers and Mr. James Moncreiff, advocate,
are strenuous for the doing away of union of affairs in the
Church altogether.   Dr. Nicol and President Hope are as
earnest for the present state of matters.   Considerable talent
was displayed on both sides of the house, but none seemed
to be convinced by the arguments of their opponents, and
the vote might have been called for in the morning, and the
members on each side would have been, I suppose, the same
as they were at eleven o'clock at night; but, then, what fine
speeches would have been lost!

"I attended a meeting for the advancement of religious
education in the Highlands and Islands of Scotland—Principal
Baird in the chair, and Dr. Chalmers croupier.   The Principal
acquitted himself well, and Dr. Chalmers made a brilliant
address, though I did not recollect much of it afterwards.
The Doctor smothers his meaning with words, and dazzles
the mind of his hearers with figurative language.   Principal
Macfarlan also spoke well, and Dr. Andrew Thomson, and a
Mr. Campbell.   There were nearly a hundred at supper.   I
addressed a short speech to Principal Baird, after Mr. Campbell, who roused my patriotism and kindly feeling towards
the Caledonians.   I breakfasted one morning with Mr.
Henry Mackenzie, the venerable author of 'The Man of
Feeling,' and other works of great merit.   He is deaf and
very feeble, the ghost of what he was.   I had taught his son
in the close of the last century, when I was a preacher and
teaching privately in Edinburgh—*Meminisse juvat.*   Lord
Mackenzie was my pupil, and it gives me pleasure to think

of the days that I spent in the society of such excellent
persons. I dined with Dr. Carson, Rector of the High
School, a Closeburn scholar. My toast at dinner was 'Mr.
Mundell, of Closeburn Academy.' In giving it I said that
if the branches have spread so wide, and borne such fruit,
how vigorous must the root be which nourished them! If
the stars which belong to the solar system of Closeburn be
so brilliant, how splendid must be the sun which shed its
light on these luminaries! This seemed to be well received."

Mr. Wightman was extremely sensitive in his affections, and from time to time, as his college friends
and acquaintances dropped off, he felt as if his very heart
was buried along with them. Only some three months
after his making the above jotting of his visit to Edinburgh, he learned at the October meeting of Synod in
Dumfries that his excellent friend, the Rev. William
Gillespie of Kells, had a day or two before gone the way
of all the earth. He had been newly married, and, besides his widow, had left two brothers to lament his loss.
In referring to this event, "I have seldom known," he
said, " any person more generally or sincerely lamented.
He was my intimate acquaintance and true friend. A
kinder disposition never warmed a human breast—
open-hearted and liberal-minded, he was the friend of
rising genius, of unpatronized merit, and had a hand to
give and a heart to feel when distress and indigence
came before him." Mr. Wightman, in giving this portrait of his friend, was unintentionally giving his own at
the same time, and in the very words.

CHAPTER XV.

REJOICINGS AT TERREGLES—APOCRYPHA CONTROVERSY—SYNOD MEET-
ING AT IRVINE—EXTRACTS—ATTENDS THE GENERAL ASSEMBLY—
INDUCTION AT ST. MICHAEL'S, DUMFRIES—PUBLIC DINNER TO
ALLAN CUNNINGHAM — SERMON AT LOCHARBRIGGS — REFORM
MEETING—EXTRACTS—IMPROMPTUS.

ON Monday, 1st January, 1827, young Marmaduke
Maxwell of Terregles attained his majority, and the
rejoicing on that account was very enthusiastic throughout a large portion of the Nithsdale district.   The
antiquity of the family, the succour and the sympathy
it had shown to royalty in distress, and the honourable
position it had always maintained in the country, as well
as the promising character of the young gentleman
chiefly interested, doubtless gave an impetus to the
festivities of the occasion which in but few circumstances
could be realized.   The farmers on the estates of Terregles, Kirkgunzeon, and Lochrutton assembled in their
respective parishes and dined together in honour of the
day.   In the evening bonfires blazed from the summit
of every hill, far and near, and a happier New-year's-
day never closed upon a rural population.   On the
following Thursday Mr. Maxwell entertained his tenantry
to dinner in the George Hotel, Dumfries, out of compliment for the interest they had manifested in the
auspicious event.   Upwards of a hundred persons, including many of the clergy, were present, under the

presidency of Mr. Woodburn, factor on the estate. Several speeches of a high order were given in proposing the toasts of the evening, which fired the spirit of Mr. Wightman with such rapturous glow that, though unprepared, he made a most eloquent oration in reference to the family of Terregles, to whose kindness, thirty years previously, he owed his position as a parish minister. Though it was not reported at the time, yet we are enabled to give, from his own after-notes, an extract from it, showing how effectively he could speak without premeditation on a subject which filled his heart. Addressing the Chairman, he said—

"My heart is still warm with the glow which pervaded our bosoms at our last meeting. We then assembled to give expression to our respect and esteem for the family of the House of Terregles, and to our hopes that the young proprietor possessed the dispositions of his ancestors. We have good proofs from what we have heard and seen of him, especially his princely donation to the poor (£100), and the hospitality with which he is now entertaining us, that he is a branch of the kindly and wide-spreading tree under which our fathers sat so comfortably and so long. The landlords of the family of Nithsdale have been none of those hard and severe taskmasters who required bricks without materials, and who, if they received the rents of their lands, were reckless of the welfare and comfort of their tenants. There are persons—they can hardly be called men—whose very looks have a freezing and withering influence, and who suffer nothing near them to be green and flourishing; who, with more than Gorgon efficacy, petrify every living thing on which they turn their eye, and scatter sickliness and sterility through all their joyless wake. But, Sir, there are

others, and we can say this from long experience, whose presence inspires confidence, and whose countenance has an
influence like that of the sun, which makes the flowers of the
field and the blossoms of the wood display their fairest
beauties and send up to heaven their choicest odours. Such
were the worthy persons who have endeared to us their
memories, and such, we confidently hope, will be the noble
youth who is the principal object in every eye to-night. I
do not envy him his large possessions, but wish him a corresponding largeness of heart the better to enjoy them, yet I
congratulate him on a rich inheritance and the devoted
attachment of so many thousand hearts. The fires of joy
which we lately saw burning on so many heights—those
pillared flames (pyramids, indeed!) which almost extinguished,
for the time, the lights of the firmament—the shouts which
made the welkin ring—the gratulatory sympathies of three
or four parishes—what were they? What were the shouts
which rent the air of assembled Greece, or the less generous
vociferations of a Roman amphitheatre, or the confused noise
arising from the fields of war? What are all or any of these
compared with the exhilarating sounds now heard within
these walls! What a mighty engine may this attachment
become in the hand of liberality guided by a benevolent
heart! What energy may it give to the ' Power of Cultivation!' On such a fulcrum this lever might level or remove
mountains. The harmony of this and the former meetings
has already been noticed. We are consolidated into one
precious metal—a kind of Corinthian brass, not, like that
which bore the name, produced by the fire of desolation, but
by the flame of devoted affection, in which every deleterious
element is melted away, leaving nothing behind but what is
sterling and pure! I have no favour to ask ; I dwell among
my own people, and enjoy more esteem than I deserve. I
have now and then an opportunity of casting a filial and

heart-winning glance to the sky-mixing summit of the mountain on which I followed my father's flocks (the Shepherd
now of a nobler charge!), and brushed the dews from its
blooming heath, chasing the humming bees and coy butter-
flies from flower to flower; sometimes fortunate enough to
lay hold of a lamb as it slumbered on its mossy couch, but
much disappointed that it did not consider me a friend, as it
bounded away from my arms to gambol on its hills again!
Ah! happy heaths; ah! pleasing scenes, I feel a momentary
bliss from the freshness and fragrance which your gales bring
to me redolent of joy and youth, and even in the winter of
my life breathing a second spring.   And when the wintry
hand of death shall chill this heart which now beats with
such transport, I wish to be considered not only as a Christian
minister, a character which I am anxious to sustain, but as
the son of a farmer, and of a farmer on the estate of Maxwell
of Nithsdale."

Mr. Wightman's address was received with the utmost
enthusiasm, and added largely to the enjoyment of the
evening's proceedings. As we have said, it was entirely
unpremeditated—a pure effusion of gushing benevolence
towards the family on whose account they were assembled, and whose hospitality they were enjoying. He
was always particularly happy in these extemporaneous
outpourings, even much more than when he had time
to prepare; and what added to the power of his oratory
was the vehemence of his feelings, the tone of his voice,
and the artless gesticulation, by no means the most
refined, with which his delivery was accompanied. He
carried out fully the maxim, that whatever is worth
doing is worth doing well, and cast his whole heart and
soul into all he undertook to say or do. He had a

sincere affection for the family of Nithsdale, and never forgot the gratitude he owed to an eminent member of that house in conferring upon him the long-desired designation of a parish minister, after great realization of the saying of Solomon, that "Hope deferred maketh the heart sick." He never forgot his friends, and could not cherish enmity even towards his foes, if such he had.

The opening summer of this year was as unusually cold as the immediately preceding one had been hot. Snow was on the ground during all the months of spring, and even in May it was lying one foot deep in the open plains, retarding agricultural labour and the progress of vegetation. On the third of this month Criffel stood towering to the clouds white from base to summit, reminding one of Horace's description of Soracte, when he says:—

> "Vides, ut altâ stet nive candidum
> Soracte, nec jam sustineant onus
> Silvæ laborantes."

The snow and the drift blasts, however, soon passed away, the bending boughs in the woods resumed their normal position, the sun shone out with compensating effulgence, and the grass sprang up with almost visible rapidity. The result was that the harvests turned out far beyond expectation, rejoicing the heart of man and beast. Nature had exhausted her quiver upon suffering humanity, and she now seemed disposed to make reparation for the distress inflicted.

Coincident with the unusual atmospheric heat of the previous year, another had arisen, or rather come to a crisis, equally violent, and destructive of a higher vitality than animal and vegetable existence, but which showed no symptom of abating, as the other had entirely done. It waxed hotter and hotter, till it culminated in an explosion which made sad havoc of Christian principle and feeling. This was the "Apocrypha Controversy," the leaders of which were the Rev. Dr. Andrew Thomson and the Rev. Henry Grey, both of Edinburgh, both able ecclesiastical gladiators, and both determined to carry on the war to the utmost extremity. The question diverged into abusive personality and inveterate recrimination in the *Christian Instructor*, edited by the former gentleman, and in a series of letters signed "Anglicanus," patronized by Mr. Grey, and afterwards acknowledged to be from the pen of his wife. The language employed was discreditable to both parties, and so violent that the Presbytery and the Synod had both to interfere. Mr. Wightman was very indignant at the unseemly contest, and gave vent to his ire in the following effusion:—

" Religion condemns the vexatious affray,
  Maintained, as reported, 'twixt Thomson and Grey.
  She never takes part in the settling of creeds,
  Where bigotry bullies, and charity bleeds;
  Nor drinks of a cup in those banquets unhallowed,
  Where gnats are strained out, and where camels are swallowed.
  Her cause is not furthered by man's vengeful ire,
  And needs no assistance from faggot and fire.
  Her weapons of warfare are brought from above,
  All tempered with Mercy, and pointed with Love.
  She warns us the *beam* to remove from our eye,
  That thus we the *mote* in our brother's may spy;
  And tells us that gifts the most costly are vain,
  Unless we the fierceness of anger restrain;

> Our body, from zeal, though we give to the flames,
> 'Twill never atone for opprobrious names.
> Before we the fame of our brother bespatter,
> Both sides we should clean of the cup and the platter.
> The cymbal's soft tinkle, the trumpet's loud sound,
> Will not soothe the life-blood that cries from the ground.
> The Father of Mercies can never delight
> To view the red field where His ministers fight.
> To Him belongs vengeance and He will repay,
> Without the assistance of Thomson and Grey."

We believe these lines appeared in one of the local journals, with the signature "Litera Tristis." They are deserving of reproduction, as affording another evidence of the peaceful and genial character of the author in all matters of religious strife. But we now turn to his diary, as important events are in view:—

"Saturday, 22nd May, 1830.—The weather has been fine for a good while, and now is cold and windy. The vegetation is suffering, although it is further on this year now than it usually is a fortnight after this time. I will be at home to-morrow preaching, and on Monday will go to Edinburgh for two or three days to see the General Assembly. Dr. Singer, of Kirkpatrick-Juxta, is to be Moderator of the Assembly. He and some of my friends, I understand, are intending to request the Senatus Academicus of Edinburgh to confer on me the degree of D.D. I presume that I could get that honour from any of the three other Universities; and if my dear *Alma Mater* refuse me this distinction, I must console myself with the conviction, that, like Cato, I deserved it. Having for some weeks past been rather remiss in my reading and professional studies, I resolve, *Deo juvante*, to be more diligent in future, as long as health and strength continue, convinced that my happiness depends much on the faithful application of my time and talents, such as they are, to the sacred duties connected with my sacred profession. So help me God! His Majesty the King is thought to be dying. This is a memento to me, for he and I are of the same age, sixty-seven years, and on the 12th day of August next we will be sixty-eight years old, if spared. The Duke of Clarence will succeed his Majesty as Sovereign of these realms."

Mr. Wightman had naturally a great regard for the University of Edinburgh, where he had gone through his whole curriculum of study for the Church, and the coveted degree from that quarter would have had additional lustre to him. As an evidence of his affection he had, twenty years previously, presented to the Theological Library of the College a magnificent copy of the Hebrew Bible in twelve volumes, very rare, in a mahogany case, and which, at the time we write, is stated to be "in the finest preservation." It is a very small edition, "Par op. Rob. Steph., 1554.—La netteté des caractères et la commodité des volumes, la font rechercher des Curieux et des Amateurs.—De Bure."

He was ten days in Edinburgh, and saw many of his clerical and other friends; but though the degree was mentioned to the Senatus, at least to the Theological Faculty, from some cause or other nothing came of it.

"Wednesday, 30th June.—The King, George IV., died last Saturday, the 26th, and same day, at Largs, Dr. Scot, my worthy co-presbyter! Kings and priests are mortal—but there is an everlasting King, and a Priest for ever. The weather is warm to-day, almost for the first time this season. Both May and June have proved cold months, and the crops have suffered considerably."

U

"Friday, 2nd July.—The weather is now warmer, and there has been thunder to-day. I have sometimes these twenty years past thought of publishing the Service of a Communion Sabbath—if not the Services of the Preparation, Communion, and Thanksgiving Sabbaths, but works of the kind have been published by Mr. Wright, of Borthwick, and others, and I may never accomplish my design."

"Monday, 16th August.—Charles X. of France has forfeited his right to the throne by his arbitrary measures of late, and he is now skulking in secret in the Netherlands. The Duke of Orleans is likely to be king, and a modification of the Ministry to take place. The present times will not bear arbitrary rulers. The nations are being shaken with a revolutionary spirit. Our new king, William IV., is shaking hands with his subjects, like an honest English tar!"

"Monday, 30th August.—King Philippe of France is very popular at present, but I fear he is too familiar, for there is an excess in this, as well as on the other side. The French are not at rest yet, nor Spain (nor some among ourselves). Our own good King William is rather too much the sailor instead of the sovereign! *Bonum sit!*"

"Friday, 17th September.—A grand ethereal arch appeared in the sky about eight o'clock at night, reaching from north-west to south-east, almost to the horizon at each end. It was white and of a fleecy appearance, continuing about fifteen minutes. It was beautifully defined on the azure canopy, and the stars were seen through it, as they were seen through the ghosts of Ossian. Saturday was calm and cloudy. Sunday was one of the most stormy and rainy days I have seen, and the Nith rose to a great height. Carts were seen going to carry away corn from the banks."

Mr. Wightman attended, as corresponding member, the Synod of Glasgow and Ayr, which assembled at

Irvine in October of this year, and at which several
dignitaries of the Church were present—such as Dr.
Burns, of Paisley; Dr. Macfarlan, of Glasgow; Dr.
Dewar, Dr. Laurie, and others.   A kind of heresy, of a
Mr. M'Lean, respecting the humanity of Christ, occupied
the attention of the Court almost three days!   Another
heresy (that of Mr. Campbell of Row) was expected to
be discussed, but from some informality it did not come
on, and was left to be disposed of by the following
General Assembly.   As was to be expected, great talent
was displayed in the debates which took place during
the long sederunts, but Mr. Wightman being a stranger
took little part in the discussions.   He merely observed
that he had come from the folds of Israel to revisit the
camps of his brethren, like David of old, and he found
them all well, and at their post, arrayed in polished
armour.   His remarks gave great satisfaction to his
brethren of the Synod, one of whom said his speech was
like an oasis in the desert, it afforded them such refreshment!   From Irvine he went to Glasgow, but we must
let him describe his journey in his own words:—

"I went to Glasgow on the Friday, along with Mr. Campbell, minister of Row, who is charged with peculiar views
regarding salvation and our Lord's coming.   We travelled
pleasantly together in the coach, along with two others, a
gentleman and a lady.   On the sun rising in a fine blue sky,
Mr. Campbell, looking out and seeing the sun, said with a
tone and an air of mild enthusiasm, 'So shall *He* come!
Fair as the moon, clear as the sun, and terrible as an army
with banners!'   He and I talked over many things with
temper and charity.   He said that 'he had not specially
prepared himself for the pulpit these two years past,' and

added that 'a minister should be always preparing.' I said that I prepared two days every week after being thirty-three years in the ministry, to which he replied, that 'the Spirit helped his infirmities.' I told him that I had read all the Hebrew Bible, with the commentaries of learned men. He smiled and said these were poor helps; he had aid from above. He said he believed everything was as he asserted. I did not doubt it, but said *belief* was not a sure foundation to build the *truth* on (speaking of human belief), for many had been so disordered in their imaginations as to think and say that a part of their body was glass, and such like. On passing a lake where the trees on the borders of it were apparently inverted in the watery mirror, I said, 'These trees seem to be growing downwards in the water, and if you were to *believe* so, that would not *prove* them to be so.' He smiled with much good nature. I said, 'You will wonder how far behind I am in the career of spiritual perfection and know-ledge.' 'Yes,' he said, 'I do wonder, and I think it is a pity that so much benevolence should be in such darkness regard-ing spiritual things.' I told him that I would oppose his views in next General Assembly. He said, 'I wish you may be directed to do all to the glory of God.' I could say no more. Having staid all night in the Buck's Head, a good inn, I spent Saturday in seeing the town, the Museum, the Arcade, the New Rooms, &c., and bought several books and pamphlets of the day. I called on Principal Macfarlan, and engaged to preach for him on Sunday afternoon, which I did, and also in the evening, in a large church, to some thousands, and caught cold. Returned by the coach on Monday—attended our own Synod, at Dumfries, on Tuesday —the induction of Mr. Wallace to St. Michael's on Thursday, and was much pleased with the appearance of my young friend, Mr. George Greig, junior, who conducted the services of the day."

The following General Assembly was a very sad and important one, several cases of the gravest character requiring to be considered and adjudged on; amongst others, that of Mr. Campbell of Row, just adverted to in connection with the Synod meeting at Irvine. Mr. Wightman took no prominent part in the discussion of this case, except in giving his vote against the accused, probably from the friendly intercourse they had had in the coach to Glasgow, and perhaps also from the overwhelming evidence he saw brought forward, and which he could not conscientiously gainsay. Mr. Campbell, after a very affecting address by his father to the Assembly, was deposed from his sacred office by an almost unanimous vote, only six members voting in his favour. The heresy also of Edward Irving was taken up by the venerable Court, and it would seem that Mr. Wightman took part in the discussion. A Mrs. Willard, an American lady, distinguished as the author of a History of the United States, and other literary publications, was present on the occasion, and in a journal of her tour in France and Great Britain, published two years afterwards, she thus refers to the matter:—" After some minor affairs, another subject was started, as if it were done at this time to gratify my curiosity, already awakened. It was the subject of Mr. Irving's heresy, which not only interested my feelings, but those of the members themselves— brought forth their divisions of sentiment—produced sound reasonings—and struck out fine flashes of oratory. The orthodox party, the leader of which seems to be Dr. Macfarlan, Principal of the College of Glasgow, were in favour of silencing the accused, while the Liberal party, at the head of whom appears to be Mr. Cook (I believe the celebrated lawyer of Edinburgh), were for more moderate measures. A clergyman, who, I was told, was a Mr. Wightman, and of the orthodox party, clothed his ideas in beautiful language. 'Though the fruits of heresy,' said he, 'are fair to the eye, yet its roots are bitter and its shade is poisonous.'"

Another case came before the venerable Court in which Mr. Wightman took a conspicuous part, and contributed much, it was acknowledged, by a felicitous *jeu d'esprit*, to smooth asperities and bring the matter to a harmonious issue. The Rev. Laurence Butter, minister of Lethendy, had been very severe in his remarks with regard to the presentation of the Rev. Mr. Nelson to the parish of Auchtergaven, in the Presbytery of Dunkeld. After several members had expressed their opinions of the presentee in very eulogistic terms, Mr. Wightman rose and said that the other members of Presbytery had behaved in a brotherly manner to the presentee, and their speeches did honour to their heads and their hearts, but one member appeared to him to have hardened *his* heart against the admission of Mr. Nelson to be his co-presbyter. He hoped, however, that he had been now *melted* by what he had heard and seen in the Assembly respecting the merits of the presentee, and that he would now join his other brethren and give him a cordial reception. It was recorded of certain tribes in Arabia, that when they receive a stranger into their tents they, as a mark of welcome, pour a cup of *melted butter* on his head, and so, he trusted, it would prove with regard to the parish of Auchtergaven, that they would welcome their young minister in a similar manner, and that he would conquer any opposition which had been shown, not with the weapons of the hero whose name he bore, but with those of kindness and diligence in the discharge of pastoral duties.   The concluding part of the speech, however, was drowned amidst the laughter excited by the *butter* pun—perhaps rather too gay a demonstration for a deliberative assembly of reverend divines on matters of grave importance.   The result was favourable to the presentee, and in due time he was inducted into the parish according to the rules of the Church, proving himself to be a workman needing not to be ashamed.   He was long minister of the parish, and universally acknowledged to be a most assiduous and faithful shepherd of his flock.   We are not aware if this incident was publicly noticed at the time, but it contributed materially to the settlement in Auchtergaven. Mr. Wightman often remarked to us that he regretted his appearances in the General Assembly, as he was never prepared with a speech, and only threw in a word or two like oil upon the troubled waters, when feelings of asperity or animosity disturbed the equilibrium of the Assembly.

The church of St. Michael's, Dumfries, having become vacant by the decease of the venerable incumbent, Dr. Scot, the congregation anxiously looked about for a suitable successor, and immediately fixed their attention on the Rev. Robert Wallace, assistant minister of Kirkpatrick-Durham.   He was considered the most popular preacher in the Stewartry, and a few weeks previously had conducted the services at the ordination of Mr. Begg (now Dr. Begg of world-wide fame), in Maxwelltown Chapel, with great ability, solemnity, and eloquence. So great, indeed, was his fame as a preacher, in connec-

tion with the popularity of the young minister about to
be ordained, that many hundreds were that day unable
to gain admission to the church, and had to return home
disappointed.   A number of the members of the Dumfries Town Council were present, and delighted beyond
measure with the talents Mr. Wallace displayed, and
the impressively decorous manner in which he had conducted the whole services of the day.   After the funeral
of Dr. Scot, a meeting of the congregation was held, at
which it was unanimously agreed to petition the Crown
in favour of Mr. Wallace as their future minister.   It
says much for the promptitude and liberality of the then
existing Government, that within ten days from the
occurrence of the vacancy, the *Gazette* had the following
announcement:—" Whitehall, July 7, 1830.—The King
has been pleased to present the Rev. R. Wallace to the
Old Church and Parish of St. Michael's, Dumfries, in the
Presbytery and County of Dumfries, void by the death
of Doctor Alexander Scot."   What Ministry could then
be in existence who thus acted so promptly and so
deferentially to the wishes of the congregation?   Was
it Whig or Tory, Liberal or Conservative, in its politics?
It does not matter which, for it was highly creditable
in its wisdom, whatever the character of its politics.
Still, who had the administration of affairs?   Well, in
looking up, we find that it was the Duke of Wellington.
In due course Mr. Wallace was inducted into his charge,
and from that day till the hour of his death he was
highly esteemed, not only by his own congregation, but
by all of every sect in the town and neighbourhood.   In
his latter days, when incapacitated for pulpit duty, one
of his rural parishioners, the mistress of a farm-house

where he was visiting, said to him, when he was lamenting his inability, "O Doctor, were ye but to gae up to the pulpit and shake your head at us, we would be pleased!"

Allan Cunningham was entertained at a public dinner in Dumfries on the 22nd of July, 1831, under the presidency of Mr. M'Diarmid, of the *Dumfries Courier.* A very large number of gentlemen assembled on the occasion, among whom were many of the neighbouring gentry, to show their esteem for the poet, and to encourage him onward in the path of fame, as a credit to the district of Nithsdale. Mr. Wightman was there among the foremost, to show his respect for one he had been proud of five-and-twenty years before, when young Allan had consulted him as his parish minister on the method of study he should pursue in the opening of literary and poetic life, and he now recited an ode of welcome to him, of which the beginning ran thus:—

> " He's welcome within Scotia's pale—
> He's welcome to his native vale—
> He's welcome to his friends and me,
> For much we longed his face to see.
> The Nith in lambent beauty glides,
> To blend with Solway's briny tides;
> The landscape all is fresh and fair,
> And bland and balmy is the air;
> Glad Nature seems to swell the strain
> That welcomes Allan back again!"

Mr. Wightman's own health was proposed in flattering terms by the Chairman, who spoke of him as " a poet and a fosterer of talent in every shape, who had marked the dawn of Mr. Cunningham's genius, and directed his young ambition in the proper channel." Mr. Wightman,

in acknowledging the compliment, remarked "that if
he had ever plumed in any degree the smallest feather
in the wing of rising genius, or had in any measure confirmed the generous purpose of early virtue, the thought
shed a halo of pleasing reflection around the evening of
his days, and made him truly happy." He appreciated
the compliment very highly, the more especially that it
was given in the presence of Allan Cunningham.

"Sunday, 31st July, 1831.—Mr. Wallace, minister of St.
Michael's, is to preach this evening at Locharbriggs, about
six o'clock. I intend to hear him. He thus shows his willingness to do his duty, though he is not able to keep up the
eclat which he now enjoys since his induction to the charge.
Non equidem invideo, miror magis—adeo turbatur agris.
Mr. Wallace is a good, well-meaning man. Sunday evening.
—I went at six o'clock to hear Mr. Wallace, as I intended.
Many of my own hearers went from Kirkton and other
places in the parish. The village of Locharbriggs and the
adjoining houses poured forth their inhabitants. Many
persons from Dumfries ('lads and lasses gay!') came trooping
to the spot where the sermon was to be delivered; about a
thousand people I dare say assembled. A rude tent, of
which a cart composed the principal part, was placed in the
corner of a field near the high road, where, it seems, the Rev.
Mr. Blackadder, whom my friend Mr. Crichton so well
describes, once held forth. I placed myself close by the tent
that my rev. brother might not see me, lest this should have
discomposed him during the delivery of his partly unpremeditated (for such it appeared to be) discourse. A psalm was sung,
a serious and loosely constructed prayer followed, another
psalm was sung, and an apology was made for want of time
to prepare himself for such an audience. 'It is not by might,'

he said, 'but by the Spirit of the Lord of Hosts, that you
have met for prayer and praise, and I trust you have already
profited, yet I will humbly endeavour to offer a few meditations on a portion of Sacred Scripture.' He then read seven
or eight verses of the Twenty-fifth Psalm, and lectured verse
by verse, or clause by clause. The observations were exceedingly indigested, but the whole unction of his voice and
manner secured to him a very favourable hearing. He could
not but say that they might not be all of the right sort of
hearers, tares were permitted to mingle with the wheat, even
to the end, yet he hoped with regard to all, &c. A serious
prayer, touching the several heads (if such they were) of the
lecture, and a psalm closed the exercise. Mr. Wallace gave
notice that he could not promise that he would be ever able
to repeat such exercises, but he wished, when entering on the
charge of a large parish, to give them all an opportunity of
hearing, at least once, the voice of their minister. The scene
was interesting, and reminded me of the olden, and perhaps
the better, days of our forefathers. Mr. Wallace, on seeing
me, said he wished he had seen me at the beginning; but
this was a compliment, for he could not mean that I was to
preach."

We have seen the interest which Mr. Wightman has
all along taken in political affairs, though he always
avoided making any public appearance with regard to
the topics of the day, and contented himself with a few
observations in his diary. During 1831 the Reform
Bill was in progress, and causing great agitation throughout the land. Public meetings were everywhere held
in town and country to discuss its merits, and by many
it was regarded as the great panacea for all their
troubles. It could not be expected that a parish so

close to the county town as Kirkmahoe would be unsus-
ceptible to the influence of excitement which was daily
fomented by the numerous demagogues who had an
unbounded gratification in holding forth to their fellows,
and, accordingly, means were adopted for holding a
great parish meeting to consider the subject, and to
give it their approbation. One morning, before Mr.
Wightman was out of bed, two of his elders called and
desired to see him on most important business. They
were immediately admitted, and said they had a favour
to ask, namely, the use of the church for a Reform
meeting. He told them he was sorry they had asked
what he could not conscientiously grant, as far as he
could prevent the church from being desecrated by
disputes on politics. They said that all would go off
peaceably. He hoped so also, and was well assured that
from persons of their sense and moderation no riotous
symptoms would be shown. He observed that the cause
of freedom was in no danger in this country, that an
excitement prevailed at present which had no need of
any additional stimulus—a stone was rolling which had
no need of the touch of even their little finger, for it
would roll perhaps further than any of them wished.
He had a country, a religion, a property, and a life, as
well as they, and must consult for these to the best of
his judgment, which, after all, might be wrong, but he
claimed the privilege of thinking for himself. They
said his refusing the church would not stop the meeting,
and would disoblige the parish, to which he replied he
could not help that. The meeting was held at Quarrelwood, and was numerously attended, upwards of 400
persons of all classes in the parish being present. Mr.

Leny, of Dalswinton, disapproved of the Bill before Parliament, and proposed, as an amendment, that they should petition for a more vigorous and efficient measure; but a show of hands unmistakably demonstrated that he and his supporters were in a striking minority, which had been foreshadowed from the beginning. The whole affair might be considered valueless, as the Bill was already virtually disposed of in Parliament, and the opinion of such a meeting could do little good, perhaps as little evil. No doubt the conduct of the majority was calculated, in some degree at least, to alienate the heart of a liberal-minded and kindhearted landlord, and to introduce among the inhabitants of a peaceable parish animosities not soon to be allayed. After voting addresses to the king and to his ministers, the meeting broke up. A few weeks afterwards the office-houses of Dalswinton were burned to the ground, and rumour, which is always rife on such occasions, did not hesitate to attribute the event to the excited feeling shown at the previous meeting. This, however, was not generally believed, though there was satisfactory evidence afforded that it must have been the work of an incendiary. It was thought sufficiently important to inform Earl Grey of what had occurred, but it does not appear that his lordship took any steps in the matter to discover the offender.

There is something affecting in the following entry in the diary, which says much for the tenderness of Mr. Wightman's heart and his affection for old friends:—

" Thursday, 10th February, 1833.—A fine day, after much rain. My servant David is still ailing—his wife, my first.

serving-maid, is to be buried to-day. They have lived long together in a cottage almost at the door of the manse. David has been with me thirty-three years, and Margaret Haining, his wife, served me several years, some before and some after the marriage. She was an active and faithful servant, and I cannot but feel serious when I am called to attend her funeral. She was the first who spread my tablecloth after I had a house of my own. A certain degree of nervousness often depressed her spirits, but did not sour her temper, and she was an affectionate wife as well as a kind neighbour. This much is due from me to one who had my interest so intimately at heart. I fear her husband may not long survive her. Then I shall be helpless with regard to almost every secular matter!"

The infirmities of age are now beginning to tell upon him, and we find frequent mention of loss of memory, feebleness in the limbs, and such like, which is not to be wondered at in a man of seventy-two. Still he thinks himself as fit for pulpit duty as ever, and at stated periods holds his diets of catechising as he was wont to do. Nay, more, he has just published a volume of lectures on the Thessalonians, and has distributed 300 copies *gratis* among his parishioners and friends.

"Tuesday, 11th February, 1834.—After three months of wet and windy weather, fine, sunny, and genial days have come—the face of Nature looks like Spring, and the air is balmy, bland, and refreshing, inspiring what Milton calls 'vernal joy.'—Alas! my comparatively frozen heart and rigid limbs cannot now, as erst, sympathize with the gladness which such seasons impart to the young and vigorous; yet still, let me be thankful. I can without pain perform my pastoral duties, and participate in the happiness which good company, good weather, and a good conscience communicate to the frail race of man. I pray that I may be enabled to go down the vale of life with sober and easy steps, and at last to lay myself down in yonder lowly bed under the shadow of the Almighty, resting from my labours and my humble works following me—not to plead merit at the throne of justice, but to bear some shadowy testimony to the wish which I had to do my duty and to trust in Him who is able and willing to save all those who put their confidence in Him! The public mind is still under excitement, and society is shaking to and fro; both civil and church matters are scrutinized and searched with a keenness and severity quite extravagant. What the agitation and shaking will end in, I know not, but doubt alterations will be made, in the ardour for new things, which will not answer the expectations and auguries of the theoretical speculators. The Lord reigns, let the earth be glad!"

The following impromptu was thrown off on reading a paragraph in a local newspaper, eulogizing Lord Brougham for his speech on the Poor Laws, which was characterized as a "great maelstrom" of vast expanse, sucking everything into it:—

CHANCELLOR BROUGHAM.

"What are the speeches of Chancellor Brougham?
I've heard them compared to a mighty maelstrom,—
Now what's this maelstrom? I'll tell if you will,
'Tis a stream wide and sweepy to drive his own mill!"

Another was to the following effect:—

LORD GREY.

"A Radical, groaning, said, 'What is Lord Grey?'
A Tory replied, 'Troth, I cannot well say.'
'I'll say it myself, then,' the Radical cried,
'His lordship's a cheat, that can ne'er be denied!'"

On being asked to translate in verse the Roman maxim, *Ne sutor ultra crepidam,* he immediately wrote down without any hesitation:—

"*Ne sutor ultra crepidam!*—The Latin's very good,
   Although the sentence wants a verb which must be understood.
   Now, *sutor* means a shoemaker, and *crepida* a last,
   While *ne* and *ultra* signify the line must not be past.
   Each tradesman or practitioner will always prosper best,
   When the line of his own business is not by him transgressed."

He took great delight amid the glow of social converse to throw off such things as these, always finishing with such exclamations as "Vive la bagatelle!" and "Dulce est desipere in loco!"

CHAPTER XVI.

THE PATRONAGE QUESTION—PETER JOHNSTON OF CARNSALLOCH—
RECEIVES THE DEGREE OF D.D.—PROFESSOR GILLESPIE OF ST.
ANDREWS—AN OLD MAN'S DREAM—CHURCH MATTERS—EXTRACTS
—IRENICA—VETO ACT PASSED BY THE GENERAL ASSEMBLY—
ASSISTANT AND SUCCESSOR APPOINTED.

THE Reform agitation had scarcely subsided when
another important matter seized the public mind and
stirred up the bitter waters of contention, so true is the
poet's line, "One prospect lost, another still we gain."
This was the Anti-Patronage question, which invaded the
land and brought distraction into the Church Courts,
but which was warmly supported by the great mass of
the people, under the belief that if their point was
carried it would effect as great a cure for their ecclesiastical diseases as the other had done for their political
ailments. In almost every parish large and excited
meetings were held for the purpose of denouncing the
evils of Patronage, and of demanding unfettered independence in the appointment of a minister not only as
a privilege but a right. Pamphlets and printed speeches
on both sides of the question fell thick as leaves in
Vallambrosa, ending not unfrequently in bitter per-
sonalities, and severing friendships the most intimate
and endearing. One of the ablest and most active
ministers on the popular side, in Dumfriesshire, was
the Rev. Dr. Henry Duncan of Ruthwell, who, from the

x

platform and the press, endeavoured to bring confusion upon his enemies with a tongue and a pen of immense power. He wrote a series of letters, which appeared in a local newspaper, to the Rev. Dr. Cook of St. Andrews, declaiming against a pamphlet this gentleman had published on the previous General Assembly's measure respecting Patronage. Mr. Wightman makes the following jotting with respect to the series:—

"Friday, 17th October, 1834.—I observe with regret a series of letters by my rev. brother, Dr. Henry Duncan, minister of Ruthwell, to Dr. Cook of St. Andrews, upon his pamphlet respecting Patronage. Dr. Duncan writes with great keenness, but with considerable appearance, and with much profusion, of disinterestedness and candour. I am sorry to find such insinuations as the following made against my friend Dr. Cook, viz.:—'There must be in your statements, or reasonings, or in both, exaggeration and special pleading of the most extravagant kind'—'the only excuse that your best friends can make for you is, that you have written under the exaggerating influence of excited feelings' —'a practised reasoner knows well to make the worst appear the better cause,'—and can 'overwhelm an obnoxious measure with captious objections'—'a special pleader can place such a measure in a disadvantageous light'—'prurient imagination'—'a measure illusory'—'authority of a name,' —and 'of party influence.' Now, I would ask my friend Dr. Duncan why, in the present state of public excitement, speak so much and so loudly of 'popular infusion'—'popular principle'—the Church rotten at the core'—'menial pedagogues'—'Court sycophants'—'mountains of difficulties resolving into clouds'? May not these clouds be impregnated with fatal lightning? Were it not better to use milder language?"

From this it will be seen on which of the two sides
Mr. Wightman stood, though he did not publicly enter
the controversial list. "I cannot agree," he says, "to
give the people the privilege of rejecting a candidate
without giving any reasons why—or to leave the
ministers of the Presbytery the privilege of judging of
the objections. In short, there is a confusion, a com-
plexity, and a conglomeration of regulations which
render the whole *rudis indigestaque moles*. The
learned and modest preacher will retire from the arena,
and the lists will be filled with ignorant ravers, or with
disingenuous candidates. *Horresco referens!*" The
fruits of the agitation appeared first within the bounds
of the Dumfries Presbytery, in the rejection of Dr.
Duncan's own son as presentee to the church of Urr.
The circumstance seemed so striking to Mr. Wightman
that he threw off the following impromptu on the
subject:—

THE PATRONAGE QUESTION.

"The Patronage question is now fairly settled,
  And all our Church moderates are vanquished and nettled;
  The deed was achieved by a series of Letters (?)
  And the driv'llers have found they have met with their betters.
  The Letters, I ween, are not powerless or silly,
  No *Trolli impar congressus Achilli.*
  For length, and for logic, their merit is equal,
  And, weighed in the balance, are not ' mene tekel.'
  They have silenced for ever the Dean of the Thistle,
  Who now on his thumb at his leisure may whistle!
  But ah! what is specious is not always best,
  Nor every plan perfect when put to the test.
  The Patronage measure, that grand interim Act,
  Which gave so much pleasure, was far from exact;
  The Letters which vanquished the moderates and Dean

Soon proved to their author a woful black bean.
His son was presented to the parish of Urr,
But against his admission arose a demur.
A band in the parish, as firm as old Cato,
Refused him their *Call*, and presented their *Veto*,
And now they rejoice that the great letter writer
Has found, by their firmness, that—bit is the biter."

Another disputed settlement followed soon after in the case of Mr. Cunningham, presentee to Eskdalemuir, in the Presbytery of Langholm. In one view there was a small majority in favour of the presentee, and in another view some of the alleged majority had no right to vote, or had died, or had removed from the parish. Certain dissentients protested on the ground of a small majority, but they did not take appeal, by which neglect it was evident they had lost their cause. Matters turned out in the Church quite as Mr. Wightman anticipated. A clap-trap style of preaching became prevalent among the young aspirants to the ministry, which was exceedingly popular with a certain class of hearers. Mr. Wightman takes notice of this in his remarks upon a preacher who had officiated for him, who had once been a schoolmaster in the parish, but was then at the head of an academy in Liverpool. He had formerly preached in Kirkmahoe pulpit, with "great acceptance" to the minister, but now he had changed his manner entirely, in accordance with the new *regimen* of things, and not altogether to the same satisfaction. The following note is given at the time:—" Mr. —— is a fine speaker, and a good man, but his style of preaching is a modification of fanaticism, and his manner is too theatrical and extravagant for the pulpit. I regret to remark the tone and manner of preachers since the new

law of the Church took place. Show instead of substance, sound instead of sense, pretence instead of propriety prevail, and seem to carry all before them!
Modest unpretending merit may retire from the arena,
and leave the contest to be maintained by those who
can meet 'the spirit of the age' with a brow of brass,
unabashed obtrusiveness of manner, and self-conceit!"
We do not believe that all these remarks had reference
to Mr. ——, but to preachers in general whom the
exigencies of the time had called into existence.

The following memento in reference to an excellent
man, who was widely known and esteemed, may be
interesting to some as a just and generous tribute of
regard :—

"Wednesday, 17th Feb., 1836.—A very cold, frosty, and
blowy day. Was at Carnsalloch to breakfast. Mr. P.
Johnston is now eighty-six or eighty-seven years of age, and
almost entirely blind. He is an interesting and excellent
man, standing on the ground that divides one age and
period from another, or system of thinking and of manners.
He is the most accomplished human being in this part of
the country. I have been long acquainted with him,
and have received many marks of his kindness and attention. Thirty-eight years have elapsed since I came into
the parish, and became a frequent visitor in his house—
thirty-six times I have dined at Christmas, and almost as
many on New-Year's Day, in Carnsalloch. Some person,
after his death, will read something concerning him to the
following purpose :—'He was very extensively acquainted
with the wide compass of ancient and modern literature, and
his deep and accurate knowledge of books in various languages
was equalled by his enlightened and discriminating judgment

respecting the living manners of the busy world. Mr. Johnston was a profound and elegant classical scholar, a warm
admirer of the Fine Arts, and an acknowledged judge in
matters of taste and polite literature. The history, laws, and
constitution of his country were familiar to him, and his
richly-furnished mind was deeply imbued with the mild and
liberal spirit of Conservative patriotism. He was ever ready
to support the best interests of society, civil and religious,
with an enlightened zeal equally void of ostentation and of
guile. As a gentleman, a scholar, a relative, and a friend,
he was highly esteemed, and as a landlord, the universal
respect of his tenants bore a pleasing testimony to his
character. His accomplished education, and his habitual
intercourse with the best informed and most polished members of society, gave to his character a dignity and a grace
which those most qualified to judge universally admired.
His condescending attentions to young persons, when they
mingled in the family circle at Carnsalloch, will not soon be
forgotten by them, and the elegant hospitality of his well-
ordered house will be long recollected, with sentiments mournfully pleasing, by his numerous visitors and friends. He
bore the infirmities of age with magnanimous and Christian
composure, and blindness itself did not induce him to utter
a single murmur of complaint. Though knowledge was shut
out at the most excellent of all its entrances, his cheerfulness
was in no degree abated. Like the great poet of Paradise,
he seemed to receive new irradiations from the 'Father of
Lights,' and the rich landscape of his former studies reopened
before him in its early freshness and beauty. Greek, Roman,
German, and Italian literature presented to his mind's eye
a splendid panorama, and furnished him with subjects of
entertaining contemplation and instructive discourse.'"

In the above notice Mr. Wightman has omitted to

mention Mr. Johnston's enterprise as an agriculturist, and the successful efforts he put forth to improve the land and ameliorate the condition of the people. He was the first to introduce draining, though tiles were then unknown. The trenches were filled with field stones, which everywhere abounded, and through which the surface water percolated till it reached the bottom, when it flowed away. The stones were covered with the excavated earth, and the cultivation proceeded as before. He also introduced the fencing of fields and the planting of trees, of which latter many splendid specimens adorn the Carnsalloch grounds.

We now find in Mr. Wightman's diary frequent reference to his declining strength, and to the necessity of obtaining an assistant. "I must soon apply for an assistant," he says, "and the congregation will expect one agreeable to them—a reasonable expectation—while I, no doubt, will wish to engage one agreeable to myself, also a reasonable wish. The people will think that I should sacrifice my own opinion to theirs, and this, perhaps, I may find it prudent to do. The Lord reigns, let the earth be glad, and my anxious mind be still!" We shall afterwards see that he did accede to the people's desire, and without sacrificing his own.

Long-looked-for came at last, but not from the quarter Mr. Wightman expected. On the 9th March, 1837, the post brought him the following letter:—

"COLLEGE, GLASGOW, 7th March, 1837.

"My Dear Sir,—I have very sincere pleasure in informing you that the Senatus of the University of Glasgow, in testimony of the high opinion which they entertain of your piety, literary attainments, and benevolence of spirit, did, on Friday last, agree to confer on you the degree of Doctor in Divinity. Permit me to express my hope that this compliment will not be unacceptable to you, either as coming from our ancient seminary, or as communicated by, my dear Sir, yours, with unfeigned esteem,

"D. MACFARLAN.

"Rev. Dr. Wightman."

Though the honour was welcomed and appreciated, yet it was shorn of half its glory by the lateness of its arrival, and from its not emanating from the University of Edinburgh. He was now in his seventy-fifth year, and had experienced in some degree the "hope deferred which maketh the heart sick." It came like the summer rain, too late to revive the herbage which a long drought had scorched, yet not to be despised, on account of the later crops in their progress to maturity. Dr. Wightman received many kind congratulations from friends, far and near, on his newly acquired honour, but that he did not himself appreciate it as he would have done at an earlier date, he did not hesitate to say. "I have been flattered these last two Sundays," he said, "by the apparent gladness which my congregation discovered and expressed in their congratulations on my having received the degree of D.D. It is a remarkable fact that on a person's receiving any new mark of distinction, people are apt to think that they discover some particular merit in the individual so honoured which they had not discerned before. Alas! that distinction comes so very ate in my life that it rather makes me feel dull than elevated. What could the University of Glasgow have discovered in me now that it, or my *Alma Mater* of

Edinburgh, might not have known twenty years ago? But still I am thankful.

> 'Libertas: quae sera, tamen respexit inertem;
> Candidior postquam tondenti barba cadebat!
> Fortunate senex.'

The D.D.-ship is something like an ornament on my winding-sheet, or a flower thrown into my coffin or planted on my grave! Give me, O God, that honour which cometh from Thee, the unfading crown of righteousness and of glory!" He used to attribute the delay of the degree to what he called his independence of acting and voting in the General Assembly. His friends could never calculate beforehand on receiving his support, and they were consequently *chary* in proposing his name for honours.

The following congratulatory letter was sent him by the Rev. Dr. Thomas Gillespie, Professor of Humanity in the University of St. Andrews, an old and highly valued friend. Though its date is somewhat after the time of the great event, yet we shall insert it here:—

"ST. ANDREWS, 15th August, 1840.

"My Dear Doctor,—Gladly would I have given you that superfluous title, but I could not. It was otherwise *Ordered!*

"As to Lizars, no man is more sensible of him than I am, and if I can serve him, I know I will serve the University. Call on Robertson and get a sight of his letter. I have there told the truth, which I have only done to him and you. To the other application I have made no answer. It was odd indeed if I did not listen to Wightman—the good-hearted, simple, talented, idea'd, classical, Gillespyish Wightman. I could take you all to my bosom, man! I am as young as ever, though I have been very ill with a hole in my heel, and the *rose* in my leg—not the rose of Sharon—but the idea of you and me bathing at Glenluce and Dunragit, and Hay and happiness are now vividly before me. The child you baptized has been ill for more than twelve months, and is now here. She is, thank God, getting better in the mean-time. My dear Helen, the sweet ' Elly Pye,' died last spring, 23rd May, 1839, and I wrote certain verses, burning from the heart. Ah! my dear Wightman, my original patron, my constant friend,

> 'Tu es præsidium, et dulce decus meum,'

long may it be ere I have to perform that duty for you which I have so poorly attempted for Coltart; but, if God spare me, it shall be done *con amore.* And should I go first, ——but,

> ' Cur me querelis axanimas tuis?
> Nec Dis amicum est, nec mihi te prius
>   Obire, Wightmane, mearum
>   Grande decus columenque rerum.
> *   *   *   *   *   *   *   *
>   ————Ibimus, ibimus,
>   ——— ——Supremum
> Carpere iter comites parati.'

You must do for me what I have done for others—mind! ——Shall it be in prose or verse? Say. I sometimes think of sending you a copy. Shall I?

"I regret your infirmities, severe as they are, yet much has been done for older people than you. You have grand stamina. I should like to see you once more, and may do so this season. My two daughters, Cath. and Maggie (Pye!), are now at Mitchelslacks, and would be glad to see you. I hope you may meet.

"As to the Kirk, she is gaen gyte. I have helped her on,

and must now stand by her; but I have all along openly and publicly proclaimed my disapproval of disobedience to the civil power. But you know I am a Covenanter to the core. I wish you would preach a sermon in behalf of a monument to the Covenanters. I send printed papers. Or get Brydone, Kirkwood, or Dunbar to do it. Perhaps Greig would lend a hand.—God bless you, Wightman.

"T. G.

"Rev. Dr. Wightman."

It had been arranged between the two, that whichever of them died first the survivor should write his epitaph in prose or verse. There is a fine expression of delicacy in the lengthened dash above when Dr. Gillespie is reminding his friend of the agreement. He could not venture to say that he would perform his part, but did it in "expressive silence" with a blank. It is in reference to this that he jocularly asks whether it is to be in prose or verse, and if he will send him a copy beforehand, to show how it will be done. We are not aware whether, after all, the agreement was carried out.

The following poem was written after spending an evening at a friend's house, where there had been fine singing, accompanied with the piano and the flute, and was sent to Mrs. Morin, of Dumfries, who, when Miss Newall, was a charming vocalist, and often delighted Burns by singing his songs during the poet's frequent visits to the house of her father, Mr. Newall. It is entitled

AN OLD MAN'S DREAM.

"Threescore and sixteen rolling years
Have o'er me wheeled their rounds,
But still my age with rapture hears
Sweet Music's magic sounds.

" Last night, when Sleep his poppies shed,
    And wrapped me in his pall,
Methought I was by Friendship led
    To Saint Cecilia's Hall.

" The Muses there, in bright array,
    Around me seemed to close;
Apollo, too, the god of day,
    In Fancy's vision rose.

" The notes of Harmony there flowed—
    I stood in wonder mute;
My soul to her sweet influence bowed,
    Subdued by harp and lute.

" Anon by Fancy's potent wand
    Another dome was reared,
And to my sight another band
    Of minstrels soon appeared.

" A sun-bright halo shone around,
    Fringed with ethereal fire;
The harp of Orpheus seemed to sound,
    And great Apollo's lyre.

" Forms, old and young, before me stood,
    And vanished in their turn;
A lovely form, in mournful mood,
    Now warbled ' Anna's Urn.'

" My heart then felt a smarting twinge,
    A palpitation sore;
The door turned quickly on its hinge—
    I saw these forms no more.

" The lark, sweet herald of the morn,
    Had waked the vocal throng;
The blackbird whistled on the thorn,
    And all I heard was song."

The poem was accompanied by the following letter:—

"KIRKMAHOE MANSE, 25th August, 1838.

"My Dear Madam,—I have enclosed the verses which were so fortunate as to meet with your approbation—no paltry boon! The alterations are more agreeable to the classical taste, but my heart was in my flute from the beginning. The present copy is certainly more correct, but nothing is added to the heartfelt conception of the whole composition. The Captain's conversation suggested the happiest thoughts that are in it, and my own sympathies took fire at his torch, which has, I own, put more vigour into the lines than the age of seventy-six years had of itself. He spoke of ' halos of recollections,' of ' flitting forms of other days,' of ' Banquo's ghosts,' &c., &c., and fanned the *last lay* of the minstrel whose rude harp must now be laid aside!

> ' Give me, great God, a grateful heart,
>   For all the mercies on me showered,
> For friends devoid of guile and art,
>   To cheer me when the prospect lowered.
> For lengthening out life's span so long,
>   For brightening *thus* its setting beam,
> For teaching me by night a song,
>   And making life a pleasant dream!'

Here I drop a tear, sacred to the memory of the past!—I could not help it—but I am not a ' weeping bard,' or a ' prophet of ills.' Farewell!

"JOHN WIGHTMAN.

"Mrs. Morin."

The ecclesiastical horizon had for some time past been portentously overclouded, and every day the prospect was growing darker than before. The two parties in the Church were becoming more and more isolated in their positions, violent in their doings, and uncharitable in their speech, till at length the General Assembly, by a majority of forty-two, brought itself into collision with the Civil Courts, in carrying the case of the independence of the Church. Dr. Wightman was greatly grieved at the unhappy state which matters presented, and felt it difficult, in the gloomy aspect of affairs, to decide what was best to be done. He thought that by remaining tame and passive, the clerical influence of the side he supported was too apt to be circumscribed beyond what was right, and by being forward and noisy in their claims they were in danger of alienating those whose favour it was their interest as well as their duty to conciliate and secure. Accordingly, we find in his diary jottings of the following nature :—

"Thursday, 1st Nov., 1838.—I regret to observe so much misunderstanding and controversy among our brethren in the Church. This is too like a symptom of disease and of dissolution. Our Establishment is receiving some shocks and shakings. I wish these may be for good. We have enemies enough *without,* and we should endeavour to have charity and peace among ourselves. While our enemies are digging round the walls of our Establishment, and trying to undermine its foundations, we ought to keep peace within the house, and not contend about things of little importance as to essentials and fundamentals."

"Sunday, 2nd June, 1839.—I am myself to preach to-day, the first time after my illness, two short sermons, thirty minutes each. The majority in the General Assembly have ventured to disregard the decision of the House of Lords regarding the Veto Law. *Bonum sit!* I wish heartily that the collision had never taken place, for we enjoyed a latitude in our way of thinking without giving offence to any party.

But now, when the law is declared, and explained, and applied to our case, our Church Establishment seems to be endangered by the decision of our Supreme Ecclesiastical Court. I would have been in the *minority*, though with some irksome feelings regarding the position of our National Church!"

"Sunday, 15th Sept., 1839.—Showers—light and shade! unpromising weather for the harvest, yet its labours are advancing apace. I am to preach on the Birth of Christ and on Christian Contentment to-day. Public affairs are still in a critical condition. Crowds of discontented people harangue on the inequalities of fortune, on the burden of taxes, and other grievances. Our Government has fostered such murmuring by coquetting with the leaders and fomenters of these complainers, and it is now too late, perhaps, to use coercive measures, so that matters are in an unsettled and tottering state. The Church is not much better, I fear. The two parties are not yet reconciled to each other's views. *Revivals*, as they are called, it seems are going on in different places, especially in the parish of Kilsyth, and in the town of Dundee. My friend, Mr. William Burns of Kilsyth, is a pious man, and his son has caught a portion of his father's zeal, hence such excitement arises, and I hope much good is done. But I am somewhat doubtful regarding these remarkable and extraordinary movements, such as groans and screams in the church, and noises which drown the preacher's voice, and induce him to stop in his discourse till the confusion is over. I like the more sober and unobserved expressions of piety and holiness; but let me hope that God is there!"

"Saturday, 18th April, 1840.—The day of James Thomson's funeral, and of others in the parish and neighbourhood. While I attend the burials of others, Lord, enable me so to improve these dispensations as to consider my own latter end, and to apply my heart unto wisdom! The Church still in confusion—Presbyteries divided, and the cords of love slackened, if not in some instances broken, for the time. Give me, O Lord, meekness and forbearance, and Christian love of the brethren, and goodwill to all!"

"Sunday, 3rd May, 1840.—A very warm, even hot day, as many days past have been, yet the earth green, and the young crops coming up fresh and verdant, the ground comparatively full of what Shakespeare calls 'foison.' I am to lecture on the 24th Psalm, and preach on John xiv. 18. The Church is still divided, and the two parties not in a very charitable state of disposition towards each other. I had thoughts of writing, and even publishing, "*Irenica,* or Conciliatory Thoughts on the Position of the Church." But matters are not favourable at present for such things. We are looking for a legislative measure on the business, but surely it would have been better to have agreed among ourselves.

> 'Quis furor, O Civis, in quo discordia fratrum!
> Bella geri placuit nullos habitura triumphos?'

> 'O Navis! quid agis? fortiter occupa portum.'

> 'My thoughts, I must confess, are turned on peace!' "

This *Irenica* he prepared, but we are not sure that it was ever published. Numerous pamphlets were flying about at the time on the Church questions of the day, and he had a strong desire, as was always his wont, to throw oil upon the troubled waters, though they were sometimes too boisterous to listen to the voice of the charmer, charmed he never so wisely. We shall make an extract from the manuscript of the intended anodyne, which was first ventilated in the form of a speech on the Veto Law in the Presbytery of Dumfries. After some

introductory remarks, Dr. Wightman entered upon the
subject in the following strain:—

"The Sacred Record gives rather a general outline than a
detailed system of Church government. It is one of the
excellences of Holy Scripture that it is adapted to the various
forms in the mechanism of society. It lays down a few, and
only a few, leading features of Church polity, and leaves the
form to be observed or extended as shall be found necessary
or expedient in after times. The frame may be preserved,
or fitted up more fully, as the Church may judge, according
to the state of society and the complexion of civil government in any place or country where Christianity is professed
and practised. In the times of the Apostles the actors were
all inspired persons, miraculous influence was also employed,
and we ought to be cautious how we apply the conduct and
the measures of these times to our own circumstances and
cases. And while we attend to the spirit of Church polity
of that period, we should consider how far the times and
circumstances are similar, and adopt such plans as suit the
age and country in which our lot has been cast. Much
obscurity rests upon the early period of the Church, and
reasonable doubts have been entertained with regard to the
genuineness and authenticity of some of the productions
which have influenced the opinions of many well-disposed
and candid judges of antiquity. They come nearest the
great and benevolent design of Bible law on this point who
attend more to the spirit than the very letter of the inspired
Record in Church government matters. So much has been
left to the discretion and wisdom of the office-bearers of the
Church that many pious and learned men have been of
opinion that there is actually no precise law in Scripture on
the point.

"After the Reformation our Church polity was in general

Y

formed on the model of the Church at Geneva; and that
Church itself adopted much from the character of the Re-
publican Civil government there, so that our Church government from the beginning received considerable colour and
complexion from the laws of men as well as from those of
Holy Scripture, and it was intended to be thus characterized.
Distinct traces of the origin of our Sessions, and Presbyteries,
and Synods, and Assemblies may be discovered, not only in
the arrangements of the Mosaic economy, and in the directions of the Apostles, but also in the forms of government
prevalent where Christianity existed. In those times of our
Church when the people had the greatest influence in the
appointment of ministers, except during the short periods
when they had almost all the power, and the utmost disorder
prevailed, there were four things which entered into the
matter—the nomination, the examination, the collation, and
the induction. A reasonable consent was always considered
an essential element in the appointment, but even the First
Book of Discipline itself, which has been termed 'a devout
imagination,' was not so imaginative as to think that the
people's consent or dissent was to supersede and render
nugatory the 'judgment of godly and learned men,' who were
to examine the presentee, and to judge of his talents, life,
doctrine, and utterance. And when nothing tangibly repre-
hensive could be found in these, those who refused to receive
him were to be compelled to do so by the censure of the
Church and the authority of the Council, so tenacious were
the 'godly and learned persons,' in other words, the Presbytery,
of their just and reasonable prerogative, to decide in a matter
so important as the care of souls. . . . . The measure
called the Veto was an apple of discord thrown, in an evil
hour, into the Courts of our Israel. Many of my brethren who
differ from me on other points are no sticklers for the Veto,
and all that they contend for is what they call Non-intrusion.

"Now, we all agree that the people should have their rights, but some of us contend that they are asking more than they can receive as the Constitution stands. A reasonable consent was always conceded to them in the appointment of ministers, but not that they should control the Presbytery, and endeavour to obtain a person to be their minister who had not the Presbytery's sanction, or to refuse obstinately and undutifully one who had. But the Veto encourages this kind of conduct, and by apparently enlarging the freedom of the people, actually hurts their real interests by depriving them of the benefit of the counsel and experience of those who are better able to choose a pastor for them than many of them are able to judge for themselves. . . I ask, in the name of peace, why should we deal in charges and criminations, and in hurling those hand grenades, filled with such inflammable materials, which may be employed against those by whom they are used? And why should we give even the shadow of insubordination to those before whom we ought surely to set an example of *subordination* and order? The judges of our land are the accredited interpreters of the law, and if we be dissatisfied with any of their decisions, we should try by all constitutional means to get the matter adjusted, and a new law made. It is by the efficacy of the law, and a due regard given to its decisions, that our houses are our homes, where we can sleep in security, knowing its eye watches over our safety, and, under an overruling Providence, protects our persons and properties from the rapacious grasp of unprincipled cupidity and the midnight ruffian. When the demon of discord is now stalking abroad shaking his bloodthirsty brand, when the torch of incendiarism is casting its lurid glare on the shades of night, and when anarchy is looking with a scowl on the venerable institutions of our country, and grinning a ghastly smile at every sound of strife among us, the ministers of the Church surely ought to seek peace, and endeavour to strengthen every cord of unity and love."

The speech from which the above extract is taken was delivered in proposing that the Presbytery of Dumfries should overture the General Assembly to rescind the Veto Act, to let the patron present, the people object, and the Presbytery judge and decide. He was resolutely against that measure, as he thought he saw in it the seed-sowing of discord, and contumacy, and strife. He was a member of the Assembly when it passed into an interim Act much against his will. His feelings were so deep and intense on the occasion that he could scarcely find words to give them utterance. He had on former occasions been thoughtless enough to indulge in some little sparklings of fancy, which, though proceeding from the utmost good nature, and the most profound deference to the Supreme Court, cost him the loss of the full confidence of the House when any matter of very grave and solemn interest was under discussion. When he rose on the present occasion he felt, or thought, that though the Moderator turned his face upon him, yet he did not give him his countenance. Lord Moncreiff had introduced the measure with all the vigorous energy and acknowledged talent so generally associated with his name, and shook the Assembly with a deep and powerful flood of eloquence almost irresistible. Dr. Wightman said that the matter must have much obscurity in it, for the perspicacity of the learned lord himself was at fault, and he could not see his own way. It was " puzzled with mazes, and perplexed with errors." He eulogized his lordship's late venerable father, and noticed the Life of Dr. Erskine written by Sir H. Moncreiff, who in that work expresses his opinion that the bone of contention regarding patronage ought not to be raised from the grave where it lay buried. He called the Veto measure, with its motley mass of regulations, in the words of Ovid, "*rudis indigestaque moles*"—a crude and indigested heap; and in the language of Virgil, "*monstrum cui lumen ademptum*"— a giant without an eye, a blind Polyphemus; adding the phrase of Shakespeare, "It is not, and it cannot come to good." The House was not disposed to listen to a display of Latin quotations, and observing that others were anxious to be heard, he resumed his seat. He sat in anxious silence, inwardly grieved to mark the fervour the measure met with, and at the close of the debate he gave vent to the fulness of his heart in the oppressive lament of the Mantuan muse—"*Telis nostrorum obruimur oritura miserrima cædes*"—we are vanquished by the arms of our misguided friends, and a sad massacre will ensue.

The affairs of the Church had now assumed an alarming aspect, and seemed hastening on to a crisis, which soon came, first in the suspension, and then the deposition, of the Strathbogie ministers.

"Sunday, 30th May, 1841.—I read yesterday with much concern that the seven suspended ministers of Strathbogie were deposed on Thursday by the General Assembly. I always thought some way of escape would be found for these brethren, whose sole fault was that they obeyed the laws of the land, instead of the rules of the Church. It was a bold step in the Assembly, and will not be generally approved of by the country, especially by those who do not study deeply the Church rules, but judge from common feeling. I sympathize much with the deposed brethren, as they did only what I think I would have been disposed to do in their case and circumstances. Different minds have different views of things. This decisive measure will make a deep and strong sensation in the country, and will be viewed differently according to men's opinions and habits of thought. May God grant that it may be overruled for good, to promote respect for the order and discipline of the Church, and prevent it from giving a grinding and oppressive spirit to the dominant party of our Church. A Fast will likely be appointed by the Assembly, and both parties will be called upon to humble themselves before the Most High for their faults and shortcomings. Peace be within our Jerusalem's walls, and in her ordinances! I am old, and must soon close my eyes on this earthly scene, but for the sake of my friends and brethren, I say, Peace be within thee!"

While expressing such opinions as these with regard to the majorities of the Church, he was far from impugning their sincerity in the views they held of their power, as members of Christ their great Head, in what they considered spiritual things; but he thought their zeal had gone beyond their knowledge, and had led them into a labyrinth of confusion and irregularity from which it would be difficult for them to escape.

The afflictions incident to old age are now beginning to tell upon him with increased severity, and his diary is full of lamentings over his inability to do his duty as in the past. He feels a numbness in one of his limbs which he cannot get rid of by all the means he can employ, and he imagines it a premonitory symptom of approaching palsy. There is something affecting in the

plaint he makes in the view of a coming Communion:—
"I feel pretty well, and in tolerably good spirits, but
oh! how changed and how languid from what I have
been in former days, and on such occasions as the
present! Great Father of mercies, give me strength in
Thy service, let my sun go down serenely, and let Thy
servant at last depart in peace!" He had long been
talking of having an assistant appointed to relieve him
of part of his pastoral labours, and he is now determined
to carry out his resolution as speedily as possible,
although at the same time he says, "Such is my im-
providence, losses, and lendings, from year to year, that
I spend all my stipend on myself." This was indeed
true so far as losses and lendings were concerned; for,
as we have seen, advantage was often taken of his
good-natured generosity, and many considerable sums
borrowed were never repaid. Inside the board of an
old copy of Mead is written, "This is all I have got
for the loan of ten pounds, but, poor fellow, Mr. ——
had nothing more to give. He is a good preacher
and an excellent man, but has had difficulties in his
way." Very few, we fear, could be found to give such
a testimony, and express such sympathy in similar
circumstances of loss.

He was extremely desirous that, whoever his assistant
might be, he should be appointed with the consent of
the people; and as several young men had officiated for
him from time to time, perhaps not without an eye to
the situation, he was sensitively afraid that there might
be a diversity of opinion in the minds of the congregation. However, matters towards an appointment went
harmoniously on, and at the unanimous request of the

parishioners, with his own entire concurrence, the Duke
of Buccleuch presented the Rev. James Wilson, who
was ordained his assistant and successor on the 9th of
September, 1841. This was of the greatest importance
to him, as it relieved his mind from anxiety, and his
physical frame from the fatigue inevitable in discharging the duties of the pastorate in an extensive and
populous parish. He would occasionally, when in good
spirits, drive to some neighbouring church on a Sunday
forenoon, and take the duty unexpectedly for a brother
just as he was robing for the pulpit. Such surprises as
these he used greatly himself to appreciate in receiving,
as showing a friendship and familiarity very agreeable
to his nature. If a funeral sermon was required for a
late co-presbyter, or any of his family, he was certain to
be asked to perform the duty, which afforded him a
melancholy gratification. He had preached so many of
these, and of course always printed them "at the
request of friends," that he had acquired a kind of
monopoly in such things, and he felt a little chagrined
if in any case he had been overlooked. He always
spoke favourably of the dead, according to the old
Roman adage, so favourably, indeed, that he was sometimes twitted for his generous eulogies. The Rev.
Walter Dunlop, of Dumfries, meeting him one day after
he had lately given one of these, said, with sly humour,
"Dr. Wightman, when I die, I would like you to preach
my funeral sermon." "How so?" "Because I ken ye
would ca' me nae waur than I am."

CHAPTER XVII.

RECEIVES THE FREEDOM OF THE BURGH OF DUMFRIES—ENTERTAINED
AT A PUBLIC DINNER—CONGRATULATORY LETTER FROM PRIN-
CIPAL MACFARLAN OF GLASGOW COLLEGE—THE DISRUPTION—
ASSISTANT LEAVES—EFFORTS TO KEEP HIS PEOPLE TOGETHER—
ANOTHER ASSISTANT APPOINTED—PRESENTED WITH HIS PORTRAIT
—A DIRGE—REV. DR. MACLEOD OF MORVEN.

IT was very gratifying to his kindly heart, now that he
had in great measure retired from the active duties of
the pastoral office, to find that he was not neglected by
the public at large, but, on the contrary, honoured by
undoubted marks of their respect and esteem.   Nothing
crushes the spirit so much as to be cast aside as a useless
member of society when vigour fails, and nature refuses
to do the work she did of yore, forgetful of the past,
however estimable that may have been.   Among the
first of these kind tokens of regard was his receiving
the freedom of the town of Dumfries at a magistrates'
election dinner, when Provost Fraser, in a highly
complimentary address, presented to him the honorary
parchment, with the seal of the burgh attached.   As
an additional honour he was requested to preach in
St. Michael's on the following Sunday before the new
magistrates, called their "Kirking," which he did with
great goodwill, unction, and solemnity.

Another honour was conferred upon him in the following year, of still wider significance, and of greater

importance in his estimation. This was a public recognition of his past services for the general good not only within but beyond the bounds of his own ministerial domain. On the 12th of December, 1842, he was entertained at a banquet given in his honour in the King's Arms' Hotel, Dumfries, at which many of the most influential inhabitants of the town and district were present, several of them having been his pupils in the Grammar-School upwards of fifty years before. James Macalpine Leny, Esq. of Dalswinton, presided on the festive occasion, and made an admirable speech in proposing Dr. Wightman's health. He said—

"I rise to propose the health of the Rev. Doctor in honour of whom we are this night assembled. Dr. Wightman having spent his youth and manhood in this district, his virtues and his worth necessarily became known to a large circle of admiring friends, who have been long desirous of offering him some mark of their respect and approbation. The confidence and friendship of those amongst whom we live, the esteem and regard of our friends and neighbours, I believe to be, next to a good conscience, one of the highest gratifications, and one of the strongest incentives to a good man. These, it is confessed on all hands, Dr. Wightman has long enjoyed, and does enjoy, in an eminent degree. The manner in which you have marked these sentiments, and the great assemblage here this night, how much do they add to their force, and confirm their truth! He is here surrounded by some of those friends with whom he had formed in youth the most tender ties; and I am sure they will give me leave to say he was not a hard taskmaster. He is also surrounded this evening by a great number of those with whom, in maturer life, he formed more conspicuous ties. But, above all, he would have been surrounded this evening, had they not been engaged elsewhere for a similar purpose, by those amongst whom he has spent the latter and better portion of his life, in imparting those consolations, and receiving that confidence and affection which it is no less the duty than the delight of a Christian minister to reciprocate. Dr. Wightman's piety and meekness, his generosity and kindness, and his unostentatious charity, have endeared him to all who have come within his sphere, but in an especial manner to that parish in which he has, for upwards of forty long years, been a faithful steward; and I believe that no eulogium which I could pass on the Rev. Doctor would be so acceptable to him as the declaration which I am here authorized in the name of that parish to make, that he has been to them a useful and an acceptable pastor. And what he has been to that parish in particular he has been, though in a less degree, to the whole surrounding district.

"Delicacy, and respect for Dr. Wightman, forbid my entering into details, and I am sure it is not your wish that I should offend against either; but before I conclude I may be permitted to observe that Nature bestowed on the Rev. Doctor some of her choicest gifts, which from his earliest youth he cultivated with the most sedulous enthusiasm. Deeply has he drunk of the Pierian spring; long has he been known as an eminent scholar; and I can well believe that those who knew him in his early life, who appreciated his taste and eloquence, his poetical genius and luxuriant imagination, may have anticipated for him a distinguished niche in the temple of fame—nay, even those who knew him but casually in more mature life may have joined in some such anticipations. But we, so conversant with him, know that his humility and timidity formed an insuperable bar to such aspirations. The Doctor, indeed, in his quiet walk through life, has culled a few of those flowers which seemed to cluster around his head, and in some of his fugitive pieces he will be long remembered by many of his friends. But even now the quiet and peaceful tenor of his pursuits is not without its advantages and reward, for we see him here in his eightieth year, if I may not say in the enjoyment of unimpaired health, yet I may say in the enjoyment of comparative health and strength, and of unimpaired understanding. I know that on this latter point he is querulous and desponding, and often complains of decay, as he was doing one day to one of his aged parishioners, who adroitly replied, giving the apt illustration, 'Na, na, Doctor, ye are just like a horse-shoe, aye the aulder the clearer.' That such may long continue to be the case I know to be your wish, as it is that of many hundreds who could not possibly be with us this evening. Giving the Doctor this earnest assurance of our respect and regard, I propose his health."

The toast was received with the utmost enthusiasm, and the speech introducing it was cheered throughout.

When the excitement had somewhat subsided, Dr. Wightman rose to reply, and, after some preliminary observations, said—"When I look about me and see so many dignitaries of the town and country—so many lights of the Church and of the Academy—so many luminaries of the Law and of the Press—so many of my co-presbyters, and friends, and acquaintances—I am led to consider with myself what those qualities may be in my character which have gathered around me such a bright halo of approbation, in which my humble orb is hid, as the planet Mercury is lost in the solar blaze, or rather receives a lustre from the splendour of the coruscation of lights with which it is surrounded. I am not sensible of having done anything to deserve this unequivocal demonstration of esteem. I have never extended the boundary of science, enriched the repositories of knowledge by any ingenious invention or useful discovery; nor have I ever taken a prominent part in matters of Church or of State. But, with a peculiar sensibility, I have recoiled from public notice, except when professional duty required me to act otherwise, and have courted the tranquil walks and pursuits of private study and parish work. There are patriots and philanthropists of distinction, benefactors of mankind, whose public spirit and usefulness resemble the mysterious water of the Nile, spreading health, and plenty, and fertility over the whole country, feeding and employing millions, calling forth the various talents of the mind and virtues of the heart; whereas my usefulness has rather been like some brook in the valley, refreshing perhaps the shrubs, and plants, and flowers on its margin, while it pursues the noiseless tenor of its way, forming, it may be, an agreeable, but still only a lowly, feature in the landscape.

"You give me credit for considerable learning and scholarship, and I accept the compliment as not entirely unmerited. I will not detain you with expatiating on my moderate acquaintance with theology, history, philosophy, or poetry, and with ancient or modern languages; nor will I now say how often I have read the Old Testament in the Hebrew, or the New Testament in the Greek original; or speak of the excursions I have made into different fields of science and literature, and the rambles which I have occasionally taken round the base of Parnassus. Some lofty geniuses there are whose efforts in advancing the interests of the arts and sciences are like the majestic motions of the eagle, that king of birds, 'sailing with supreme dominion through the azure deep of air,' scorning to alight to rest his wing on any perch lower than the towering Caucasus. But the exertions of my genius have rather resembled the motions of some bird of feebler pinion, wheeling its humble flight among the groves or woodlands of the plain, and perhaps cheering them with its warbling. Whatever might be my literary attainments, I have endeavoured, ever since I became a parish minister, to bring them all to bear as much as possible chiefly on professional usefulness. I considered a Christian minister to be like a traveller who loves his country and his home, who marks in his journeys whatever might be an improvement if transferred to his own country or domain, and applies it accordingly, were it only to embellish his native village, his house, or his garden. The principal views and aims of a minister in his reading and observation should be to enrich his pulpit and parish instruction. His heart should be in his ministerial work and his soul on his lips. The young, the aged, the poor, the sick, and the dying ought to engage his special attention.

"In the welfare and happiness of young persons I

have always felt a deep and lively interest, and the
frosts of eighty winters have not so chilled my heart as
to prevent me from still feeling warmly on behalf of the
rising generation.   I hope that I have sometimes been
of benefit to the young by counsel or conversation, or by
lending them books or otherwise.   I hope that I may
have at times contributed, with less or more influence,
to plume the young wing of aspiring genius, and what is
still more desirable, to fan the glowing spark of early
piety.   I hope that I may have watered the plant which
was to become a tall cedar on our Lebanon, a stately
palm tree by the streams of our Zion, a green olive tree
by the walls of the sanctuary, a tree of God in the midst
of our Jerusalem.   I hope that by a 'word in season,
like a nail in a sure place, I have occasionally been the
instrument of fixing the generous purpose of well-doing
in the tender breast of youth.   I hope that I have sometimes encouraged the young traveller in life's journey, in
pursuing the pleasing and peaceful paths of wisdom, and
cheering him as he climbed, with eager foot, the arduous
steep, while he urged his way to where her august temple
shines afar inviting his approach.   I hope that I have
been happily instrumental, on some holy occasions, in
directing the inexperienced voyager in this 'sea of
troubles' to keep his eye on the bright star of Jacob,
that heavenly cynosure, that his frail bark might escape
the rocks, and shoals, and whirlpools of destruction with
which the perilous navigation of life abounds.   I most
humbly hope that, with the lamp of the Divine Word in
my hand, I have brought the light of comfort into the
chamber of distress and the house of mourning, and
have, with a gospel promise, smoothed the pillow of the

bed of death, and brightened for a few moments the fixing eye which was soon to close on the cheerful light of day. I fervently hope that I have in such trying hours encouraged the immortal spirit while yet lingering in its earthly tabernacle, and trembling on the brink of eternity, to lean with humble confidence on the staff of the Divine Shepherd, in passing through the valley of the deadly shade. If these things have been so, these— these are my trophies, my laurels, my riches—laurels that shall not wither, treasures that shall never fail. For, if these doings and endeavours have been animated and inspired by the good spirit of grace, they will, I trust, follow me beyond the narrow limits of this diurnal sphere into that bright and blessed world where moth and rust corrupt not, and where thieves do not break through to steal. I then might say with the sage of antiquity, who had escaped with personal safety from the burning city—*Omnia mea bona mecum porto*, and might, unmoved, leave behind me a world in flames. In such retired and unobtrusive, but, if rightly discharged, most useful duties, I have passed four-and-forty years of peace and comfort in the sweet vale of Nith, where my humble services have been amply rewarded by the kindness of my parishioners, from whom I have received tokens of gold and silver as marks of their esteem, which I value more than both.

"But I should recollect that I am now in Dumfries, and here I stand a free citizen of this ancient burgh, for I have received the honour of citizenship from the hands of its excellent Provost. Dumfries! how many sacred and time-hallowed associations are connected with this magical dissyllable! Dumfries! here I received a part of my education, and have both publicly and privately taught; and I know not how many provosts, and bailies, and deans, and town-clerks, and municipal authorities, and high officials, and worthy citizens have received lessons from your humble servant; how many young admirals, and generals, and captains have meekly submitted to my authority! Here I have assisted in administering the sacrament of the Holy Communion above thirty years in both the Old and the New Churches twice a year. Here I have borne a part in the examinations of the public schools of the place for upwards of forty years, and have felt much delight in marking the development of the young idea, and the putting forth of the tender buds of hope. Ah! the images of things that once were now powerfully arrest my thoughts. Venerable ministers of the gospel, excellent instructors of youth, now no more in this world, pass in shadowy glory before my mind's eye. And what a brilliant sweet company of ingenuous youth flit, in mystic vision, before my fired fancy! Some of them have grown old among us, and some of them are here contributing in doing me honour.

" Mr. Chairman and Gentlemen,—I stand before you an aged minister of eighty years, enjoying some good measure of health of body and soundness of faculty; and I attribute this, under Providence, in some degree, to the regularity and temperance which I have been enabled to observe. For, to use the words of the great Bard of Avon,

> 'In my youth I never did apply
> Hot and rebellious liquors to my blood,
> Nor did I with unbashful forehead woo

Z

> The means of weakness and debility;
> Therefore my age is like a lusty winter,
> Frosty, but kindly.'

The countenance you have this day given me has gladdened my old heart. It has shed a cheering gleam over the evening of my days, and brightened my setting sun. I recollect a stanza on a grave-stone in the churchyard of my native parish, in memory of an aged minister. The first two lines are descriptive of my present condition. They ran thus—

> ' As of the setting sun we say,
> He larger looked at close of day.'

And infinitely happy should I be if the other two lines were realized in my case—

> ' And then sunk from our view, to rise
> In glory bright above the skies.'

My sun is now on ' the verge of the sky,' and your kind regards, and *cheers*, make it now send forth, as by reflection, a kind of parting beam athwart that fair hemisphere through which it has seen many circuits, and from which it must soon sink for ever. It was said of our great Reformer at his grave, ' There lies one who never feared the face of man.' I hope that I have never felt that fear of man which bringeth a snare, yet I would rather it should be said at my grave, ' There, beneath that yew-tree's shade, rests the dust of one who never willingly or wantonly gave pain to a human heart.' In conclusion, if I had the privilege of some ancient patriarch, and could convey a blessing in the close of life, I would now lay my hands upon your heads, and impart to you the best blessings of Heaven. But I will do what is in my power, and I fervently wish that He whose blessing maketh rich without sorrow, may bless you all, and that your kind and generous hearts may never feel distress."

This was certainly a wonderful speech for an old man of fourscore, and delivered without a single' note to assist his memory. It need scarcely be said that he was enthusiastically applauded when he resumed his seat. He received many congratulations on the honour which had been done him on the auspicious occasion, from friends both near and at a distance. The Rev. Dr. Macfarlan, Principal of the University of Glasgow, sent the following complimentary letter:—

College, Glasgow, 24th Dec., 1842.

" My Dear Sir,—Most grateful do I feel to the unknown individual who forwarded me a copy of the *Dumfries Courier* of the 19th inst., and in so doing gave me the very gratifying account which it contains of the preceding Tuesday and its festivities. I need not tell you how soothing it is to receive such a compliment bestowed by those who have enjoyed ample opportunities of knowing him who is its object, and are well qualified to appreciate his character, the more especially when it is their spontaneous act, and unalloyed by the degrading consciousness of its having been gained by artifice, dissimulation, or flattery. Still, in my opinion, it reflects higher honour on those who have the good sense and good taste to pay the tribute of respect, not to ephemeral celebrity, or pompous parade, but to a character tried and ascertained in the noiseless field of local and Christian duty, during a ministry embracing nearly half a century, and a life

extended to the unusual period of fourscore years. The
piety and fidelity, the conversation embellished by literary
acquirements, and enhanced by the warmth of unfailing
charity, must sooner or later obtain their reward, even in
this world—and well is it for those who become the instru-
ments by whom it is imparted. Not only have they done
what in them lay to cheer your declining years with the
meed of well-earned praise, but have read to our younger
brethren a most salutary lesson, by which I trust many of
them will profit. Be assured, my dear Sir, that I sympathize most cordially in every favourable feeling which was
expressed, and every kind wish that was breathed, for your
prolonged health and comfort, and that the more lonely I
daily find myself in the world, the more fondly do I cling to
those remaining pupils of the old school, who, like yourself,
adorned what I must call the better days of our Church, and
still survive to exhibit a sample of what those days produced.
It added not a little to my gratification to observe that the
chair was filled by my friend Mr. Leny of Dalswinton, who,
in taking that situation, and discharging its duties in the
way he appears to have done, has earned an additional claim
to the esteem of all who know him.—Believe me, my dear
Sir, yours most truly and faithfully,

"D. MACFARLAN."

The whole affair was one of the most pleasing to all
concerned in it that could be desired, and was of course
most grateful to him on whose account it was carried
out. He might well have used to a certain degree the
language of aged Simeon, and have desired to depart in
peace, but his work was not yet done, his portion of the
vineyard was not yet finished, and therefore he must
abide a little longer, till the night come when no man
can work.

While thus, as it were, reposing on his oars after a long rowing voyage on the sea of life, and enjoying a well-earned *otium cum dignitate*, his whole heart and soul were absorbed in the Church of his fathers, and his incessant prayer was for her welfare and peace. These, however, were seemingly far distant, and by-and-by the clerical contention attained its culmination in the rending of the Establishment, and the division also of families that had been long linked in the bonds of harmony and love. His place in the pulpit being supplied at home, he went far and near doing Sunday service, endeavouring by all the eloquence he could command to reunite broken households, confirm waverers in the good old paths, and smooth asperities everywhere, by words of kindly counsel, and by reviving old associations when divisions were unknown. But all his efforts were of little avail. Matters had attained such a height, crimination and re-crimination had been so indulged in, and every one was so competent to lean on self-reliance, that his beseech-ings, and entreaties, and sometimes even tears, were all in vain. Many felt for the old man, but thought they had a duty to perform, beyond the reach of any secular influence however friendly, and which lay altogether between their consciences and God. He saw this and bewailed it, but at the same time allowing the freedom of judgment to others which he claimed for himself, he gave them his parting advice, and left them to follow the bent of their own opinions, in accordance with the Apostle's exhortation, to "let every man be fully persuaded in his own mind."

In his own parish of Kirkmahoe disaffection had begun to appear, and a change was evidently being prepared for, which greatly grieved his generous heart, as he looked upon the people with a parental eye, having baptized the greater portion of them, and married not a few. What aggravated the case was the translation of his assistant, Mr. Wilson, to a neighbouring parish rendered vacant by the secession of the incumbent, leaving him comparatively helpless in the season of his greatest need. Instead of immediately appointing another assistant, he thought to rally all his people around him by performing the public duty himself, and thereby lead them to reciprocate the affection he himself cherished towards them all; but in this he was mistaken. Other influences were at work which he could not overcome, and by persisting in these a number of persons became alienated, and finally separated from the Church in which they and their fathers had been baptized. We have the best authority, however, for saying, that had Dr. Wightman immediately appointed an assistant when his first one left, no separation in the parish would have occurred. As we have said, he resolved to do the preaching duty himself, when he was quite unable for the undertaking. His voice was become weak, and his articulation indistinct, so that little benefit could be derived from his services, however much he exerted himself to proclaim the Word of Life. Stranger ministers poured into the parish in defiance of all ecclesiastical rule, and met with considerable success, for, as our informant, an intelligent F.C. deacon, resident all his life in the parish, said—"We were glad to have a sermon from any minister, and had Mr. Wilson remained among us, there would never have been a Free Church in the place."

Many young probationers proffered their services for a Sunday or two at a time, which were gratefully accepted, and neighbouring ministers were kindly obliging to do what lay in their power in behalf of their aged friend. One of these latter is deserving of special notice on account of the readiness with which he frequently gave his aid, and of his acceptability with the congregation. He had often preached on ordinary occasions for long years before, and his assistance on sacramental seasons was always forthcoming and duly appreciated. He was now called in to take full charge in dispensing the Communion when it came round, and to perform other duties less prominent but equally needful. This was the Rev. Hugh Dobie, minister of Kirkmichael, whom Dr. Wightman had always regarded with sentiments of the highest esteem. Mr. Dobie was everywhere popular as a preacher. His sermons were noble structures of substantial theological masonry, fitly framed together, and without any meretricious ornamentation. His doctrine was severely orthodox, and in treating his subject he gave no rein to the imagination, feeling his work was too solemn and important to admit of anything addressed to the fancy rather than to the heart. His style was simple but polished, and every sentence showed the utmost care both in its construction and teaching. His delivery was clear, measured, and articulate, and the earnestness which pervaded all he said kept the audience in breathless attention. He was punctual and reliable in all his professional engagements, and on sacramental occasions when he was to assist any of his brethren, his presence could be depended on within three minutes of the appointed time, however far he had to travel. Such a minister was deserving of appreciation, and he had the happiness of being highly esteemed wherever he was known.

After nearly two years' length of this state of things the present writer was appointed his assistant and successor, and the old minister never preached in his own pulpit again. Still he occasionally officiated elsewhere, and was highly gratified when he saw a good audience before him. Amongst his latest jottings we find the following:—"I was much gratified by seeing Holywood church full to the doors, and the people there closely adhering to the Church of their fathers." He still kept an eye upon the doings of Government, and praised or censured as he thought necessity required. On the Maynooth Grant Bill he thus reflects:—"I believe Sir Robert Peel, and those Protestants who support him, do not wish to injure the cause of Protestantism in its establishments and institutions. His aim is peace to Ireland, but he seems not to understand fully the sense of the Articles of the Church of England, and the *perfervidum ingenium Scotorum*. While he, in his youthful travels in the North, marked the pulsations of the great Atlantic, and the mighty swellings of Corryvreckan, he overlooked the ardent feelings of the nation, and their attachment to the religion of their country. The education of the people and the clergy, I have hitherto thought, and often affirmed, is the best antidote to bigotry and superstition, but I have been lately tempted to hesitate, and I find that there is at least one exception. The Bill will pass, I think, and may do good, though I fear otherwise."

He was greatly pleased with another mark of esteem

shown him at this time by the ladies of the parish, who
had on several former occasions during his ministry
similarly testified their regard for him as their minister.
This was the presentation of a full-length portrait of
himself, painted by John Maxwell, Dumfries, whom
Thomas Aird characterized as "the best likeness-taker
on earth," and certainly in this case, as in others, the
testimony is fully verified, as a more faithful and life-
like picture never came from an artist's easel. On
receiving the gift from a deputation who waited upon
him, he gave expression to his feelings in the following
terms, his voice tremulous with emotion, and his heart
full of affection:—

"Ladies of the Deputation—The elegant portrait with which
you have so highly honoured me inspires the warmest gratitude, which I cannot adequately express. But, at the same
time, it reminds me of many shortcomings of which, though
they have been overlooked by the kindness of my parishioners, I am deeply sensible. During the period of eight and
forty years in which I have been minister of this parish, I
have always had before my mind a fair model of a degree of
perfection in the discharge of pastoral duty, public and
private, which, with all my wishes and endeavours, I was
never able to realize. But I have the satisfaction to reflect
that my professional duties were always my principal concern, and that I was generally engaged in some exercise
which, directly or indirectly, bore upon those duties. For
nearly forty years I never used a single note in the pulpit,
and never came before my intelligent congregation on the
Sabbath without much careful study. I have often grudged
the time spent in committing my discourses to memory, as
I thought it might have been more profitably employed in

household ministrations, and other exercises belonging to the sacred ministry. But with all my imperfections I ever met with decided marks of esteem from all classes of the parishioners, and I will never forget their kindness. With this parish of Kirkmahoe, my humble name has been long associated, and it is my fervent wish to be here remembered after my decease. It is therefore very gratifying to me that my portrait, your splendid gift, is, with your consent, to remain in the manse, with my reverend brother, as his property, after me. It will there be seen by many, from time to time, and by some with tender recollections of friendship when the original form is wrapped in the green lap of earth, in yonder cemetery, and will exhibit the likeness of a once 'living, breathing man,' who long ministered in this parish, who was feelingly alive to the beauties of its natural scenery, and the courtesies of its social intercourse, but who, alas! always came far short of what he felt to be his duty, and what his hearers had a right to expect from him. But I feel that I must not pursue this line of thought any further, and I willingly turn to a more cheerful prospect which opens before me, and which gilds the close of a graciously lengthened ministry."

The remainder of the address was highly complimentary to myself, and therefore not necessary to be given. A duplicate of the portrait was painted by Mr. Maxwell, and presented by a few admiring friends to the Dumfries Academy, as a memorial of present and other days. Though now beyond the farthest boundary of human existence mentioned by the Psalmist, the poetic fire of former times was not yet extinguished. A very amiable young lady in the parish, endeared to all by her genial disposition, kind condescension, and Christian liberality, was taken away by death, and in the midst of the universal regret he gave expression to his own feelings, and those of all around, in strains which sound like the song of the dying swan:—

IN MEMORY OF MISS JANET JOHNSTON OF CARNSALLOCH.

" Peace, gentle shade, a Muse of humble fame
   Devotes these verses to thy honoured name.
   If Piety availed from death to save,
   Thy dust had never occupied this grave.
   If Charity the ruthless foe could charm,
   That heavenly grace did all thy bosom warm.
   If Beauty ever claimed that wondrous power,
   Death's hand had never plucked so fair a flower.
   If Birth that quality had e'er possessed,
   Thy death so many hearts had not distressed.
   Ye tender Relatives now cease to grieve,
   Let heavenly hope your sorrowing hearts relieve.
   She, whose untimely loss you so deplore,
   Still lives in bliss celestial evermore.
   Her footsteps following, through heaven's free grace,
   You yet in glory shall behold her face:
   And through eternity shall share her love,
   With blessed spirits in the realms above!
         So sang the Muse of fourscore years and four,
         And thus employed a solemn evening hour."

Advanced in years as he was, he still kept up a correspondence with several leaders in the Church, and one of these, as we have just seen, was Principal Macfarlan of Glasgow College. Another was the Rev. Dr. Macleod of Morven, who kindly sent him a long and interesting account of a tour he had made in America, as one of a deputation in the interests of the Church of Scotland at the time. We make no apology for presenting an extract from the letter, only we hope the writer of it will not call us to account for doing so:—

"MANSE OF MORVEN, OBAN, April 29, 1846.

"My Dear Sir,—I reproach myself very much for delaying so long to reply to your letter, at the same time I am fully persuaded that yourself would, if aware of the circumstances in which I have of late been placed, find at least some apology for my silence. On my return from the *Far West* I had much to do at home, as you may easily suppose. My own parish, though not a populous one, is rugged and extensive. It presents a sea coast of nearly one hundred miles, and there are only about five miles of continuous road throughout the wide extent of it. You can at once suppose that such a parish required no small exertion on the part of the minister after an absence of six months. Such exertions were the more arduous on my part that I had met with an accident on my travels in the West, which for the time deprived me of that physical fitness for the wilds of Morven, for which the eloquence of Candlish—and he can be eloquent —would not compensate. Other duties also devolved upon me. I hold the offices of Presbytery and Synod Clerk, and also that of Synod Factor, an office rendered necessary here, from our holding under the Crown a right to the revenues of the bishopricks of Argyll and the Isles, and to the emoluments of vacant benefices, all which we apply, as required, to pious uses. Nor have I been idle in the cause of the Church under existing circumstances. I thought that having journeyed, as with my brethren I did, eleven thousand miles in the cause, amidst the backwoods of America, I might for a time rest on my oars at home, but rest was not allowed me; and thus have I held Church meetings since my return in almost all the parishes of our bounds, the labour of which during stormy winter no one can estimate who is not acquainted with the insular character of this country. These meetings have, I think, been of much benefit. They were in every instance well attended. . . . . Possibly few or none have been reclaimed, but the Church people have been confirmed and comforted, and thus rendered less open to the agitation by which they are from day to day assailed. Here such efforts are requisite, and ought to have been made further, for we have not, as with you, pamphlets, newspapers, &c., to enlighten, and we must thus have recourse to other modes. Here, though we have our difficulties to contend with, from the conduct of the rude, ignorant, and vulgar agitators sent among us, who adapt themselves to the prejudices of the populace in a way we should be sorry to imitate, we, on the whole, get on pretty well. There is in many of our churches no sensible diminution of the congregation, and all our schools are well attended. I remember well the scene with the Gaelic School Society to which you refer, and I gratefully bear in mind your kind and fatherly feeling on that occasion. Would that the Assembly had then listened more attentively to my counsels of warning! Had they done so our Highlands were now differently situated in regard to the Church. It was the Gaelic School Society, the most ——— with which I was ever acquainted, that prepared the Highlands for the Secession, by acting in direct violation of the principles on which it was professedly established. We are now done with it, but, alas! not in time. The progress of the Secession has been in the ratio of its influence. In the Lewis, where the teachers were dominant, there are not out of the town of Stornoway 110 Churchmen out of a population of 18,000!! But if it has injured the Establishment, it will yet injure the Free Secession. A power has been called forth which cannot be regulated. The lay preachers will *set up for themselves*, and the people will become Congregationalists. So far as we are concerned, however, let us go onward in our course, acting on right principles, and leave the result to His wisdom who can overrule all for good.

"Our Mission to America was attended with much pleasure, and I hope with much benefit. The Church there is strong, and would gain strength if we could but send out ministers, and, above all, ministers of the right sort. I had much comfort in meeting some of our poor Highlanders, and it would rejoice me if I could repeat the visit. Our labours were arduous, and less enlivened by the novelty of the country than you can suppose. The country in general is tame in the extreme. Except the Hudson and Lake George in the States, Quebec and the Thousand Islands in British America, there is no fine scenery—none of our own bold peaks and islandic glens. Even their woods are not in beauty to be compared to our own. I will not speak of Niagara, the grandeur of which neither painter nor poet can depict. Its Falls must be seen, and a sight of them compensates for all the toil and trouble of the voyage. We saw a little of the States, and had the honour of shaking hands with the President in *his own house* at Washington—and half an hour thereafter, the horror of seeing the Slave Market under the very *nose* of the Capitol. The sight indeed was a sad and a revolting one, and indicates a sad perversion in the American character. We were much struck with some of the cities of the Union, and especially with Philadelphia, the public buildings of which are not surpassed by any in Edinburgh. Boston, from the character of its institutions, is a most interesting city. These are on a great scale‧ and ably conducted. In no country does education appear to have made greater advances than in this Northern State of the Pilgrim Fathers. Where, for instance, can we find the female operatives of any of our manufacturing towns fit to conduct a periodical? and yet here they do so in a way the most creditable. . . . After all, however, the Yankees are not a literary people, though literature is more open to them than to us. Our best works are published by them, and at a price to us quite tantalizing. The people, however, are too much engaged with trade and politics to attend to matters of refinement, but they are advancing, or, as they say, 'going ahead,' and they will, in a short time, vie with us in literature, as in other matters. . . . . I cannot conclude without thanking you for your kind remembrance of me, and expressing my heartfelt satisfaction that God, who has prolonged your day of life, has blessed the evening of it, and enabled you, while attending to the things that belong to your own peace, to evince so deep an interest in all that concerns that Church in whose service you have so long and so faithfully laboured. Need I say that I shall at all times be gratified to hear from and of you. I fear that my letter will appear as if written in the Gaelic. If you have at any time been in communication with my brother at Glasgow, or my nephew at Dalkeith, you will own that we are a family not blessed with the gift of legible writing. At all events, I hope you will read and believe that I remain, with very great esteem and respect, my dear Sir, yours most sincerely,

"JOHN MACLEOD.

"Rev. Dr. Wightman."

The length of this extract will be excused on account of the interesting details it brings before the reader of an important tour in a far distant land, at a critical period in the history of the Church of Scotland, and written by one so eminently qualified for such a mission as he describes. It may also be mentioned that another reason for quoting it is, that it was the last letter Dr. Wightman received from a clerical friend on ecclesiastical affairs, and one which he often perused with peculiar pleasure.

CHAPTER XVIII.

THE MINISTER'S MAN—GENERAL CHARACTER—DAVID HENRY—IMITA-
TION OF THE MINISTER—FAMILIARITIES OF THE CLASS—FAITHFUL-
NESS AND SINCERITY.

THE "minister's man," long an indispensable and a
well-known appurtenance of the Scottish manse, must
now be almost reckoned among the things that were.
Not that the minister now serves himself any more than
formerly—that he has laid aside the dignity of his profession, and takes an hour in the stable, and another in
the coach-house, to make all trim, before going to the
Presbytery, or to help a neighbour at his school examination or Communion. The modern *servant* is not like
the *man* of old. He has no idea of being at the manse
longer than to qualify himself for a situation where a
pair of horses are driven and a suit of livery allowed:
hence he never amalgamates freely with the household
of the manse, or takes a family interest in its concerns.
He is either leaving or desirous to leave, and is looking
less to the benefit of his present than his future master,
and much more to himself. Again, in many cases no
man is now kept, because none is necessary. He is
found a burden, and is therefore dispensed with. While
everything has risen in value, the minister's income
remains stationary, and far behind. Household expenditure, children's education, domestics' wages, and
tradesmen's bills are all increased, but still the same

unvarying stipend must be accountable for all. Therefore the horse has been disposed of, the glebe is let in
grass, the "man's" engagement has not been renewed,
and the minister now walks the distance which he used
to drive before.

Yes, the "minister's man" is now no more; and, under
the impression that the character and usefulness of the
class merited something more than merely having
"*Fuimus*" inscribed on the last one's tombstone, we
would now affectionately cast a stone to their cairn, by
recording a few memorials of their day and generation.
If the "man" had faults and foibles not always overlooked
and sympathized with, his virtues and responsibilities
obtained for him the general respect of the parish; while,
in the estimation of many, as well as himself, he was
regarded next in importance to the minister and elders.
Never in a hurry, and accustomed " to crack" with every
one he met, he was a leading chronicle of the various
ongoings of the district, past, present, and proposed. His
office, too, gave him an opportunity of gaining information which many were anxious to obtain, such as who
was to preach in the minister's absence next Sunday,
who were to be the assistants at the forthcoming Communion, when was such an heritor's child to be baptized,
and who were all the grand party at the manse a few
nights ago. Such information, it was naturally supposed, he alone could furnish, and with a fawning
obsequiousness many set themselves to work the oracle.
With a pliant yet dignified air, he would lean against
the stone fence, strike a light for his pipe, and satisfy
the thirst for knowledge to the best of his ability with
some gratuitous comments of his own, often the most

2 A

acceptable of all. In reply to any apology for detaining him from his work during such social interviews, his logic was very peculiar and conclusive—" Anither day's comin', an' if it doesna come the work will no be necessar'."

Such was the character and the saying of David Henry, who, it will be remembered, entered the new manse of Kirkmahoe along with his master on Christmas, 1799, and had continued with him during the whole of his incumbency. Though we may not say that he was altogether a model "minister's man," yet he was a very faithful representative of his class. Our acquaintance with him extended over several years, and we had ample opportunities of discovering the weak as well as the strong points of his character. It is generally understood that every "minister's man" is named John, but our friend was christened David, and was always addressed by his acquaintances *Dawvat*.

His whole heart was devoted to the interests of the manse. He might not always have looked with the same economical eye as his master did to the performance of the daily duties required at his hand, but still he saw them accomplished in his own style and way. A man might be unnecessarily called in to dig and plant the garden in the spring, The stubble land of the glebe might take six days to be turned over instead of three, and the ingathering of the harvest might be participated in by a band of reapers, one-fourth of whom was amply sufficient for the work. But it was thought that there was always time enough and stipend enough for all. At mill, or smithy, or coal-hill, time was entirely forgotten in the flow of gossip which ensued respecting all things in general, and parochial matters in particular, while all was invariably attributed to the considerate plea of resting the horse.

David was accustomed to have recourse to a *ruse* for the purpose of saving himself the fatigue of thrashing. This was to get the boys of the neighbouring cottages to compete at the flail while he sat by regaling himself with his pipe. The reward held out was that he who thrashed the greatest number of sheaves was to have the gratification of riding the old mare to watering—a coveted privilege, which was often gained by considerable bodily labour at the flail.

From his long affinity with the manse and the church, and the many opportunities he had had of hearing all the ministers preach within a wide circuit, he assumed a right to be considered a good judge of preaching, both as to doctrine and delivery. He was versant in all the technical terms commonly employed when pulpit ministration was under discussion, acquired, doubtless in great part, from overhearing his master, of whose sentiments in such matters his were generally the echo. One of his stereotyped deliverances, with regard to a preacher who had impressed him favourably, was very grandiloquent in its style, and ran thus:—"He had great theological profundity, uncommon logical acumen, strong originality of idea, a felicity of illustration, and an overwhelming flow of eloquence." One day, complimenting ourselves on our pulpit discourses in rather a left-handed way, not long after our settlement, he said: —"Your introduction, Sir, is aye grand—nature then feels your approach, Sir—its worth a' the rest o' the sermon; ye should mak' it a' introduction—ha, ha, ha!"

It should be mentioned that David considered himself in alliance with the Muses, and consequently a child of Nature. He had composed several pieces of what he called poetry, one of these being on an old beggar found dead in the snow, in which the details of the poor man's supposed sufferings, mentally and physically, were minutely described, but we are sorry we cannot give a specimen of the dirge. We remember that it was very fair, all things considered. No doubt the inspiration was caught from his residence in the manse.

It was not unnatural that his master should be, in his opinion, the *facile princeps* of all the ministers within his ken, and many a considerable portion of his sermons, and also of his prayers, he could repeat *verbatim*—giving the pathos, unction, and intonation with very striking resemblance. He was as perfect a master of the "drant" as if he had been trained to it from his youth. As some may not understand the term we shall explain it. The *drant* was a peculiarly solemn drawling whine or intonation, made use of in the pulpit by the Scottish clergy till about fifty years ago, which was supposed by both preacher and hearers to add considerably to the effect of the whole service of the Church. And so much was this regarded by the people as a *sine qua non*, that, as we saw in the case of the Rev. James Thomson, Cameronian minister at Quarrelwood, they refused to listen to their new minister, the second Sunday after his ordination, because he declined to adopt the *drant*, of which his predecessor was a proficient, and insisted on addressing them in his natural voice.

But we were speaking of David's ability to quote his master. We shall give one example of his powers in

this way. One fine summer day we were seated beside
him on the *dickie* as he drove the minister into town,
when he began to dilate upon the descriptive powers of
his master, who was under cover behind us, and out of
hearing. "To hear him on the gude Samaritan, Sir, is
remarkably fine. The composition is beautifu', and
makes ane realize the scene, it is so graphic. I could
let you hear a bit o't if you like, for I hae heard it many
a time, and my memory is gae gude." Receiving our
cordial assent, he slackened the reins, stuck the whip
into the hold, and *Inde toro* . . . *sic orsus ab alto.*
"The wounded traveller lay in the forlorn condition
already described, in the bloody way, which to him was
like the valley of the shadow of death. He might now
see nothing but the frowning cliffs of the desert, and the
shadows of the evening lengthening out. He might
hear nothing but the discordant cries of wild beasts of
prey interrupting the awful solitude and silence of the
place. At length we may suppose his listening ear
caught the sound of a passenger's foot, and his weary eye
lifted up might discern a human form advancing. But
might it not be another robber, a ruthless murderer,
coming to extinguish the few remaining sparks of the
vital flame which yet glowed within him? It was not a
robber. It was not a murderer with such intent. It
was a priest of the Most High God, a professed servant
of the Father of Mercies—of Him who raises up the
bowed down, and who will have mercy rather than sacrifice. This priest might have been one of the great body
who dwelt at Jericho, and who performed in their turns
divine service in the temple at Jerusalem, and he
might have been now going home after doing duty in the

sanctuary of Zion. Did he bring his religion with him
from the altar of God? Did his heart burn within him
by musing on the divine law which he had been reading?
Was it warm with charity, and did he put forth his hand
to relieve his fellow-creature in distress? If he could
not give relief to the body, did he endeavour to comfort
his mind? Did he pour the consolation of that religion,
of which he was the minister, into the fainting breast?
Did he supplicate the hearer of prayer, and soothe the
seemingly departing spirit with the sympathy of a pious
heart, and with the prospect of a better world, where the
souls of the good rest from their labours, and where
sorrow, and pain, and death are no more? No! when
he saw him, he passed by on the other side."

"Magnificent! David, magnificent! Go on."

"It's really gran', Sir, but if ye only heard himsel'."

"Could not be better, could not be better! Go on."

"But another passenger comes—a Levite, also a minister of religion; but what could the unfortunate sufferer
now expect? Would this man act a kinder part than
the other? But does he not come aside to see him more
distinctly? Yes! He thus only shows more the hard-
ness of his heart, and having excited a hope which was
disappointed, he also passed by on the other side. Thus
a priest and a Levite, both ministers of religion, passed
by this unfortunate person without giving him any
assistance. How is religion wounded in the house of her
friends, when her professors, and especially the ministers
of her ordinances, disregard her doctrines, and violate
her precepts. Disconsolate indeed was the condition of
this wounded traveller. Every ray of hope might now
be departing with the last beams of the setting sun.

Night and death might seem equally at hand." We were now approaching the town, and further description was necessarily at an end.

David's criticisms of his master's sermons were not always of the most favourable kind, showing that he was not destitute of original discernment. On one occasion, when the minister had been preaching in a neighbouring pulpit on the passage of the Israelites through the Red Sea, and thought himself that it was a discourse of no ordinary merit, both in matter and composition, as he was driving home in the evening he inquired of David what he thought of the sermon on the escape of the Israelites. "Thocht o't, Sir? 'deed I thocht nocht o't ava. It was a vera imperfect discoorse in my opinion. Ye did weel eneuch till ye took them through, but whaur did ye leave them? Just daunerin' on the sea-shore, without a place to gang to—as unsatisfactory for them as for us. Had it no been for Pharaoh, they had been better on the ither side, where they were comfortably encampit, than daunerin' whaur ye left them. It is painful to hear a sermon stoppit afore it is richt ended, just as it is to hear ane streekit out lang after it is dune. That's my opinion o' the sermon ye gied us to-day." "Very freely given, David, very freely given; drive on a little faster, for I think you are daunerin' too." To which the reply was given, "The beast's gaun fast eneuch."

When Dr. Wightman was leaving the school of Torthorwald, at the close of an examination day, the boys began to climb up behind his phaeton to have the pleasure of a swing. The Doctor, who was always kind to the young, said to them that he knew the boys of

Torthorwald were good boys, that they did not swing on carriages, and always did what they were bidden. "Humph!" said the man, who had taken his seat with reins in hand, "they're just like their neebors, an' nae better. I hate sic palaverin'. Drive awa, Mall."

The familiarity which existed between the "man" and the minister sometimes resulted in expressions and deportment of rather a peculiar kind. The minister of Torthorwald one day sent a message to his man desiring him to go and sow a certain high field behind the manse, called the *bank*. It had escaped his notice that the day was boisterous, and not well suited to such an operation. John made his appearance in the study very unceremoniously, and decidedly not in the best of moods, when the following colloquy took place:—

"Did ye sen' me word, Sir, that I was to saw the bank the day?"

" I did, John."

" Weel, it just shows that ye ken naething aboot it. Wha in a' the world ever heard o' folk sawin' in a day o' wun like this? It's ridiculous madness."

"John, do you know what Solomon says on the subject—'He that observeth the wind will not sow.'"

"I carena a snuff for what Solomon says; but I like common-sense. He kens as little aboot it as yersel'. It's very easy for you and Solomon to sit at the fire there and tell folk to do this an' that; but, my faith, I'm thinkin' that if baith you an' Solomon were sawing the bank the day, in this sou'-wast wun, ye wud mak' a bonny han' o't. Solomon an' you thegither wadna mak' a richt man atween you." With which expression of opinion, and some indistinct mutterings to himself, he

departed as rudely as he had entered, without waiting
a reply.

The minister of Tinwald had a "man" who had been
long in his service, and who was often more plain than
polite in addressing him, arising not from want of respect, but from familiarity, connected with a natural
irrascibility which he did not trouble himself to restrain.
In order to arouse his temper, various tricks were played
upon him by the boys of the neighbourhood when going
to school and returning. The minister becoming aware
of this, thought he would prove, by ocular demonstration, whether it was so or not. One day, when the
"man" was engaged in garden operations, he kept pop-
ping stones at him over the wall, to the great annoyance
of John, who began to swear in a very infuriated manner.
Alarmed at what he heard, the minister immediately
appeared at the garden gate, demanding a reason for
such profanity and blasphemy, stating that it was the
minister this time and not the boys. With an oath
which we shall not repeat, he said—"Minister, or no
minister, he should not throw stones at him. He would
leave the place first." The minister was only too glad
to beat a retreat.

The Rev. Mr. Lawrie of Kirkmichael had a man-
servant who was not overscrupulous in his choice of
expressions in moments of irritation, pretty frequent
with him when matters did not go according to his
mind, and he had often been rebuked by the minister
for his unguarded speech. But though he humbly
submitted to admonition, and always promised greater
circumspection for the future, yet his memory seemed
very defective, or his old habits were stronger than his

resolutions, for his irritability remained the same, and his hasty utterances under it continued unchanged. One evening the minister thought he heard an uproar in the kitchen, and hastened to see the cause of the disturbance. On approaching the door all was quiet, and he stood for a moment still, when, to his horror, he heard a wild exclamation, which we shall not quote, and he instantly rushed in to prevent murder. There was, however, no one present but the man, who was busy at supper. "What's ado, John, what's ado?" "O naething, Sir, naething ava, but thir sowens is unco ill to catch." "But, John, I surely heard profane swearing before I came in." "Maybe ye did, Sir, maybe ye did, but I dinna think nae ither body heard ony." John was supping cold sowens with a horn spoon out of a pewter plate, which is a most difficult operation, as well as a tantalising one for a hungry man, but he had been so intent on the pursuit of the slippery fugitive, which always slid round the dish and eluded his attack, that, losing temper, he unconsciously expressed his disappointed feelings in the manner indicated on the minister's approach.

At an annual district ploughing-match in Nithsdale, a "minister's man" in the neighbourhood, who had been a great prize-taker in his youth, felt the old fervour return, and ardently longed to show "how fields were won." His master, however, was not at home, being in England, to grant him leave to renew the feats of his younger days, and he took the responsibility upon himself, went, and carried off the fifth prize. On the minister's return, glancing at a newspaper, he saw what had been done in his absence, and immediately summoned his man. "John, how is this? I see you have been at the ploughing-match; who gave you leave to go?" "Ye werena at hame, Sir." "Well, you ought to have written me." "I didna think it scarcely worth while, Sir. We were gey weel forrit wi' our ain ploughin', an' I thocht it would be nae harm to gang." "That may be; but how are you so far back in the prize list as to be only fifth? I am quite ashamed of you, and you ought to be ashamed of yourself." John's blood rose at this depreciation of his honours, and he rashly and irreverently said—"Weel, Sir, ye may be ashamed or no as ye like at my doin's, but I'm thinkin' that if ye were at a preachin' match, wi' ither five-and-thirty in the fiel', ye wad come in for nocht ava."

Notwithstanding these familiarities to which we have alluded, and perhaps because of them, there was a deep current of affection for his master in the heart of the "minister's man." No member in the whole Synod was considered his superior, if his equal, and none more worthy of being made a D.D., if he had not already obtained the honour. At any hour of the day or night he was entirely at his service. When sickness visited the family, either in its head or any of its members, no kinder sympathizer was to be found; and when the sad event came which could not be averted—when the minister's labours were brought to a close, and he was carried to the grave like a shock of corn in its season, there was no sincerer mourner in the whole parish than the "minister's man."

CHAPTER XIX.

THE good old man had now nearly completed his eighty-fifth year, and he wanted but a few months of having been fifty years minister of the parish. His parishioners, the greatest portion of whom he had baptized, had resolved on giving him a jubilee entertainment, and were about to begin preparations, when he turned ill. It was proposed to erect a large pavilion in one of the retired glades on the banks of the Nith, and the two principal heritors, Sir Alexander Johnston of Carnsalloch, and James Macalpine Leny, Esq., of Dalswinton, were expected to be the presidents on the occasion. Invitations were to be sent, far and near, to all the Doctor's leading acquaintances, and he had himself, in joyful anticipation of the event, invited several friends, and had received assurances of their intention to be present. A special invitation was to be sent to Professor Wilson of Edinburgh, whose glorious revelling among the glens, and the braes, and the lakes, and the streams of his own native land would have well accorded with the festive scene, and have lent a charm such as none other could confer. He had sometimes visited at Dalswinton House, and it was therefore thought that he might be prevailed on to come. Other

distingués of the Scottish metropolis, who had paid
short annual visits to the moorlands of the parish on
the twelfth of August, were also to have invitations.
The members of Presbytery, of course, were to be there,
with whatever friends they chose to bring along with
them; while from the neighbouring districts and the
county town, in all of which the Doctor was not only
well known, but highly esteemed, it was confidently
anticipated that no fewer than two thousand persons
would be present on the festive occasion. In order that
this great fête might be carried through in the most
felicitous manner, a public meeting of the parishioners
was about to be called for the purpose of electing a
committee to make arrangements and conduct the
whole. But much frequently happens between the prospect and the attainment : so was it here. The venerable old man, on whose account all this was to take
place, had been for some time complaining that his
limbs seemed not his own in his usual visitations
among his people—that he felt a numbness pervading
them which he had never felt before; but he said, with
a kindly smile, that "he trusted he would yet tread the
April gowan, and, if that were so, he might see another
winter before he should go hence." He did tread the
April gowan as he desired, but long ere the winter had
come the grass was growing green upon his grave.

Notwithstanding the boisterous state of the weather,
he would not confine himself to the house, but, ever
anxious to be engaged in his Master's business, he
would wrap a handkerchief round his throat, put on his
greatcoat, take his black staff in his hand, the gift of a
friend, and sally out, down to the widow's cottage at

Lakeside, and from thence to the Bowness family in Springvale. During one of these visits he caught a cold, which he said he would drive away doing his duty, and would walk it out; but his duty was to have kept to the house and his easy chair by the study fire. It continued its hold, as if unwilling to be shaken off, and medicines of various kinds were administered, which wrought a mitigation but not a cure; however, he did not despair of getting round, and of being chief guest at the great entertainment which awaited him on the anniversary of his ordination. His feet and ancles began slightly to swell, and two reddish itching spots appeared below the calf of one of his legs; but he bathed them frequently with salt and water, and thereby kept them from spreading. By assiduous perseverance in this treatment they at last evanished, and great was the old man's delight at having thus vanquished and dislodged the foe. But though they had disappeared, they had not left safety behind—they had only retired for a little, again to return more insidiously, like the Greeks of old, when they withdrew from Tenedos, to come back under the quiet moon and accomplish the siege of Troy.

His cough increased, and every suggested prescription was administered, but all in vain. The enemy had gained possession, and would not be expelled. He was no longer to be seen as usual, lingering among the garden flowers and the shrubbery, or taking a stroll to a retired part of the glebe called his "Mount of Observation." Reclining in his easy-chair, or extended upon the sofa by the parlour fire, he would peruse at intervals the publications of the day, and point out their several merits or defects when we called to inquire after his welfare in the evening.

Inward debility daily increased, and faintishness about the head became more frequent; but he did not despair of recovery, and his spirits were sustained by the flattering consolations of his friends, who often too easily believed as certain what had no stronger foundation than their mere wish or desire. But though he was thus prevented from visiting his parishioners as usual, he was seldom entirely alone. Frequently and numerously they came to sympathize in their turn with him who had so often consoled them under their afflictions, and offered prayers in their behalf to Him who is the hearer of prayer. He always expressed himself much gratified by their attentive and kind inquiries, for his heart had always been wrapped up in his flock, and his desire was that of the Shunammite of old, "to dwell among his own people." These friendly sympathies, which they now manifested so feelingly towards him under the infirmities of age, and in the season of trouble, he felt were an ample reward for all the services he had rendered them, as they were indubitable evidences that his labours, under the blessing of Heaven, had not been in vain. Such interviews were very solemnizing and impressive to those who witnessed them, and spoke an edifying lesson to the heart. Change! change! no abiding! was the thought which filled the soul, as the hoary-headed sat beside him, and talked of the days of youth, when he had united them in the ties of wedlock —baptized their children and their children's children —held diets of catechising and examination in their several districts—admitted them with pious exhortations to the table of Holy Communion—and accompanied the remains of many of their kindred to the house appointed for all living. At such recitals, how the eye of the venerable man of God kindled up with the fire of former years! and then the big tear trickled from furrow to furrow down his wan cheek, at the remembrance of so many endearing scenes, which had given joy to his heart, and which, under the dispensations of an inscrutable Providence, had been followed by others peculiarly painful and sad. But these were only for a moment, the sunshine followed the shower at irregular intervals, as is sometimes seen on a lowering winter day. These visits of his people were necessarily short, the feeble state of his health, and the excitement produced by the appearance of every new visitant—for he wished to see them all—induced him soon to extend his hand, and with his usual "God bless you!" bid them farewell.

One day important business required his presence in town, and it was thought that, by muffling well up and keeping the phaeton closed, he might venture in and out without sustaining much fatigue. The weather was far from propitious, the day was a very disagreeable one, the wind was sharp, and a drizzling rain came on in the afternoon. He returned much exhausted, regretting he had been obliged to leave the house. In the evening he baptized a child, the son of his biographer, which was brought to the manse, but the duty seemed almost too much for his strength, and at the close of the ceremony he was assisted to his easy chair, wearied like a worn-out soldier after a long and successful campaign. This was the last professional duty he performed, and all present

instinctively felt the conviction that he would never
sprinkle the baptismal water again.   He retired to rest
at a much earlier hour than usual, and never left his bed
till he was carried out for burial, three months after he
was laid down.   All was silence, sadness, and gloom
about the manse during that deary period; all betokened
a change; all silently, but surely, intimated that the
master was preparing to "fall asleep."   In the lobby
hung his hat, as when his hand had left it, yet not
altogether so, as it was growing hoary with dust, showing
it was no longer brushed by the breeze.   In the study,
too, there was visibly a change—not in his books on the
table, for they lay in the same position as when he laid
them down, and his chair was also in the spot he left it;
but there, beside that folio Bible, from inside the boards
of which peered out the leaves of two manuscript sermons, lay piles of unread newspapers, and unopened
letters, silently intimating that he to whom they were
addressed was waiting to learn different tidings and
answer a different message from a higher source than
his fellow-men.

His friends, ever solicitous about his recovery—for
they hoped against hope—were unremitting in their
attentions, and anxious, as well as frequent, were the inquiries not only of neighbours but of those at a distance.
Day after day, rich and poor, old and young, tapped
gently at the manse door lest the bell might disturb the
invalid, and kindly asked in a half whisper, "How the
minister was to-day, and how he had rested during the
night?"   With an ear quick as it ever was, if not quicker,
he heard the gentle commotion, and desired that all
inquirers should be introduced into his room, that he

might see their countenance, grasp their hand, and reciprocate their sympathy, for his heart was united to his flock as the soul of David was united to Jonathan; and his affectionate sister, the ever-watchful attendant by his bed, gratified his desires in all things, though she saw that such frequent interviews, however short, tended to increase his weakness and produce fatigue. This was too evident, also, to those who called upon him, and, seeing it could not be avoided, they adopted other means than personal visitations for learning the state of his health. Jenny, at the well, as she drove the cows to the field, or passed along to the village on some household errand, afforded frequent opportunities of receiving information how all fared at the manse. One told another, and that one a third, and in this manner the daily bulletin was made known. The venerable old man who was the object of all this solicitude was not long in perceiving the change, and in remarking on the apparent inattention of his friends, and all within the bounds of the parish he considered such. We shall not soon forget the look he gave, and the tone with which he on one occasion said, "They are tired of me now— they are thinking I am too long here. Oh! when shall the day break and the shadows flee away!" We assured him it was not so, and explained the reason of the seeming neglect; but though he replied, "Well, well, be it so!" it was evident he did not consider it a sufficient excuse.

In the meantime the season for dispensing the holy sacrament of the Lord's Supper in the parish came round, but it was evidently impossible that he could either preside or be present. It was, however, a solemn and an anxious season to him, and though absent in body he was present in spirit. On the morning of the Fast-day, a neighbouring minister who had come to assist went up to his bedroom and made some inquiries respecting his condition. "O what a morning I have had!" said he, "preaching and praying with my old friend Mr. Greig, in the Kirk of Tinwald. I was assisting him at the Sacrament, as I used to do of old; and, O! but we had a crowded congregation. But the dream makes my heart sad, for it is long since I saw my worthy friend's remains laid in the clay!" The remembrance of bygone days came like the sunshine of heaven upon his soul, or the return of a long-absent friend, and, unable to conceal his emotion, he wrapped his face in the coverlet and wept.

His strength gradually declined; a few minutes was all the time he could sit up in bed during the day; his appetite was gone, and he would lie for hours without uttering a single word, though many were the anxious looks of those who attended his bed. The former swelling in his limbs returned, the consequence of various maladies which kept him under intense suffering, but he uttered no complaint. Resignation to the Divine will he knew to be his duty, and he well exemplified it in all his distress. The Bible, which had ever been his constant companion, was now his comfort as he approached the shadowy valley. The fourteenth chapter of John and the eighth of the Romans were his favourite portions of meditation, and were read by his special request when the throne of grace was approached in prayer.

He could rise no more—helpless as a child, he lay as he was laid, and what nourishment or cordial he could take was administered without raising his head from the

pillow. His medical attendant declared he could do
nothing more, and he committed himself to the Great
Physician, in the peaceful assurance that "God was his
refuge and strength, a very present help in trouble."
One evening we paid him our accustomed visit, and
recalled to his recollection some of those precious Scripture promises which he had himself so often repeated at
many a death-bed during the course of his ministry.
We engaged in prayer. On rising from our knees he
made a feeble effort to extend his hand, but he spoke
not a word—he could not—his heart was too full for
speech, and "the big tear stood trembling in his eye,"
declaring the emotion of the soul within. At nine
o'clock we wished him "good-night," and went away,
considering him not much weaker than for several days
before; but a change was at hand. The clock had just
struck eleven, and we were about to extinguish our bedroom light, when a loud knock at the door, hurriedly
repeated, made us dread the worst. On opening, our
fears were confirmed. A sudden tremor had seized his
whole frame, and had continued for an hour so violent
that the bed shook beneath him, and could not be kept
still; and while faithful David, who had served him for
nearly fifty years, went off with all haste to the town for
medical aid, a neighbour came requesting our immediate
attendance at the manse. No time was lost; and though
two miles had to be travelled over, half an hour had not
passed when we stood by the side of the dying minister.
And what a change had taken place since we left about
two hours before! The tremor had ceased, and he was
breathing heavily, evidently having come through a
violent struggle. Reader, have you ever seen the return

of a vessel which has encountered a hurricane at sea, just as she is entering the long-wished-for, haven, and while amidst the last foaming breakers she receives a shock which makes her very innermost timbers quiver— weak and disabled she enters the calm waters of the harbour, and is safely moored at her destination? Such was the idea suggested to our mind by the scene before us. His speech was gone, but he was quite conscious. We sang the 121st Psalm, "I to the hills will lift mine eyes," &c.—supplications for heavenly strength to aid him in passing the swellings of the Jordan were presented, and the look he gave us afterwards showed he had heard all, and expressed his confidence in God. David returned from the town without being successful in his object, and as every half-hour showed a gradual change in the features of the dying man, we all continued around his bed, and solemnly awaited the summons of death.

The gray dawn of the morning broke upon the neighbouring hills, and peered in at the chamber window; but though it was the middle of a beauteous summer, a sombre sadness came with the reflection of that morning light. The lambs were heard bleating in the adjoining fields, but there seemed a melancholy in the sound, like a mournful lament, saying, "Ah! why will ye die!" Poor Tray crept stealthily into the room as if conscious of the approaching event, and desirous to take farewell of his kind master, who had often fondled him like a child. Placing his fore-feet upon the bedside with a piteous look, he would have sprung in had he not been restrained; and when it was found necessary to put him out, he lay down outside the door and howled mournfully and long, yet no one could think of removing him further away. Death was evidently near—the pulse was becoming fainter and fainter—the breathing inconstant, sometimes deep, heavy, and difficult; again gentle and scarcely perceptible. The scene was solemnizing and affecting. Around the dying man stood sincere friends, faithful, if few; his only sister, ten years younger than himself, his two domestics, David and Jenny, his nurse, a kind-hearted woman, and ourselves. The two servants did not seek to stifle their sobs or conceal their tears; these were the effusions of affectionate bosoms, and came gushing forth without hindrance, the manifestations of sincere sorrow on behalf of a master they had long served—David, as we have said, nearly fifty, and Jenny thirty-three years. There was one whose grief was too deep for tears, but who gazed upon the ghastly countenance with all the affection which could inspire a sister's heart. She shed no tear—she spoke no word—but she looked what the voice could not utter, and we often heard a sigh. The last moment seemed now at hand, and leaning over the couch we repeated the words of the fifth hymn, commencing with "The hour of my departure's come." When it was finished we looked narrowly at the half-closed eyes—our look was feebly returned— he had heard it all. We looked again to make sure—he was gone—there was life no more—the pulse was still— the heart had ceased to beat—the eyes were sealed in death. Thus departed from the world this pious, learned, and generous-hearted man of God, to reap the reward of his labours and enjoy the pleasures at his Father's right hand for evermore. As we closed his eyelids, and wiped the cold sweat from the brow of the dead, his sister repeated the poet's line, "Some pious drops the closing eye requires"—and looking up we perceived the tears trickling down her cheeks. He died on the 14th of July, 1847, in the eighty-fifth year of his age and the fiftieth of his ministry. After staying a short time, as we could do no more, we left the manse, deeply impressed with the solemnity of the scene just witnessed, and desiring, when our earthly pilgrimage is run, "to die the death of the righteous, and to have our last end like his."

The morning of the funeral at length came, calm and sombre, mournfully harmonizing with the feelings of the bereaved inmates of the manse, and appropriately introducing the scene which that day was to witness. Externally, all had been in a state of unbroken quietude since the eventful morning when the good man's spirit took its flight to higher worlds, but nimble fingers had been busy within. Orleans and crape had been speedily converted into weeds of woe, while muslins of various textures and forms contributed important aid in deepening the melancholy which overhung the countenance and shrouded the heart, but relieving it somewhat, like a storm-cloud edged with silver on a winter day. While decorous solemnity pervaded all things without, great had been the assiduity within in preparing for the funeral obsequies, but all was now completed, and the sigh came forth without interruption, deeply drawn from the inmost recesses of the soul. On the previous evening the old joiner and his son came over from the village to arrange seats for the company of mourners expected on the following day; and as several hundred invitations had been issued, for the minister was widely known and

respected, it was evident no apartments about the
premises could accommodate them all.   As the weather,
however, seemed promising—the middle of July being
pleasant and balmy—it was proposed to place benches
across the green plat in front of the manse; and a fitter
spot could not have been selected for such an occasion.
One side was sheltered by the back of a range of offices
covered with wall-trees of the pear and plum, grasping
it in their wide embrace.   The other side was hemmed
in by a high wall, similarly bespread, and betokening
an abundant harvest of luscious fruit.   In the centre of
this enclosure stood an apple-tree of forty years' growth,
towering like a cedar of Lebanon, and always reminding
us, as we passed beneath its shady boughs, of our boyhood days, and

> " Tityre tu patulæ recubans sub tegmine fagi."

On this grassy sward benches were easily and comfortably
arranged, and should the following day prove unfavourable, they could speedily be removed to a commodious
granary contiguous to the place, while other apartments
could be speedily brought into requisition.   The morning
came, calm and sombre, as we have said, and fears were
entertained for a rainy day.   Often was the eye as well
as the heart turned towards the heavens, and many were
the wishes expressed that the hidden sun would reveal
his beauty.   Still it lowered, but, nevertheless, the hope
was still cherished that the day would not turn out wet
or otherwise disagreeable.   The hope was fully realized,
for at noon, the hour of meeting, the gloominess dis-
persed, the sky cleared, and a brighter sun never shone
upon our sin-blighted world.   The company now began

to arrive, and soon every seat was occupied. Many
contented themselves with standing-room, in preference
to sitting, even could a seat have been found. Several
reverend brethren from other Presbyteries and of various
denominations were there; and many sorrowing friends
from far distant parishes, who had left their homes
early in the morning, also appeared, showing symptoms
of far travel and fatigue. When all had assembled, to
the number of nearly four hundred, a solemn and impressive prayer was offered by the venerable Dr. Dunbar
of Applegarth, who had preached his first sermon in the
parish upwards of forty years before, and who, along with
his friend, the Rev. John Crocket of Kirkgunzeon, now
standing by his side, had presented their deceased friend
with a handsomely bound copy of " Zimmerman on Solitude," in memory of the event. The deep solemnity of the
tone of prayer, the noble and venerable heads of the clergy
standing around, and the devout demeanour of the whole
assembly, reminded us at the moment of the descriptions we had read of the communion gatherings of our
Covenanting fathers in the times of old. A considerable
number of pupils from Dumfries Academy were also
there with their masters, to show their regard to the
memory of one who had so long and genially presided at
their annual examinations. After refreshments had been
served, and another solemn prayer offered by the father
of the Presbytery, the Rev. Dr. Thomas T. Duncan of
Dumfries, the hearse slowly moved away, followed in
regular order by the relatives of the deceased—the elders
—the ministers—the heritors—the schoolmasters—the
parishioners—the strangers—and the masters and pupils
of the Academy referred to. The scene was one of the

most imposing and impressive character, not soon to be
forgotten. All along towards the churchyard, on every
height, were collected hundreds of people who looked
pensively on, and many shed tears of heartfelt sorrow.
Old matrons were there in their weeds of widowhood,
leaning upon a staff, and a grandchild beside them;
young maidens were there with some neckkerchief or
ribbon of mourning; and sportive boys now stood
thoughtful and reverential, with their heads uncovered,
while the funeral procession moved slowly along.

In a retired nook of the churchyard, and close beside
the church wall, a spot which he had himself selected
many years before, and where he had planted a small
yew-tree and a rose, as it were the one to cast its shade
and the other its perfume over his mouldering dust, was
committed to its kindred earth, to await the morning of
the Resurrection, the mortal part of the venerable
divine, who for nearly fifty years had been a father and
a friend to his people, sympathizing in all their sorrows
and sharing in all their joys. Tears dropped from eyes
unaccustomed to weep, as the coffin was lowered down
into its place, and many a hoary head was uncovered as
the grave closed over the dead. When the green turf
was smoothed down, and the last sad offices were completed, men, women, and children lingered around the
newly-covered grave, and there sobbed their sorrow,
unwilling to bid farewell to the lone tenant of the tomb.
One by one the mourners moved away, for some of them
had far to travel ere they reached their homes among
the hills; and that night, around many a cottage hearth
and farm fireside, reminiscences of the departed were
rehearsed, concerning baptisms, and marriages, and

burials, and catechisings, and Communions; while the
evening worship ascended in a holier strain, and with a
deeper solemnity, than it had done for a long time
before.

It was looking forward to this event that one Sabbath
evening in autumn he stole away unperceived into the
churchyard, and there, seated on a grave-stone beside
the yew-tree and the rose referred to, he poured forth
the following strains, mingled with many a tear:—

CHURCHYARD MUSINGS ON A SABBATH EVENING.

"On this sweet Sabbath eve the heavens serene,
  And solemn silence reigning all around,
Come, Contemplation, sanctify the scene,
  And let me feel that this is holy ground.

"Death's trophies everywhere here meet my eye,
  And graves of every length and breadth are here;
The rich and poor, the old and young here lie,
  The high and low, the false and the sincere.

"In yellow lustre shines yon setting sun,
  Which late, in golden glory, ruled the day;
Those leaves, once fresh and green, now sere and dun,
  Wear the sad livery of dire decay.

"Then let not man, in pride of youth and health,
  Hope to escape the universal doom;
No rank, nor fame, nor dazzling glare of wealth
  Can move the ruthless tyrant of the tomb.

"But to yon corner let me now draw near,
  For there my dust I have resolved shall rest;
Let every meddling fancy now forbear
  To mar the musings of my thoughtful breast.

"I now have reached the term of eighty years—
  An age, by heaven's decree, vouchsafed to few;
A lengthened period—yet it short appears,
  When thus surveyed in retrospective view.

" Man's life, how short, even at its farthest line,
    With dread eternity's extent compared!
Then, in that little which remains of mine,
    Oh! let me strive for death to be prepared.

" Soon must I close my eyes on day's blest light,
    On yonder circling hills, and Nith's green vale;
Ah! soon must I be wrapped in death's dark night,
    And this warm frame assume his 'ensigns pale.'

" Then farewell flock, and friends, and kindred dear,
    And welcome, for a time, this lowly bed,
Where Friendship may perhaps let fall a tear,
    If haply hither by remembrance led.

" Here shall my flesh ' in trembling hope repose '
    Till Nature's elements shall melt away,
And Nature's God the wonders shall disclose
    Of the tremendous Resurrection day!

" Within these walls the minister shall preach,
    And prayer and praise to heaven's high throne ascend;
But my cold ear the sweet sound will not reach;
    No voice from here with Sabbath hymns shall blend:

" Yet well for me if, in the courts above,
    Amidst adoring choirs of spirits bright,
My soul shall celebrate redeeming love
    In glad hosannahs with the saints in light.

" But oh! what faults and failings, saddening train,
    Crowd on my mind and fill my heart with fear;
Unless my soul be washed from every stain,
    At Christ's tribunal how shall I appear?

" Father of lights and mercies, God of grace,
    Forgive them all for Thy Beloved's sake;
Let shine on me the brightness of Thy face;
    And what Thou'dst have him be, Thy suppliant make.

" So shall the evening of my life be blest,
    And humble hope my dying hour shall cheer;
So shall I gain the everlasting rest
    Where Thy own hand shall wipe off every tear."

The venerable Dr. Duncan of Dumfries was appointed by the Presbytery, at the request of the relatives, to preach the funeral sermon, which he kindly consented to do, though suffering from the infirmities of age; and when the Sabbath came, the church was filled to overflowing by an attentive congregation, many of whom were in deep mourning. After an impressively solemn discourse from 1 Peter i. 24, 25, Dr. Duncan paid an affectionate and faithful tribute to the memory of the departed minister, his old friend, which greatly affected all present as well as himself.

Thus closed the obsequies of Dr. Wightman, a workman who needed not to be ashamed, and who rightly divided the word of truth amongst those committed to his care. He ever exemplified in private what he taught in public, aware that he who united the man and the minister, the private Christian and the public teacher, in one living embodiment could alone be a successful herald of the Cross. None knew better than he did the importance of combining example with precept, in order to influence the minds of others in receiving spiritual instruction, that knowledge which maketh wise unto salvation, the truth as it is in Jesus. No minister ever manifested to his flock more conspicuously his continual remembrance that life was a passing scene, and that they were all journeying to a land, a heavenly Canaan, promised to the Israel of God. His aim, therefore, was diligently to perform the work given him to do before the night of death should approach, and the darkness of the grave descend. His Master's will was his chief and only concern. His great care was how he might best establish the Kingdom of God in the heart—how he might win souls to Christ. Thus occupied, he had little thought about temporal comforts; he saw one thing was needful, the welfare of the soul, and that he endeavoured to provide. He remarked to one who visited him on his death-bed, that " this world's gain never lost him one half-hour's sleep during the whole of his life." What an admonition to let the heart have but a slight hold of this world's possessions, riches, pleasures, and honours—to set the affections on things above, and not on things of the earth! He lived in the faith of the gospel he preached, and he loved to ponder on the glories of the New Jerusalem, and the blessedness of the land afar off, towards which he was hastening. Every death around him he regarded as a personal warning to himself, to be on the watch for the coming of his Lord. His feeling, perhaps too feeling, heart would not permit him to stand long by the sick-bed which he visited, when it was not in his power to mitigate suffering, but sincere and fervent was the prayer which he there offered—kind the sympathies he expressed—soothing the consolations he imparted to the sinking spirit—and patriarchal the blessing he gave as he left the chamber of affliction and the house of woe.

But not only was he ever mindful that this world was not his home, that he was journeying to a land of which God said He would give it him—he endeavoured to impress on others the same solemn and important truth. His language to all was, " Come thou with us and we will do thee good." Goodness of heart was the most prominent feature in his character, and was eminently conspicuous in all that he said and did. Nor was it confined to his own friends, his own parishioners, his own congregation. He regarded all men as brethren, of whatever country, rank, or condition of life. Generous and benevolent towards all with whom he had inter-course, he waited not to know who were of Paul, who of Apollos, who of Cephas, before he exercised that virtue of his nature; but, trusting they were all of Christ, he endeavoured to do good to all men as he had opportunity. Often did he say that the sun never went down upon him in his wrath, and yet his patience was sometimes sorely tried by those who were strangers to the bene-volent affections. Though advantage was sometimes taken of his generosity by the unprincipled and the deceitful, yet he was willing rather to suffer loss than to think there was one so debased as to impose upon his charity, or that the really destitute should suffer through the imposition of others; but though none were excluded from his benevolence, the virtuous, the industrious, and the pious shared it in an eminent degree. Widely loving all, he was widely loved in return, but he naturally wished to be most respected by his own flock. Other parishioners might be good, but they were not like his —other congregations might be attentive, but none so attentive as his own. No fields were so green, no land-scape so fair, no woodlands so beautiful, and no people so dear as those of his own rural parish of Kirkmahoe. And although he might have been removed to another part of the spiritual vineyard in the course of his ministry, yet he desired to spend and be spent among those who had received his first affections, and in the midst of whom Providence had cast his lot. But, en-dearing as were all these to his affectionate heart, he

could not abide with them for ever.   A change came over
the scene.   The fields, however, still remain as green as
before, and the landscape, with woodland, and streamlet,
and hill, and valley, is still as beautiful—the flock, too,
are still as worthy of being loved, but he is not here to
enjoy them.   He is numbered with the dead, and the
red-breast finds shelter from the winter winds in the
long grass now growing above his grave.   A handsome
monument was erected to his memory by the parishioners,
with a suitable inscription at the head of his tomb, and
there his remains now rest, with the yew-tree and the
rose entwined at his feet, and his beloved sister Mary
by his side.

GLASGOW: R. ANDERSON, 22 ANN STREET.